# THE PLAYER KING

EARL ROVIT

# The Player King

NEW YORK HARCOURT, BRACE & WORLD, INC.

*first edition*

*Library of Congress Catalog Card Number: 65-11993*

*Printed in the United States of America*

FOR H. S. R.

"He told us the most troublesome thing was that Monsieur le Prince claimed he was already dead and refused to eat, on the grounds that the dead did not eat."

—SAINT-SIMON

(*translated by Sanche de Gramont*)

# THE PLAYER KING

# Inscape

So why are you writing?

A pimple is why I am writing.

Because of a pimple you're writing?

Because of a pimple I'm writing. A wonderful language! With the voice a question becomes an answer, an answer becomes a question. English it isn't. (English it isn't?) Yiddish it's not. (Yiddish it's not?) Subjects and predicates leapfrog and somersault and the incredulous shrug in a vocal inflection plays hobbledehoy with subjunctives and optatives. Prose letters scrambled on a white page like black Polish peasants preparing a pogrom in the snow rush into the silence—the white-flaked curve of the knout and the hollow scream choked forth from the womb of words where the knife will not cut and the lash does not fall. English it isn't. A black year on my enemies. They should suffer the sins of alle Yidden.

So come back a minute. What's with the pimple?

The pimple? Is a pimple is all. Like any pimple, but it's on my nose. A simple pimple. On the tip. And it sits there—a pustule of venom. The puckered kiss of mortality. A small red spit the color of blood on a nose which is not small and which is comically my very own nose.

So get rid of it. An electric needle and a shot of novocaine—in two minutes and a Band-aid you're a man with no pimple. A world of modern science and medicine and you make of a pimple a Mount Sinai already. You got Blue Cross?

I did already.

You did what?

Not once but twice I did. I hired the needle and it burned in my flesh and I smelled what I was like in an incinerator and it's back.

Ooooiii! The pimple is a growing pimple. It's—you should pardon the expression—malignant?

Don't ask.

And so—because of the pimple which will not stay put, you are writing?

You express it with precise incision. I grow a pimple and I write. Or, more accurately, a pimple swells up like a large pomegranate seed and grows me, which is that which writes. A capsule esthetic, neatly and logically huddled into the groined vaults of a very small pimple. I smelled my own tissues and cells in flame and I knew my death and I chose to meet it with erection, not resurrection. A choice, mind you. Not a spontaneous reflex. Not a whim or a compulsive urge. A choice of my own cells and tissues which had been condemned and which rejected the sentence.

Why such a mishmash about the choice? So what's the difference between did you choose or were you chosen?

A man with a pimple like mine, he needs his pride. So even if it's false, he needs it all the more. But right now I could stop. I could let the paper fall and quiet the typewriter and cut the pimple and let the pus flow over my lips staunching my mouth. I could but I choose not to. I choose to sit and sweat with the typewriter because I want to. Or because I *will* to even when I don't want to. That's why I insist.

You'll excuse me, it's a small difference.

It's a small pimple too.

So I won't argue. The pimple is why you write. Is it also *what* you will write? I ask because these things are very interesting to me.

In a very small sense—a small metaphysical corner of sense—it is *what* I will write. But by itself, this would be a misleading answer. More accurately, I will write a novel.

This is even more interesting. You are aware, of course, of the problems?

Some of them I am aware of.

You know the problem of form?

I would have thought you would bring up the problem of good and evil first.

Shlepper! I hope we understand one another better than that. You know as much about good and evil as a baby. The problem of form is something else.

I know a little bit about it.

Where did you learn?

I've read a lot.

Too much.

I've taught some courses.

Oi shlecht!

And I've got my pimple.

Maybe the pimple will save you.

I'm hoping so. If it's an honestly malignant pimple, maybe it will give me my rhythms and counterweights. Maybe it will pulse and throb like an esthetic seismograph, pushing me on and holding me back. Here, anyway, I have no choice. I can't depend on a dominant metaphor or a sonnet structure or a framing ideology. All I've got are the fatal tides of my own blood. It's not a very novel idea.

Don't apologize. Especially when you're being coy. No novel ever came from a novel idea. You're going to write a realistic novel?

Be more concrete, please. I don't know what those words mean.

Your novel? Where does it come from? Have you lived it? Do you make it up? Does it transmit messages? Is it a mirror? A window? A radar set? Are your characters people? Symbols? Allegories? Dream projections? Is your plot cyclical? Linear? Dialectic? Are you going to incarnate a vision? Enflesh an apocalypse? Will it *mean* or will it *be*? Are you afraid of women? Do you hate women? Are you grotesque, classical, romantic?

These are very difficult and embarrassing questions.

These are *significant* questions. Any good *Paris Review* interviewer could think of dozens more. And you have to present a specimen of your ink-blotted manuscript before you can qualify. I'm only trying to help you, you shouldn't be a disgrace when they come with the tape recorder, deceptively smelling from Martinis.

Couldn't I just show them the pimple and tell them to read the novel?

They wouldn't touch the pimple with an iambic-pentameter pole. And they'll have read the novel. And taken notes on it too. As well as your Master's thesis on the parody structure in the plays of the Wakefield Master. And the obscenities you scrawled in the men's room of the old Copley Plaza. You got to be ready with the meanings or they'll wash you out cold.

I suppose you're right. But couldn't I go to St. Tropez or Dubrovnik and just hide?

They'd find you. They have expense accounts.

But I can't answer those questions. They're not fair.

They're the current fare, you should excuse me. They're the lead pennies for the three-headed dogs that patrol the outstyx of Publisher's Row. You want a foundation grant, a writer-in-residency, a National Book Award?

I want to write a novel.

Look, don't make like Thomas Wolfe with me. You're way over thirty. You want to play this game, you got to stay with the rules.

Well what'll I do?

It's simple. Throw them off. Spray horse radish on the trail. Fill up their noses so they can't sniff up your ass. You're a Jewish refugee, aren't you? So go into evasive action.

Drop the metaphors and speak plain to me. Unless you're going to write my novel for me. Are you, by the way?

Don't worry. I'll help.

Well then start helping on this problem.

It's simple. Write first, at the beginning of the novel, as though you were being very honest, very sincere, why and what you're doing.

I see. Like Gide. Like we've been doing.

Like we've been doing. And then write a critical review of the novel.

Before the novel itself?

Don't make such fine distinctions. The form has dissolved, burst, splattered. Orpheus is dismembered. It's your (our) novel, isn't it? You can do anything you want to. Write the review first and you give the *Paris Review* boys a Wellington kick in the ass. And you convince the screening committees of the Foundations and Writers Conferences that you're hip and safe—articulate—a shaman in an academic jock strap. *Commentary* won't be able to ignore you. *The New Yorker* might use you for travel fillers. Young English instructors with bad Weismuller tests will swing on your wordy vine from East Nebraska State to Southwestern Illinois Business School. You will be a shock of recognition in the elevators of the MLA. I see you, J. Pressed and inviolate, in *Wilson's Bulletin*, alphabetized in *Modern Fiction Studies*, catalogued in the State Department for cultural export.

My concupiscence runneth over.

No irony, please. It went obsolete with The Bomb. You will be a serious grotesque in wild static fury. You will speak directly the shrieking dreams that disengage themselves from the waking moments of the day. You will refuse to huddle within the real fictions which we use to hide ourselves from the terrors of the Super-Real. Inebriate of *are*, art thou, and debauchee of *do*.

I begin to perceive, oh guru. I'm a vaudevillian of the interior consciousness. I throw triple somersaults across the bottomless maw of the libido without a net. I am the crucified clown of the esthetic high wire.

The esthetic why higher.

Thank you, the why higher. I weep at the weddings of the flesh and I laugh at the bitter word. My cloak is stiff with the eternal blood and my mouth is a wound.

You're getting on to it. Let your periods roll a little more. It helps for quotation purposes.

The Christ and the Faust recede to the wings—bulbous Shakespearean shams both. Two thousand years have weakened and shadowed their archetypal forms and they cling together for paltry substance. Victim and Victimizer fused in the blood transfer of ages. Feeble now and gorged to satiety, they moan in loveless embrace, a bloated beetle and its burden. The Passive Principle slouches into supine passivity—the Eternal Feminine impaled and unregenerative under the vertical thrust of History, spent, expended, bank-reft and barren, breastless, zestless, wholly unholy, and at rest.

That's better. Now a little less intellectual and more glandular.

And the Promethean fire, quenched and unsmoldering, limp as old celery on the dry belly of the desert. Passive-active, female and male, nymphet Christ and Faust the old ram—an inert and hardened callus of ultimate dual compliance. The willing and the will wedded and swelling to the ashen fruit of the won't. The audience bored in their seats, twitching with jaded annoyance in the prisons of their expectations. The Show has reached the showdown. The fail-safe mechanism has failed unsafely. Galactic explosions in the nerves herald the whimpering end, the acid search in the parking lots for the shiny car all gone to rust, sitting on tires that peel black strips of age on the gutted concrete. Home is nowhere and the driver is locked to the wheel, his foot heavier and heavier on the gas pedal as he seeks in mad mileage the blissful rending of metal by metal, the slow hemorrhage of grease and oil, the almost inaudible hiss of the deflated lung and pneumatic heart.

Too purple. Use a cookie cutter on your edges.

But enter the Wandering Jew, for the first time in history usurping the dead center of the dying stage, scuffing the writhing Christ-Faust (flotsam and jetsam intertwined) to one side like a stage prop out of place. He stands and his smile is the breadth of the proscenium arch, but his teeth have been filed to needle points and they shine in the light. Victim and Victimizer—their last act—expire in the final sexual sigh of the assault that has structured the world for twenty centuries, but no one sees them, no one notices their passing. The accepted gods of the past are the refuse of presence. Because the Wandering Jew has taken off his cloak (the mysterious greasy black of the ghetto, the usurer's pit, the worn entrails of the peddler's pack) and he is naked revealed for the first time. There is a white scar on his side which has healed into a pious caricature of the comic mask. His chest is broad and pelted, and his upper arms glisten faintly as though with oil. He is circumcised and the hair on his legs has a shadowed darkness which barely covers the musculature of calf and thigh. The feet are strangely pale and long-boned, and he rolls from heel to ball in dark reminiscence of the Mourner's Chant. The face? The face is impossible for words to describe.

No tricks. This isn't a Sophomore Creative Writing course. Describe the face or don't mention it at all.

The nose is a Spanish synagogue, furrowed and beaten by the Inquisition, but hawked and curved in accordance with the Holy Law. The cheekbones are high and arrogant in their thrust, the mouth set and slightly tensed between thin, but not overthin, lips. The eyes are gimlets of sky, black as night, cerulean as the cloudless day, coruscating, overcast, opaque. The long blond hair falls to the shoulders, meeting the soft curling beard at the apex of the collarbone. A river of greenish light washes back and forth across his features and he bends his head far back and he laughs. The audience is trapped by the laugh, is caught in its guttural resonances, is striated with fear and forgiveness, is absorbed into the greenish-black of the laughter, its million hands drumming slowly the beat, its million pulses dreaming slowly the respiratory starts and halts of the laughter that buries the Christ-Faust into one unmarked and unremarked shallow trench.

A little easier on the alliterations. And modulate your key. You know, something more prosaic. Build some suspense for the common reader. You do want a common reader, don't you? Someone to read the feshtunkeneh thing?

I don't care. The novel is all written now. There's nothing I can do about it. And all I need is one reader. You or me, common or uncommon, it doesn't make any difference.

Don't be so noble. Do you mean it *really* is written?

In a way. The beginning is the end, that kind of thing. The rhythms have begun, the pimple is throbbing.

You know what you're going to do?

No, not in that explicit sense. I'll learn by going where I have to go.

I suppose you're just going to follow your nose?

I might as well. Or my prose. Nose, prose, they come to a point in the same thing.

Just one more question, hochim, and I'll leave you be. Or become.

Yes?

You've said the *why* and you've said the *what,* but you've left out something. Granted, between your nose and your prose you're all committed to this thing. And I have a special interest too. But why should any normal human being who is not you—why should he read your novel?

Why not?

Don't be glib. Say why.

Well, normal human beings don't read novels at all, so they surely won't read mine. And abnormal human beings are liable to do anything. But I would hope that there might be things to be enjoyed, to be laughed at. It might be fun.

To read for fun?

For fun.

Maybe you'll go into paperback. A sordid spine.

Maybe. And then, too—

What?

Most people have pimples of their own in secret and far-away places.

Ah!

Maybe not on the tips of their noses. Maybe in the armpit, the inside of the groin, on the walls of their mouths. You know.

Momser! Who the hell do you think you are? The Messiah?

No. Weren't you watching? *It died already.*

# Journal

*16 April:* Two days after Easter. I wonder if He's still in a trajectory of ascent. When me they fly I am the wings. The Parisians couldn't care less. A half-million Frenchmen returned to Paris last night, vacance tout complet, Citroën, Peugeot, Simca, Renault, bumper to bumper, fender to fender, spiraling whine of horsepower wailing into Les Grands Boulevards, baby carriages lashed to the roofs and the children squashed in the back seats like Brussels sprouts, faces empty with holiday exhaustion. *Started the novel yesterday* and I have never actually believed in it before. I think I can push it through this time, all the way, if I can keep the pressure steady and not bear down too hard. Like Gieseking chiseling at Handel. Like swimming fifty yards under water, conserving the last air for the breakthrough to the top. I know I can do it this time if they'll just let me be. Paris should be diversion enough for Eva and the children so that I don't have to bleed out my energies entertaining *them.* We'll just have to put Mark into a kindergarten before he destroys all the bisque and majolica in the neighborhood. I got furious with him yesterday and Eva wanted to know what I expected from a five-year-old anyway. Well at least a modicum of discipline and order. Children don't have to be animals unless they live with animals. Lily is worse. I'd put her in a convent if they handled three-year-olds, but it wouldn't be fair to the Holy Catholic Church. I've always been ineffectual with her. Eva came back from the Louvre all crazy over the Da Vincis, especially the Bacchus and the Baptist. She said he was the only painter whose shapes echo like Shakespeare's. Supper was almost an hour late because we had to wait for her. It would seem simple enough to time one's trips on the Métro so that you'd know how long it takes to get home from where you've been.

Actually that's not quite accurate. I began to dream this thing more years ago than I can remember and I have old fragments written in Chicago, in the Schwarzwald, on the Welsh coast, and almost everywhere else we've been. But they've denied me a future up till now, and for the first time I can write into a time funnel where I know I have four blessed months to burrow into. You wonder whether what's out the window ever comes inside and gets on the pages. The fat rain on the Goethestrasse, the idyllic blue of the bay at Ischia, the endless soot of Paris. Maybe there's an indirect metamorphosis. No, of course not. All the worlds exist, but they have to come inside my head to be realized. Like I walked around Montparnasse looking for Joyce and Hemingway but there wasn't a trace of them. Just two American college boys rolling a garbage-can cover down Rue Notre Dame des Champs. This incredible city absorbs its past like a woman and the scar tissue is imperceptible to the naked eye. Which is what I shall strive to be, after all. A naked Emersonian eye.

I don't even have a carbon. One shot only. The kind of stupid romanticism that I wouldn't even try to defend. Lafcadio sticking a penknife into his thigh. The kamikaze school of writing in the Age of the Doctors (Spock, Seuss, & Salk). But it *testifies*. It says that there is one and only one of these things and, hence, it is unique and precious. The way Eva feels after she's done a line drawing and it has the rarity of having knifed out its own peculiar and eternal space in the universes of time. But it's going to be damned anxious not to have another copy under lock and key. Especially with two wild children in the house and Eva could give them my manuscript for paper airplanes if she weren't thinking.

Received the expected but undesired rejection of my James & Emerson piece this morning. They took the trouble to write an incoherent defense of their judgment, as though I cared for their gratuitous pedagogy. Oh, how I must have grilled their livers for them to have bothered to instruct me! They just can't understand that esthetics and morality are merely different labels for the same area of experience. So whatever I said about *form* was ipso facto lugubrious. And they'll never see that I don't give a turd's interest for biography and literary history. (Men have no histories and the life of mankind is just a play.) The man is the man; it's as simple as that. When he lectures, he's a teacher. When he writes, he's a writer. When he makes love, he's a lover. And all his actions and inactions should be ideally directed toward the free and complete possession of selfhood. Art is the path of the creator to his work, as Emerson so justly said. But why must they superimpose on this plain and simple truth some restrictive and overunified definition of self? What terrifies their skin? Only a mystic would have the right to say me nay, and all the mystics were vaporized at Hiroshima. Lord, Lord, I'm getting tired of waiting for them to catch up with my last year's footprints. It's lonely here in the future.

Had a surreal cup of coffee with Doren this morning, like Raskolnikov and Svidrigailov whispering madnesses through the transom of a closed door. In his dark labyrinthine way—the basement corridors that he closed off when he first perceived the line between darkness and light—he poses the same problem on an emotional level. The responsibilities of love as against the responsibilities to self. In the extremes—he runs to the extremes for his safety's sake—the dangers of moral cowardice (you give too much of yourself away) or moral callousness (you harden into a stalactite self because you haven't given enough away). But why does it have to be extreme? If you trust in the rightness of the bloodflow, and you feel that you know its currents for you, why should you seek knowledge in any other way? Controlled discontinuity, I would say. Nor is this the substitution of one paradoxical axis for another. Controlled discontinuity of styles and gestures. Moods, structures, and responses. The faces that face and avert. The only danger is that derangement which leads to suicide (it has many forms), but the risk is necessary. Doren plays the role of risk-taker, but his gambles are all predicated on the securities of everyone else's responses. He has an odd contemptuous affection for me, but I fear that I cannot read his plans for Eva. Or does that mean that I fear I read them all too bravely?

A recent article somewhere warning Americans to drop poker for chess on the grounds that our nuclear age makes the bluff-and-showdown metaphors too rigid for international diplomacy. Claimed that chess was more flexible and more susceptible to sacrifice and compromise. I'm not even sure that

Americans still possess a poker sense, but God help them, sweet Jesus, if they slump into the effete sophistication of chess. The movement from the existential to the ontological always signals the death of vitality. The poker player without a very immediate sense of Otherness has lost his shirt before he sits down to the table. The chess master always plays with and against himself, the first baroque Onan, soft-fingered monster of pallid narcissism. No sense of the Other at all. How To Blow Us All Up In Six Easy Lessons. The King's Pawn's Opening.

So we swing toward the Summer Solstice (I should be sighting a sleeve of light at the other end of the tunnel by then) with all hands more or less on board, fair blowing the winds for France, a clean ream of white paper ready to receive the blessings of the coming months. A cautionary note, perhaps, useless as are all admonitions. One crawls around within one's consciousness like a many-legged spider, testing the inside membranes with the tiny pressures of hirsute feet. It's a real risk, you know. A foot-pound too much and the walls could break. A miscalculation in the terrible darkness (the dead center of self is without light), a forgotten turning, a stress erroneously weighted, and the spider will wander out of time and into time, blinking its sudden eyes and puffing out into dirty cotton, dry like a parched pod. You've been there and you remember, but you forget which slip of the foot hurled you down. The few things which you learn from experience have ever to be relearned. And the rain it raineth every day.

A cold Paris spring, but the damp chill in the air is good for remembrance and thought and the dank pyramids of the imagination. Doren's dark vision of the city is a nice counterweight to Eva's silvered joy, but I must shake my head free of both and create my own secrets.

# One

Shape up, voyageur; there's lots of sail in the harbor and any one of them can go out on the lee tide if the inner wind whistles right in the rigging, but you've got to be big and you've got to be trig.

But the day the wind blew and the sail flew hard, I wasn't big or trig, just a little soft maybe, like butter, sitting on a white plate in the middle of the kitchen, that Letha had forgotten to put back in the icebox. I was sitting a little like the butter (although I didn't know it then) in my regular station on the bench facing the Frog Pond in the Common. I was nicely in the sun and about halfway through a package of Ry-Krisps which I'd feed me and the pigeons on during that summer. The crumbs had made my hands a little sticky in the sun and I'd given up on turning the pages of Géza Róheim's *The Gates of the Dream* and given myself up to the pigeons and the water jetting out of a spout in the middle of the pond. I was on a mythology-depth psychology kick that summer, always on the verge of finding impossible answers to impossible questions. I'd go from Freudian to Jungian like a ping-pong game in which I was the ball, and just when I was ready to back a mammoth uncastration building program for the collective psyches of the world, the goddamned Omphalos would sprout up like a cauliflower in the middle of the Racial Memory and I'd start worrying again about my little world and me. So I was sitting there watching the fountain and kind of idling my head around as the spray would arch into the sky and then break into an umbrella fall until the breeze would catch it and scoot it around everywhere. We were approaching the end of a hot August and the kids, mostly Italian from the North End, were ducking under the water, breaking the spray even more, and shining like light-colored olives in the middle of a big concrete salad plate.

Letha was in New York, "renewing herself in the galleries," and I was living in and out of our apartment which was now graced by the incomparable presence of my mother-in-law, that Mrs. Newsome made flesh, that maternal Jewish glacier, Sylvia–Sheva (or, as I privately muttered from time to time, Shiveh). Mama Sheva was ostensibly there to help out with the kids and the meals, but except for her frequent protestations that "tomorrow" she would make the potato kugel which was her one claim to culinary fame, we all lived on scrambled eggs with the white threading through like viscous strings. Letha's letters—according to pattern, long and frequent at first, trickling into hurried postcards from one or another museum—her letters seemed to indicate that the "renovation" was relatively successful. She seemed, at least, to be able to convince herself that she was "seeing" again, that she had not become irrevocably removed in time from the young painting student of ten years before who had been the summer shrine of the Art Students League, the knowledgeable but unknowing receiving set for the lusts and admiring yens of half the beards and part-time bohemians of Greenwich Village and Morningside Heights. At least as I read the letters and conspired in my memory for the images brought current, the "renovation" seemed dangerously successful. I meanwhile was supposed to be hard at work cataloguing the ergs and nuances of Jonathan Edwards' dialectic of moral freedom within a deterministic universe—a pursuit for which I had little talent, less patience, and no desire except the overriding knowledge that if I didn't get my dissertation done now, I would be forever doomed to the legion of forgotten men—the unbayonetted Beau Gestes of the Freshman English sections, eternally on assignment at the parapets of the run-on sentence and the dangling modifier. The fact that the University had given me a summer research grant to complete the work ("It's really for your own good, David. Of course it doesn't mean anything, but it is, after all, the union card to The Profession.") didn't help my natural lack of assiduity at all, either. The gift was quite palpably a threat, and although nobody likes to be pushed, people always seem to think that I'm an exception to the rule. So they push and I budge not. Not at all. And sometimes even when I would like to.

Anyway, it was all very rational and practical—this summer separation for a freer expression of personalities, etc.—but kosher? Not on your life. Actually, although dear Mama Sheva didn't know it because dear Mama Sheva rejected the possibility that there was a world beyond the mirrors of her own silver fingernails, Letha was on the point of explosion and I was nearing that contraction to absolute zero where all the molecules are supposed to stop moving and the earth's axis must grind to a slow and shuddering halt. It's hard even now to describe clearly. I mean she was there and all, round and ripe and ready as hell, but not for me. And I couldn't make the connection, like when you scrape the key all around the lock but it won't slide in—except this particular lock sighs a little and moves away and the key goes back into the pocket, cold and loose among the small change. But it wasn't sexual, I mean, or it wasn't only sexual. The kids were big enough now so that the bathroom didn't aways look like a laundry established primarily for weak prostate cases (the Cloaca Maxima I used to call it in its balmy days), and they were busy enough exploring their own little universes so that we were able to live somewhat more free of them. But we clocked too many hours sitting cold and separate together, going about the routine chores and talking and sharing everything except anything that might have touched us individually and basically. So when this proposition came up—and it may even have been me who first brought it up—Letha grabbed at it with reluctant rapacity, pleading with me to make her go even while she protested her want for the four of us to stay together. It was the easiest coaxing I ever did to get her on the train, suitcased, moneyed, and as delicately shaved and perfumed as though she were going off for a check-up from the obstetrician.

So it had been maybe three weeks and I'd taken to walking from our place on the Fens down to the Common to read a little and watch the fountain and feed the pigeons and forget that goddamned mind, Jonathan Edwards, and maybe I'd duck into one of those air-conditioned bars off Park Square and sit with a beer and the baseball game, and it wasn't bad, it was just a kind of slowed-down waiting. I guess I knew and I didn't know what I was waiting for, but the mind is such a tricky thing that you don't ever really know what you knew or, for that matter, what you know either. Edwards has a multileveled discussion on this point, but he loses me, so maybe he wasn't sure either. So I'm sitting there on my favorite bench with nothing much in my head except the sun and the play of broken water, when the nuntius arrives, sidling up the walk like a black cringing clam. There were probably close to a quarter of a million people in and out of downtown Boston that day, and how Strogoff managed to meet me in the Common is a question that still startles me into a sweat on some nights, but meet me he did and there was even something inevitable and imminent in the direct oily ooze of his walk from God only knows where (maybe he'd been fingering the cheap Italian-styled sport shirts in Filene's basement or wandering the marble lobbies of the cloak-and-suiters on Kneeland Street)—to me on that particular bench. One of the back slats was broken off and the wounded wood was dry as dust.

He sat down next to me and in the same motion was wiping his face with a coarse handkerchief, pushing his hat brim back from his forehead. I noticed that he'd gotten balder since I'd seen him last (what funeral? what food-swollen bar mitzvah?) and his heavy black suit smelled of raw naphtha. He had the look of a man who was enjoying himself wonderfully, who had scraped the noodles aside with his spoon and discovered completely by surprise that there was a pale-yellow egg in his soup.

"So, nu, Dovidle, wie gehts? Long time no see."

I grunted more or less sociably. His observation was incontestable and I couldn't care less.

"Such a pleasure," he continued, sucking invisible noodles through his teeth. "A whole year yet I don't see you or your wife and then in two days, with a distance a whole two hundred miles in between, both you and Letha I see."

And I knew it then. I knew it with every vertical prickle on my flesh, and the back of my head and neck froze hot and I made some kind of a smile and I waited, although I knew he couldn't tell me anything more than I had already got.

"So look, Dovid. Me, it's none of my business, but as a husband myself, speaking as a husband to a husband, I think a husband should know."

Every time he said the word "husband" his mouth pecked forward as though he were taking a decorous bite out of a hot dog. I started to say something, but he had his spoon on that egg and he could no more have been stopped from delivering his message in full than I could really have let him be stopped.

"Believe me, Dovidle. If I were in your place—which God forbid—I'd want you should tell me. And with no flimsy-flamsy. But direct and to the point."

I started to break in on him again, but obviously my only existence for him was as an audience and he had evidently rehearsed his little speech until it was absolutely word perfect. I could see him coming back from New York on the train, practicing his face in the broad glass window, testing his lines, his expressions of fraternal solicitude with alternate grimaces of stern and painful honesty. He might even have gone twice or three times to the men's room, bracing himself by the knees against the stained white toilet bowl as he chose from the possible attitudes of justice, kindness and mercy, each intermingled with a delicious prurience which gave a sustaining glow to his drab skin.

"So I'll be direct, I'll be brutal direct to you. I'm in New York yesterday for the business and I'm staying like always at the Toffit and who do I see coming out of a room on my own floor with a man—not a man even, Dovid, but a goy—who do I see but your Letha? Believe me, Dovidle, better I didn't see, but I seen them. Him touching and leaning all over her like she was a bed— Oi, I knew all about it in a minute. It was a lot of monkey business in that room— No, let me finish the story. It's to the point and I decided right away that you should know, and I was going to call you anyway tonight, you shouldn't suffer from being ignorant. So I says to myself, Strogoff, you should better look a little around—a regular Charlie Chan yet. And I find out they're registered at the desk as man and wife—a Mister and Missus C. Greene from Garden City, New Jersey, but they're checking out that afternoon. How can you know what to do? But I decided there and then that I would tell you personal the entire geshichte. Could you imagine, Dovid, a nice Jewish girl like that?"

I suppose the world should have merry-go-rounded as it does in the epiphany scenes in the cheap movies, but so far as I can tell nothing special happened to me. In fact, I remember staring curiously at the raised red veins on the flanks of Strogoff's nose. He had a really magnificent nose, thick and sculptured like a prize turnip, and the corded veins were architecturally massive. I wanted to ask him if those veins ever throbbed, and if they did, did he ever think that his nose might have an independent life of its own. I had a quick fancy of Strogoff tucking himself into bed at night, pulling the covers neatly under his chin, and then when he began to snore, his nose leaping off his face and—I don't know—nosing around, I suppose. I slid an invisible mask on—over my face, but under my skin, if you know what I mean. It wasn't anything I thought about; it was something I did so automatically that part of my brain was surprised to find it done. The features of David Riegel, A.B., M.A., just one unwritten dissertation away from Ph.D., were impassive to the outside world—firm, unrevealing, composed in casual dignity ("Coo, old chap. You say the bomb scored a direct hit? And not even a piece of the children left? Poor Cornelia, it's as well it was instantaneous. She could hardly have stood up to it, you know. *Too* bad."). Strogoff had burrowed his face forward toward me through the heavy heated air. Sweat glistened on him like sardine oil and there was an obscenely conspicuous fleck of spittle incongruously pendant on the flange of his right nostril. The lieutenant in charge of the vice squad must probably exude the same kind of smell when he examines the pornographic materials that his lusty myrmidons shovel onto his desk. I realized that I was supposed to say something, so I played it Cary Grant.

"Yeah, Strogoff. So what else is new?"

His expression didn't change but a little blankness moved under his facial skin and he tried again. "You're not understanding me, Dovid. What I'm trying to say, it's—"

"Sure, sure, Strogoff. I get the message fine. I know all about it."

"Oh," moaned Strogoff, obviously disappointed that he was not the first to make it from Aix to Ghent, but still happy with anticipation of the genuine real-life drama that was unfolding right before his very eyes.

"Sure, Strogoff," I continued, climbing wildly inside my mind for something to say. "Sure. You see—you see, Letha and I—" I leaned confidingly toward him and I would swear that I saw those incredible nose-veins twitch a whole quarter of an inch. "Letha and I have—made a little arrangement. Yes—a little arrangement. You see, this guy you ran into at the Toffit— He's Letha's brother. They were very close as kids and—"

"Brother?"

"Yes, he's her brother. They were very close as kids—maybe *too* close, you know—and they get to miss one another, and—"

"Dovidle, the hip that Letha was rubbing against that guy. This was not the hip you rub against your brother."

"Yes—yes, Strogoff. They've always been very close, you

see. Blood and water, or is it oil and water? You know what I mean?"

Strogoff shrugged my obstacles out of his way with the rigid cowcatcher of his powerful intention and steamed up the track. Those rehearsal hours in the train were not going to be wasted. "Look, Dovidle, I know just how you feel, and I want you should understand that I sympathize with you right down to *here*." He caressed his stomach as though he were suffering from a little gas. "If it was me—which God forbid—I'd sit shiveh for her, but it's none of my business except I wanted you should know the whole facts of the truth. And if there's anything I can do to lend a helping hand, you know that Strogoff is right *here*." He tapped at his collarbone meaningfully.

"Well, that's very nice," I said, getting awkwardly to my feet with the Ry-Krisps in one hand and the Róheim in the other. "And it was very nice of you to tell me that you saw Letha and maybe the three of us can get together one of these days. And your wife, too." I nuzzled his vest with the sharp corner of *The Gates of the Dream*. "Mustn't forget your wife, eh, Strogoff? Old friends, new brooms, you know—" I was already moving down the path when Strogoff grabbed my arm.

"Dovidle, what are you going to do?" He had pushed his face close to mine and I had a sudden impulse to see if I could pull his nose off. "What are you going to do?" he repeated.

"Well—" I looked past his nose into his watery eyes. Flakes of yolk were crusted in the corners. "Well, I might just dig a hole and stuff your head in it. See if we can get a crop of spring turnips next year. Or onions. Or noses. You know what I mean."

And while he stood there swearing—albeit with pity—at me, I marched down the walk slowly, erectly, with my shoulders back, my chest out, my chin jutting smartly to the front. My heels clicked on the pavement, my book was tucked neatly under my left arm and the package of Ry-Krisps was at a forty-five-degree angle to my body. I took a sharp by-the-right-flank-MARCH, pivoting cleanly on the toes of both feet, paraded over to a large litter basket and dropped the Ry-Krisps in. The basket was almost empty, a crumpled cigarette pack, some hard orange peels and a used contraceptive. "Jesus," I remember thinking, "some guys are awful neat."

The fountain was still streaming in the middle of the pond (why shouldn't it have been?), but the breeze had picked up and the shattered water broke into an erratic spray under the movement of the wind. The kids were chasing the fall of the spray, but the wind, as though party to the game, had set up an eddied whirlpool of air which made the spray elusive and diffuse. I walked all the way around the pond noticing vaguely that the black-clad Strogoff was nowhere in sight. Then I headed for Boylston Street where the sun was glinting on the tops and sides of the ever-moving line of traffic and the effect of the noise and the shine and the movement was that of a great scaly dragon breathing a fire invisible and searing.

I must have covered a fair distance because I know that I stopped in one of those Fun Palaces in Scollay Square near where the Old Howard had once so humbly stood, and put a dime into a rusted peep show. It was one of those machines which flip a series of yellowed pictures toward the eyepiece, and although each picture is itself innocuous, the general momentum is supposed to be suggestive. The eyepiece was so dirty and the pictures and revolving mechanism so overused under the mountains of dimes which adolescent lust of all ages had invested that I wasn't sure whether I had paid for "The Dance of Young Spring" or "Lather in a Roman Bath." I threw three lopsided canvas baseballs at a row of stiff sawdust dolls that looked like Strogoff and I missed them by successively wider distances. I stood near the excavation work that was bringing the new expressway-skyway over the downtown area and I very deliberately mused philosophically (not Edwardianly) on the inexorable processes of time and change. Scollay Square was depressing with its watered root beer and shattering neon that seemed to be on the verge of leaking into leukemia. This Scollay Square, erstwhile grande dame of whoredom, port of call for every gob in every navy of the world during the thirties—and, above all, during the war—reduced to old cronage, become a skinny old hag selling rotten apples on the sooty street.

Oh, how often had I stuffed my lunch into my green baize bag and headed for the Square rather than to high school. A quick stop at Joe & Nemo's for a sandy hot dog and a beer and then the delicious sneaky entrance (if you could reach the ticket counter with your money, you were an adult) into the Howard, where the show lasted from eight in the morning until forever. What triumphs of theater had I witnessed there! Hedy Lamaar in *Ecstasy* (the cut version), the statuesque Lois de Fee, and the torrid-topped Margie Hart with the green loincloth that accented the marble white of the most beautiful body in the world. The endless parade of bovine strippers and choristers whose ultimate expression of sex and provocation was the inexpert shaking of the fat on their asses while massaging the stage curtain with their thighs until, in spite of yourself, all you could think of was some fat middle-aged ladies toweling themselves after a shower. And the humor. Who has ever really learned to laugh who missed Mike Sachs or Jimmy Savo when burlesque was at its height (or depth) and you were fifteen or fourteen and the double entendre associated with the word "balls" was sufficient to stimulate a paroxysm of risibility? And the inevitable crooner, sweatily suspended from the fixed microphone in the wings, booming out the overemphasized beat of "Jealousy" (it was the only song he could sing all the way through), while the matrons of the chorus chewed their sticks of gum and stomped like circus horses on the pseudo-Elizabethan lip of the front stage. The Old Howard, where Oliver Wendell Holmes (the young judge, of course) had a private box for his own use and where the first row was always composed of bald-headed men who tried in vain to pinch the flesh that sagged to their fingertips, and the second and third rows were the bailiwick of old garlicky Italian women who slept or slapped their children during the whole show waiting for the clowns to take their turn. The comics were more often than not Yiddish in their gestures and punch lines (how Jewish thy contempt for the goyim—the consumer, the client, the enemy), but there was always a "pasta-fazoo" thrown out for the Sicilianas and this was enough to justify their waiting one two three hours for the comedians' bitter return. Ah, Old Howard, I thought, we were both young and innocent in our apple dreams and only titillated naïvely by the possibilities of life.

I remembered that hot spring day when Al Penori and I had cut classes before Latin (there was to be an impossible quiz on the hedges of the Nervii) and we had sailed off for the O.H. to spend the morning and then over to Fenway Park to watch the hateful Yankees luck out another win over our darlings, our loves, and our prides. The dark cool of the theater was a shock from the hot sidewalks and the fetid swamp of the subway. We stacked our book bags next to our seats and settled ourselves with the acne on our faces and a package of Milk-Duds. I was in the aisle seat "to spot any ready broadies" that might enter alone, it being a generally accepted adolescent truth that no woman under the age of fifty would come into the Old Howard unless "she was dying for it." A man came down the aisle and although our book bags were right in the middle of a yellowed patch of light from an underhung aisle lamp, the man tripped and fell clumsily to the floor. He was slight and vaguely mincing in the feline grace with which he turned a clumsy fall into a controlled pattern, and I began to burn with that embarrassment that even then assailed me when I was on the margins of a scene or a drama. He got up and his features were menacing as though he were folding them into an angry shape.

"That's a stupid sonofabitchin place to put your groceries."

His whisper was pitched high and I couldn't decide whether he was really angry or not. Faces were turning around to look at us and I didn't say anything.

"Move over, kid," he said, pushing into our row. "I think I sprained my ankle."

Al and I shifted one seat over and the man sat down holding a slender foot between his hands. He wore silk socks with vertical silver designs on them and he massaged his foot tenderly, mewing softly under his breath. My face was hot with some strange shame and I tried to watch the screen. A movie was in progress—one of those movies that seemed to have been shot on old film with swift pictures of trees and bending grasses and every so often a distance shot of running girls with white scarves streaming behind them. The man kept mewing, a little more loudly now, and I tried to quench the shame by saying something that would put an end to our unresolved scene.

"I'm really very sorry about that bag," I said. "I specifically put it in the light where anybody could see it."

He stopped his mewing and looked at me in a flat way like a cat interrupted in licking itself clean. "That's all right, kid," he said. And he smiled with his mouth as soon as he had stopped speaking, but there had been no smile while he had looked at me or while he had talked.

I tried to concentrate on the movie, but I was too conscious of his being next to me and too aware that my shame must be compounded before it would cease. He didn't wriggle around in his seat or mumble the way some people do at the movies; he was just *there,* the way you know somebody's in the room with you even though you can't see them. So I wasn't surprised to feel his hand on my knee, where it began skidding up my leg like a soft paw, although I did get cold and prickly with embarrassment and fear. I shifted my leg to warn him that I knew what he was doing—as if there were any doubt that he knew I knew—but the hand returned almost immediately. At almost exactly the same time, Al had sensed that something was going on, and he pushed his young and ugly face with the round windows of his glasses glinting from the bright screen over toward me, grunting an undecipherable question. The man leaned toward both of us from the opposite direction with his hand still on my leg.

"You kids care to go to a place I know for a little wine and a little time?"

His face was very tight and he seemed to be talking as though the words were twisted out of his mouth from an orange squeezer. Long afterwards I got the notion that this was something he was doing not because he wanted to, nor because he was forced by passion to, but almost as though it were something he had to do as a punishment or penalty. And I realized that his proposition wasn't directed to me and Al at all, but maybe to the general air, to the whole audience, to everything that wasn't himself. But my immediate world was smaller then, and the shining alabaster of my adolescence was being defaced with slime.

"Get the hell out of here, you homo bastard," I said in a voice throaty with shame and purposely loud so that people would turn around.

"Yeah, get out of here, you goddamn fairy, or we'll slice you up," echoed Al.

People began to react to our small commotion and the man stood up lithely from his seat. His ankle seemed to have been restored to full functionality as his body arched delicately over us. His face was a blotched white in the flickering reflections from the screen, but he projected an air of odd dignity as though he were suffering for us in spite of us. And I felt terribly decreased and urgently deficient in some strengths that I couldn't put a name to, but which I knew myself to be without.

"It's been lovely meeting you sweet young things," he said, looking down on us, but speaking, as before, as though to some auditor that he alone could see. "We must do this another time—sometime." And he bowed with a grace that even then I knew was grace and he walked up the darkened incline to the exit.

When Al and I left the Howard, after forcing ourselves to stay for another hour because we had arranged it that way, the early afternoon heat sucked up by the Square and the whooosh-claash of the traffic made a too-bright too-noisy world that we were impotent and lost in. Later, in the center-field bleachers at Fenway Park, I tried to connect the spurious bright green of the outfield with the rocking dark subway ride to Kenmore Square and the dank dark of the Howard. Doc Cramer was playing center field and the round circles of the "8" on the back of his shirt were inky against the white linen screaming in the sun. I watched most of the game trying not to look directly at the players because their uniforms were too sharply bright and my eyes blurred and could not focus well. The splitting crack of a well-hit ball made my head ache and I wallowed in a dank fuzziness where the white delineation was an unjust assault on youthful senses, overtuned and awry.

Ah, yes, Old Howard, I thought with self-pitying tears behind my eyes. We were both young and innocent together then—Old Howard and Young David—twin despoiled virgins amidst the putrescence and sad debris of life. And poor Penori, dead, someone told me, at Salerno. The giant teeth of the excavators rip new wounds in the flanks of Scollay Square and the grey steel supports of the skyway stretch like death over the onetime opera house which is now history and the onetime Penori who is now history and the onetime Davie Riegel who watches through the eyes of time his other self, red and silent in spirit, groveling on the foul floor between the rows of seats, chastened and crushed amid the candy wrappers and wadded gum and spent lust of the burlesque house.

I must have covered a good distance that afternoon because I remember stopping for a cup of the good Joseph on Commercial Street and later browsing through the paperbacks in South Station. From there I must have walked in the brutal sun all the way down Stuart to Copley Square and then down Boylston to Mass Avenue. My gait was leisured, but still with a slight hint of the military in the set of the shoulders and the regularity of the stride. I supposed that a trained observer would have guessed that I was a Colonial officer—Indian service, most probably—on temporary retirement into mufti, but so habituated to the steel discipline of The Service as to be incapable of slouch or slump. Behind the mask of my march, however, my mind began to make infiltrating stabs at the numb knowledge in the middle of my brain. I found my feet stepping to the rhythm of "Peter, Peter Pumpkin Eater, Had a Wife and Couldn't Keep Her," and grotesque images of giant orange pumpkins and the inner rounds of Letha's thighs filled me with a flaming nausea. I pulled the reins up tight on my mind, trying to clench off the insatiable flood of vile associations—lewd ugly fascinating pictures which teemed and boiled like obscene minnows in a fish hatchery. Naked entangled legs and breasts taut with passion, the brownish nipples stiff and scaly to the palm of a strange hand, the animal grunts and moans of desire rising to a hungry flesh-biting pitch to subside in a hissing spent tide, stomachs flabby, loins wet and limp, mouths distended and sate. I felt hollow—cored like a grapefruit.

As though I were holding my son's hand on a trafficked street, I carefully led my mind away from the terrible center of my knowledge, hoping that the periphery would be easier to navigate. Man cannot bear too much reality, as the man said. And only the eagle can gaze directly into the sun. The periphery was if anything worse. The brutal collision of bodies, the eager swallowing of penetration was not so horrifying, or it didn't have to be. It, at least, was impersonal—a bruising need of the flesh—bodies on bodies—foreign bodies, heavenly bodies, nobodies at all. You could think in terms of the phony wrestling exhibitions that Paul Bowser used to promote at the old Arena, where he had to give the tickets away so that there would be somebody in the audience. Orgasm was orgasm, as physical as spit, as vomit, as tears. A simple physiological excretion, understandable as a system of tensions and discharges. Once in a troop train, going through Montana, a soldier who had never walked on anything but concrete and polished wood before he was drafted announced to the whole train in a voice tremulous with wonder, "Hey! There's two goddamn cows screwing over there!" And I hadn't known immediately why everyone laughed so hard and so long. The sex itself, the corking of the bottle, was a picture that I could accept with some calm as a physical and not very meaningful thing. But not the long series of feints and withdrawals, of thrusts and parries that must have led up to it, and the moments seconds hours after with the recurrence of the passion flashing like a lurid glow in the dark of courtship.

I knew Letha well even if not too wisely. Seduction was out of the question unless it was mostly on her side. The meeting (How did they meet? How hard for a pretty woman to meet a man?). Letha with her young-girl face and the voice and body which she could unfold like a greeting card (mother of two well-fleshed children and everyone automatically calls her "Miss" without thinking). No, the twentieth-century seducers are always the female, probably have been forever. Her hands moving across a table like quivering animals, the way she must have used her body to touch, to burn, to draw closer and closer. Even Strogoff—and no lightning rod he—had caught the moist electricity of her charge on Mr. C. Greene (sea-green and dapple-dawn drawn falcon in his riding o'er the heavy air). But the cold deliberate calculation—arranging for a room, down-facing the ratty room clerk, standing on the wall-to-wall carpeting while the boy tests the key, switches on the bathroom light, leers at the nonexistent suitcases, and opens the curtains which so soon will draw close and darken the bright contours of a different reality. The first time they hold hands, the first time his arm sidles around her waist, his fingers smoothing the plump fold of flesh which her too-tightly notched belt pinches, the first kiss with the mouths groping open, their legs slightly apart, she pushing her breasts and leaning upward into him. It doesn't happen in a moment of impersonal physicality. It takes time, and the mind and the memory only extinguish in flashes. Where was I then in Letha's mind? Was I dead? Without being? Am I dead right now? When he squeezes her hand with joy or rage or desire and the ring on her wedding finger pinches the skin with a pain that she must feel, am I still dead and the ring just a golden provocation like the black stockings the Petty girls used to wear to make nakedness more naked? What in hell is love that it can hurt so bad? And why did we have to be made this way? God, oh, God, you sonofabitch!

That way lies madness, someone else said. So what? What good sanity to be the vessel of woe? Madness maddened is an answer. Slice the cords of care! Rip up the binds that bond! Rage, rage against the dying of the light! Easy, Riegel old boy. Riegel wasn't built in one day and Riegel isn't going to collapse in one day, either. Look at the magnificent company you're in. Roger Chillingworth and Alexey Karenin, sweet brothers under the skin. I say, get thee to the marketplace; Anna is mounting the scaffold with a scarlet "A" on her breast and I shall finger my short-cropped beard like Basil Rathbone and the cuckold will disguise himself as the learned herb doctor. Weeds from my garden, anyone? Ratsbane, nightshade, mandrake root (get with child), love vine. What a country club we have—exclusive—The Horns—the funniest clowns in the history of civilization. Riegel and Chillingworth and Karenin and Leopold Bloom, oh, modern Odysseus. You can take your beery Dublin, bitterly bitterly Boston one time more. You read too much of the night, Riegel, old gull; take a day off and go out to Suffolk Downs and watch Frou-Frou split a gut in the third race. Put out the light and then put out the light. Light. The light and the dark. Oh, what a goddamned nasty joke, that comic hateful play. Othello was right and the poor dark bastard didn't even know it. Maybe Cassio, maybe Iago, probably both of them, and whoever the hell else was moving scenery behind the wings—all of them were getting into her pants. And she so sweet and demure and cuddly, the white angel of Shakespeare's great period. Angel, my ass! That handkerchief was the real clue—the cover-up, the wispy scrim of lace to adorn the crotch so the fair hairs would make a triangular target for any doughty lad with the want and the will. Othello the simp, the patsy, the miles gloriosus with his heroic past of derring-do. Daring don't, better. Wasn't he a brilliant warrior, no warlock he? Hadn't the Duke sent expressly for him to straighten everything out—so wide his fame? And hadn't she adored him and fronted her father's wrath for the pleasure of hooking her little pinky under his warrior's belt? He had history and memory on his side, but the poor stupid dusky male mind never knew that history and memory are masculine and white angel Desdemona was alive only under the handkerchief. It's betrayal-deep under the handkerchief but not a centimeter of time. Hail, brother Othello! At least you never knew, and you are easily the most comical of cuckolds, because you thought you were merely a murderer.

Whoa! Not without some self-pity (just enough to lubricate the mechanism nicely) I used two hands to yank my mind away from the direction that it was accelerating toward. I was standing in front of the old green Viking with the rough rune engraved on its pedestal that had been set up in this grassy corridor down Commonwealth Avenue between the two lines of traffic which never cease their daytime flow. Countless classes of Boston schoolchildren had been brought devoutly to view the rune, just as they had been brought devoutly to gape at the dinosaur in the Museum of Natural History (now Bonwit Teller) or the Forsythe Dental Clinic ("Yippee, Mom! Fourteen cavities and trench mouth!") or a rehearsal of the Symphony under Koussevitzky or Paul Revere's house or the Hall of Flags in the State House. Reeking with dead history and culture was mellowed corrupt red-bricked Boston, and no boy, even if he were Jewish, could grow up in the City of the Inhuman Bean without being deeply affected by it. The names themselves—sentimental, hackneyed, untarnished in a meretricious setting—were enough to people the streets with an unassailable glory—but, most wonderfully, a glory not wholly unreachable, even for a Jewish boy. The Mathers, Franklin, all the Adamses, the Jameses, Santayana, the Lodges, and now the Irish heresy of the Kennedys. And the prime regent too, the most resplendent name of them all, the kingly Emerson. So many had succeeded so well that how could one not be convinced that one too might become a Boston name!

The afternoon traffic reached a driving pitch of regularity in the stop and start, the snarl and whine of engines, the spasmodic horns and the insulting, nonindignant yells of drivers ("Hey, lady! Weah'd yah get yah license, Seahs and Roebuck!"). It was as if two swift-flowing rivers had cut me off on the grassy island and I and the rune populated a truncated world of lonely pain and silent resistance. I sat at the foot of the pedestal noticing that the blue dye of my book had stained my sweaty palm and my handprint was ineffaceably white on the cover. The rune and the ruin, I thought, visitors both to Boston, exiles both and expatriates both, but where was I exiled from? It was like coming home to sit in this place, to watch the moving world and know that I was separated from it by a sparse distance that no comet could traverse. How many windows had I leaned out of, watching and smelling and feeling to the outside, longing from my thirsty pores to connect, to make contact, to bruise with my flesh and spirit against something. Against anything. Everything. The nights and the days, the heats and the colds, the rains and the hot vacuum suck of the sun had wrapped me in an envelope from which I could see and hear and yearn acutely, but within which I was imprisoned as surely as though I had heard the great key churn in the lock and watched the casual warder saunter away. Within windows with my elbows scraping soot from the sills, leaning my upper body dangerously out and wanting to fall into some air some pavement some adamant otherness that would make me lose my separateness. It was an old feeling and I had long ago discovered that it didn't pay to sit inside it too long. Rune, I said, accept a small croon from a ruin, and I hummed softly below the river flow of the traffic:

"I am a saint without a taint
Like Mary's Joseph long ago
Oh ain't it quaint to be a saint
While all the sinners fall so low."

A middle-aged woman, very modish in beige linen, in fact so much the Beacon Hill dowager that she could only have been a Sodality lady from Mission Hill or Southie, strolled by the monument, and from the tight lips which she screwed at the sight of me, I knew she thought I was drunk. I got up and brushed my pants off and made a deep bow to her.

"Sure and pahdon me, ma'am," I brogued at her. "Fayther O'Brien has got himself the shingles and I think it may be contagious."

I bowed again and crossed the street toward Mass Avenue, leaving her with her lips still tightly screwed but somewhat more twisted than before.

I suppose I must have known where I was going from the moment my nostrils had reacted to Strogoff's black naphtha'd suit, and all this walking around in the humid Boston afternoon without the living blessing of an east wind from the harbor had been an elaborate parentheses, a stumbling, wandering prologomenon to my facing Father Abraham. I thought wryly of Edwards' poor chained will when I discovered that I was outside the familiar Abraham's Fruits & Vegetables, a wizened two-door shop set between a Chinese restaurant and an Express laundromat almost catty-cornered across the street from the Christian Science Mother Church. Why there should have been such a shop in that part of Mass Avenue, and how it had been able to stay in business even before the octopus growth of the chain stores and the supermarkets, no one really knew (or cared). The shop had actually been there forever, established some months before Richard Blackstone had planted his orchard and settled his legendary library on one of the Boston hills. Father Abraham had always been, and it was authoritatively rumored that his first cash sale had been corn to Massasoit. When I had worked for him in the afternoons while I was going to high school, he had been just as old, his long beard just as clean and curled at the ends, his face just as pink and unlined. And I knew as I stood in front of his shabby show window with the geometric pyramids of grapefruit round and yellow against the streaked glass that I had laboriously come to a beginning; that I was starting to react, to shuffle my feet slowly in the blooded sand, to rock on my toes and begin to seek a stance for my soul. Father Abraham was the first act and I had had to come here but I had been delinquent in the coming.

He was sitting in his rocking chair, a homemade monstrous thing fabricated out of orange crates and barrel slats with two pieces of felt on the arms, his head thrown back and to the side on a specially rounded wooden brace, also padded with felt, so that while he rested in his chair next to the cash register, he could watch the whole store and the two squares of light which gave him a double view of the outside world, his beard flowing easily down his arm coiling to rest on a box of prize tomatoes. I hadn't been in the store for over four years, but he looked as though he hadn't budged in all that time, and the tomatoes had the same red waxy shine which set off the dramatically unbelievable whiteness of his beard. His eyes recognized me without surprise, those incredible Jewish blue eyes that welcomed the world without censure and lost themselves in the secure depths where his heart pulsed. He was wearing his faded cotton work coat which fell down below his knees when he stood and which buttoned down the front with large yellowed clasps. The sleeves were extra wide and when he raised his arm in slow greeting, his salutation was an unmistakable benediction.

"You are welcome here, David," he said, and although I knew his voice well, I was once again shocked by the feminine sweetness of its tones—a sweetness strangely enhanced by its guttural resonances. I dragged a small fruit crate across the floor and sat in my old place at his feet, my chin braced on my hands at about the same level as the prize tomatoes.

"You are always welcome in my eyes, David," he repeated. "And especially when you come in a time of trouble."

That was my first directional upset. I had planned to talk delicately around my sea of troubles, sticking a precarious toe in from time to time, but I had forgotten Father Abraham's intense directness. "I didn't realize I looked so much like an animated illustration for a CARE ad, Father Abraham," I said. He didn't smile.

"Tsoris is beyond cosmetics, David. It's not meant to be hidden if it's honestly carried. And this is a good thing. For without unhappiness in the human soul, love has no entrance there. And where love cannot enter, the countenance of the Almighty is turned aside."

"Well, it's not all that cosmic." I fidgeted. "In fact, I guess it's kind of trite. Even Biblically trite, you know." And then I said it right out without knowing that I was going to. "My wife has been playing Bathsheba, you might say, and— And I'm the wrong David in the story."

I watched his eyes carefully to gauge his reaction to this, but there was no reaction. Neither shock, nor pity, nor contempt. His eyes were sweetly serene and I had a quick image of my trouble plunging like a heavy stone into the placid blue and disappearing beneath the surface without a ripple or a splash or the slightest disturbing tremor. If you didn't know him well, you might have thought he had heard nothing; but you knew him well and you had learned that almost nothing escaped him. Since he uttered no word and offered no response, I told him briefly what had happened and he listened as an ice-blue lake might have listened to the winter moan of the trees and the frosty rasp of the winds through their unleaved branches. He sat unmoved and I waited for the speech that was coalescing in the deeper waters far below the surfaces which shone and glistened from the late afternoon light of the double windows. He shifted very slightly in his seat and began to talk in a gentle low voice as though he were chanting a private canticle.

"When an orthodox Jew rises in the morning, he gives thanks unto the Lord that he has been created a man and not a woman. You know that, David, but do you know why he offers his thanks?"

"Sure, I remember that. It's because woman is supposed to be more or less an animal. The bearer of passions and uncleanliness. Almost trafe. And the pious Jew could just as well be thanking God that he's a man rather than pork. It comes to the same thing."

"Oi, oi, oi." Father Abraham rocked with disgust. "How am I going to teach you anything when you don't know anything to begin with? So constipated your brain wasn't when you were a boy not yet a man. The Jew thanks the Almighty that he is a man and not a woman, as he would offer thanks for being a man and not a sunrise. As a sunrise cannot delight in itself, so a man cannot delight in life except in terms of the Female. Thus the gratitude of the Jewish prayer is a gratitude for the gift beyond price. The man humbles himself in appreciation of the crown of creation, the jeweled Eve, who brings the dance and delight of sex to the blessed Garden. Note well, you ersatz teacher, that Judaism for three thousand years has mocked at celibacy and asceticism. We know nothing about the castrated pleasures of living without women on this earth and less than nothing about a Female Principle canonized into some celestial sexlessness. Our Marys are Miriams and our holy men are full-blooded, wholly living men. The pious Jew, the *intelligent* Jew, makes this prayer of thanks as a testimony to his pleasure in being a human male."

Father Abraham dropped his arm which he had been using

as a forceful baton and let his fingers tenderly press the ripe red tomatoes at his side.

"All right, all right. So I'm not qualified to give a Commentary on the Morning Prayers. What does this all have to do with me?" His roundabout detours into the Scriptures irritated me. I wanted good clean sympathy and I was getting education.

"Not so fast, David. So sure, you got some nasty hairs across your ass." He touched me kindly on the knee and returned his hand to the end of his beard, twisting the white hairs like the fringe on a prayer shawl. "But where the heart is involved, it is important that the mind also involve itself. Otherwise the heart will blow up like a bomb. You feel; this is good. Then you must think. This is also good. And then, on the basis of your thought, you must feel a more complicated feeling. This is the best way. And this is the cycle of growth and life which the God of Jacob has bestowed upon mankind. Let us, for a text, examine the beautiful story of Adam and Eve which presents so wonderfully the whole aching drama of man and woman. You will remember that the Almighty put a heavy sleep upon Adam, and while Adam was in deepest slumber He removed his rib and fashioned therefrom the blessed Mother Eve. So, what does this signify to us? On one level this wonderful image expounds the truth of man's blessed fortune in receiving woman. Out of Adam's sleep was created Eve, the lustrous gem of Creation, the deepest dream of man made physical for his enjoyment. But there is a lower level to the meaning of this image as well. The creation of Eve is accomplished by stealing something away from Adam. Adam is something less after the appearance of Eve, just as he is something more with his increased possibilities of living. And more, because she is the image of his deepest dream, she is also the living body of his deepest fears and terrors and anxieties. Ach, David, the sages of old knew well that the rounded bottom of every beautiful dream is a nightmare and the beauty of Eve sits on a black irrational ugliness which is the lifespring of all beauty."

"Fine, fine. That's all very fine, Father Abraham." I was angry at his callousness to my shame and suffering. Why didn't he give me some pity? "Fine and dandy. I've even read it all in a book somewhere. But my Eve has stolen not only my rib, but my heart. She gives me just the nightmare without the dream. Maybe woman is around to delight man, but I can't take any pleasure in not being the man that my woman delights. For Christ's sake, how could she do this to me?"

"Ach, David, David," sighed the old man. "Still you are thinking with your glands and not with the divine spirit that the Almighty planted in you to know the difference between the light and the dark, between the fruit of love and the fruit of bitter ash. I am an old man and I have perhaps forgotten the foolish flesh pains of children, especially that most childish pain, the hurt of the little pride. More humble you must learn to be, before you can again become a man."

He looked away from me as though my face might be an embarrassment to his blue eyes. Then he turned toward me again and his voice was electrically kind, but the words stung and slapped like wires.

"*Your* Eve, you say. *Your* woman, you wail. No, David, not yours. Hers perhaps, and the Almighty's to be sure, but not yours. The only true gifts, David—the gifts of making life, the gifts of making love—these are gifts of giving and no taking. Ah, nebbish, you have sinned badly and I pray that you can find it in you to forgive yourself."

I was sure that I had taken the wrong bus, that I had bought a newspaper and found it to be printed in illegible type. I had sinned and he prayed that I might be able to forgive myself. And Hitler and the Ku Klux Klan. I felt terribly wronged, terribly misunderstood to be so falsely accused.

Fat tears of righteousness welled in my throat and my tongue tasted like fish scales.

"That's not fair at all," I cried. "It's she, not I. I gave and she has taken away. All. All I gave. I wadded myself up into a neat package and I put it in her hands and she tossed it in the gutter. Me, the kids, our life together, our *us!* She had no right to do this. No woman has that right!" My arms were trembling and although these were not the words I wanted to speak, they leaped like salt from my mouth. "My God, Father Abraham. What about the Ten Commandments?"

His eyes never changed but the position of his body was enough to demonstrate his disappointment in me. That he had been willing to discuss with a man and found himself nursing a child with a splinter in his thumb. But his voice was deceptively serene. "Poor David. Poor poor David," he crooned, and since this was the first sympathy he had offered, I didn't care to weigh his words for sarcasm. "Poor David. Over thirty years old. Surrounded by women since you were born. Mother, cousins, aunts, girlfriends, daughter. Over thirty years old and you still know nothing about women. Are you *ever* going to learn? Didn't you even peek at them when they were undressing?"

He rocked back and forth creaking the wood of his homemade throne as though he were intoning an inaudible prayer.

"Shut up your hurt pride for a minute and listen to what I'm telling to you. Like a stuck calf you lament and you quote at me the Ten Commandments as though you were a cheap lawyer. Woman is the gift of life, the conceiver, the nurse, the holy temple of joy, the final tender deliverer. The pagans of old were not so stupid to connect the woman with the moon—inconstant, fickle in its phases, but fixed and regular in its cycles of revolution. Would you command the moon with a Commandment? Oh, David, the ancient prophets of Israel knew well the nature of this precious Eve. The holy tablet of the Law which Moses carried down from Sinai, this has nothing to do with Eve. These are the laws for the male descendants of Adam who lost a piece of himself in the making of Eve. What does woman have to do with laws? She is complete in herself and is her own law. It is the crippled Adam with a piece sticking out of him who must try to comprehend the Law in order to complete himself so that he may truly pleasure in the gift of life."

I was bewildered and insidiously betrayed by the direction to which Father Abraham inexorably pointed. Unfair, desperately comically wildly unfair. And yet deep down in some unknown base of me I felt dirty and terribly naked. But the words from my mouth as before came involuntarily.

"I don't understand. I don't understand at all. I remember my mother at the head of the table on Friday nights. The white tablecloth. The dishes gleaming and the red wine under the Sabbath candles. In shul we sang a welcome to the Bride of the Sabbath and my mother was a queen at the table. I don't know this Woman you talk about—without law and wildly free. My mother was as holy as the candles and inviolable as the tablecloth. She was the true Eve, not this other."

"David, David, David. You foolish pitiable thing. And with the strong royal name you bear. All my life I have studied the Law, studied the Talmud and the Midrash, studied the people who have with such a blessed fullness entered into my life. And what have I learned in my old age? I have learned that the study of life is the study of Woman. You betray your princely heritage and you make me worry about the scattered generations in Unser Amerika. In the shtetl it wasn't so good, but the young Jew wasn't so stupid, either. You are a man, David, not a woman. You have an obligation to *think*, to move your hands and mouth in response to your *thought* not just your bladder, not just your pecker, not just your animal nerves. If the Almighty, Blessed be He, in His wonderful wisdom created Eve as a plaything for Adam, it is the responsibility of Adam to learn how to play. And not as a child plays, but as a man of thought plays. You—ech, you are a nudnik."

In my pain and outrage at his unbelievable tirade I could say nothing. I waited like a prisoner in a deep well who hopes forlornly that some light may drip down the dark sweaty walls.

"Yes, sure, David. From time immemorial our Jewish people—our Jewish *men*—have created the image of Woman that you mumble over like a baby. The Bride of the Sabbath. The pure robes of chastity and calm. The dutiful daughter who squeaks out 'Ein Keluheinu' with her fluffy white skirts hardly covering her ass and her skinny legs bare and shuddering like a chicken. The Mother, the matriarch, the mammoth cook who loads a dinner table like magic with a forspeise, with thick soups, with a chicken and four vegetables. Who gives to each guest a glass of tea as though he were a god to be served. And who for dessert worries that some crumb of the feast should remain uneaten. And you—you believe in this image? You, a married man and the father of a daughter?"

I was caught unguarded in a truth that I had never dared to acknowledge even to myself. "Well, I—I always thought Letha was different from other women. I—"

"Chrrrr, gaylem," Father Abraham gargled and squinched his nose as from a bad smell. "You have the blessed fortune to marry a real woman and you spend your life apologizing to yourself for her. No real woman lives in that manmade image and no real man believes that such a slave picture is anything more than a funny mask which man puts on woman for man and woman to play with. Woman is wild, is without law, is the coat of many colors for man to delight in. She bounces like a ball with weights inside and neither she nor the man ever knows which way she's going to bounce. She is a marvelous toy, not a machine. And her pleasure is in being played with.

This she calls love and duty. Play with her and she is Paradise. Force her to play with herself and she will bounce away for somebody else to play with. Oi, oi, oi, oi! You must have killed her spirit, you possessor of a machine."

I decided that the old man had gone mad. Nothing he said made any sense, and yet there was nothing that was not some insane truth. I wanted oracular advice, some commiseration in the eternal ascetic rock, and he whipped me like a dog.

"David, David," and the old man's voice was a singing gentle chant. "I talk to you like this in the belief that you are not yet completely dead. I knew you when you were a boy alive and I am trusting that your life still flames somewhere inside you."

"I'm sorry, I don't know. I don't know anything, Father Abraham. I am hurt, of course, but I'm all confused now. You talk about play and you turn everything upside-down—"

"The best kind of play, David. And the best position. If we all stayed upside-down a little more, the world would be more topside-up. But let me return to the wonderful Adam and Eve story again. If a man could truly understand that story in its divine fullness, the Almighty would close up his lips and seat him at His own right hand. After Eve is tempted by the serpent—after she eats the serpent with her other mouth, as the poet says—why does Adam, Adam the man of thought, why does he rush to join his sin with hers and bite into the forbidden apple?"

I thought over the question, trying to become that Adam of heroic haste, and I remembered John Milton with his baleful wedding night and stupid daughters and a seminar on *Paradise Lost* that I had gotten an "A" in.

"Well, Milton says that it has something to do with Original Sin and determinism and self-sacrifice, but— Well, I think he was a damned fool."

"Yah!" Father Abraham spat. "You and Milton. Two castrated Puritans who choose to sleep with an exclusive icebox and make the whole world pay rent. If you would only try to *think* instead of squeezing your self-righteousness into neat academic turds, you would see that the blessed Adam is beginning the play. He knows that Eve cannot sin as a ball cannot be guilty of breaking the window that it smashes. And he knows too that Eve is a delight to him in all his senses. So he pays a small price. He eats the forbidden apple, and he ties a string to his Eve, a string of play joining groin to groin, and he opens the great comedy of mankind with all its disguises and deceptions, its sexual explosions and tender warmths. Oi vay, what a player, that Adam! He teaches Eve nakedness—what could she know about nakedness without him? She who is always naked. But even he can't teach her shame, God bless her. He teaches her the roles of Mother, Daughter, Wife, Mistress, and he keeps changing the dance through all the parts, but he never stops dancing. When the archangel drives them from the Garden with a fiery sword and Eve's thighs are unstrung and there is no light in her face, that Adam—he *dances* under the sword! This is a man who plays! With his head. With his blood. With his body. This, David, is a man with a sense of humor, and he would be ashamed to own you as his son."

There was obviously no use arguing with the old man about Adam and Eve. In fact, his obsession with sex was a little shocking, almost obscene for a man of his age. I couldn't any longer remember what I had been seeking from him, but I knew that I had knocked on the wrong door. And I guessed it was about time to be getting out and back into the understandable currents of my misery, when the shop door opened and two large middle-aged women entered. One was short and the other was of average height, but both were very large—comfortably large. Their faces wore that pleasant grossness which is almost always a mark of well-intentioned stupidity and frustrated complacency. I could easily imagine them spending every afternoon of their lives in darkened movie palaces, filling up handkerchief after handkerchief with shallow queenly tears. They came into the store and prowled the bins with an air of casual proprietorship. Father Abraham greeted them familiarly.

"So, good afternoon, ladies. You're a little late today, but I would wait open for you even in the dark."

The taller one scrubbed her pink face to a brighter, blotchier pink with a shredded Kleenex. "Sure, Father, and isn't today a turrible hot one?"

Father Abraham leered at her with stage lasciviousness. "It serves you right, Missus. Always I'm telling you that you wear too much clothes for the weather. Like a mummy you wrap yourself up and your skin sweats out its anger." He winked and I saw a startlingly clean-bearded goat in the chair. "So what can I do for you, ladies?"

The shorter woman was inspecting a box of melons, picking up one at a time and pressing the tender skin for soft spots. She would fondle and discard and fondle again another one before throwing it back into the box. Without looking up from the melons she spoke to her companion. "You were looking for a nice avocado, weren't you, Loretta?"

"Yeah, Father. You got a nice avocado for a cool salad? Hot day like this, it's all I can eat."

The nice avocado was chosen, neatly wrapped, and paid for, and the two fleshy women left the store. Father Abraham crowed a good-by to them.

"Today a nice avocado. Tomorrow a nice lemon. Never more than one thing. They come into my store not to buy, not to talk to me, but to feel my fruit and vegetables and to remember life with their fingers. That's why I keep my tomatoes out of their reach. They can't be trusted with tomatoes. Ah, women, they're wonderful!"

The shadows had stretched out on the sawdusted floor and I was conscious of having sat long in my cramped paralysis. I was uneasy at this long lecture and I wanted to think about something else. The old satyr smiled benevolently at me and I was sorry that I had come.

"So, nu, David. In spite of yourself I shall help you. In spite even that you do not want to be helped. I shall help you to help yourself."

Balt, I thought. That's just all I need. But aloud I still had to argue. "It seems to me that the trouble is not my helping *myself,* but that everybody else seems to be helping *himself* to whatever the hell he feels like."

Father Abraham looked quizzically at me and picked up a tomato in either hand. "There are two ways to eat a tomato, David. There are two ways to do most things."

He made a quick fist with his left hand and the red pulp spurted from between his knuckles staining his white coat. Then he lifted his right hand above his head, bent his neck back, and squeezed the other tomato so that the juice streamed into his open mouth. His Adam's apple worked up and down like a yo-yo and red trickled on his throat and into his beard. It was the most disgusting sight I had ever seen.

"One more lesson, David. One more lesson from the wonderful story of the Garden of Eden. Adam is the great player, the man of thought, but even he had to learn this lesson from the wrath of the Almighty. After Adam and Eve have discovered their guilt and their nakedness, Adam fears the Lord and hides himself behind a bush when the Lord calls him by name." Father Abraham spit some tomato seeds from between his wide-spaced teeth. "It is only after the Lord has thundered out His call that Adam reveals himself from behind the bush saying, 'Here am I.' 'Here am I,' David. The most wonderful words in the whole blessed Book. Do you understand, David? No hiding in bushes. No irony. No wisecracks. 'Here am I.' A small voice uttered with fear and trembling. But with directness, David. Directness. Ah, this Adam, he was a *man.*"

He looked at me sharply and weighed the uncomprehending blankness of my expression. "Some people, everything they got to learn the hard way. For you, David, nothing comes easy. Anyway, I'm going to help you. My grandnephew, a fine bocher, is entering into the Yeshiva in New York, and tomorrow at ten o'clock at Back Bay Station, he will meet you for a traveling companion. Together you and Ziggie Solchek will go to New York like another David and Jonathan."

He leaned back in his chair like a retiring Supreme Court Justice, very pleased with himself, the red stains on his beard shining like the measles.

"*What?*" I was thoroughly taken aback, certain that senility had at last avalanched on the old man's head. This was the first thought I had had about actually going to New York myself, and the wild notion of ferrying some kid to an advanced Hebrew school was beyond all comprehension.

"Myself, I'm too old to go with you, David," Father Abraham sighed regretfully. An acid light gleamed for a moment in his eyes and then expired. He smiled, remembering the old joke. "And besides," he said, "who'd watch the store? With Ziggie at your side, it will be just as if I were there. Genug. I must lock up for the night and you must have many things to do."

He raised his arm in rabbinical blessing, effectively forestalling my unuttered expostulations, and without leaving his chair ushered me out of the store. "Remember. Ten o'clock, Back Bay."

Ten o'clock, Back Bay. Bend the rock, black tea. Have a cup tea, David, you'll feel much better. A little tea on the stomach, it's very settling. Not my cup of tea at all. Lithe and white in tennis flannels and the pock-a-pock of the furry balls pinging off the rackets leaving imperceptible skids on the episcopalianly greened courts. Seagreen seagroined courts of love. Forehand to backhand. A little more English, please. Foreskin always wins. Ace. Deuce. Change courts, Love equals nothing. Game set and match. Pure Protestant white flannels (a little more English, please), always sharply creased no matter whatnot. No matter what muscle flexes, what bone breaks beneath. Protestants don't sweat, not in Boston. They tennis and canoe and tea dance and make genteel perfumed love under creased white flannel sheets and without a tear of sweat. In Boston. Red-brick monolith sailing between rivers of Catholic-Jewish-Negro sweat—massive dry blood bank floating out to sea with genuine cobbled streets and bunkered beaconed hills and Copley Square for tea. Play with her, David. Play and play and play within the play. Drip it the heathen sweat the codfish smile adores. Oh, deadly beautiful thy minarets, O Boston, thy bastions, thy turrets, thy impregnable portcullised walls. Oh, deadly beautiful. Oh, beautifully dead.

Second- and third-generation immigrant children with sweat-gnarled names that old Thayer, the Latin master, would wince over in the roll-call as though someone had offered him a gerund when he was looking for a passive periphrastic. As though someone had offered him a dripping half-sour pickle to garnish his tomato consommé. Papalopalous, Lento, Kritzky, Bevilacqua, O'Toole. How he labored with contempt, almost hidden behind his tinted glasses, crumpling us under the whip of his sarcasm like an Egyptian overseer on the pyramid detail. We started with the wrong blood is all, the right sweat but the wrong blood. Beyond us forever a true appreciation of the rolling hexameters of *The Aeneid* or the holy resignation in the *lacrimae rerum* of the decadent Romans. But parse we could and parse we would. And we sweated our logarithms, the genealogy of the Merovingian kings. And we memorized and declaimed Burke by the hod-load and drew endless maps of the Peloponnesian War (I remember the maps, but I don't remember who won), and we learned to emulate the casual Brooks Brothers look (from Rogers Peet to Brooks but never to Hickey-Freeman) without being mistaken for high-class traveling salesmen. We became precisioned machines of cultural acquisition, scraping the patina off the cobbles of the past like our accented fathers, the cleaners of the genteel streets. And to us, as to our fathers, the violet panes on the bow windows were forever opaque, even in the sunset. And the porte-cochere was ever shut. A little more English, please.

We went in gangs to Beacon Hill on Christmas Eve and some caroled the madrigals of the ruthless knife or rang the bells that tinkle in the dark cortege. We hotly applauded the latest heretic-conformist at Ford Hall and argued moral rearmament in cramped Oxonian apartments in Cambridge with our collars buttoned down over our brains and our opinions crisp with unitarian starch. The night that the Junior League paid their dutiful respects to Emerson in a salvationally antiseptic hall on upper Marlborough Street and you got carried away and tried to show what that cunning heart really meant by "Only he can give who has; he only can create who is," and you sinned a sweat on your Oxford collar and the truth was moistly apparent to one and all (especially to one) and nobody even cared and you knew then that the war was lost even though you had won every battle. To be born in Boston not a Peabody is to lose all the Peabody battles. To be born in Boston a Riegel who wants to battle the Peabodys is to lose all the Riegel battles. But there may be one treacherous way between, delicate and devious, the way of the Judas with fallen silver. You lead two or three lives simultaneously and you never let yourself or anyone else know which one you're leading at any or every time. The Protestant Jew at home with the family, spraying your acquired cultural contempt around the living room like an Aerosol bomb, making the mother and the father uneasy with pride and fear and alienation. The Jewish Protestant in the bleached Anglo-Saxon world, accepting with decorous deference the stiff Victorian rules of Hoyle, but arrogantly assertive of your right to administer these rules more effectively than the dead hierarchy—those without even the external vestments of the trade. But always the alone-life as well, emergent from under the layers of reverie or cigarette smoke or the long sensual walks up and down the streets which wear a sheen of rain on the concrete and your heel prints fix suddenly and fade before the echoes of your steps have ceased.

And now a cuckold on top (or bottom) of it. Screwed, blued, and tattooed—U.S. PRIME CHOICE stamped on the upper thigh, the great hook in the ear and you hang in the modern crucifixion position like meat marked, weighed, and priced for the special purchase. Caveat emptor. All well and good to play the social game. The commitments are calculable and the most you have to lose is a disposable social mask. But the other game goes groin deep and you're down to the next-to-last mask and the press of body to body is as honest as flesh can cling. My Wife. Ma Femme. Meine Frau. You can't say those simple couplings without declaring an affirmation. The words are too few and too single-syllabled for ambiguity, for the saving nuance, for the hooked inflection which raises an invisible shell to protect the seared identity. If one of the ways that you answered that awesome question "Who am I?" was with "MY"—and it was, God help you—whither goest thou now? Let God thunder from out of the pillar of fire, "RIEGEL!" and you can surely say "Here!" But, "HERE AM I"? How? All the Riegels explode in a snickering shrapnel-burst and each fragment demands to be whole and here, and each has his multitudinous "my's," but where is there a collective "my" or "I"? In pain, answereth the prophet. In pain and fear and the scoop of foreboding that renders you shitless. Bullshitless, respondeth Riegel, or one of him. Pain is universal, not particular. By its very nature it is indefinite rather than definitive. Pain is only a question, never an answer. That's what doctors are for. Correct, saith the prophet, and therein lieth the answer. No. Therein lieth Letha. Carrying the key to my identity between her legs and too callous, or not bright enough, or too spiteful or just plain egotistical to keep her thighs together the way any decent girl would. Denied three times before the cock crew, but Lord the cock did crow and Golgotha is a nearer place than any Jew should know. I'm spent, oh cock, and crackéd is the day. Ten o'clock, Back Bay.

And, indeed, I was there. Dressed in my four-year-old wash-'n-wear Haspel with a regimental striped tie, somehow brushed and shaved and conscious that my face had only aged the normal twenty-four-hour period between one sunrise and the next, bewildered as I was bewildered the day of my father's funeral that so much can happen inside and there are no physical signs to manifest anything to the outside, and that if one could or would turn off the faucet of his memory, even *he* would know nothing of what had happened and he would be, because he is always being changed, finally changeless like a seamless rock in the flow of the tide. The home-parting was simple enough after all. The statement "I'm going to New York for a few days to look after Mama" was enough to accomplish the actual going as though the words themselves labeled an actuality in the world and all sensible inhabitants thereof—especially children—accepted the finality of the words with the ingenuous indifference that a monumental equestrian statue aspires to in bronze reference to the pigeon droppings on his shoulders. Mama Sheva expressed solicitude for herself and her increase in hardship. ("I don't know. You kids. I must have been crazy when I had my kids. Daddy and I never spent one night away.") But the wind was from the east-northeast and the only bad smell she could catch was from her hair spray. The children themselves shrugged off this new fillip of fortune with the self-enclosed superiority that children automatically assume toward the eccentric orbits of their guardian planets. I tried to feel something in the parting, preening my face like the incomparable Garbo's in that heart-breaking scene where she sneaks in the predawn Petersburg winter to kiss her beloved Seryozha, but Marvin was buried in a comic book and Rosalie was practicing her handwriting on a large mauve sketching pad, using green ink and rounded script letters like in the perfume ads. Rosalie Riegel. Rosalie Maureen Riegel. Maureen Regal. Rosla Lee Regal. Maureen Lea. Mlle. Maureen Lea, Couturière to the Queen.

"Papa, how do you spell 'couturière?' "

"I don't know, honey." And then, with unnecessary spite, "Ask Nana. She's a woman."

"I already asked her. She said to ask you since you're so smart."

"Actually, dear, nobody spells it any more. In fact, it's a sign of very bad taste to spell it. Especially out loud."

"Oh, I see." Rosalie was at the age of great sensitivity to breaches of taste. "Papa, what exactly does a couturière do?"

I gave a loud stage sigh of satisfaction and pulled Rosalie up on my lap, holding her with both my hands on her shoulders.

"It's a strange and wonderful coincidence that you should ask me that very question on this of all nights in the year, my dear one, because I just happened to spend the day with one of my oldest friends, the famous couturière Helaine of Argentaine, and I asked her the very same question. We were sipping a delicate Pommard at a lovely shaded bistro near the Fish Pier, she very chic in pink tulle sprayed with Arpège, I casually but nattily appareled in my gold-and-vermilion foulard. Helaine, says I, seizing on a nook in our conversation, what exactly does a couturière do when she's couturière-ing? Why Professor says she, I'm surprised that a man of your round worldliness should be ignorant in such an area. Well, Helaine, says I, slightly nettled by her sarcasm—she has never forgiven me for marrying your mother, you know— Well, I says, I have of course a general idea of the area in which or on which the couturière operates, as does any man of my experience, but— And that area is what? challenged Helaine, throwing the gauntlet of her upthrusted bosoms at me and zeroing in on my face so that I could see the reflection of the blue paint of her eyelids in the pale depths of my Pommard. It was an unmistakable challenge, Rosalie, a desperate dare directed at my pristine virility and a subtle threat to your mother's right to that virility. And I'm proud to be able to confess that I had the raw guts to accept the challenge with the same spirit of defiance with which it was hurled. A couturière, riposted I, operates on the area of the derrière."

Mama Sheva picked her head up from her nightly occupation of licking and pasting into her album her latest collection of Israeli postage stamps. I pinched Rosalie's thin behind tenderly, putting her back on the floor so that I could walk around the room at my lecture pace.

"The derrière is one of the great underdeveloped areas in the world's understanding, Rosalie. I could weep tears for it. And you, Marvin—take your head out of that trashy book for five minutes—you too can learn from your sister's innocent query. Men have for centuries devoted an astonishing amount of disproportionate energy on far less significant areas of human comprehension. We have chartered the murky profile of the vast ocean beds. We are measuring to the final erg the quiddities of the Van Allen radiation belt. We have assembled mammoth libraries and museums for the desperate cataloguing of the world's history. Which is, after all, merely a profile in time. But what do we know beyond the barest surface impressions about the human derrière? Great painters and sculptors have given us in God's aplenty analyses of the physiognomies of beautiful men and women. The female bosom in our time has suckled a veritable industry of meretricious advertising and merchandising. The stomach, the inner organs, the diseases of the flesh, the extremities both north and south have received their due and undue attention and, in some cases, even obsessive worship. But who, alas, will champion the shapely, the all-encompassing derrière?"

I breathed a short sob of despair and outrage, lit a cigarette, and climbed a notch higher in my fancy, listening to my rhetoric as though I were safely separate from my words, savoring to the full the self-pitying distance between what my words were saying and what they were so patently echoing by not saying.

"Regard, for a moment, mes enfants, the derrière—stripped to its essentials, unadorned, undisguised with cosmetics and ointments, with salves and depilatories—naked, indeed nude, to the sympathetic analytical eye. Yes, I know that you are young yet, but the apple does not fall far from the tree and you too will sit one day in judgment on the cruelly abused derrière. Lessons should come early lest they become homily. They should be learned posterior, if I may say so, not anterior to experience. Oh, children, you will forgive a foolish passionate man his madness, but what the blessed Elizabethans used to call 'the bum' sits, as it were, upon my brain and squashes me into an abject humbleness. Oh, derrière, oh, globéd fruit, oh, twin hemispheric rounds, with what regal glory dost thou enthrone thyself on this our pumpkin world! Before a man can stand, must he not sit? Was it not old wellrumped Montaigne who murmured low that the indubitable seat of kings was but the seat of kings? And how do we normally regard this seat, this curved bump, this undeflatable pillow on which our arrogant torso seeks its rest? How, I ask? With disdain and sniggers of contempt—snuff that snigger, Marvin!—with pinches and gooses of arrant superiority. Look at the words we dare associate with the noble derrière! Bowels, hemorrhoids, piles, anus, bottom, behind. What, after all, is the derrière *behind* anyway? This noble split world, cracked down the middle in manifest hieroglyph of Adam's fall, we have the temerity to look down upon because it forever resists man's prying capacity to behold. Oh, mendacity and prurience, incestuous breeders of such a baleful, wailful pride! No man, my children, can stand behind himself, and affronted beyond endurance by the ultimate defeat of his longings—because he cannot view his own derrière—we extract our petty revenge, our five or so foolish pounds of flesh, by playing the spiteful fox and contemning that which is our soul and sole support."

The children were listening with polite attention ("Papa's being entertaining again") and Mama Sheva was giving about equal time to me and her El Al commemorational issues, amused and tolerant of my hyperbolic behavior. I was getting tired, however, and already declining back into my depression, so I prepared to tie up the package neatly and quickly.

"Let us together, then—the four of us—let us seek to redress the hideous injustice and lack of under-sight which ages have wreaked. You know of the mystic science of phrenology—the examination of human behavior in terms of the bumps on the cranium. Let us inaugurate a *Magna Instauratio,* a Scienza Nuova, a revolutionary methodology for the human understanding. Let us be the Marx and Engels, the Freud and Jung, the Four Horsemen of the new future. Compatriots, disciples all! I give you *Assayology,* the science of the under-understanding. Each ripple of flesh on the derrière is indicative of an inner psychic wrinkle on the soul. Fingerprints, dreams, ink-blot tests, marriage licenses—they all can lie! The ass, never! The demonstrable shape of the behind, ranging from the great cumbrous pear shapes which sit like Etruscan jugs to the demure impossible Valentines that are the delight of the advertising people, but the bane of the bowels. Each shape, professionally assayed and tested for lubricity and flexibility, divulges beyond a shadow of a doubt what amativeness, longevity, intelligence, acquisitiveness lurks behind the behind. Show me a pear-shaped bottom and I will have you a deliberative person, settled and meditative, heavy with thought and digestion. Give me a behind that is ovoid, tight at the ends, and elongated, and I will have you a nervous thwarted soul, squeezed into a paralyzing tension between the forces that desire to relax and the forces of restraint. Ah, mes enfants, this is an historic moment—a moment worthy of a Polaroid-Land camera. Three wise men some two thousand years ago rode after a star on their asses, and tonight we can finally see that the truth they sought was not in their star, but in their asses. The derrière beckons—a fuzzy plum ripe for the picking, and we will follow to glory. Could a man but scratch the surface, possess, as it were, just a piece of it, he would be more opulent than Midas of old. But woe betide that miserable wight who has the fortune to get a piece of it and have it stolen from his grasp. His misery is manifold and the very stars weep spears for him."

I had picked up a candlestick from the mantel which I was using to punctuate my periods, and with my peroration complete, I thrust it Statue-of-Liberty-like toward the ceiling and marched out of the room. Behind my back I could hear Rosalie asking patiently, "Nana, what *does* a couturière do?"

So, indeed, I was there. Nine forty-five A.M., Back Bay Station, ticket tucked securely in the little pocket inside my right-hand suit pocket. I checked every three or four minutes to make sure it was still there, in case maybe an invisible vacuum cleaner had sucked it away or the cardboard had been chemically treated to make it dissolve or I had merely dreamed that I had bought a ticket and put it in my pocket. I had a miserable dread—always did—of finding myself with the conductor asking for my ticket and I being unable to give him one. I know people who will habitually board trains without tickets, and I know that it is quite legal and allowable to pay one's fare after the train is already moving and the buildings and telephone poles are slipping backward in ascending acceleration, but I have never been able to do this. The very thought of having lost my ticket—even though I had extra money in my pocket—would make my flesh creep with sick sweat and my level of angst become critical. And I felt obscurely shamed at this perversity. To whom could you confess such a monster? It fit not at all with the image I aspired to, but I was impotent in its clutch. I could have saved ten per cent by buying a round-trip fare to New York, but with a bravado that was a burlesque of bravado, I burned my bridge behind me and felt the corrugated edge of my one-way ticket safe and square-cornered in my pocket. The smell of the burning bridge was in my nostrils as I looked around the platform for the Yeshiva boy who was to be my train companion. "Aleph, Beth, Gimel, Dalet, Who put the ham in the rabbi's salad," I chanted, searching for some pale-ivory wraith, black-garbed and forelocked, whom I must attempt to keep swaddled from secular shock until I got him safely to New York.

The platform was fairly empty, a half dozen or so people who were obviously *not* Ziggie Solchek and were even more obviously going to no Yeshiva nowhere. The oversized hands on the station clock crept closer and closer to ten and still nothing that looked remotely like Father Abraham's grandnephew. God alone knows why I was waiting for him, but then it was the same knowing God who alone could have understood how I had gotten into my situation in the first place. A camp counsellor giving diaper changes to a rabbinical student before he launches himself off to confront his wife for her adulterous behavior. A ruptured duck of a husband playing stork in the duck blinds before he resumes his comic role as—as what?—as pigeon. The tabloid history of David Riegel, modern Arthurian cuckold, filmed on location in hysterical Back Bay. Popcorn and garlic wreaths distributed at the door. Suddenly and simultaneously, two bursts of noise swept along the platform. The whirling egg-beater sound of the ten o'clock from South Station roaring to an airbrake-screaming halt at 10:05, and the cackling of three porters rolling steamer trunks, airplane luggage, canvas bags of large and small variety, with tennis rackets, golf clubs, a hockey stick, and most incongruously, a neatly tied up volleyball tenuously affixed to the cascade of luggage. The two processions steamed up the track on parallel lines, capturing the attentions of the people along the platform in equal quantities. I checked my ticket again and resurveyed the waiting passengers. Solchek was nowhere to be seen. I gave one more look, half of relief, and I joined the line that was attempting to clamber into the car, snaking with ducked heads through the three porters who were trying to unload the luggage into the train. The carnage was magnificent. An elderly woman was poised with one foot on the train step, the other on the platform, thrusting a shopping bag at a dangerous angle before her. Suddenly a ski pole, hurled javelinlike by one of the porters, hooked the handle of her bag, sending the contents everywhere, splitting the brown paper like a wound. Crocheting, carefully wrapped presents for the grandchildren, a red enema bag, clothes, and sandwiches fountained in a garish mess. People shouted and shoved and the locomotive brakes hissed steam like an angry cat. A train guard rushed up to inspect the scene, his open

Hamilton watch brandished in his hand as though it were a weapon.

"Goddammit! You know this heavy stuff goes into the baggage car. We're a minute'n a half late already!"

"Watch ya langwidge! Theah ladies present heah!" This from a little woman pressed like a straw flower between a steamer trunk and a large man.

"Y'all argue with *him,* boss. He want dis stuff heah, not theah."

The spokesman-porter pointed behind the crowd at the owner of the luggage and everyone turned as on stage cue to examine the originator of the confusion. Indeed, he would have been worth looking at even in calmer situations. He was lounging against an upright girder smoking a cigarette in a long silver holder, scanning with undisguised indifference the stock quotations in a crisply rolled *Wall Street Journal.* He was wearing a bright-orange slack suit with black sandals and a jet-black beret rakishly slung to one side of the head, topped with a screaming orange pom-pon. He was tall and thin and his face had silver tones that oddly matched the cigarette holder. His hair was very long—so long that he wore two clumps of black curls over his ears and curving down his cheeks. When he deigned to notice the crowd's interest in him, he sauntered over to the car, coming directly to the train guard who was still clutching the opened Hamilton watch as though it were a talisman of the carnage.

"Now, now, old chap," he said, patting the guard's watch gently with his newspaper. "This train is already three and a half minutes behind schedule, and unless it leaves in one minute I shall have to cancel my reservation. Why don't you just give these boys a hand with the baggage and see if we can run a railroad here today." He climbed gracefully through the parted crowd up the steps and then turned with an afterthought. "Oh, yes. I'm expecting a visitor. Would you inform anyone that might ask that Mr. Solchek will be in the Pullman." And he disappeared down the corridor leaving a vacuum in his wake which only another orange-and-black apparition could have filled.

I took my seat in the day coach in a shocked haze. So this was my Yeshiva bocher, my Jonathan-to-be, my diaper change, the prospective Virgil to my Alighieri. Oi, oi, Father Abraham, here you really got yourself a prize tomato. Better I should sit this one out. From that bimbo you could get nothing but trouble. But by the time we were in Providence my curiosity and my realization that in about four hours I would have to find a direction to act upon made me ready to confront Mr. Solchek. I found him sitting in a swiveling Pullman chair, an emptied brandy glass on one overstuffed arm, the silver cigarette holder in an ashtray on the other. He looked to be about twenty-five—some five or six years younger than myself—but there was an absorbed experience to his look which made me doubt that I would ever grow old enough to acquire it. I introduced myself tentatively, still half convinced that there was some ridiculous mistake of identities somewhere along the line, but his response left no question.

"Well, Daddy-o, so you're the cat that Uncle Abe wants me to take in out of the rain. Give me some skin, chum, and take a load off. Where in hell have you been since Boston, weighing mailbags?"

We shook hands and I sat down. I was still lost somewhere in my mind, trying to find some correspondence between this so obviously wealthy hipster and my rapidly dying image of a black-clad Yeshiva student with black-pointed shoes, black round hat, and curling forelocks.

"Care for a drink?" he asked, ordering me one with a negligent wrist even as he asked me. "They water their Hennessy on this run, but if you double-shot them, you can't tell the difference. Me, I just got to drink this morning far-a-way.

Couldn't face Old Man Pee Em otherwise. Woke up feeling like the Andrews Sisters had been squatting all night on my back teeth pissing on my tongue. And they're so square, man. They don't even piss on beat."

I rolled my glass in my hand, inspecting the clear brown glow of the liquor as though I might find some answer there to my bewilderment.

"Keerist, man! You're sure a talkative one. You *do* talk sometimes, don't you?" He felt my wrist with his long fingers. "Well, if you're dead, it must just have happened. You're still warm."

"Wait a minute," I blustered, feeling like a Mongoloid idiot. "I didn't—I don't understand."

"Don't understand what? You don't really think that the Andrews Sisters can piss on beat, do you? Come on, man, say you're a little *forlorn,* but not absolutely gone-lost!"

"All right, Solchek, come off it! I'm told to meet a Yeshiva student and I catch instead a Park Avenue hoodlum. So I'm confused is all." Goddammit, why do guys like this Solchek, completely in control of the space they occupy, always make me feel and act stupid and defensive?

Solchek chuckled musingly. " 'Park Avenue hoodlum', huh? That's not very good, not very fast, but it's an attempt. Maybe we might get along after all. I just wanted to find out whether rigor mortis had set in or whether I had a live corpse on my hands."

"Yeah?" I grunted, feeling like a primitive slug with my tail caught in the branches. Good Lord, why doesn't he put the needle away? I wasn't up to playing games and he had me thoroughly off balance. "So have you reached a conclusion yet?"

Solchek looked at me without smiling, looked in fact as though he were examining a piece of fabric. I noticed then how deceptive his eyes were. They looked brown at first—a healthy sunny-boy brown, but the color went deep beneath the surface picking up glints of yellow and green and even a smoky violet as the layers went deeper. And the muscles of his face conspired with the high cheekbones and thrusting aquiline nose to form an instrument almost from which his eyes could focus like high-powered lenses. Solchek was obviously more of a character than his hipster dress and talk would suggest. He displaced his twelve or so cubic feet of volume with the cruel angularity of a knife. Or, rather, he didn't so much occupy space as seem to be poised in a moment of air, using both the moment and the air as things to act upon. There was no waste or relaxed surplus of flesh or gesture in his whole demeanor—no more or less, that is, than there would be in a precisioned machine.

"Well, Daddy-o." Even his hipster drawl was crisp. "Since you inquire, I would judge that rigor mortis hasn't quite set in yet, but unless you finish your drink and have another one, you might begin to stink a little."

And, Jesus Christ, I did not like this arrogant, uncuckolded man at all, but I had to agree with him. The web of memories and self-promises that was the design of my futile attempt to make sense out of me was pretty tangled and rotted. I finished my drink and had two or three more, no longer tasting the liquor, but only enjoying the languorous feelers of passivity which it spread like a vine inside my body. I had by this point given up my responsibility for myself—as undramatically and as surely as one slips off an ice floe into the warm black of the broken sea. I was spinning away from any center the way a child surrenders his unique momentum to the pitch and whirl of the merry-go-round, trusting in the painted wooden horses and the obsolete creaking iron to bring him around and safely home. Solchek rang the steps on my merry-go-round with a carrousel of talk—bright, flashing talk like ice cubes in a pitcher of Martinis. I drank and grunted companionably, only half listening to his stream of anecdotes and observations, becoming more and more settled and warm in the direct center of the bottom of my brandy glass. I could tell with my half-awareness that he considered me four-dimensionally square, that he would no more have bothered with me than with the local Brownie unit were it not for his uncle. And yet, beneath his manner, he was trying to be gentle and kind. Our talk was a monologue on his part—a steady delivery of judgments, aphorisms, staccato conclusions on life, art, and the pursuit of happiness—half hipster and half cultured don in his accents and allusions. It was exactly the kind of talk that always irritates me, because it excludes the possibilities of conversation, placing the speaker on a promontory of distant wisdom from beneath which I want to catapult poisoned arrows. But the brandy was swift in me and I could feel myself nestling into my Haspel and there was that unfailing telltale of a hiatus between my making of words and the bounce of them off my eardrums and I knew I was drunk and I didn't care. The unaccustomed opulence of the Pullman gave me a spurious ease with Solchek and I made a mistake that I'm usually very careful to avoid. I tried to match his language and his unwonted rhythms and with false heart I assumed a familiar connection between us that neither of us believed in.

"Ziggie, old man. Tell me the score on one thing, will you? What gives with this Yeshiva bit? What kind of a ploy are you making with that?" I leered amateurishly (I have never learned how to leer), expecting but not receiving a communication of camaraderie.

"It's quite simple, David. I'm entering the Yeshiva in Brooklyn to prepare myself for a study of the Holy Books. That's all. No bits, no ploys. Quite straight."

"Come off it, Solchek, you hot cool cat. Don't hand Papa Riegel that shit. What *really* gives? That Halloween costume of yours wouldn't get you into a minyan, much less a Yeshiva. Come on, level with me."

I wasn't that drunk that I couldn't see that my tack was stupid and offensive, and that the one sure way of tangling with Solchek was to pretend to a friendly community that didn't exist. But he remained gentle even though it cost him a noticeable effort.

"Just relax, David, and don't try so hard. If one of the ancient prophets were alive today, do you think he'd wear a toga and a long beard? Would he talk Aramaic or Hebrew? I mean, man, you either feel or you don't feel. And what you wear and how you speak doesn't have a hell of a lot to do with what you feel. And—" he adjusted the leather strap of his sandal—"and, I feel. So I'm going to the Yeshiva."

"All right, all right, so peddle that ancient prophet crap. You might as well make a little modern profit on it." I giggled too loudly and very much alone. "All right, I'm a little drunk. *But what the hell do you feel?* Do you feel that you're one of the Chosen People and God is a special volcanic rock and if you get in the right position, lava is going to come out of your mouth? Do you feel that a Covenant was made and a Covenant was busted and you're going to be the handy Band-aid that will make everything just peachy fine? Or do you feel that six million of the Chosen People—shit, they had to be chosen. They sure in hell wouldn't have volunteered—that six million were burned like trash in zippy-quick ovens and you're going to use a little Easy-Off so that the burners won't shine with grease? Jesus, you're a great feeler, you are. Me, I don't feel nothing."

Ziggie had left his chair and had been standing at the broad window watching Stamford slip behind us while I harangued him. He stood for a while without answering me and then he returned to his chair.

"Look, boy," he said, and his anger was rising like lye in a dirty sink. "I could talk nice to you, but would you know any more than you do now? I could tell you that it's none of your bloody business—which it very much isn't—and maybe you'd shut up. Or I could say that all women are stinking itchy to get the pants off piety, like the Magdalene tearing her fingernails to pull off Jesus' loincloth, because a woman can't stand for a man to be married to something that isn't female, and every broad is convinced that she personally has the stuff to defrock the frocking priest, and *that's* why I'm going to Yeshiva. But the actual point is why the hell do you have to have reasons for everything? When a steamed-up chick climbs into bed with you and throws a thigh across your leg, do you worry about *why* you want to get on top? Why does it bother you so much that you don't know the 'score'?"

He made an obscene fish shape with his mouth on the word "score" mimicking my expression, and I hoped that I didn't really look like that when I asked him. He lit up another cigarette, exhaling his disgust, and moved around the chair as though he were circling a deep hole.

"Riegel, let's get clear between us right at the beginning. My uncle briefed me on your misfortunes and I agreed to help out if I could. But long ago I made it a rule not to let some cripple cripple me. If you want me to help you, I will. But not if I think you're going to use me as a crutch and swipe my good legs for your rotten ones."

My drunkenness disappeared like the explosion of a nauseous bomb. My outraged humiliation was on the bottom floor at last and there was no cellar to plummet into. But there was also a wave of joy too, because for the first time in this whole madness I had something physical—somebody physical—to get mad at. We were both standing in the overstuffed Pullman burning at one another above the emptied brandy glasses, he with cold white anger, I with red fury, and the slightly scorched green Connecticut landscape sliding backward as a frame for our drama. I thought of Uncas and Magua locked in death struggle (Bruce Cabot playing Magua and I as Uncas), but I shut off the whimsy of my mind and funneled all my blood into my fury.

"You second-rate punk! You bumptious beatnik! You acne-souled juvenile! Who the hell do you think you are, the incarnation of Shirley Temple?" My voice rose by steps to my large lecture-hall volume until I had reached stereophonic fortissimo and each word that I shouted across the six-inch gap that separated our faces was a new spurt of kerosene for my anger. "Who in good God's name asked for you? Who in good God's name asked for anybody to butt into my life? And if I wanted anybody, why in hell should I get a squirt in orange pants who's seen too many Marlon Brando movies?" I noticed vaguely that a clump of stewards had gathered at the Pullman door, but the fact registered only on the retinas of my eyes. I grabbed Solchek's upper forearms with both my hands and jerked him down into his chair, shouting even louder. "I don't want you! I don't want nobody! I don't want nobody at all!"

And then with nothing in my hands except my own spent and shaking fury, I saw myself red-faced and absurd in a wrinkled suit spitting loud sad sounds into the air ("Papa's being entertaining again") and I prayed for merciful disintegration on the spot. "You stupid sonofabitch, Riegel," I prayed. "You stupid stupid sonofabitch." And then Ziggie, who had been cold and composed and imperviously enclosed through all of this, did a beautifully generous thing, and I shall remember its beauty forever, long after we are all dead and vineyards are growing wild where humans once walked. He put his long hand up to my cheek and smoothed it tenderly, and it was as natural and unambiguous a movement as a hand can make. And he said with no sarcasm and no sentimentality, "What a lovely voice you have, Dave. What a superbly lovely voice."

I don't know how or why that did it, but it was perfect. It scooped up our little world—an iglooed impasse in a racing Pullman car—and tossed it billions of miles into space, connecting it to the vast dimensions of light-years and galactic arcs, and it burst the immeasurable tons of wall that had locked us, freeing us from ourselves and for ourselves. I sat down again and we both lit cigarettes. I noticed that, with the performance come to an unhomicidal finale, the stewards were leaving the door to the car.

"Thank you, Ziggie," I said, looking directly into his eyes as I spoke so that he would know from how deep my words had come. "It's very kind of you to say." I blew a jet of smoke operatically toward the ceiling. "At least it certainly impressed the kitchen help. But you should really hear me on Herbert Hoover. *There* I even surpass myself."

We talked easier after that, I in one sense relieved and in another increasingly anxious as the train sped closer to Grand Central and the ridiculously intense pain that called me there. Ziggie—and from then on, he really *was* Ziggie for me—assumed a true community between us, and, as I have rarely done, I accepted it eagerly.

"Actually," he said, "this Yeshiva business *is* straight, but I don't completely understand it myself. It's a little bit like Mallory and the mountain. The Yeshiva is *there,* so I've got to give it a whirl."

I nodded sympathetically, wondering why Mohammed didn't try a Yeshiva—or an ice axe. I didn't really understand, but I was willing to go along with whatever he said.

"I know it's odd," he said, ordering another pair of brandies. "But that's the way the matzo crumbles. I'm a Jew. And I don't know what it means to be a Jew. Maybe all it comes down to is a special kind of heavy diet or a peculiar sense of humor or an acquired condition of alienation. I know what it feels like to be a Jew, but I don't know what it *means*. And Jesus H. Christ, I can't afford not to try to find out."

We toasted his pledge of attempt and he continued. "Hell, David, everybody that isn't a Jew knows goddamn sure what it means to be Jewish, but I've never talked to any Jew who could tell me something that made sense. And what you said, too. Six million poor bastards were incinerated like trash for being Jewish, and the fat potato-fed cretins who pulled the switches and hammered out the gold teeth and sorted the underwear into sizes—*they* knew what being Jewish meant. I am not a sentimental soul, David, but I owe it to some of those six million to try to find out what they burned for." He finished his drink in a gulp and smiled. "Besides, I wouldn't be surprised if it turned out to be kind of fun, too."

I had a quick series of kaleidoscopic images of Ziggie with his orange suit and black beret, bouncing his volleyball past long-bearded men swaying over parchment scrolls. I raised my drink in salutation. "To Yeshiva," I intoned. "Bo-ray p'ri ha-go-fen."

Meanwhile the landscape out the window had changed from rural to suburban, and the train rocked by the platforms and parking lots of the commuter stations that stretched from Norwalk to New York City. Port Chester. Rye. Pelham. Riverdale. Blurred faces and attaché cases postured like foolish chess pieces as the express raced by on an inner track. The heights of the buildings rose and the canyonlike tunnels through which the train roared increased in frequency and length and I remembered why I was going to New York and I tried to think about what I would do. It hurt to. I was enjoying Ziggie and the brandy and my unexpected holiday and I hated to remind myself that I was engaged in a search, a crusade of vengeance, an attempt to make errant life come to terms with me.

"I don't know how much Father Abraham told you," I began, but Ziggie waved me off casually.

"Lots of time for that business," he said. "I've always liked this view of New York. Like looking at the raw plumbing under a modern pink-enamel toilet bowl." We were just short of entering the great tunnel that burrows into the rock heart of Manhattan. "He told me enough so that you don't have to tell me anything right now," he said. "Riegel, aged brother, just plan to put yourself in my Semitic hands for a few days and we'll see what happens."

We plunged into the blackness of the tunnel and the train lights glared into yellow half-brightness and the throb of the engine echoed and resounded off the curved womb walls of the underground passage to the secret center of the city. I felt suddenly that man is always the smallest delicately carved box inside an endless series of Chinese boxes—that as my heart throbbed deeply in the tunnel of my chest, so was everything in some way just another dark heart inside a larger black place. And the whole complicated concatenation from corpuscle to cosmic dust throbbed in an inaudible harmony as it hurtled with accelerating frenzy away from whatever it had once known, relentless and cold, toward something that both was and was not an alien heart afar.

# Journal

*26 April:* Shakespeare's christening day, I think. It's oddly consoling to be able to mark a day in terms of an anniversary. As though this gave you an insurance premium on a continuity into the future. Cheap illusions, tawdry sunglasses for the mind's eye, Doren would say. But he obliterates the past in order to deny the future completely. And he refuses to realize that this is an effective negation on the present as well. Orgasm is the pinprick of the past which moistens the future, I would say to him. And he would snicker as though I had told a dirty joke. Hélas, my work is out of time anyway, and it seems to be marching well. And the household has a minimal solidity, like the Flying Dutchman in the eye of a hurricane. Mark is far better off in school (all the toys are unbreakable), but Lily is still to worry about, although not, thank God, the demonic incarnation that Doren insists he sees. She is in pain much of the time, a psychic pain against which she has no resistance and which she has not yet learned to siphon away. Mark never suffered from this. *Proposition:* Pain is ubiquitous in life for everyone (it *is* life), but we only recognize it as pain when we become conscious of its congestion within us. Mark is a relatively free funnel for energy flow; it enters him and leaves him. He acts with it. Lily will have to develop some special techniques of action—a mode, a métier, a system of forms through which she can make a bundle of her energies and discharge them under her control. She rarely laughs calmly and naturally. (Neither does Doren. Perhaps this is their link of violent gloom.) She will have to become an Apollonian in order to live with the Dionysian flow, but she will always *seem* Dionysian. Mark will appear pure Apollonian in his easy tractability, and yet he is much truer Dionysos. Doren claims that the Nietzschean artist must inevitably fossilize into the marble forms of Apollo in order to preach the Apocalypse. Everything returns to paradox and Judas is the true Savior of man because he is the only one to have made an eternal sacrifice. Ah, mon vieux, you could have made a Pope's fortune in the days of the scholastics with your unerring sense of quiddity. And, of course, it's all nonsense. Which is to say, art.

I pilgrimaged the other day to the Place de la Bastille, thinking to find there the sacred hulk of historic slavery and symbolic freedom. I knew just what it would look like. A massive grey scar out of Carlyle by way of Dickens. And I searched the curving streets for an hour only to be told by a baffled policeman that I was a couple of centuries too late. "La Bastille, monsieur? La Bastille, c'est partout. Ah, le *prison?* Pardon, monsieur, c'est *pouf!*" *Pouf*, indeed. Slavery and freedom and the modern *pouf* to the spirit that the self wallows in like De Sade with his evil roses. And Doren tries to sell me Henry Miller as though I were a buyer on the *pouf* market. I don't know why he needs it, but I have *pouf* enough in my own soul and its neighbors. I don't need any more, either in movie or tablet form. The human obligation has always been the struggle for humanity. Not for divinity, diabolism, or animality. And to be human is enough of a butterfly for any madman to chase.

But I have been having wonderful Dostoyevskian conversations with Doren, who is caught on the fulcrum point between murder and suicide—the only proper political position for our time. (Isn't it incredible that as the world has tightened into savage social knots of struggle, metaphysics has replaced politics? When we knuckle into The Last Great Cramp, esthetics may be the only cure.) Doren and Eva and I have become serried into magnetic patterns which conjure up the fantastic rhythms of our thought, talk, and heady drink.

> *Murder:* To assert finally and positively the claims of self, the claims of the operative ideals in action. To defend the adamantine wholeness of self from compromise, invasion, and slow rot. To kill in order that life may live. To kill out of recognition that The Other exists, because its being may always be an illusion unless one can actually hear the dull rattle of death in its throat.
>
> *Suicide:* The affirmation of love, of community, of becoming. To die in order that life may live, as one must die in the begetting of life, as one must always die to a worn-out moment of the past in order to be future-free. To die to prove that life is because it was.

But the paradox clamps down again and the mind wriggles free and lost. Is Judas the murderer and Christ the open sacrifice, or is Christ the eternal murderer and Judas the loving lover betrayed? There had to be one unseized *other* behind the long table, shadowy but not completely concealed. He too had to sip of the wine and break the bread. Thy rod and thy staff they comfort not me. Forsake thee not my Torah. It should have been Da Vinci with a slow mad green smile, pointing a third way from both the Baptist and Bacchus. Good Lord, I'm strangling in half-knowledge.

Physically I'm quite tired. I walk three to five miles a day and Paris is so much to respond to, so full of movement and whirl that it's like working in the middle of a pinwheel. We went to Chartres and Fontainebleau and I have covered the Latin Quarter, the Bastille, Les Iles, Les Halles, the Palais Royal, Trocadero and Passy on my American rubber soles (my American robber soul). The writing goes steadily but my mind does not stop when I snap the typewriter closed and everything seems sucked into the uncontrolled spin of my pinwheel brain. But I think I have a good grip on my energy limitations and if I do go mad, no one will know it except Lily. And she has always been convinced that madness, not ripeness, is all.

Consciousness is such a compounded fracture. I suppose this is Freud's recognition that civilized man is diseased—a suppurating wound sternly rejecting all cures, tragically in love with its own tumescent death. I buy a baguette at the boulangerie, I soothe my daughter's tears, I watch Doren and Eva parrying across a plate of fruit and cheese. On another level I compose pictures from the palette of the city. The rear-angle view of Notre Dame where it looks like a great mother ship sailing in and free of the stone which forms it. The fine gritty rain settling like dirty gauze on the trees and statuary of the Tuilleries. The Pont de St. Louis from which you can see the two currents of the Seine breaking their flow and gently sidling the quais. And the novel lives a life in my awareness even more secret and more alien from the other levels, sucking its dark life from what, from where. I act, I see, I think, I feel, and every tremor of energy keeps within its own terrible track, self-determined and wholly discrete. My God! We have the effrontery to define insanity as the incapacity to keep our prisons of awareness solitary and unconnected, as though this were not health and the other sickness. Who is truly mad—I or the psychotic who lives in one complete simultaneous mental world? Only in sleep is there an end to these racking divisions. I dream no more, or, at least, I am not aware of my dreaming. My sleep makes consciousness completely porous. The tracks all join and opaque images—nonverbal, nonpictorial, silent—offer themselves with full and rendered wholeness to my total experience. Past and future, memory and promise, selfhood and otherness make one sensuous pulse. Maybe this is why I cannot recall having slept and dreamed. Such consciousness—total, immediate, and utterly enthralling—would have to transcend waking perception. And perhaps this is the true profile of God.

And I feel a persistent arrogance here in Europe, a strange sense that I am less innocent as an American than any European who walks these streets no matter what hideous sufferance he has borne, no matter what evil he has fondled in his hands. That I have seen the promissory note presented for redemption a hundred times and seen it a hundred times returned as an inept forgery. Doren and Eva think me naïve (I sometimes think that *they* are children), and of course I haven't been conquered, invaded, occupied, ravaged, and spiritually looted (unless now by my own dreams). But yet—and how can I say this without claiming more than my rightful share?—the American begins with a single historical fact that is only now commencing to plague the European. The American has never been crushed in a war; *he is himself a war.* Ripped at by a Maenadic fury of contrary obligations and definitions, he has had to learn to believe and not to believe, to care and not to care, to retreat from his victories and advance over the warm blood of his defeats. He has had to learn to live with the dangers of not seeking a self while all the voices of exhortation scream at him to try one on for size. Fat old Ben Franklin was the first Yankee diddler-peddler abroad, the canny innocent of Passy, the poker player in the salons of whist and euchre. And for the deprivation he did them, the French honored him with a street. We remain fluid in our age—a not entirely desirable thing; but they are fixed in their youth. Isn't it far more innocent to be placed, defined, ascertainable? What is the real difference between a Grande Marque and a radioactive isotope?

The children sleep and Eva has gone to the theater with Doren and I am depressed under my worlds. And sometimes I would choose not to bear them if the choice were merely to the will. But they are my worlds—poor paltry things—and no one else's and every man is sunk beneath his own unstandard weights and measures. And if I can sustain myself, am I not in some small way contributing to the collective strength of mankind?

Hypocrite moi! I am an intellectual cannibal of abstractions!

# Two

Exactly when the *pitch* started I can't right now remember. It may have been in the Pullman or it may not have begun until later that day, but somewhere within this time my sensory responses were subtly transposed into another key, a duodecaphonic scaling which gave a weird ambience and intensity to almost every impulse that assaulted me. It was like living in a surrealistic landscape beneath the rush of a Chinese waterfall. Ordinary objects—a newspaper kiosk, the curl of cigarette smoke, a strangled voice from a closed telephone booth, things you normally take for granted—burst out of their backgrounds humming with an intrinsic queerness and provocation. It was as though every commonplace thing demanded to be worshiped as a miracle, or at least reverenced for being precisely what it was. And, at the same time, queer things—ridiculous, incongruous, normally incredible things—presented themselves to me with a bluff insouciance that two days earlier would have prostrated me like a violent accident. If now I can see (or think that I can see) that nothing is accidental and, at the same time, all is sheer accident, then I could only react to everything as inevitable and miraculous. In an odd way I was reliving a situation analogous to that of the legendary Jewish salesman from Des Moines who wakes up in a Chicago hotel room after a classic bender with the boys. He finds himself squeezed between two gigantic Negresses in a single bed, all three of them stark and immensely nude, the signs of the evening's debacle littering the rug and the bed in monumental disorder. From the depths of his hangover and his dim comprehension of his plight, he crawls over the mountainous flesh of one of his companions in order to arise from his bed of morning woe. In the process he disturbs her slumbers and she clamps his arm in an iron clutch. "Doan you-all mess wif me, white mahn," she growls. "Ah is jus the brahds-maid." Or, to put it in more literary terms, I was caught between Coleridge's old mariner and Wordsworth's gatherer of leeks and both were equally familiar and extraordinary. For evil can bless and ice will burn and categories of experience are always outside of experience.

At any rate, we were swiftly settled into Ziggie's apartment on Christopher Street—the suitcases and trunks unpacked, the ski poles and volleyball carefully placed in the back of a closet, the books neatly shelved in the large cases which circuited the big front room. While Ziggie efficiently put his house in order, I envied him his books and wandered the cases trying to puzzle out the eccentric contours of his personality in terms of the books he cared enough about to truck along with him. Alas, the mystery was only compounded in the contradictions which his juxtaposition of titles recorded. He had the predictable worn stacks of Modern Libraries, the scattered heaps of shiny paperbacks ranging from Anouihl to Zen, but the real books—the hard-cover and oversized books—fought transcendental battles in language, culture, subject, and point of view. Wilhelm Worringer stood next to Mircia Eliade, Toynbee and Ortega y Gasset glared at each other around a slender volume of Ramakrishna. Balzac had a whole shelf to himself, as did what must have been the entire catalogue of the Bollingen series in dark bindings with little gold spine ornaments. Freud and Jung and their respective camp followers pushed their psychic weights at one another, while Ouspensky ignored them all from a higher shelf. All the disciplines seemed to be represented. Wittgenstein bulked large in the middle of an enormous armoire-type bookcase, surrounded by Husserl, Heidegger, Jaspers, Marcel, Sartre, Merleau-Ponty, and Buber. Huizinga, Auerbach, Curtius, and Spitzer dominated the philological corner. The Frankfurt school of Lukács, Marcuse, Adorno, and Benjamin crested a little inglenook which was pyramided on the Leipsic edition of Goethe and the collected works of Marx and Mann. The Russell-Whitehead *Principia* sat three-volume firm in the middle of a series of shelves in which most of the books were composed almost entirely of mathematical symbols. Large, fantastically expensive art books half-buried the Victorian poets limply bound in vellum. A thin volume of Bialik nuzzled the formidable buckram of Heinrich Zimmer and Giambattista Vico. The complete Frazer *Golden Bough* was symmetrically balanced by the complete works of the Marquis de Sade. French symbolistes, the bittersweet Germans, the precociously acrobatic Italians jostled and shoved, stood silent and made deprecatory shrugs with their spines. I felt that the walls were covered with African masks and Polynesian thunder gourds, that the prow of a Viking ship jutted above the window and Giordano Bruno burned in the next room. It was a library to dream about. A library to dream ravaging nightmares where the screams were in ten languages and the price of admission was the casual acceptance of single-minded chaos.

Ziggie was carefully Scotch-taping a brownish photograph to the wall above his desk. "Jesus," I said. "You sure got a helluva collection of books."

"The fruits of a misspent youth," he said. "See anything you want to read, just help yourself."

I walked over to the desk to see whose photograph was going to adorn the place of honor in this intellectual pantheon, fearful that it might be Albert Schweitzer or Gandhi. The face seemed nineteenth-century, but it wasn't familiar to me. "Who is he?" I asked.

"The only American writer worth a fart in the British Museum. Don't you know who he is?"

I examined the picture more closely, canceling out the faces that it wasn't. It assuredly wasn't Poe or Whitman or Melville or Mark Twain, and it occurred to me that for all its wealth and heterogeneity, Ziggie's library was very sparse in Americana.

"I don't know who he is," I said. "Emily Dickinson, maybe?"

"She wasn't bad," he admitted. "Compared to our other lady writers. Henrietta James. Emilia Hemingway. Willa Faulkner. No—" He smoothed the paper against the wall before sticking on the tape. "This is Trumbull Stickney. The one American writer that even America couldn't turn to crap. Though he had to die quick to escape it."

"Trumbull Stickney?" I had a vague recollection of a Stickney stuck between a Stoddard and a Tuckerman in some anthology summary that I had once memorized. "Are you giving me the business?"

"Business? Have you read him or are you just making academic noises?"

"Well, I don't actually remember reading him, but—"

"You read him. You read him and then I'll argue with you. Why, man, this cat was absolutely *clean*, absolutely pure. Like chromium. You know, not a goddamned thing wasted. Everything just where it had to be. Take a line like 'It rains across the country I remember.' Hell, that's not a line, it's a tidal wave. It's a cosmological orgasm. It isn't poetry, it's metapoetry."

"Well, yeah—it's a very nice line," I hazarded. "He didn't—he didn't publish much, did he?"

"He didn't have to. Not old Trumbull. Why, he did things with language that we're only beginning now to guess at. He's sort of the Willard Gibbs of poetry, you know. Man, he *intuited* generational grammar before it was invented, and he's one of the few writers in English to understand the function of silence in writing."

"Silence?"

"Sure, silence. Look, you listen to me." Ziggie addressed me as though he were giving a Sunday-school lesson to an Australian bushman. "Every sentence, prose or poetry, is made up of words, right? And each word is separated from every other word by a tiny space in time, right? In printing we simulate this time break with a physical space, a blank piece of white on the page. Now that's clear enough, isn't it?"

"Sure, but so what?"

"Well, most writers are used by these space breaks. Or at least they act as though they were completely unaware of them. But really great writers—a chanter like Homer or a speech writer like Shakespeare—they don't forget the human voice. They can make those space breaks function as *silence*, not only between their words, but between their sentences and paragraphs and even bigger units. Look, just listen to the sound of the silence *around* the words in this line: 'It rains across the country I remember.' Jesus, you get a guy like Trumbull Stickney and he even uses the silence between his poems. Between his books even. And this means that he's writing even when he's not writing."

Ziggie had a vaporous look in his eyes and there was a deep smoldering fire searing hot beneath the surface and his arms curved semicircularly in a movement of gathering in.

"Believe me, David, that's the true immortality that a really great artist can achieve. Not that crappy fame how he lives on in the hearts of his countrymen and the third-grade reader in P.S. 36. But a guy like Stickney, he can live forever as long as he keeps silent, and if he's dead, he can't do anything else. Or a painter like Hobbema, who uses unpainted space in the same way."

"Hobbema? What the hell are you throwing me? Who is he?"

"I'm sorry, David." Ziggie smiled condescendingly and let his arms fall to his sides. "I keep forgetting that you're a product of the American graduate-school system, so how in the hell would you know what I'm talking about. Hobbema is just the same kind of immortal in painting that Stickney is in poetry."

"I don't know anything about painting," I grunted belligerently, implying that I knew enormous amounts about other things. I didn't like being patronized, but I couldn't be sure what Ziggie's angle was—whether he was putting on an act or what. But there was that savage prophetic fire in his eyes, the serpent look of the pedagogue gnashing yellow blackboard chalk between his teeth.

"Look, David," he said in let's-be-reasonable tones. "Take music, for example. When you hear music, do you listen to the notes or the intervals between them?"

"You listen to the notes, of course," I said, pleased to find a small rock that I could put my weight on.

"Wrong!" he shouted triumphantly. "You listen to *between* the notes. You listen to the silences."

"*You* listen to the silences. I listen to the notes." I began to whistle "Oh, say, can you see—"

Ziggie modulated his attack again, elaborately casual in his unconcern, but I could sense that I had somehow managed to paint myself into a blank corner. "Let's not argue ourselves into an emotional dead end, David. Let's see if we can get at this in a simpler way. Bartok is a great musician, right?"

"Right." How could I afford to say no?

"Schönberg is also a great musician, right?"

I spread my palms in the age-old peddler's gesture of stubborn compliance. "Bartok and Schönberg are both great musicians. I wouldn't choose between them." I hoped I wasn't going to have to be more specific about them.

"All right. Fine. We agree. Now. When you hear Bartok and Schönberg, do you listen to their notes or to their silences?"

"Notes," I said.

"No. Silences," he thundered.

I was firm. "Notes. Not silences." I enunciated my words with elocutionary care.

A satisfied smile on Ziggie's face signaled my forensic disaster. "Good," he said. "You're a bloody liar and I got you by the bloody short hairs. *Nobody* can listen to Bartok's or Schönberg's notes. They'd go out of their goddamned minds. The notes and the chords aren't even meant to be heard. That's why they flat out into dissonances and screeches. Why, Bartok has a cello piece that would crack the brain like a pile driver if anybody ever really listened to it. As a matter of fact, you couldn't do it even if you wanted to. The ear shuts itself up like a fungus. Sure, you hear echoes of the notes like shadows that the eye catches on the fringes of vision, but you don't hear the notes themselves. You hear the silences. And that's why they're great pure musicians. Their things can only be listened to *musically*. You can't whistle it like Bach."

"Are you saying that Bach isn't a great musician?" I knew I had been sunk but I wasn't quite ready to strike my flags.

"Oh, he was a great musician all right. But great for his silences and not for his notes. He had to throw melodies in there for the fat burghers to dance to. Bartok and Schönberg—and the deaf Beethoven, of course—these are the first musicians who have the purity to write straight music without the crap."

I didn't want to argue any more, especially when I didn't know who was on first base. "Maybe I listen to the silences and I don't know that I'm doing it," I offered as a truce gesture.

"Sure, David. Don't worry about it," Ziggie said quietly, the light subsiding from his eyes. "You read a little Stickney some time and see how you like it."

He sat down at his desk, arranging blotters and papers into complicated private patterns, and I walked over to the front window. The curtains were a pale pink that reflected an anemic blood hue on the windowpanes, and I looked down on Greenwich Village through appropriately rose-tinted glasses. The afternoon was on the verge of becoming evening and I still hadn't made any move toward finding Letha. It was as though the sum total of my energies had been expended on getting me this far and I was enervated beyond taking another step. I had an address in the East Sixties where she had rented a room. This was the address to which I had mailed my cheery letters—cheery, chatty, carefully avuncular, yearning letters. I knew that I had, at least, to check on the address, but I knew also that she wouldn't be there. I knew that her room would already be occupied by somebody else, that her suitcase would be down from the closet and the room swept bare of her touch, her scent, the intangible feel of her flesh, which inevitably transformed any room she lived in as though something of her sprayed out of her pores and coated the mirrors and the windowpanes, adhering to any surface, and what was left over would just hang in the air, static and a little cloying, so that if you walked from one wall to the other you sometimes felt that you were brushing away a tenuous web of femaleness, of presence, of Letha herself. And, as effortlessly as it came, so swiftly would it go. We had lived in many rooms and I was constantly amazed at her capacity to possess a place—and, in turn, to leave it in a denuded state as soon as the books were in their boxes, the mirrors swaddled in newspapers, the giant bed frame unscrewed and dismembered like an angular corpse awaiting the cortege of the moving men. Nor was it only through furniture that she could do this. Her antique red brush on the dresser, a favorite book, a post-card print of Van Eyck's *Pietá* which would be propped up where the cruelly forgiving eyes could be widely vigilant—these were sufficient in themselves to make an impersonal place into an extension of the smell of her soul and her sachet bags.

No, she would not be at the address and the landlady would have no information about her. But the landlady would remember her, and the sharp rapacious face would whet itself into that knowing double-edged look—the kind of look that boasts of a feral intellectual superiority to the childish games that one plays for tourists and transients out of malicious pleasure and economic need. She wouldn't quite say, "The small brunette with the affected accent? The one who carried—no, who had carried for her—a portfolio of art stuff? Kind of pretty in a showy way? No, she don't stay here no more. A week. Maybe two weeks ago. And good riddance too. No, she didn't actually *do* nothing. Nothing you could catch her for.

But—well, Mister, I don't like to run that kind of place." She wouldn't say those things, but she would somehow communicate them through her constipated clench and the Gothic outrage in her Judgment Day face. And you could look at the sloppy Victorian drape to her long skirt, and the coffee-stained cardigan with large agate buttons that made her look like an impressionistic haystack, and imagine the twisted blue veins on her flabby thighs and the black mole beneath her breast with maybe a coarse brown hair or two sprouting like a potted palm in the desert of that ample decrepitude. So you would smile a courteous smile and thank her for her manners and leave your name and address to be crumpled and thrown away before the door closes and scuttle out to the kindly sidewalk where at least there is life in the streets even if it is only neatly deposited dog shit in the gutter and rainbow splotches of oil on the hot asphalt.

As though he had been tuned in on me, Ziggie called indolently from the desk without turning his head around or interrupting his own methodical arrangements. "By the way, David. You get a chance, write down your wife's address. And the name of this guy who is supposed to have been seen with her. And look—" he turned around in his chair—"don't bother about these mundane marital matters for a couple days. Leave us see what Papa Solchek can do as a leg man."

As I began a protest he waved me aside. "Fact is, David, I really would like you to learn about silences. Your motor has been overrunning, I'd guess. You got to learn to slump the way a dog does in front of a radiator. Take a little vacation from yourself. Get rejuiced. Hell, man, you're as empty as a stud bull after a hard day on the farm. Relax awhile and let old Ziggie drive the wagon a spell."

So I wrote down the address and the letters that spelled C. Greene, swearing impotently at myself, naming me coward, time-server, buck-passer, craven shmuck. What kind of a man could or would slough off this kind of job? *The Cuckoldry of Smiles Standstill Riegel* by Henry Whatsworth Shortboy—an Epic Poem of American Heroism circumcised into unrhymed dactyllic hexameters.

"Go to the damsel Liletha, the loveliest maiden in Boston,
Say that a blunted old husband, a man not of deeds but of humor,
Offers his bed and his bounty, offers to take on all comers . . ."

That's what I am. The tallithed phallus of wonderland. Everybody's carefully curried poodle relieving my bowels in neat heaps beyond the curb, squatting tremulously on a ninety-year leash while the traffic roars by and the taxis swerve ever so slightly to shave my quivering ass and make my tender eggshell heart vibrate like a weak power tube. But, goddammit, I am tired. My coils are rusted. You ain't young any more, Riegel. Oh, no, you ain't.

So with deep shame and glad relief I gave Ziggie my papers of temporary deliverance and announced that I was going to sail about the watery part of the world for a bit. He gave me his extra apartment key, telling me to use everything as though I'd paid for it. I flooded my hair before combing it, and putting a little soap in the water because I was way beyond a haircut, redid my tie, and prepared to affront the city. Then I remembered a question that I had meant to ask.

"This silence business, Ziggie? Wouldn't it mean then that everything that happens is unimportant? That it's the things that don't happen between the actual happenings that are really important?"

He tapped his cigarette holder against an ornate bronze inkwell at the back of his desk and he squinted at me. "Well, in a way," he said. "If you could impose a rhythm of some sort on time and space, that might follow. Or something like it."

This suggested a whole line of possibilities. Nothing but possibilities. Impossibilities became themselves impossible possibilities. Why action, anyway? Or, on the other hand, if a man spent his life dodging action, what good his passive contemplation? I reached toward some hook of polarity or undulation—a system of rhythm which would require an eternal Siamese war—but for the moment I contented myself with the opportunity of giving Ziggie just a touch of the needle that he'd about worked to death on me.

"Then, Ziggie—speaking purely academically like us graduate-school types do—wouldn't death be much more important than life? Doesn't life sort of get in the way of pure clean death with all that sloppy clutter?"

My eyes molded a death's head on the columns of Ziggie's neck and I stripped flesh from his fingerbones, hearing the silences that his stark-white knuckles sounded in the shadows of the room.

His skull wagged in thoughtful hesitation. "It might be so. It might be so," he said from the muffled vault of the death I had given him.

The flesh congealed slowly from the tip of his jaw to his high-sloping brow, crowning itself with shiny black hair, and the brown eyes gradually filled the vacant sockets like slow coffee in a cup, and then the lips which could bleed again were moving.

"It might just be so, David. Where are you going?"

"Oh, nowhere," I said. "I think I'll drag me a cup of coffee or something." I paused on my way over the threshold. "I'll try to see if I can drink between the coffee and the cup, though. I shouldn't want to be an embarrassment to your pedagogy." And I went out.

The streets were busy with the late shopping-for-supper crowd—worked-out men and women stopping at tawdry expensive groceries to buy cans of tuna, ready-to-eat beef stew with frozen heat-'n-serve buttermilk biscuits and the inevitable leaky pint of ice cream—or, ascending a level of desire, spumoni or baked Alaska. The slow leak of the great American dream from the home-made ice cream cranked in a wooden bucket to the slickly packaged, overpriced frozen good or bad that could be bought and served immediately. One Instant Culture, Just Add 2 Cups of Anything & Shake like Hell. Don't get pundity, Westbrook Pegler, I warned me. Let people be. Let them be and buy and not care. Let them scrape the bottoms of the cartons where the melted gelatin sticks to the cardboard—the saccharine dregs of our civilization on which we frenetically choke, trying to satisfy our innocent frustrations. And who in hell are you to identify with the castrating Protestantism that clips the eagle's wings and screech? Colonial American furniture, old-fashioned telephones in knotty pine to be used as decanters for Manischewitz wine. These white-washed people scoured clean of the thick incense of suffering—what in hell are they to you? Imagine Herbert Hoover, the canny inventor of the vacuum cleaner, the stalwart Mandarin of the FBI—imagine him draped in a prayer shawl beating his breast and dipping his engineered fingers into the blood-wine of the ten afflictions. God help you, Protestant America. Your bowels are just too clean for me. Miserable and lowly enough art thou, Roderick Riegel, with your Ellis Island beard and old-clothes men, but a far far better thing this than the other—the despairing guilt-devoured confrontation of the self-righteous sin with the justice of a Calvinized rubber-stiff God. You Lysol culture. If I couldn't laugh at your twisted testicles and vinegared vulvas, I'd have to drown in a sea of tears. Ach, philosophe. So wise, so Olympian, so transcendentally compassionate. Remember what you are. You are the man. You suffer. You are here and not somewhere else. You walk the streets of an alien city in a land which is the New not the Old Jerusalem. All cities and countries are alien to you and none more so than where the oranges are grown for export and the sun-browned sahbras play hide-and-seek with the sun-drowned Hasidim. You have no place. You just attach to the horizons like Scotch tape until something yanks you off and throws you in the ash heap. A split-level in Orange, New Jersey; a prefab California ranch in Coral Gables; the brick upright coffins of Detroit and Shaker Heights with a powder room behind the stairs and a bar in the basement recreation room. Everywhere you adhere, assume the garments of the showcase manikins, the predigested foods of the supermarkets, the clipped hair of the smooth-skinned animal in the cage. You paste your Community Chest Red Feather to your window and electrify your neighbors with the Edison glory of your Christmas tree. Kikes and sheenies are temporarily obsolete. Only the bloodless can survive. Sex and religion—like hunger and thirst, defecation and perspiration—are deep-frozen and dormant, market-researched and distributed in the mindless automatism of heat-'n-serve, wash-'n-wear, drip-'n-die. And you, Jew. You're worse than the others because you know better. They elect, but you are chosen. They will burst like a boil, oozing through the drains of the mental hospitals, gutted on the knives of the built-in disposal units, but you will consume yourself as the brittle leaf of the last autumn day, sere and juiceless, mere shreds to the careless winds that list not where they blow. Ach, philosophe, so wise and detached and so deftly screwed up.

I had been walking quickly, glancing in store windows at displays of handmade jewelry, chessmen, sandals, serapes—crossing streets on impulse to peer into rough niches of darkness that led to courts and basement apartments. The sidewalks became more crowded as evening advanced and I remembered that I was in the Village, the cultural sediment of American life. I wanted company. I wanted to touch some other human beings to whom I was nothing but an indiscriminate cipher, an indefinable integer with a voice and an ear. I wanted to talk and to listen and to build a temporary soul in the void swamps of my being. Temporary, that was the word I grabbed onto. I wanted to be temporary. In time. Averted from the obligations to the timeless and the out of time. Some yards farther down on my side of the street I saw a metal replica of a coffeepot, grotesquely patterned on an obscene mimicry of copulation—the crooked spout driven by clockwork to penetrate and withdraw from a large brass cup. Refreshing to the last drop, I thought. Poor rotted urn, poor unfilled Keats.

The coffee house was smoky and overlaquered, its walls adorned like an Egyptian tomb with shoddy paintings, its tables dropsically handmade by hands far better suited to typewriters and interoffice telephones. The coffee house (its vermilion painted sign announced it as The Libido) was rush-hour full with a cross section of Village types—the tourists who looked like tourists; the tourists who were disguised in black turtle necks and crotch-tight pants; and the tourists who were the indigenous lease holders of this shabby sonnet world. And the last group had a glossy sadness all its own, absurd and profound in its insouciant innocence. The art students looking like walking collages in their paint-smeared ensembles; the young, impossibly bearded poets in white shirts and sloppy sweaters with unwritten ironies singing in their heads and printable filth under their fingernails. The older inhabitants—commercial artists, wordsmiths, admen, fanatics, wealthy culture mongers, academics, unemployed actors (which of them was not a fully employed actor?). The transient permanent world of the frustrate who pour culture into a bottle and suckle for gain or for loss, slurping on Freud and Michelangelo. And yet, in spite of its patent phoniness, there was a real excitement, a genuine quickening that was not polluted by the contrived artificiality of its mechanism. Those who believed and those who came to sneer their disbelief were engaged in a semireligious dance of confrontation, and if the idols were spurious and the worship hypocritical, there was at least the barest possibility of a congregation and a splinter-shivered chance of ersatz communion and atonement. For Christ's sake, Riegel! Grand-uncle Maimonides is dead and the old lens grinder has long since curled his toe bones in a Dutch cemetery and you ain't either corpse. Sit down and have a cup of coffee and let someone be Aristotle who's more Greek than thee. More Greek than thee, less Jew than you, I repeated to my mind's adoring ear. The cosmos breathes in the release of the sphincter muscle and what the world calls fart the soul knows well as art. Poetry sings in the bleeding of thy wounds, Riegel. Thou belong'st here.

The one large room was crowded and I looked for an empty seat which might offer sanctuary. In a corner flanked by an immense bullfight poster and an expertly wormwooded corner abutment was a round table at which only one person sat—a man in his forties completely encased in a green raincoat. I maneuvered my embarrassment to the practically empty table, indicating by deaf-and-dumb signs and pitiable snaky contortions of my upper body my desire to sit down. Egalitarian democratic America, friendliest, most generous people on God's green earth, but it is the height of usurpation to inflict yourself on another except to ask for charity. When you want to mooch a match, a cigarette, a ten-dollar bill—when you want a girl or a hot meal or a vote or a donation to yourself—you can assault anyone with dignity, sacrificing nothing of your self-esteem. But may the good Lord take compassion on you if you want something that brings you into a position of equality with a stranger. His hackles bristle in defense of his squatting rights; your neck creeps in a red tide of humiliation even as your fingers grip the legal charter. It is as though that which is your right becomes an infringement—a selfish amputation of the other's—while that which is not your right becomes a gift through the indifferent magnanimity of the stranger whose reward is the self-reflection of his own largesse. De Tocqueville must have had something to say about this, I thought. And he didn't even know anything about sit-ins or freedom rides. But the man at the table suffered my intrusion as a European would, passively recognizing my claim to at least one of the empty chairs at his table. I sat directly opposite from him, settling into the smoke and the varnished walls and speech hum of the cafe.

He was stirring his coffee abstractedly, seeming to be absorbed in a scrutiny of the bullfight poster. He read the announcement aloud, pronouncing the words sonorously—more, I thought, with an Italian than a Spanish accent.

"'Extraordinaria Corrida de Toros.' Extraordinaria. Always extraordinaria. Nevair ordinaria. Nevair without 'seleccionados toros.' The impresario thinks he's at the butcher shop. Looking for sausage meat. Zees one and zat one. Sí. Sí. No. Sí. Ah, bueno. Seex good ones. Anyzing else today, señor?"

I thought his soliloquy was for his own benefit, but the fixity with which he regarded me while he talked suggested that I was not only allowed to sit at his table, but I was expected to be a privileged companion as well. I was to engage in conversation with him. I tore off the edge from the hand-printed menu and mumbled something, pretending to study the menu so that I could look at him more closely. He had a great quantity of rippling sandy hair brushed over to one side of his head, and his skin, an unrelieved pink from the lobes of his ears to the tip of his upturned nose, was blotchy in the cheeks where his veins clustered. His glasses were perfectly round, with glinting metal frames, and when he moved his head the lenses caught the light, giving the upper part of his face both a mystery and a quickness of play and expression that may not actually have been there. The most striking aspect of his appearance was the raincoat, lizard green and weathered, tightly sealed up to the chin by tarnished horizontal clasps. Its collar looked like an old World War One collar, separating the neck from the torso with a corrugated military finality. Beside him on the seat was a tightly furled umbrella—a black Neville Chamberlain umbrella with the ferrule enameled bright electric red. The day had been warm but not particularly humid, and I could as little imagine the reason for the raincoat and umbrella as understand why he kept so lobsterman-sealed in the relatively becalmed atmosphere of The Libido. I had a sudden thought that he might be stark naked under the raincoat and I imagined the startling pink of his nudity at the coffee-house table, somehow wretchedly unhealthy in the vast blotchy expanses which his face foretold. All this while he was looking directly at me with that impersonal friendliness with which a teacher regards his students, and when my eyes finally met his, he tapped at my menu meaningfully.

"The good Lahd created man in His own image, and now the good Lahd is dead. Man is dead also."

Holy Jesus, a religious nut, I thought, but aloud I agreed that what he said was very likely so. He merely waited for my voice to cease and he continued, indicating the roomful of patrons with an awkward thrust of his elbow.

"Dead. They're all dead. They sit there and they don't fall down. But they are quite truly dead."

He sipped at his coffee as I signaled my order to a passing waitress. Then he picked up his spoon and jabbed it toward me. "Do *you* know how the good Lahd died? Do you ever think about it? Don't you ever worry out your parcel of the shame? Do you know how He died?"

The spoon leveled off in the air, pointing directly at my inoffensive nose, and it hung poised there in a meaty red fist. The clatter of cups and conversation made a surrounding amphitheater for our table, but there was a deadly center of silence between me and the spoon of my companion. And I knew that his question was not rhetorical, that the spoon was a summoner, a pointer like the delicately carved ivory fingers which rabbinical scholars use when they read from the Torah. My first impulse was to redden and avoid this intrusive man with some polite apology, some evasion, but the spoon collected me and beckoned me out of my hiding. Everybody speeches me, I thought. Maybe I got an extra-big ear. Strogoff and Father Abraham and Ziggie, and if I go to the men's room there's sure to be some cracker making a speech to the toilet paper and I'll get me another lecture. To hell with them all, goddamn it. I can get into the act, too. It's a free country. A permissive lunatic asylum.

"Yes, friend," I said. "It just so happens that I *do* know how the good Lord died. And since you ask me so politely, I'll be very happy to give you an almost eye-witness report." My voice was angry but not rude, and the spoon retreated from my nose and made bivouac in the coffee cup.

"In the first place," I said, "and contrary to persistent rumors, it wasn't murder. It was a cut-and-dried case of suicide. The good Lahd just killed himself. And in the second place, man *is* dead, but he didn't commit suicide. He—poor old fornicating mankind—was murdered in ice-cold calculating blood. And, friend, you're obviously a pretty bright boy, so you can put two and two together and get the same answers that I get."

I took a theatrical puff on my cigarette, but the red face and the flashing glasses didn't move from their fixed outrage.

"Sure, friend," I continued. "I'm glad you asked me about this. I'm sick of keeping it a secret. When the good Lahd killed himself, he clobbered mankind into its slow grave the way the recoil of a shotgun blast might knock a lamp off the table, but the big goddamned corpse, it don't care. It got what it wanted and it lays out in state like Lenin under the glass, and what the hell does it care about us lousy maggots who kill ourselves trying to be alive—but what the hell, we were dead before we were even born at all. And *that's* how the good Lahd died, if you really want to know."

The spoon came up again in the red fist and the pink face with the glasses shining like revolving mirrors came forward in a tight, anguished lurch. His voice squeaked a little in the baritone registers, but it was measured and it was furious.

"Hideous. Heinous. Blaspheme. Lie. That's a very bad lie. *You* hammered nails into Him! *You* shoved a spear into His side! *You* gave Him a cup of vinegar to drink and thorns to make His head bleed. And when the sun hid itself for shame, *you* felt your life run out in you, and you knew that you had killed yourself and you died weeping. And that's the God-awful truth of how it happened. Pride! Man and his puny stinking pride! Logic and reason! Pride! Weights and measures! Pride! You couldn't weigh Him and you couldn't hold His length with a ruler. So you murdered Him. With nails and a spear. Your story is terrible. A lie!"

The spoon made a marionette dance in the air to emphasize the stressed words and then it poised motionless at my nose again. I wondered whether it was my particular nose that bothered him or whether he was like this with all noses. A nose fetishist. Proboscis sadism. An extreme case. I took a sip of my coffee, which the waitress had left on the corner of the table as though fearful of approaching too close, and I returned his speech, mimicking his emphases.

"*That's* a hideous heinous lie. And you know it, too. God couldn't be murdered. He was too big, too smart, too much in the know. He was no loser like us, man. He was God. The Big Fixer. The Master Mind. The Primordial Daddy-o. No snot-nosed punks could do Him in with nails or spears or spikes or bombs. Not unless He arranged it himself. And if He arranged it himself—if He decided that He wanted to go all the way, it's only because He was looking for the biggest bang. SMASH! and the rest is silence crap. Maybe He got bored. He'd been at it a long time, you know—working His will, seed timing and harvest timing. Yeah—yeah, that's it, He was getting bored. The classic ennui. No kicks any more in being God, no real challenges, nothing. Or maybe some of the God juice was leaking out of Him, evaporating maybe—slowly, gradually, a drop every hundred years, something like that. Not enough to show, you know. Not enough to spoil anything. Nobody would have known about it for maybe a billion years, but what the hell, He was God. He *knew*, man. He'd been God a long time and maybe He didn't like to think that someday He'd be a has-been. A shelf all to Himself in Cooperstown. No bench for Him—even if the bench was an eternity away. So let's say He knew, and He was big enough—if He wasn't who the hell is?—big enough to handle the knowledge. So the hell with it, Jack, says He. Let's do it up brown. Let's die the way a God dies—no bangs, no whimpers, just one goddamned good joke. So He arranges the scenery real nice and He sets up the kill and He frames the snot-noses and punks and goes out with a goddamned laugh that still shudders the skin of every living son whose death He doomed. And don't hand me that crap about murder, buster, because this is the way it would have to be and you know it. And that's why you have to hate Him, too, isn't it?"

I brought my coffee spoon dripping out of the cup and held it at the en garde position. His spoon rose to parry and we crossed spoons lightly above an ovoid ceramic ashtray.

"My name's Riley," he said. "The coffee stinks here but sometimes I meet interesting people."

"I'm David Riegel," I countered. "I'm a tourist, myself."

"We all begin that way," he said, the light splashing off his glasses so that I had no chance to read his eyes. "Even I began that way once." He fingered the top clasp of his raincoat as though this movement explained something. "But people don't have to stay that way."

"Don't have to be tourists always, you mean?"

"Don't have to. Most do, but nobody has to."

He slipped his hand under the flap of his raincoat without disturbing the seam that the tight clasps made, so that I still couldn't see what if anything he wore underneath. The quick gesture was to bring out a flat package of Player's cigarettes and a steel lighter molded in the shape of a large bullet. I decided that if he wasn't wearing a shirt, he must have had pockets sewed into his skin.

"Are *you* no longer a tourist?" I asked.

"Nope. No more. Had it a long time but I finally got rid of it." He lit his cigarette in a great burst of flame and he blew the smoke out of his mouth and nostrils at the same time.

"Is a tourist the same as a pilgrim?" I asked.

He thought for a moment. "Yup. Tourist, pilgrim, seeker, traveler, student, inchworm. All the same word. All the same thing."

"Well, then—what are you *now*? If you're none of these things that are all the same word?"

He smiled. It was a genuine delighted smile that his whole face collaborated in and I was surprised at the whiteness and evenness of his teeth. "*Found!* That's what I am now. I'm found!" He paused and grimaced his dissatisfaction. "No, that's not right. I should say I've found, not I'm found. That is, I *have* found, not I *am* found. That's the big difference. You see?"

"No, I don't think so," I said.

"Never mind," he said. "You're still a tourist. And you're a very clever man, but you don't really care anything about God, do you?"

"No, I don't *think* I do, really. Unless I don't know if I do. It's just never seemed to me terribly important."

Riley played with his cigarette in the ashtray and then brought it up with the same jabbing motion he had used with the spoon. "Why'd Hemingway commit suicide?"

"Jesus," I said. "Talking with you is like playing Information, Please." I countered his cigarette with my spoon. "Name me five great homosexual Popes who never learned to speak French."

His cigarette jabbed again. "Please. I mean it. Talk mustn't be cheap. You're a thoughtful fellow. Why do you think Hemingway committed suicide?"

"I really don't know," I said. "It bothered me a lot at first. Maybe he just wanted to see what it felt like. There was this guy in the army with me was like that. He used to put the barrel of his M-1 in his mouth with the butt between his legs on the floor and just hold on to the trigger with his left thumb. You'd come in on him in the squadroom in the dark and find him like that, sitting on a bunk, his eyes closed, his thumb on that trigger. He'd get everybody crazy till you'd want to kill him. And he wasn't a morbid guy either. He used to say that the taste of the barrel made him know how much alive he was, because he could taste how dead death was. Hemingway might have been something like him. Maybe he got to like the death taste better than the life taste. Or maybe he got a spasm in his thumb. You can't know about these things. Especially with a complicated guy like Hemingway was."

"Maybe," Riley said, "he didn't want to be a tourist any more."

"Maybe," I said. "Or he got fed up because he couldn't write or he couldn't hunt or swill wine or screw all night. Or maybe he decided that his life was just short and happy enough—as it surely was. Or maybe it was the way he found to pay off his old man. Or the Catholic Church. Or women in general. Or the critics."

A large hand jolted my shoulder and a voice of baritone joviality interrupted me. "Maybe the poor bastard had the misfortune of running into our friend Riley and he took the only sure way out."

I turned around to see what flesh surrounded the voice. Two men and a woman had joined our table and were scraping chairs and sitting in a babble of sophisticated expostulations. The man who had interrupted me was heavy and short-cropped. He wore his salesman's suit with a kind of familiarity that suggested a symbiotic relationship—the tweed and hound's-tooth taking on a sheen from the low pumping of his blood beneath the white skin at the wrists and ankles, his footprint stealthy and rubbery in the scuffed chukka boots. His male companion looked like a ferret—his clothes were unobtrusively dark around the shocking white of his shirt front, his hair was black with a dull shine and smooth to the skull as if it had been poured on his head from a bottle, while the flesh tones of his face were dully white in an almost obverse shadow to the general opacity of his appearance. The woman was tall and she gave the impression of slenderness so that you were surprised to see that her individual parts were not thin but almost plump. She wore a yellow smocklike affair yoked at the shoulders and tightened in the waist by a lightly knotted crimson tassel. Her face was plain, delicately formed, and dominated by her eyes—great round hazel eyes like those of a horse or like yellow grapes. I didn't know that I was staring at her until she centered her eyes on mine and held them there expressionless. I didn't even know that she was beautiful until I had looked at her long enough to see her all together, because there wasn't any single or even conglomerate thing about her that would hit you just like that.

"Howdy, Padre!" It was the boom of the jovial baritone,

who grabbed one of Riley's red hands with his own well-cared-for athletic ones. "Come on, Riley, introduce us to your latest Hemingway victim." The man winked at me. "Old Riley went into esthetic menopause when Papa made with the big POW. He wants to be Saul of Tarsus to Ernesto's swan dive. But us Philistines love him just the same."

Riley retrieved the hand as though it had been permanently spoiled, slid both his fists into the diagonal pockets of his raincoat, and hunched himself silent on his seat. I thought I saw his lips curl around the unspoken word, "tourist," but he said nothing. The large man was neither offended nor surprised. He turned toward me with genuine welcoming friendliness.

"My name's Millcote. Roger Millcote. I'm in advertising up the street." He gestured at the ferret. "And this is John Weir. He paints. That is—" he gurgled over a stage chuckle—"he paints and makes money at it." The ferret made no sign of response. "And the lovely lady is Rennie. Sometimes she works for me." I had a moment of speculation on the multiple ambiguities of that remark, but the girl was reading the small print on the bullfight poster and I couldn't see her face.

"I'm David Riegel," I said. "And I'm a tourist and I just happened to sit down here, but I won't bother you if this is a private party."

"Oh, sit down, Riegel," said Millcote. "You're from Boston, aren't you?" I nodded. Millcote smiled at the girl, flicking his finger at the nipple of her breast that was somewhere under the loose folds of her dress. "I can always tell a Boston accent," he said. "In my business you get to be an expert on all kinds of things." He ordered extravagant desserts with imported cheeses and coffees for the whole table as though he were Father taking the family out for Sunday dinner. The waitress wrote down orders with a careful pencil. She took him seriously and he respected her for that.

"Yessiree, Rennie," he said when the waitress went away. "You notice how that Boston accent is usually joined with a kind of nineteenth-century manners? No offense, Riegel, but—" he turned toward the girl—"you see now why we have to mock up a completely different standpoint of valuation for our New England accounts? Like that Krampax promotion that almost lost us the whole goddamned contract when the Boston people got ahold of it. No kidding." His arm drew in the whole table, inviting us to share in the comedy of the ridiculous Boston accounts.

"We had this helluva presentation for a new Krampax 'Get Un-Quainted' promotion, you know. Thoroughly checked out with the MR boys—but in depth, sample reactions from all over the country, the detail men just wild on it. Oh, it was a real sweet job, a gas. We get this very good-looking gal done up real nice in a gold lamé sheath and pose her with a boa constrictor coiled around her thighs and belly. He's all puffed out and working hard on her and we're getting the maximum appeal from the sheath on where he's squeezing and where the sheath is straining and her hairdo is just as set as an iceberg and her make-up is right in place and the expression on her face is that cool society don't-screw-me look—and I mean it's all there in the picture—the above and below, the strain and the restraint. Underneath in that expensive invitational script is 'WHEN THE SQUEEZE IS ON, KRAMPAX WORKS LIKE A CHARM.' You get it? Charm? Snakes? Oh, it was a sweet job. So we print up fifteen thousand of these damn things in life-size cardboard with fold-back supports so they could stand inside the doors of every drugstore in the country. Jesus, the kids would've eat 'em up. And then these prehistoric New England squares put the no-go on the whole damned thing. Said no self-respecting druggist in their territory would use them. Then find some unself-respecting druggists, says I. Sell 'em to the discount houses. Oh, I put up a real fight, a last-ditch Nixon Donnybrook, didn't I, Rennie?"

He looked toward the hazel-horse beauty for confirmation but she gave him the same no-expression that she had given me. I guess he never noticed because he went right on talking.

"Believe me, I was mad. You guys make fun of PR, but, shit, it's an art like anything else. Jesus Christ, I had been *living* this Krampax campaign for three months. I was as much tied up in the menstrual cycle as any woman could be and I had sweated with this whole thing, stinking detail by stinking detail. You think it's easy to get hold of a boa constrictor in New York City? Even a tame one? And these stupid Boston bastards—no offense, Riegel—washed the whole sonofabitching thing out and we had to compromise with the standard shot of the broadie in shorts jumping high enough so her titties show while she pounds the hell out of a tennis ball. Christ, I mean you sweat and you slave and you create something new and the bastards won't let you live."

Millcote slumped in his chair in mock collapse and I decided that he must be one of those parodies of real people that New York was famous for. Neither Riley nor the painter had paid any attention to his harangue and the horse-girl had become rapt in the contemplation of a pebbled salt shaker, which she rolled in her long hand like a cherished talisman. No one spoke for a long minute and then Weir, the ferret, cleared his throat as though to spit and began to talk in a monotone as though he were all alone, addressing his mirror or the darkened recesses of a closet with the door slightly ajar.

"I painted seventy-eight dog turds today. Yesterday I made two gross of phony ink blots. Tomorrow it can be anything. Maybe fake bloodstains for virgin sheets. Or brown-rubber chocolate candies. Or ashtrays shaped like toilet bowls. Or cancer smears for party favors. It doesn't touch me. My hands work. My eyes measure and grade the light. I work and I am not touched. I am a working machine and I give not a fuck. I mold plaster and mix paint and I make anything but I do not touch what I make with me."

He kept on talking, his voice going lower and lower into his chin, and he could have been on an empty stage with no audience in front of him. The five of us sat at a table which might have been a temporarily closed community of some sort, but we were each alone and nobody's voice reached anybody else's ear. There was a long two or three minutes of silence and then Rennie broke it, bringing the salt cellar down heavily against the table with a sharp glassy crack. The others ignored her and she concentrated on me.

"Well, Riegel, what's your excuse? How do *you* earn your dying?"

Her enormous eyes focused on mine and I felt a slight current tenuously connecting us.

"Me? I have no excuse," I said. "I am a great unpublished writer."

She winced a little, scornfully. "You don't look fairy enough to be a poet," she said. "Or are you one of those sneaky ones?"

"Just try me," I said with a bad imitation of the famous Hemingway kudu-killing grin. "I happen to be working on a great unpublishable novel. But don't let it worry you. I don't usually mention it."

"Oh, a novel," she said sarcastically. "What's it like, this novel? A precious Frenchie bibelot with concealed cloacal meanings? A hard-hitting satirical sweep at the Amurrican way of life? Another painful reminiscence of a young man's initiation into dirty sex and evil women?" She was becoming interested in the cleverness of her own flow of words.

"What are you?" I asked. "Bennington or Sarah Lawrence?"

"Oh, you're the human-observer type," she said. "Indiana Summer School of Letters. Bread loaf. Aspen, Colorado. Two books of Kenneth Burke and a sophomore course in economics. What's your novel like?"

The current was a little stronger now, herself seduced by her own sophistication to a point where she needed me to prove that sophistication valid. I was enjoying the game and I was under no obligation to give anything away.

"Well, actually I have a kind of interesting idea," I drawled. "It's a novel about writing a novel about a novel. There's a story and a diary, you see, and they get all mixed up. The hero of the story is living in Paris trying to write this novel. You don't know what it's about or anything, and he has these long conversations about nothing and how he's making out in the city and descriptions and such. You know, Paris in the rain and like that."

I gestured explainingly with both my hands and knocked over my coffee cup. A slow brown tongue dribbled from the overturned lip, staining the table and wetting the yellow dress where it smoothed over the thighs. Without thinking, I grabbed a napkin and began to rub at the stain. "If I was Walter Raleigh, I'd take off my coat," I murmured gallantly. Rennie stopped my hand and did the job herself with a handkerchief dipped in a glass of water.

"I'm sorry," I said. "One of the reasons I don't like to talk about my novel is it gets me all excited."

She shrugged. "Don't worry it, Riegel. Fifteen dollars to the cleaners and you won't be able to tell the difference." The water made a Rorschach blotch on her lap, but I decided that the associations were too loaded to have much clinical value.

"Back to your novel," she said. "What's the diary for?"

"Well," I said, improvising hastily, "that's the beauty of the thing. The diary tells the real story. From the *inside.* Kind of like from the Freudian preconsciousness. And the gimmick is that the diary is a much more interesting story—more *fictional,* you see—than the actual story. You see, in the diary, this guy is hunting for this girl who's run off with this man. But it's all *allegorical* on this level."

Rennie pursed her lips. I figured that I'd managed for the moment to pull her slightly beyond her depth.

"I think I get the picture," she said. "It seems like a variation on Gide's *Counterfeiters*."

It had to be Sarah Lawrence after all. "Precisely," I said. "But Gide's is an intellectual destruction of reality. What I'm trying to do is work an *emotional* destruction of reality. You see the guys in my story and my diary don't even know one another. The only link between them is the reader. That makes all the difference."

"Oh, I see." She smiled uncertainly, impressed. "I can understand where that might be so."

Our companions had finished their coffee and pastries and were fixed in inertia under the café noise and the smoke of the evening crowd in The Libido. A strange swarm of bedfellows, I thought, savoring the appellation in regard to Rennie. Riley had not opened his mouth since our private conversation, turtled in his green raincoat, nurturing his unremitted outrage from behind the shielding lenses of his glasses. Weir the ferret made a leprous smear against the dark background of the wall behind him. He had subsided into a silence that was as removed as his earlier monologue. Millcote was breaking cake crumbs between his fingers, rolling them into little pellets and snapping them against the raging bull in the wall poster. The ribbons on the banderillas stood out straight in the artist's wind and one of the cake pellets moist with whipped cream stuck to the great black hump of the bull.

"You know what the big mistake is?" I caught Rennie's attention from the cake pellets and brought it back to me. "Let me tell you what it is. Right at the beginning, right where language starts, that's where the mistake is. People got to supposing that they were nouns. You know. Nominative, accusative, that kind of noun. And from this basic grammatical stupidity, they built a completely unrealistic psychology and philosophy. People aren't nouns. At best, they're adjectives and adverbs."

I saw that I had lost her again under her eyes. "Wait a minute, you just think about it," I said. "Look at everybody around this table. By themselves they don't exist. No nominative, accusative, or anything. They have to be coupled with something else—something that isn't themselves—before they can even come to life. Just like an adjective or an adverb. It's very simple."

"Sure," Rennie said. "Are you an adjective or an adverb?"

"I'm an adverb. Men usually are. Women are mostly adjectives."

"Sweet of you to say so," she said. "How can you tell?"

"Men," I said, "have to ally themselves with force, with motion, with a cause or an idea that has some distinct dynamism in it. Hence, they're adverbs. But women tend to take on meaning by fixing on some solidity or motionlessness. They generally adhere to something that's distinctly *there,* something that's relatively stable." At any rate, some women, I thought.

"Well, then, what about sadists and masochists?" Rennie argued. "According to your definition, they'd have to be nouns. 'I hit the ball. The ball hits me.' Pure nominative and accusative, straight out of De Sade by way of Krafft-Ebing."

She wasn't stupid, that Rennie. Sweet old Sarah had tied her up into pretty little educational bowknots. "Of course," I said. "And that's exactly what's so pernicious about the false grammatical analogy in contemporary psychology. Sadism-masochism, victims and victimizers. Bullshit. It's as rigid and unempirical a system for understanding human behavior as astrology. You start with the myth that people are nouns and you can demonstrate any kind of monstrosity as though it were logical. Perfectly normal men and women go around telling themselves, 'Grrr, I'm a sadist. I get my kicks out of hurting people.' And other equally nice people tell themselves with great self-pity, 'Alas and woe is me, I'm a masochist. I only find pleasure in feeling pain. Hurt me a little harder, please.' Absolute nonsense. While all the time, all people really want to do is to couple with other people. To modify and be modified. Reserving their God-given adjectival or adverbial right to uncouple at the end of a sentence or a paragraph and find another person or thing or time to stick to. Jesus, people are possibilities, not grammatical categories! Don't you agree?"

Rennie inspected her stained dress, which had dried into a faded swatch of pale yellow. "Good Lord, Riegel," she said. "You go all around Robin Hood's barn to get to the same place that everybody else is at. But it's not a bad line."

It seemed to me that the currents were fairly sizable now in spite of her veneer of unconcern, and I remembered that Ziggie had advised a vacation for me. For Christ's sakes, Riegel, be an adverb for a while. You've served your time as an accusative noun. And then some. Rennie picked up the salt cellar and deliberately cracked it against the table to get the attention of her friends.

"Are we going to sit around here all night? Let's go get drunk somewhere before I lose my mind. Or what's left of it."

Millcote brushed the cake crumbs carefully to the floor and massaged his sticky palms. His whole face wrinkled as he thought, his brow pleating up like a schoolboy's. "I got it, baby!" he cried, his forehead perfectly smooth again after his labors. "I got a great idea. Janie Putter is throwing a party tonight to celebrate her third month of living with Leo Farina. Jesus, everybody will be there. She makes a real swinging party."

No one responded but Millcote was already out of his chair, riding his new idea like a magic carpet. "You know Janie

Putter, John. She's got the biggest ass in the art world. And Leo might be able to nudge some work your way."

Riley sat unmoved while the others collected the debris of themselves from the amazingly cluttered table, Millcote crumpling a bill under the ashtray, Weir rising from his seat like a wraith of a balloon. I found myself moving with them in the scraping of the chairs and the arranging of rumpled pants legs.

"I'll see you again, I hope," I said to Riley.

"In another country," he replied.

And he didn't even follow us with his eyes as we left, Weir and Millcote making a prow up the aisle toward the door, I riding their wake with my hand on Rennie's hip, which was warm and rising to my palm.

Janie Putter and Leo Farina must have been inordinately proud of their three-month bedlock, because they'd gone all out to throw the swingingest party they knew how. Leo's studio—an enormous loft behind Houston Street—was cleared for revelry—the floor partially swept for dancing, a monumental drafting table pressed into service as a bar, even an orchestra, a five-piece makepiece, untalented and loud, organized from the motley of the guests. Roger Millcote may have been guilty of a slight exaggeration when he insisted that everybody in the art world would be there, but enough and varied eventually made their appearances so that only a pedant would have quibbled. I knew nothing and cared less about "the art world," but living with Letha for almost ten years, I had picked up enough information—a name here, a faded reputation there, a new movement everywhere—to be able to appreciate the splendor of the rich fruitcake which was offered for my delectation. And I had Rennie as well to see to it that I didn't miss any of the more savory and exotic pieces which minced in and out of the spicy batter. However, two factors were in constant operation throughout the evening to befuddle an absolutely accurate report on the orbital gyrations of our party. First, the band—untalentedly loud, as I have mentioned, and demonically indefatigable in their motor and respiratory capacities. Their range was awesomely wide, dredging back into the lint of the past to bring up mossy curios like "Begin the Beguine," "The Isle of Capri," "The Object of My Affection," and desperately contemporary seizures of endurance in wrestling with the compulsive noises of the twist and the bossa nova. When one plucky bandsman was just at the point of suspiring his last breath into a clarinet that had begun the evening pointing proudly at the skylight only to waver and droop limply against a sweaty shirt, another guest was ready to grab the instrument and apply a fresh measure of spit to the reed. The music never ceased, never relaxed from its decibellic peak, never really departed from the simple syncopation which all the would-be but never-were musicians had drudgerously learned in their youth. The effect of this unrelenting audial barrage was to create a surreal unmoving background for the evening in which landmarks in time sank below the surface of the sound like weighted corpses into the sea. The other deranging factor was the bar, or, more precisely, my increasing relationship to the bar. Janie and Leo knew well the economies of mass distribution; their bar was a perfect application of the Taylor System. Dixie cups, a lined-up battallion of gin bottles at the ready, quantities of ice, and wholesale-sized jars of olives. The one drink the house offered was a dry, a veritably dehydrated, Martini. And since the evening was warm to begin with, and the music and increasing body heat aggravated the warmth even more, I quaffed liberally and well and managed barely to tread water, as it were, in a great liquid blur of gin and music, bumping my forehead from time to time against whatever olives bobbed into my proximity.

Certainly, everybody who was anybody—as well as many who were not—was there. The silver-haired satyr, Hermann Gans-Glunik, now the crown prince of the painting world, with Pollock and Kline departed to some nether shore. Rex Soxo, severely intellectual as he demonstrated vector analysis to a clump of admiring Columbia students. The great black hulk of Lucien Schwarz. The precious ballet grace of Yokigaru. The whimsical Judas glance on the Christly face of the sculptor, Angrinini (his socks had slipped beneath the counters of his shoes but his beard burned with black fire). And the big money people of the younger generation. Jonas Asphalt, as furry as a Teddy bear. Harry Montaine, vaguely strangling in a loosely knotted tie that accented his protruding Adam's apple and made you wonder why, if he was making all that money, he didn't spend some of it on food. And striding around the floor like a paced panther in a tight purple sweater, riding pants, and spurred boots, the exotic sculptress, Samurai. And the eager not-yet-arrived, greedy in their self-announcements, but with uneasy eyes and with the fear sweat under their arms. And the biggest gallery people—Snijas smothered in his own fat, Knadle, Bella Bonbaum, the rat-faced Manfred Loewenstein. And seemingly all the important art editors and critics, the careful men with the sharpened pencils who spitefully withheld their admiration from all save their particular chisel or brush. Fogarty was in histrionic transport over the latest cement mobiles from the hod of Habib Hussein. Chaim Spero gestured into the crowded air to suggest the unfathomable volume in a new technique of miniatures by Max Ansen. Everybody who was anybody stayed antiseptically clear of anybody else who might have been somebody, preferring to rotate in little satellite worlds of their own where their small greatness could be reflected and magnified. Leo Farina's canvases were stacked on one wall, their surfaces turned toward the clean brick, and no one fingered them to see what shape they made. It was a magnificent press of people—bearded, balded, besequined and near nude. The music wheezed and pounded within and above, the gin picked the tempo to a higher harder place, and I fragmented like a shredded adhesive tape, liquorishly ready to become affixed.

At some time in the evening Rennie swirled to me from a serpent's knot of people, carrying a still-stiff Dixie cup to refill me. "Come on, David. Circulate," she said. "Mix around."

"Don' wanna mix, baby," I said. "Wanna modify. C'mon, let's couple-ate." I had trouble focusing my eyes, but it was good trouble. "Aren't there any little rooms off this big room? Like sleeping-type rooms?"

Rennie ignored my fatuous smirk. "Come on, David. You can pick up material for your novel." She was pulling at my sweated Haspel sleeve and I carefully, drunkenly, removed her hand, sliding my arm around her waist so that my right palm rode warmly on the rise of her right hip. In that position we approached a disengaged group that was gathered casually near the large open studio windows.

"Jesus, Rennie. This is the goddamnedest party I ever been. I can't get to first base with any of these women. But the men! At least three guys have thrown hard passes at me. One squiggly guy—Christ, he had a mustache he must of crocheted himself—hell, he had me so bugged I almost went and locked myself into the bathroom."

Rennie laughed. "*That* would be exactly the worst place to go. We'd have to mail you back to Boston by scrambled freight."

I squeezed her hip and made a grab for her near earlobe with my teeth. I tried to make my voice low and throaty, but the gin bubbled over it so I sounded as though I were talking through a drainpipe. "I don't take any high moral position on these things, you know, kiddo." A hiccough interrupted me. I tried unsuccessfully to pretend that it was a Charles Boyer gargle. "It's just that I prefer women."

"Don't fight it, David," she said abstractly. "You're just irresistible to a certain variety of men." She looked expressively around the room. "Which we have in large representation this evening."

We had caught on to the edges of the group by the window, some seven or eight people smoking and talking with an informal seminar air, the white scrim from their cigarettes floating gently into the cool outside night. An enormous man about my age was dominating the conversation in a high-pitched meticulous voice, which was so incongruous coming from the fat breadth of his throat that you thought at first he was cruelly parodying his own bulk. His dewlaps shook and the entiered folds of fat on his neck quivered in tapioca applause when he spoke. He was wearing a white shirt with the sleeves rolled up almost to the elbows, leaving his forearms bare like mammoth kosher salamis, and—marvelous to behold—he sported a tight pair of Levis. ("He must have got them from Jake Klugelman's Stout Shoppe," I thought. "A size-fifty waist if he's an inch.") Around his neck, the knot drooping low to the side cowboy-fashion, was a gorgeous red silk bandanna. His hair was kinky black and his skin was grainy with a dark-green tinge, like chopped liver left out in the sun. From the way the group deferred to him, it was obvious that he was, if not an anybody, then at least an almost-body. He carried his enormous weight with patent worried affection, assured of its precious value, and in my happy haze the confidence of his manner and his easy good opinion of himself was an irritation and an affront.

"Oh," Rennie said, following my glance. "The delicatessen

man. That's Phil Stein lecturing his disciples. He's just started to get a market and he thinks he's God."

". . . so there's no place else to go in Art today. The doors are all closed, see?" He closed the doors by bringing one huge fist into the palm of his other hand. The concussion of fat against flab was wet and splashy, like a whale doing bellyflops. "You know my last show at the Rokefort? Well, you must have observed the continuity in the canvases. How they march to this new vision. It's not for myself to say, of course, but I consider that show a real breakthrough. A pioneering step in Modern Art. And it's all—you might say, *crystallized* in the red and green oil I call *Contemplation Nadir*. This is a very sig*ni*ficant canvas. The climax of my thought to date."

"Oh, but that's an absolutely brilliant piece, Phil. You *know* how strongly that affects me." This from a not-so-brilliant piece, a tall thin straw-colored girl whose hair was so high and thick on her head that you knew she'd fall over from sheer weight if she bent to scratch her ankle. The other acolytes made unintelligible murmurs of ecstatic remembrance which Phil absorbed with a kind of porous satisfaction.

"You see, what *Contemplation Nadir* says—or, better, *is*," he continued, "is the one viable way out of the cul-de-sac that has beset Modern Art. In those two opposing vertical shapes with that red thrust moving laterally from both sides of the canvas, I literally *force* a new direction for Modern Painting." He shifted his monumental behind from ham to ham as though he had a bad case of diaper rash. "You see, with these carefully calculated countervailing forces in operation, I completely control the viewer. You look at that painting and you have to move right into it. There's nothing else you can do. And it opens up a whole world of new possibilities for the Plastic Arts."

A red, balding man in an expensive silk suit clapped the painter on the shoulder. "Y'know, Phil. While you was talking

I just saw it. You know, saw it for the first time. You just made it as clear as a baby for me. Smatta afack, you oughta write up your ideas in a little article or something so people could appreciate. You really ought to."

Phil Stein hitched himself up to the window sill ("Please, a derrick, a crane, an earth mover for the old sod," I prayed), the tough denim of his dungarees stretching taut across his stomach and thighs to accommodate his giant seat. His feet dangled back and forth like a fat boy's on a swing, revealing blazing red socks of the same material as his bandanna. He snapped his cigarette out of the window in a long sparking orange arc.

"In point of fact, Melvin, *The New Arts is* planning to run a piece like that in a month or two. Harriet Algae will write it up, but, of course, I've given her all the important ideas. I suggested that she approach it from the historical point of view. How far Kandinsky and Picasso carried painting until they created their own dead ends. The contemporary frustration of the Neo-Surrealists, the Actionists, the Pops—all that corny business. The way I planned the piece, the first half will demonstrate how all our modern movements have painted themselves into a corner—" he smiled knowingly at his pun and his eyes disappeared into two parallel pockets of flesh. "And the second half of the article will be devoted to my little doorway out." He sighed contentedly. "She had to have a name for the movement, so I've decided to call it 'Accelerational Passivity.' "

" 'Accelerational Passivity,' " echoed several rapt voices.

"It's the poifect name," Melvin said, beaming his delight.

I drained my Dixie cup for some booster fuel, discovered that Rennie didn't wear a girdle—at least where a girdle is usually worn—and plunged into the devotional murmur of appreciation like a boisterous seal from the wrong side of the snow tracks.

"Sure, it's a movement, Phil," I said. "And so's a bowel movement. But it ain't got nowhere to go except down the flush. You're either putting us on, man, or you're kidding yourself bad."

The group swung around like a singed cat to stare at me.

"I know I ought to keep my mouth shut, Phil," I continued aggressively, ignoring the others and targeting my words directly at the large artery which had to be buried somewhere beneath the furled bandanna. "But, Jesus, I saw your show at the Rokefort too. And I know you've got it. Sure, you got it, man. But—" I grinned a Boy Scout grin as though I were passing out free popsicles in the park—"but, man, you're just turning it to shit."

My surprise assault had discommoded everyone and Phil Stein, swinging his feet from his pinnacle of admiration on the window sill, was in a position of precarious disadvantage, able neither to attack nor retreat without falling flat on the bulging seat of his impeccable Levis. Rennie reached into my shirt pocket for a cigarette, tweaking my nipple in a gesture of avowed comradeship, and I figured what the hell did I have to lose.

"Look, man, I'm not trying to put you down or anything," I explained ingratiatingly. "If I didn't *respect* your work, I wouldn't say anything at all. We *both* know how few people there are who are doing any really original work in painting today. And that's why it gets me in the crut to see what you're doing with yourself."

The balding Melvin, he who was as clear as a baby and had probably invested a small fortune in early monuments of Accelerational Passivity, was the first to leap into the breach. "Who the hell do you think you are, Mister—"

"Riegel," I said. "Mister Rog Riegel. Like maybe you saw that ridiculous five-page write-up on me in *Life*. 'A Wild American in Paris' or some eight-ball title like that."

Melvin backed off, his honest simple face pleated with sudden worry wrinkles of bewildered defeat. The Luce machine, I congratulated myself. The ultimate weapon. There was an almost perceptible realignment in the forces of resistance as I radioed for the Panzer units to move through the torn gaping holes that my Stukas had opened up.

"No, it's like you say, Phil. In that red-and-green bit. You're right, man. The verticals and laterals *force* you to move right into it. But, man, that ain't what painting does. That's the death, man. Nail a coffin on the wall and you can crawl right into it too. I mean, that's the end, man. But the grave."

I grabbed a pencil and a piece of paper from some shelving that came up to the studio window and I jabbed at it with a confusing array of directional arrows, talking loudly and demonstratively as my pencil scored the paper.

"You see, Phil, what bugs me in that canvas is that you *had* it—" I gestured wildly at my random arrows. "And you threw it away!" I crumpled the paper like a burst blossom in my fist and sailed it out the window. The group watched it fall out of sight as though it contained a secret formula forever lost.

I stabbed at Phil's denim-stiff knee with my pencil point until the lead snapped against the tough, never-knelt-upon material. "You could have graded your texture in that top vertical just a little bit—" I made pulsing lateral motions with my hands—"and then, you see, you'd have gone right over the rim. You'd have been up and away, man. Heigho, Silver—Awaaaay!!" I danced a little pony trot to my own jangling accompaniment of the William Tell Overture within the circle of the group, whinnying a wet Bronx raspberry into the balding Melvin's ear and goosing the broomstick blonde, who wiggled unconcerned. I wheeled to a sliding stop next to Rennie. "You shoulda gone all the way on that one, Phil," I smiled. "But, instead—" I shrugged my spurious consolation—"you end up laying in shit." I turned to Rennie, whose expression of shocked admiration I had been conscious of all the time. "Jesus, Tonto honey, get me a drink, will ya? I like to die of thirst here."

Egregiously well-flanked as he was, Phil Stein was routed. He looked like a melting lard sculpture of the Rape of Nanking; tiny globules of sweat hung on the black hair prickles of his second and third chins where his cautious razor blade had feared to tread. He had been stripped of his alliances and forced into an unholy entente with the Friendly Enemy, and with the shredding rags of his pride, he couldn't even use his gorgeous bandanna as a tourniquet to stanch the flow. He took a clammy grip on the only choice I had left open for him—a kind of Yalta disagreement of mock cordiality, but with no secret resources save undying hatred.

"Well, I sup*pose* I see what you *mean*, Rog," he said, hiking himself down from the window-sill redoubt which had served him so poorly. "Although, I *can't*, of course, agree with you at all."

I do not—when it comes down to the final hiss-swish of the guillotine blade—have the killer's instinct. Even in my dream life I have avoided administering the death. I have, like Francis Macomber, elected to allow the gut-shot lion a safe return to its own grasses, and although I know that this lack will forever deny me entrance to the ranks of the rated heavyweights, I have to prefer loathing myself as a coward to discovering myself a total stranger to myself. At the same time, however, I have a healthy optimism with regard to the capacities of life to live. In its ability to absorb pain, to reshuffle the cells of its resistance, to assert the play of energies in irrational spite of logical impossibilities. I have never believed that life is a diminished thing since I have always been convinced that life abhors diminution just as surely as classical nature is supposed to have abhorred a vacuum. For death, unlike beauty, is never just skin deep, and in my gin delight I saw no reason why Phil ought not dance a little heavier and a little more bloody on the hook.

"Oh, come off it, Phil," I said. "You can't have got so close to it as you did without knowing it. And without knowing that you choked up and ran away from it like a kid peeing his pants."

I winked at the blonde insinuatingly. "Christ, he wants us to believe that he had his hand right on the old twat and all he thought was he was in church." I turned back to Phil—a grey angry impotent Phil Stein. "Fact is, you fizzled out, didn't you? Couldn't get it up. Turned cold yellow and backed off and figured you could be a big man by sneaking in the cellar door. Hell, man, I don't blame you—" I caressed his back like a good comrade, and his shirt was wet under my hand. "Ain't nobody can blame you, old soldier, but, Jesus—let's not try to peddle crap for gold."

The good Melvin was not quite ready to surrender. He had a stake in this thing, and his goodness had an investment to protect. "Look here, Mister Wriggle—" he blurted.

"Riegel," I said. "Like it almost rhymes with bagel. You look it up in that *Life* article. It's about the one thing they get right on me. But look, I ain't nobody's Mister. You just call me Rog, you hear?"

Rennie had returned my drink and I thought it only proper to ascend the window-sill throne that Phil had so gracefully abdicated.

"Well, Mister Rieg—Rog—" Melvin had trouble bending his teeth around the first name. "I don't really unnerstand. I never seen any of your things, but I seen Phil's. In fact, I buy a lot of his stuff." He had the innocent decency to blush. "Well, what I mean is— Look, I don't know too much about Art, but I know what I like. You know, I mean—you know? I mean, whatsa matter with Phil's paintings?"

"Don't worry nothing, Melvin," I soothed. "Nobody took

you for anything. You can still get your money back on Phil's stuff. If you sell 'em quick enough. What we were talking about was like on a different level."

I drained my new drink although I didn't need it and I prepared to finish up Professor Stein's lecture.

"It's this way, Melvin," I said. "Like Phil was explaining. Painting today is in front of this big goddamn wall. Like who needs it? What's it good for? What *contact* does it make with anything? Shit, you can smear paint all over that goddamn wall, but so what? You see, that's the problem—it's a so what."

Melvin nodded his head up and down understandingly like a taffy apple on a stick.

"Hell, it was a cinch for the old bastards," I continued. "All they had to do was copy what they saw. Wasn't any fat tourist with a Rollei-Flex and a light meter to tell them they got their exposure all wrong. Or they could just paint any screwy thing that people wanted to believe in. Like devils and all that holy crap. You know what I mean. Painting didn't have to *do* anything. It could just be itself. But, Christ, that kind of painting went out of business a hundred years ago. You see?"

"Yeah, yeah, sure," he said. He saw but he wasn't persuaded. He had heard variations on this theme before. "I'm not stoopid, you know. I unnerstand all that. Phil even got me to listen to Cadmium Greene talk about this business at the New School onct. But that's what this new 'contemplation series' is all about. It's the answer to all this." Melvin searched frustratedly around the group. "You explain it to him, Phil."

Alas, Phil had disappeared, his white-shirted and red-neckerchiefed bulk become transmogrified to a better, or at least safer, salt lick where the heavens did not open and the earth rend itself under the serene surfaces of a friendly cocktail party. Melvin had to appeal to me for Stein's defense.

"Sure, I know all about those theories," I said. "A dime a dozen. I've heard 'em a hundred ways. Symbols of contemplation crapola. The newest frontier. Shit, Melvin, that newest frontier is the oldest one in the book. It's the one they bury you in.

"Let me make a demonstration, Melvin," I said. I seized Rennie by the shoulders and spun her around so she was lying across my lap. And then I kissed her hard and wholehearted on the mouth and she kissed me back with a slight bite of hunger that went below the gin. The kiss had started out as a blackboard illustration, but the chalk broke and screeched its nerve-splitting joyful arc fifty fathoms below the blood and ice line.

"Geronimo!" I trumpeted, cradling Rennie on my lap. "See, Melvin. That's life! That's something happening. That's a beginning. And if art doesn't manage to *do* something, to flat out the three-dimensional world of flesh and motion and time onto a two-dimensional plane, then—well, then it's a great big *pooof*. It's had it. It might as well spend its time stippling toilet bowls. *Action!* Motion! Bursting spontaneous jellies of life! That's the only way that painting can move at all!"

Melvin was no longer his own or Phil Stein's man. He was mine, the pains of his new birth displaying themselves in fine white lines at the corners of his eyes, his manicured right hand unconsciously creeping toward the wallet in the inside pocket of his coat, and there was the slugged shock of infantile wonder in his voice.

"Yeah—yeah," he said. "When you say it I see it. I really see it. Clear as a baby. Boisting jellies of life. Jesus! And you do this kind of thing, huh?"

"I sure do," I said. "You read up that *Life* article." I was investigating Rennie's throat with my fingers, probing the cords and bones. Her throat was like a collie's, the pulse beat tremulous and deep. "Yessirree," I said. "Ole Rog delivers *action.* Pure action. I've used a Japanese brush with my teeth. Spray guns. Sprinkler cans. Once I used a high-pressure fire hose, but it ripped right through the canvas and knocked a hole in the goddamned studio wall. I've squeezed paint, leaked it, tromped it with my feet. I've mixed my own sweat and piss for water colors and once I damn near bled to death to get a stigmata effect in an abstract religious commission."

I paused parenthetically to light a cigarette. "Blood is very unsatisfactory," I said. "Its color values are minus zero when it dries." Melvin nodded knowingly.

"The whole point," I said, "is something's got to be happening. Naturally. Physically. Violently. Right in the painting. Otherwise it's dead. A great painting has got to freeze energy. It's got to lock it up and store it until somebody comes along to act as a ground. A physical detonator." I blew the cigarette smoke high in the air. My audience watched it hover as though it were weighted down with a price tag.

"My ideal painting," I said and I leaned intensely into the group. "Like it would be so energy-locked that if you, Melvin, were to come and stand in front of it and really *see* it—POOOOF!—you'd explode like a bomb. Pieces of Melvin from Harlem to Horn & Hardart's in the Battery!"

"Jesus," Melvin breathed reverently. "I'd love to see one like that."

"Well, I'm not exactly there yet," I said humbly. "But if I ever make one like that, Melvin, I'll give you first shot at it."

I shifted dramatically around on my window-sill seat, throwing my head back to gaze with ostentatious reflection at the night sky, but actually to find a more comfortable position for my thighs. Some hook or clasp or sharp button on Rennie's underclothes had been gouging at my left thigh and I wriggled out from under the prod. Rennie was warm and pleasant on my lap.

"As a matter of fact, Melvin," I confided, "I think I may say that I have been working on a new technique which may be the greatest thing in painting since the invention of the wall. And strictly entre nous, I am very very close to success."

Melvin and the others huddled closer to receive the Newest Word.

"What, after all," I orated, "is the source of all action, all motion, all energy? It's very simple. Sex. Plain old fornicating sex. Painters for centuries have tried to simulate it, sublimate it, symbolize it, transcend it. Somehow or other transfer it out of the glandular system—or wherever it is—into a painting. And they've kicked their asses all over the boards and got nowhere. But, at last—" My voice became hushed— "I'm on the veriest verge of a new technique which will employ sexual energy in the most direct and immediate way known to man. Sex-Painting! Spermism! Unpredictable, absolutely spontaneous sprays of spermatozoa exploding on a concave canvas in beautiful libidinous fury!"

The group gazed at my picture and winced with worshipful awe.

"No, no," I restrained their admiration with my hand. "Not quite yet. I haven't quite been able to perfect the dyes but it's only a matter of time. As simple and convenient as birth-control pills. The spermist pops the appropriate colors of his mood into his mouth, waits forty-five minutes for the chemicals to interact, and then for the first time in history, he really PAINTS. Pure action! Form released from its bondage to the constipation of the mind. No more a slave to the slavering cowed ego. Form and energy fused in one orgasmic rainbow. The painting which will make all painting unnecessary!"

Rennie murmured from my lap, "My hero. The ultimate sacrifice for Art and Beauty. Oh, noble noble soul."

"Greater love hath no man," I replied. "And I want you to know that everything I do I shall owe to Mother."

"My sweet Oedipus," she chided.

Her squirming in my lap was placing the Spermist Movement in imminent danger of a premature collapse before its heralded debut. I set Rennie on her feet to reduce the counterrevolutionary pressures.

"Si le grain ne meurt," I said. "Let's twist."

"Pourquois pas," she answered, leading me out to a cleared place on the floor where couples where shaking their behinds, squatting, writhing, rolling their stomachs in glazed athletic narcissistic delight. My hips were loose from the gin, and Rennie was a dedicated twister—a back-and-forth and up-and-down as well as side-to-side twister. She danced her half of the dance with her chin cocked tightly over one shoulder, her eyes half closed and private, as though she were a voyeur to her own perversities. It was a good thing that the band took a slurry rest on "Deep Purple" and I could dance upright, giving my loins some grateful surcease from the provocative assaults of the dangerous world.

"Riegel's special Martini mix," I said, nibbling toward the earlobe which bobbed a tooth distance beyond my bite. "Two parts gin, a half jigger of musk, shake liberally with sweat. Drink quickly under the heat of the opposite sex."

Rennie shook her ear away from my mouth. "Riegel, you're a pathological ham. You're impossible."

"Nothing's impossible," I said. "Everything's pathological."

"But Phil Stein had it coming to him." She remembered and giggled. "There was one time he almost blushed. And he would have if his skin could have taken the color."

"A prince," I said. "He'll be more careful the next time he runs into the Haganah. And with thine own sword will I smite thee, and thy lips themselves shall beg that no mercy be given."

It was long after midnight but the studio was still roiling with people—latecomers arriving, others leaving—the pitch of voices and body movements become more strident, more angular and grotesque, and yet more liquid also, and almost somnolent. A couple stood near us, not dancing, stiff and untouching, but whether it was hatred or agony that locked them erect I couldn't tell. A voice speaking German carried itself to my ear and the guttural spray of the consonants split a deep nerve in me, but the saxophone wailed louder and the connection was broken. Rennie looked around the room, surveying the press of people.

"Jesus, Riegel. No kidding, *everybody's* here. If somebody set off a bomb, that would be the end of the art world in America. And not such a bad thing either."

"BOOM," I said. "Except that I haven't yet seen Janie Putter and the biggest ass in the art world. And I owe it to myself to embrace all experience."

"You're just a lech," Rennie answered absently, still looking over the crowd. "Like all men. Look, there's Gans-Glunik trying to make time with that baby brunette." She laughed. "Every time he gets close enough to grab hold, some student breaks in to admire him. Christ, they're all out like groundhogs. Cadmium Greene. Tonio Telleschi. Lulu Rebbitsen. Mordecai. It sure is tulip time in Texas tonight."

Tooly-tooly-tooly-tooly-too-lip time. Cadmium Greene. Tonio Tell—Cadmium Greene. C. Greene. Seagreen and bright thy hair. A pale hollow shaft punctured a hole in my drunkenness.

"*Where's* Cadmium Greene?" I was gripping Rennie's shoulders and her face was frightened.

"Don't. You're hurting me. He's just going out the door. What's the—"

There was just a blur of shadow and shape moving through the door and by the time I wrestled through the dancers and the standers-around to rush across the room through the door to peer down the stairwell, there was no one. The landing and stairs were empty and my ears could catch no footfalls. There was just one heavily made-up woman in a white dress who was sitting on the stairs with a large black pocketbook across her lap, and she was weeping deeply and quietly through her mascara. Just a blur of shadow and shape, far across the room, moving too swiftly to be seen. Just a blur and a spastic plummet in my loins, felt and inscribed on the neural traces even before my eyes had focused and seen or not seen the blur at the door. And the gin had been no help to my depth perception either. But if the blur of moving shadow had been the broad back of a man saying his good-bys at the door, purposively pushing his way through people with coats and handbags to make a deliberate and unbegrudging exit from the frivolous music and the dance—if the blur had truly been Cadmium Greene and some lucid section of my retina had seized and retained the image of his back at the door, I had also seen that his hand was ferrying the shadow and shape of a woman before him through the door, nursing and controlling her direction like a nudging tugboat, and the woman, if she actually was one, could only have been Letha.

I chose a stair of my own to sit upon in mute companionable uncommunication with my weeping sister. I lit a cigarette which I smoked with hard long drags, blowing the smoke in diffusing curls down the empty stairwell. Oh, Riegel, you unutterable slob. Poor tired worn-out sperm painter. The big man. The big mouth. The gaping garbage can of experience. Throw anything in. There's lots of room. Broken glass, old rubber, the rotted fruits and vegetables of everybody's discarded lives. Send them. The teeming refuse of your crowded shores. Send them airmail special. C.O.D. Riegel, he'll take them. He buys everything. The original junk dealer, the old-clothes man. He overpays for everything and sits on the moldering heap of himself like a monstrous stinking fungus. With such delicious shame. With such acute self-pity. Shame and self-pity, the two isosceles legs on which the spongy heart of The Wriggle wriggles. And how do you like your blue weeping-eyed boy, mister Death?

My white-clad sharer in grief occupied her pew some four or so stairs below me, and I envied her the lower depth. She keened over her shiny pocketbook, and I breathed long desperate funnels of grey smoke down the dank shaft of the stairs, the music and party noise from the studio giving us a sea background for the wail of our broken bird wings. And then I was suddenly conscious of a third—the third who walks beside you—lounging easily and ominously against a shaky banister, mixing the thick white clouds of his long cigar with the thinner shrouds of my cigarette. He was dark and lithe—gleaming black hair, face chiseled to a fine cutting edge, his eyes heavy and filmed under intensely black eyebrows. He looked like The Frog Prince in the old fairy tale. He looked like cruel beauty twisted into man shape, and a constant nasty sneer played the perverse role of smile with his fleshy lips. And most shocking of all was the directness with which he saw and talked to me, assuming diffidently a secret rapport, a diabolic understanding between us which was as revolting as it was fascinating.

"You could do it very easily, you know."

His voice had just the slightest touch of an accent and he had the habit of ending his sentences with an unhealthy laugh, more a snort than a laugh, half laugh and half asthmatic nasal wheeze.

"Do what?" I responded, automatically keying my voicc to his so that we were almost whispering together.

He nodded toward the banister and the four floor drop to the concrete hall below. "Across the river and into the trees," he quoted, and then the sick conspirational laugh.

I looked down the stair shaft. A single naked light bulb, clumsily shaded by a spiral of red cardboard, gave the only light to the old stairs, and the shifting planes of shadow and lurid glow throbbed sinuously and beckoningly like cool water beneath my feet. I felt rather than willed the restraining clutch of my muscles to keep me seated on the step as I looked down into the dizzy descent and saw myself falling like a bird with scooping wings sucking the planes of red darkness into myself. Cool inviting indefinite. The music pushed at me, a thick interlocked wall of trebled chords pushed at me, and I rose in my spirit to ascend it.

"Why should I?" I asked him, looking directly into his heavy eyes in order to keep my gaze away from the stairs.

"Why? Why not?" He laughed again. "Perhaps to prove. Perhaps to see. We go where we have to go. To see what is there. To prove that we can. Why? Why not?"

The stairs were lovely dark and deep. And I had neither miles nor promises. This far I had walked. Another sixty feet would matter little. And nothing to redeem. Nothing my own to give that was not already superfluous. To float easily like a brainless bird. To drift, to dismember, to accept the final slow descent. Why not, indeed?

He blew a long jet of smoke over the railing and we watched it ride the impossible currents of air, diffusing in a white stain over and into the shadows.

"Why not?" he repeated, seating himself on my step, and I could smell some herb on his breath under the acrid cigar. Basilica? Orégano? "Why not? To see. To prove." The seduction in his manner was too curved and languorous, and the herb on his breath was green in the red darkness.

"To prove what?"

"To prove that one *is*. That's all." Again the laugh. "Not to be moved always from without. Not to be written like a character in a novel. To make or break one's plot. One's own fate. How else can one know?"

Across the river and into the trees. All the fragments of that other me fragmenting home. Easy soothing homeward. Shades and shadows, shifting planes of scattered being shattered home. His eyes were so heavy on mine and his taunting smile invited me to knowledge. It would have to be my own shade, I thought. How else is the spirit lightened?

"But you—" I interrupted my drift reluctantly. "Who are you? Are you my novelist? What's in it for you?"

He ignored my questions, sucking at his cigar until the end burned in a red circle of desire, and his voice had a lisping sexuality. "Why not?" he coaxed. "One does not seek death, but when the proper vehicle is offered—" he snickered again—"it would be very ungracious to refuse it. It is not so easy to find it, after all. Especially when you need to look for it." He touched me for the first time, patting my leg that was nearest him in a coldly confident caress. "You've got to be open, you know."

*Death.* He had placed the word between us, between me and the banister. And the word was alien flesh to my flesh. The word was something that was written or spoken in speeches. It was in poems, in books of inquiry. The word was a counter in an argument where the mind weaves paradoxes and lightning reversals of meaning. The word was the unreal face of my father in his coffin—unaccommodating, unnaturally waxen and composed. The faces of the dead are composed. Plotted and designed. Arranged with the cold cosmetics of alien hands. The drift of the stairs was something else, something of desire and longing. Something that life wanted. Death was not that. Death was not mine.

"I've got to be open," I repeated. "I've *got* to be open." And he must have seen that he had overreached, that he had fumbled the life in my pocket and his fingers had slipped through negligence or coarse greed.

"One is too late," he laughed. "Or too early. It is not important. There is all the time in the world. We know one another, after all."

"You seem to feel that you know me," I said, flicking my cigarette into the stair shaft, which was now a great vertical ashtray. "I don't know you."

"We know one another." He patted my leg again and the snort of his laughter this time was louder, with easy confidence. He pulled himself to his feet as though he were tired, or older than his body suggested, and the weight of his eyes made them bulge. "And I must this Babylon depart, my beauty sleep of regenerative death to seek."

And again he laughed—unnaturally, nastily—and the sound reached up to my ears above the clatter of his feet on the steps as he descended the four flights and went out the door. The woman in white was snoring softly, drunkenly, her head trustingly cradled against the stiff upright railings, and there were sooty canals running down her cheeks where her tears had recorded their unavailing descent. I smoked one more cigarette, resting my own head against the wooden banisters, searching with a strange passivity for the evasive soul which lurked deeply among the sea fronds beneath my own tears.

When I returned to the studio it was like going back into a movie that one has left to find that one has missed nothing, that the shouts and the strange jumpings on the screen repeat the same patterns and the same intensities, and you take your seat and adjust your eyes and you are back in an unreal world where everything is real except you. I plowed my way directly to the bar, methodically lined up three Dixie cups brimful, and, willing my stomach to be quiet, drank them one after another like medicine. And after a time when I was sure that I was going to be sick, the gin settled and my head flew hot and high. Rennie found me, as I knew she would, caught between her indifference and her curiosity, between her self-concern and her urban boredom. She was decently piqued at the desertion on the floor and I saw with sudden alarm that she was a dangerously tense citizen under the yellow yoke of her sophisticated style. It occurred to me that she too had her broken places, that she lived in the center of her novel even as I did in mine. And that all the practitioners of the dance—the drunk and degenerate, the eager and the meager, the twisters and the twisted—that all were huddled like precious fetuses in the centers of their novels. And all, like me, were without a sure grip on their own centrality, fearful that somebody or something would smash their novel worlds into sham and tinsel dust.

"What in hell happened to you?" Rennie said. "Boston manners, for Christ's sakes. You just left me there—standing."

"Had to see a man," I said. "I'm sorry."

"Are you all right, Riegel? You've been hitting the gin awfully hard."

"Little mother." I laughed. "You're worrying about me. That's a good sign."

She measured my face coldly, a neat housewife inspecting the moldings for signs of ants, and I could feel them creep in a long uneven line from the whorls of my ears down into the hollow of my throat. I shook my head to throw them off and a broken reed on a saxophone gave me a surcease of pitch.

"You've got to be open, baby," I told her mockingly, trying to shrug myself back into some role of seeming solidity. Everybody wants someone to lean on, I thought. A goddamn world of human tepees. Tepee or not tepee, there is no question. You hold my head and I'll pat your ass. And that's how you keep the old wig warm, I sang to myself. I pulled her toward me into the dance, stroking her shoulders and letting the long warm curve of her hips and thighs rest against me.

"Who are you, Riegel?" she asked. "What are you doing here? What do you want?"

"I'm just me," I said. "A trouble shooter for Continental Can. An unemployed statistic. I sell ladies' garters at Gimbels. I'm just me. And I want everything."

We danced slowly—soft anachronistic dances that made you remember the hidden pint in the glove compartment, the unopened package of contraceptives that you had been carefully keeping for five months, the pain of the broken colors of light that the revolving spot shattered into a great aching circle. The studio was darker from unscrewed light bulbs and the people who remained were softened into little huddles or couples blending their daytime fears into swaying columns of embrace. We danced and drank ourselves into adolescent knots of nostalgic yearning, but we did not talk and we made no plans.

Rennie's apartment was on the West Side and I sheltered her in the taxicab, our faces still glazed with the spurious hues of what teen-age dance. We leaned on one another in the elevator and I unlocked the ornate door of her apartment with a small key that dangled on a silver chain. We stood in the sudden silence of the *click*-close of the door like actors in a pageant who had dropped their lines and were wearing bright confidence like a shield against the audience. I fumbled toward her, full of uncertain desire, and she yielded against me for a fractional second and then shrank away. My touch had been her cue, the admonitory beat from the prompter's box. She kicked off her shoes and twirled away from me leaving me leaning into the air like a clumsy bear.

"You can sleep on *that,*" she said, indicating a low divan on the wall facing the window. "It pulls out if you need more room."

"I need more room," I pleaded. "Please, Rennie."

"Tomorrow's a work day," she said. "I've got to get some sleep." She wasn't talking to me, she was talking to herself, twisting the balls of her feet into the thin rug, exercising her toes as though this were their nightly outing. She stood there settling the apartment for the night with her eyes—locking and barring the windows and door, banking the fires in stove and hearth, placing the sharp knives out of reach, the box of matches away from the slow heat of the refrigerator's motor. She secured the elevator cable, the chained lids of the garbage cans in the littered back courtyard, the long narrow strip of sky between the two rivers.

"Please, Rennie," I repeated. I hated the sloppy clown's grin that my face had taken on, but I had no expression under it for a replacement. She had finished her mental precautions against the wolfish night and her toes had come home to her feet.

"Poor David," she said. "You need a sister, don't you, baby?" Her eyes were wide as hazelnuts, but they had already commenced their sleep. "I'll be your sister, David."

"Sister! Christ!" She had already turned for the farther room.

She stopped at the door and her eyes woke up for a sinister moment. I can't properly describe it, but there was pity and mocking in her look and also hatred. Slow terrible sepia hatred, mostly from her eyes, but with a whip flick from the corners of her lips as well.

"Faith and hope I got none of," she said. "And charity I ain't giving away." And then her face changed back and the sleep returned to her eyes and I could tell that I had missed something important that was lost. "You have a good sleep, Brother David," she said, and she blew me a decorous birthday-girl kiss and closed the bedroom door behind her.

My grin dribbled off my face and I could feel that my features were held together by no expression—just anatomical bone and integument, unformed and malleable as the faces of drugged patients in their comas. The gin began to throb heavy and high behind my eyes and the strange city surrounded me with hollow dangers. I turned off the light and groped for my bed, tenuously held together by the ambiguities of the uncertain darkness.

# Journal

*10 May:* One goes a far far way away and every time it's a little bit harder to get back. (To what?) Like swinging on an enormously long silver string, the unbroken umbilicus of our sanity, of our centered selves. Gloss that, Sigmund, but you'd be wrong. Or perhaps you never really get back at all; you just pretend that you have and everyone adds his tacit lie to the conspiracy and that's what other people function for in your life.

*Community:* The treacherous utopian myth of the frightened ego, the frightened ages. The unholy alliance that nurses the cancer of loneliness without making any attempt to effect a cure. Business as usual. We walk within the world, upright fears, zippered brutalities, disintegration pressed between tiepin and cuff link, seething toward an honesty which is precisely the price beyond purchase. The Garden of Evil behind us, the Disheveled City in the future, and we blind ourselves to the holy Presence that is NOW, casting lies back and forth to avoid the one meeting that we need.

Who would want to write a novel, for Christ's sakes, just to make indelible the blasting fancies of the night, if he weren't running hell-bent away from worse things? And, by the same token, what healthy animal would dare to enter another's madness except to palliate his own? Maybe only in this sense are men brothers—fellow inmates in the true asylum of democracy, where the gibbering laugh and the catatonic sigh catalogue the same library of grief.

The work goes slowly, not so much in time as in emotional drain. How many foot-pounds of pressure can the nerves really stand? What wind tunnel can accurately measure the stresses on the ailerons of consciousness? What rough beast, his hour come round again. And yet I heard Eva talking to Doren while I was opening the wine in the kitchen, and her voice was shaken by an honest surprise. "But Leo looks much younger since he's been working on the novel. It's a shame he didn't start it ten years ago." Stage dialogue to manipulate a mood.

Our Paris is on the point of a drastic change for us, though. Doren plans to leave for Greece tomorrow, the classic burning isles to receive a new sear. First step in a crescent swing through the old civilizations, the Near East and Egypt. His will be a strange loss and I measure at it with different pairs of calipers. He and Eva and myself have fallen into a wild and magical colloquy of polarities, communicating in a violent shorthand which creates rather than exchanges meanings. And it must be the presence of the third that introduces the factor of volatility. Two people quickly drain one another of their agreements and differences, swiftly exhausting the reservoir of mutual flexibility to become fixed in their responses and attitudes. The third is the principle of indeterminacy, the eccentric tangent which refuses the compromise of the golden mean. Murder plus suicide divided by two equals paralyzed nonviolence. Murder and suicide trisected creates the possibility of love. And we were there, night after night, street after walked-over street, crucifying the vertical history of Western Civilization with the horizontal slice of our three intransigently distinct egos. It is certainly true for me at least that my thought and experience were much more than mine when I was of the three. There was a clarity a rung short of beatitude, a rung short of death.

But perhaps it's as well that the scenario sends Doren eastward. The intensity of our threefold contact is denied that extra rung, and we could only reach a place bitter and devouring. And Eva has been protesting too stridently her freedom from emotional commitments. I am not thrilled by the trapezist who flaunts his braggadocio daring when the floor is well-netted below him. Women spend their lives studying survival so that they can preach recklessness. And who is net, Doren or I, or must we both lock hands and become mutual safety for the outrageous dancer on the rope? And still, Paris will be distinctly less rich with Doren pilgrimaging to the East.

One thing, however, has become certain. If I ever finish this incubus and decide to publish the remains, it will be under a pseudonym. For thematic rather than personal reasons, of course. The last Chinese mirror, which reflects the whole serried line of mirrors with their own glassed regresses. The ultimate joke or curse of attempted creation. For, look at it this way. Although—or because I don't believe in God, I am obliged to become God in my small typewriter-ribbon way. I

AM THAT I AM. It's the only thing that makes sense. His Name cannot be written in the Holy Books. The Adonai is an alter ego and nothing else—a mock king sent on the battlefield to delude and decoy the assaulting mace and the barbed arrow. HE meanwhile rests in the tent of His firmament, playing His psalter indolently, dreaming the terrible dreams which lave us in the nightsweats of Hell. Jehovah is a Yeatsian mask, an observing narrator, the cosmic reflecting consciousness of a Jamesian Divine Comedy. Who can know what HE is? And yet I have been cut by pieces of Him many times. The cockney metalworker in the Soho bar who had worked a lifetime rewriting the Old Testament only to lose his single copy in the Underground. That mad Polish Jew who fought with the French Foreign Legion and saw the whole universe in the image of a gigantic radiator. My dear dead friend who almost broke the bank with a bad poker hand and who paid up his chips when his bluff was called with a whimsical dignity that seems something more to me than a royal flush. Doren says that if we have a God, He is a God with His foot in His mouth and His Name is SNAFU. His foot may indeed be in His mouth, but only to keep Him from blurting out His true Name. And in my small comic burlesque show, I must not depart from the example of my betters. My true name will also be falsely hidden, although I doubt whether anyone would care to make a search.

Twice I have dreamed in the past week, the two dreams similar in their seminal images. I see me curved into a tailor's hunch, crudely wrapped in an ailanthus leaf of deep oily green, and I am lying on the lower right-hand page of a great big open book. The book seems to be propped up, and although there is nothing to keep me from sliding down the page, I am quite secure. I am naked under the leaf and my hair is very thick—long and curly as it used to be when I was a boy. And I have a sense of gentle waiting—waiting for the page to be turned, waiting for the print to roll along in steady black words. And that's all except for a very peculiar but not really disagreeable feeling of absolute dependence. I have no power to turn the page (I am a part of it, not apart from it) and I can't move by myself until the page is turned. The letters on the page are in motion. They run along in the jerky sweeps that the eye makes in reading, but I myself am in total arrest. I'm sure it's not a very remarkable dream (strong womb and birth symbology), but it's strange that I had it twice. Hélas, I will need a good vacation when I am through with this infernal machine of my own making. Or when it is through with me.

Meanwhile Paris has come into spring at long last and I have beaten down familiar trails through this stupendously voluptuous jungle of unfamiliarity. I can still get lost in a paroxysm of response if I deviate to the right or the left, of course, but I have learned a minimal prudence in the restraint of strangeness. We went to Vincennes, where Doren contrived to get himself locked into the dungeon and we had to rout out the guard to get him released. He was sitting on a stone in the middle of the court when we arrived and he looked furious to be free. One other evening Eva lost an earring in a sewer at the Place des Vosges and Doren and I had a long argument whether it was the King of the Cats or the King of the Mice who had clawed it away for his coronation crown. I didn't see the earring fall, but I could have sworn I saw something gleam in Doren's pocket. Twice we have started out for Versailles only to be sidetracked by three-hour-long picnics in rare grottoes where the children can pick dandelions and buttercups and we can float our emptied wine bottles on the rivers of our talk. And once I was terrified by the Eiffel Tower, looking at it by night from the Palais de Chaillot, its red rusted iron illuminated by spotlights, its four giant legs braced in a Cartesian insanity of cross tensions, an incredible imperial toy, an Erector set gone mad. Doren turned his back to it, and Eva admired herself in her hand mirror, and I was fixed like a plummet in the centered circle of all the tensions.

And the pressure stays on—steady steady steady—and all things adhere like ionized metal particles. The world changes me (violently, viciously, ruthlessly) and I change the world (tenderly, fearfully, tinily) and not the slightest erg of energy is lost in the double transaction. Ozymandias might better have cried, "Look on my despair, ye Mighty, and be Mighty," but Shelley, like all the Romantics, was sadly lacking in a sense of humor and knew only how to be sacred in profane places. To be profane in sacred places requires at least an equal dedication, and either way alone is but half a vision. My Muse tells me with rueful eye, "Write a half-assed book, will you? I got a half-assed book written last year, and the public deserves at least a whole ass, don't you think?"

# Clippings

*The New York Chimes:*

A new first novel, *The Player King,* presents the now-too-familiar autobiographical reminiscences of a sensitive urban-American Jew recording the shocks and joys of his uneasy enmeshment in the rich fabric of American life. It is the "outsider story" all over again—the chronicle of a boy on the wrong side of the candy-store window, desperately attempting to reconcile his desire for the chaste ladyfingers in the showcase with his unappeasable congenital lust for the halvah he eats at home. Told with a mordant tender humor, it reminds one of Henry Roth's *Call It Sleep*, with certain somnambulistic visitations from a sophomore course in modern philosophy. Although there are some interesting technical experiments in the narration of the novel and a moment or two of successful satire, the author's real talent is for farce. Unfortunately he conceives of himself as a serious writer and he is unable to make up his mind whether to tell the story of the ladyfingers or the halvah. The result is a sticky, half-baked Dobrische Torte. Mr. Rovit shows promise of an interesting point of view, particularly in his incisive critique of the American Jew's mock inferiority complex, and it is to be hoped that he will pay a return trip to the oven to become more firmly crusted.

*The Sad Day Review:*

. . . Another novel employing the Jewish milieu in the urban East is Earl Rovit's *The Player King*. However, in this case, the Jewish material is used symbolically to delineate that limbo world between madness and sanity, between primitivism and puritanism, between the bearded beatnik of Washington Square and the buttoned-down burgher of bloodless Suburbia. At times a penetrating Jeremiad on the juiceless eccentricities of our marginal people, the novel is insecurely plotted and irretrievably sunken under the weight of long discursive conversations that start from nowhere and take too long to return to their beginnings. The characterizations are uniformly thin, and the all-important narrator, David Riegel, never convinces the reader that he possesses a real existence, partially because he is never quite sure of the fact himself. There is a great hoopla of structural and stylistic oddities in the novel which suggests that Mr. Rovit is using his fictional scaffolding as a means of making fun of his readers. And yet one senses, almost in spite of the novel, that Mr. Rovit had something important to say; the worst thing that can be said about *The Player King* is that the novel gets in the way of the saying.

*Dime Magazine:*

A Walt Aphro-Disneyac adaptation of a Bergman film, *The Player King* is guillotined before the first curtain. Author Earl Rovit props up a straw pretender on a shaky throne of words—dirty ones for the teen-agers, Yiddish ones for the nostalgic Unitarians, pseudo-existential ones for the fake intellectuals. Gaudy, shallow, and pretentiously chuckle-headed, *The Player King* falls to the first finesse and the reader who buys the book plays the dummy hand.

*Documentary:*

Fronting with a whimsical immediacy the harrowing ambiguities of the contemporary human condition, Earl Rovit's *The Player King* takes a courageous pessimistic plunge into our modern excremental abyss and comes up with—if not a rose—at least a cultured pearl from a royal diadem. Its narrative line is a familiar Jungian one—the archetypal Odyssey of a twentieth-century Ulysses, David Riegel, educated, sensitive, Jewish—accelerated on a mad search for meaning in the labyrinth of our days and ways. He is ostensibly seeking his estranged spouse, Letha, a somewhat unrealized emblem for forgetfulness, death, beauty, meaning. It is the demon of the absolute which he rides, crashing through the fixed gates of rationality, logic, and social mores. What is a Jew? What is man? What is human and possible in this inhuman impossible twentieth century? The answers he arrives at are paradigms of paradox and powerful potentiality. Rovit takes his place on the side of the Yea-Whisperers, alert to the implacable grunts of negativism, responsive to the frustrating paralysis of will-less-ness in our time, finally resolved to essay the choice for life rather than death.

On its superficial level *The Player King* is an amusing novel, obviously indebted to the back-lashing whip of satirical scorn that one finds in the bitter poems of Heine, the outraged secretiveness of Robert Musil. Indeed, in an age of cleverness, Mr. Rovit is almost too clever. But he employs his cleverness to illuminate the stupidity of being "smart." The true comedy of the novel is an enclosing frame for a tragic comprehension of the finite misery in each quotidian moment of life. Employing a cross-tensional structure to sustain a constant shifting between maker and made, between foreground and background, between the dancer and the dance, Rovit forces the reader to reconstruct his own values, depicting with heartless accuracy the gnawing disease in health, the radiant glow on the fever mask of the terminal patient.

*The Player King* is not a pleasant book to read, but our age is not a pleasant one to live in. Both put severe emotional demands upon the reader-citizen, twisting him into his own desperate stance for identity. Rovit grips us at the pit of where we live and forces us to tally the exorbitant cost of the unexamined life. His novel makes a signal contribution to our needed assessment of ourselves and reminds us that a free liberalism of spirit requires more and further evaluations. Ultimately it is not so much as a novel that *The Player King* should be regarded, but as a human document, written by human hands and aimed at human hearts.

*The Jewish Parliament Weekly:*

There is a sad but truthful cliché that says that the most bitter and effective Anti-Semitism is that which originates from the Jew himself. What mountains of self-loathing, what diseased twistings of healthy Jewish nature could produce a monstrous travesty like Earl Rovit's dangerously deceptive *The Player King*! The ersatz labels of Judaism are pasted all over the book, but the true spirit of Judaism is as remote from these pages as it was from the Hitlerian diatribes at Nuremberg. Mr. Rovit is either abysmally ignorant of our rich and healthy Jewish heritage, or he willfully distorts the real image of Judaism for sensational commercial purposes. In either case, *The Player King* is a vicious and malicious caricature of American Jewishness which we cannot allow to be tolerated without horrified rebuke. Surely some of our Gentile neighbors will relish this nightmare lie of Jewish lust and scandalous immorality. Indeed, some of our own people, especially among our secularized youth, will discover here a tissue of falsehood and deception which they can use to blind their eyes to hide their own true Jewishness from themselves. This is a disgusting and unwelcome book, but, thank God, it, too, will pass. One's righteous anger against the book is soon dissipated, since it contains its refutation in the pathological self-hatreds of its own structure. But one is moved to pity its twisted author. We can throw his book away with disgust and revulsion, but he has thrown the best part of himself away—and he must live in the dung heap of what he has left himself.

*The Carrion Review:*

. . . and of these five, the most interesting from a purely *structural* viewpoint is Earl Rovit's *The Player King.* The novel itself is patently unsuccessful, but the author indicates in a rather clumsy manner one of the possible ways in which the philosophical dialogue and the informal essai can be adapted to the architectonic exigencies of the serious modern novel. With the failure of a truly *public* mythos, narrative action in modern fiction no longer supports what one might think of as the traditional epistemological quest of the Bildungsroman. Employing a system of multiple focuses of narration and Dos Passos-like metaphysical vignettes, *The Player King* takes a small amateurish step toward the establishment of a synchronicity of consciousness; it is conceivable that variations of this technique, refined of Rovit's jejune gaucherie, could be used to rejuvenate the presently moribund "novel of ideas" which disappeared with Mann's *Der Zauberberg* and effect a reification of . . .

*The Boston Glob:*

Earl Rovit's *The Player King* is a very confusing first novel which may have some special interest for Bostonians, since some of its scenes are set in The Hub. Although I don't think that many readers will share Mr. Rovit's attitudes toward Old Boston. The hero of the novel, David Riegel—who is not at all a "proper" Bostonian—seems both charmed and angered by his native city. In the wild episodes in which his search for his runaway wife embroil him, there are frequent mentions of Boston local color and history. I must confess that Mr. Rovit's Boston is not *my* Boston, and I would advise the author to take a more positive look at the diamonds in his own Back Bay. But it is a good sign to see that our younger generation of writers is taking an interest in the "new" Boston after such a long period of neglect.

*The Apocalyptic Trump:*

*The Player King* is the comic turn to truth.

Beauty is the bastard daughter of death. True art hastens the death of the ego. True art is the thespian stiletto thrust into the silences behind the last curtain. Polonius must be dragged through every room before our house is cleaned.

The great importance of all art is its intrinsic unimportance. We must be moved by the beauty of the temple to tear it into ruins. The only true literature is that which is not written, that which is aborted before gestation. True literature teaches man the monstrous nullity of his soul.

*The Player King* is true literature.

# Three

The late-morning light was a wash of raw iodine on my wounded hung-over eyeballs, and I foxholed for a long uncomfortable time in the pillow, knowing that the blessed unconsciousness of further sleep was impossible, but knowing also that the day would just have to wait for me before I could struggle to it. With my ostrich head under the pillow I painfully filled in the crossword puzzle of my yesterday life, incredulous at the letters that popped into their square places. Fragmented echoes of my own voice, cubistic candid flashes of little Davie Riegel playing satyr in the gardens of Bohemia, jangled like an out-of-focus stereopticon, and while I must confess to a small modicum of awed pride in certain aspects of the total picture, the effort to gaze at it whole and clear was more than I could even begin to attempt. The very bed in which I hid smelled treacherously of a strange musty other life, evoked wispy cobwebs of tweed and cigar ash which were beyond my capacities to integrate. I remembered Rennie, and my mind licked at the sepia fear her eyes had stung into me, and I cursed myself long and soulfully. I recalled the lengthy excerpt from the good Jonathan that I had tacked as a dissertational exhortation above my desk (was it only two months ago?). It imprinted itself like a black-bordered advertising sign at the side of the careening highway of my rushing thoughts: "Thus stands the cause between us, we are entered into covenant for this work, we have drawn our own articles and have professed to enterprise upon these actions and these ends, and we have besought favor, and we have bestowed blessing."

Thank you, Rabbi Edwards, you may sit down. And you, Mister Riegel, worthy Puritan divine—old lamed vovnik of Agawam—how does *your* Election Sermon grow? With wedding bells and cuckold-shells all fouled up in a row? What's your dominical stance now, oh, mighty avenger? Doctor Cackle and Mister Hide, no doubt. You certainly did your best to bestow blessing in your small Dionysian way, didn't you? Old Raunchy Chillingworth, copping a feel under the Puritan dark. Great big fat abstract Justice with a hard on. And we still beseek favor, do we not? The H.M.S. *Enterprise* is still awash on the seagreen briny. But how stands the cause between us now? Where are the rights and wrongs now? Whose role to utter the recriminations and whose to whine the apology? And how much cheap spite enfueled your aphrodisiac fires, you second-rate playboy of the western world?

I moaned and rolled over on the bed, discovering for the

first time that I was under a blanket—a faded-green blanket with a yellow fringe on it. Rennie must have covered me sometime in the abysmal night. What about Rennie? Is she in or out of this? Her eyes. The hazel horror of that look. What have I become to her that she can look at me like that? How much does it cost to get off the hook of a look like that? You touched your life to hers, not vice versa. Is she just one of those regrettable fatalities, the disinterested by-stander who gets a little blown up in the unsuccessful robbery attempt? We regret to inform you that your daughter was mashed to smithereens when our lunar rocket toppled off the launching platform. You will be pleased to know that structural adjustments in the ignition system are being made to forestall such accidents in the future. I am sincerely yours, Solomon Stolid, Northampton. Oh, bloody miserable Jesus, how can you make any sense out of a ridiculous goulash like this! Pour it in the deep freeze and carve it up into popsicles. One to a customer. Lick 'em and vomit.

A throaty wretched groan and I decided that, bad as the outside world undoubtedly was, the bed was worse. Angst and bursting bladder were too formidable for fear or argument. One more groan and one last acid retch and apeneck Riegel caught the full roseate flush of the morn on his bristly cheek and rushed to the bathroom for his late-morning ablutions. A shower and a shave later—Rennie hadn't seemed like the razor-owning type, which just goes to show the depths of my bourgeois naïveté—I found the kitchen. A note in slanted angular writing was propped against an aspirin bottle on the stove.

Dear Rog—

Tomato juice in the icebox if you can stand it. The coffee's made—just set it on fire. I'll be at the Libido around eight o'clock anyway. You're perfectly *free* not to go there. I couldn't care less. I'll probably wait until nine.

If you take a shower put the shower curtain *inside* the bathtub. I don't even know why I bother to tell you *anything.*

R. (Sister)

I did gratefully without the tomato juice, feeling a little better just knowing that I wasn't going to drink it, and I sat with the note over two scalding bitter-black cups of coffee. My thoughts got no clearer, but I felt better for the coffee and more willing to engage the day. At least I had two, or maybe three, markers to set my course by. Some time or other I'd have to check with Ziggie. And there was an almost-flesh-and-blood Cadmium Greene in the city. And 8:00 P.M. at the Libido. Somehow the last seemed more dangerous than the others. What's with this sister bit anyway? And why does it make my groin fold like wilted lettuce? You've got to be open, baby, I remembered. A small cool slogan to scratch on my escutcheon. In hoc signo vinces. I.N.R.I. We have drawn our own articles and have professed to enterprise upon these actions and these ends. Lay on, MacLife, and damn'd be him who first cries, That's my wife! Ah, Riegel, you should write that novel you spiel so well about. You are large. You contain multitudes. And all of it, as the daring French say, pure unadulterated merde.

With no malice aforethought I headed instinctively for the Village. It seemed like the symbolically right place for me now—the dirty dim-lighted place. For me and the rest of the sloppy people. Now I was an immigrant settler; always before I had been a superior visitor. I recalled my first trip when I had still been in high school. West Fourth Street was as much of a Babylon as my imagination could then encompass. With what moral revulsion had I seen the open display of signs outside drugstores: "PREGNANCY TESTS WHILE U WAIT." And I had imagined in my adolescent disgust thousands of desperate girls hiding in urine-smelling telephone booths, waiting for the results of whatever complications they must learn to live into. Teeth clenched on rubber-tipped bobby-pins, chestnut hair streaming in lank strands over apple-cheeked faces (all girls were wholesome *Saturday Evening Post* covers to me then), bitten lips barely able to frame the horrifying question: "Which one is the father? How will I know the father's name?" Babylon Village, Greenwich time, caravanserie of unwed mothers choosing names out of telephone books for surrogate patronymics. America, America, land of the free, land where our fathers died and left us alone and incomplete, oversized and undecided children. A man must kill his father before he can become a man. Our fathers die and doubtless we kill them, but we fail pathetically at manhood and our women tell us so. Why? Because we kill but we fail to kill well. We kill sloppily and we avert our eyes from our own bloody hands. Because we murder and fail to create. Because our psychic lives blank out at the sharp edge of the descending axe. Guilt is cheap (land of the free) and we are gorged on our guilt, but responsibility demands the expense of a second moral growth. Fatherless children all, floundering sloppily in a great bathtub of self-indulgence and unconfrontable guilt. Oh, Father Abraham, you had other slaves to free. The American heritage of staunch impuritanism. Every securely fathered immigrant became an orphan-parricide at Ellis Island (the one-way ticket to the blessed New World) and although the patriotic songs may say otherwise, our revered Foundling Fathers were all of them unfound. And you, Jonathan baby! You had a father and I had a father once. You walked with yours in a pasture and he told you about the unspeakable majesty of the Lord (and he himself seems to have been a very stern man) and then you went off by yourself in the woods and resurrected your father as the Unmovable Mover of the Universe. And you had a Grandfather Solomon to reckon with too, the Pope of Western Massachusetts and the Connecticut Valley, issuing forth from time to time like a papal stud bull among the heifers of your family tree. Could it have been so hard for you to rage against the Antinomian and Arminian heretics and teach the squalling papooses that they must be as little children before they could come to the Throne of the Lord? Christ, you never had to be anything but a little child dressed up in your father's leathern catechism. And I had a father too, but he wouldn't have known how to preach the majesty of anything, because he was a very sweet man. He sold newspapers on the Boston wharves when the other children were going to school, and once he swam all the way to Boston Light in a puffing, spray-spuming breast stroke and it was the one absolute conquest of his life because he did not see the world in terms of gains and losses. And he shaved himself cleanly one night in order to save ten minutes in the morning and he died of a heart attack with his face as smooth as but much more severely lined than any little child's. "To beget a son is to net a father," I wrote on the day that Marvin was born, for I felt that I had at last truly become a son, even as I passed around the new father's cigars. Ah, but David, you have to keep working on it. And every slip into sloppiness is the messy regression to the orphan, the again-loss of the father, the renewed murder. Classic introjection of the Super-Ego? No, God help us, no! I'm truly sorry, Papa.

I let myself into Ziggie's apartment with my borrowed key to find the flat empty and a note and a letter propped up on the rug immediately inside the front door. This day I shall call Note Day, I said to myself. The Day of the Notes. Blue notes, true notes, notes of deliverance, notes of seizure. The note was a single-page scrawl from Ziggie; the letter was unmistakably from Letha, fat and bulky, forwarded from Boston in care of

Z. Solchek in Mama Sheva's illegible hand. It must have come yesterday morning, I thought. Right after I left. Written a day or two before. Or a week, the way Letha carried unmailed letters around, waiting for the mystical conjunction of stamp and mailbox and divine urge to part with a piece of herself. No bitterness, I admonished myself. Your credit's run out. I made some instant coffee in the kitchen and read my messages sitting at the white-enameled table, drinking the coffee in slow gulps to assuage the ponderous drumming in my chest. The faucet on the sink had a bad washer and the drip was loud enough to hurt my ears. Ziggie's note was brief and comradely:

Dear Davyo— Got what might be a hot lead on C. Greene which will pursue tout de suite (shnell, man, shnell). Assume that you are not suffering our New York heat too badly. What Cynara are you being faithful to in your fashion? The apartment offer included a bed, you know. I will be home about 6:00 P.M. for latest communiqué—

Garcia

My heart swelled to him with gratitude for his unerring tact and light touch. Ah, Ziggie, I thought. As straight and true as a sparrow. I love you, Ziggie. A prince of politesse.

Letha's letter waited and I readied myself for its onslaught. There were five closely written pages (she always used both sides of the paper and most of the margins), and although I knew that it would have taken me three or four hours to write such a letter, carefully structuring my sentences and disputing and rejecting my rhythms and images against the too much and the too open, I knew that she would have written this in one paragraphless torrent of immediate self-exposure. The water dripped steadily from the faucet and I read the letter as though under an overhanging shelf of rock, chained by lichens and desperately seeking the dry light.

Dear dear David,

And so again I don't know who or where I am and I fasten my eyes on my fat pigeon who is nibbling a peanut near my foot (I'm sitting in Washington Square) because if he thinks that peanut is really there, then my foot must also be there, mustn't it? Did you ever notice that pigeon wings, dirty sooty blue-black New York City pigeon wings, have deep red tones under the blue-black which you'd have to suggest in the primer because any other way would be too much red? Unless you were Chagall and could paint red pigeons of the mind rather than the pigeons which sidle out of your way so you can kneel on the grass. And that's the trouble, don't you see? I don't have any pigeons or anything else in my mind. When I shut my eyes and my ears I have a quiet dead vacuum and I just don't care. I can't lead a pigeon around with me on a leash all the time to tell me that my foot is, you see. How do you learn to remember absence anyway? Oh, David, there's so much that's old and dying and I can't stand it at all. The old women who sit on these park benches like Rilke's women, hungering after their blowsy moments of youth and you're ashamed of yourself in front of them and terrified of them. You know if they see you at all that they want to bite holes in your throat with their yellow rotted teeth and pinch the round flesh on your arm until it's blue and hard like theirs. And they should, they should. And I feel that I should help them. I ought to go over to that Armenian woman with the black shawl making a reverse aureole over her frizzy white hair and arch my neck so that she can bite two holes in my throat and the poison of my blood will leak out in thin red lines and I will put on my black mantilla and be dead too. But the worst is that they don't even see me at all even when I stumble on purpose against their legs. They've even forgotten to forget what it was like. Oh, it's not fair, David. It's a bloody rotten unfair thing and I can't stand it. I never cared—never never never. Even when I thought I did and especially when I thought I should. I looked in a mirror last night and my face was absolutely beautiful, my hair was perfect and I was completely beautiful and my face wasn't at all familiar to me. It wasn't my face. Do you understand what I'm saying? It wasn't that it was different from my face, it was that I didn't have any face at all and the reflection in the mirror was a ghastly beautiful stranger who moved around and talked but as something other than anything I could recognize or even understand. And I pinched my cheeks hard and so did she and everything I did she did too, so it just meant that there was no me and I was a machine, a beautiful wretched machine like my favorite Sibyl in the basket who just wanted to die. I'm not—I'm *not* being melodramatic, and I don't want to upset you and I probably won't even mail this because how can I write you the things that I can't even say to myself and it's not fair to you to have to be my pigeon, but the mirror scared me frightfully. And I *have* been seeing. The way arms move and the way people shape themselves into designs when they talk and when they fight and even the sea-shell scallops of the ear. I walked all last night along the river and every bridge and every light was patterned and distinct. And the wonderful old walls with their corroded fire escapes like broken rusty bones and the uneven peel of the paint. Everything composed itself into a fresco of desire. I do want to care. I desperately do. I'm not strong enough to go it alone without you or the pigeon or at least God. Because there just isn't anything there at all. I got into conversation (you would say I picked him up) with a crippled man who saw me reading my Rilke and we got into a discussion. He was angry and he said Rilke was very dangerous to read, that he was very soft and he looked for God in all the wrong places, and I think I know what he meant and he is probably right, but what if that is the only way you've ever known how to be and the only way you've ever been able to look for anything. I mean, if God *is* at all, and you know that I believe he is, shouldn't he be in the wrong places especially? The people who don't need him at all always look in the right places, so he especially ought to be in the wrong places for those that have the real terror and need for him. I'm sure this is all incoherent and poorly expressed—and you've always said that if I'd had you for Freshman English I'd at least have learned how to make sentences—but I'm understanding things, I'm on the rim of understanding things. It seems to take me so long to learn anything at all and I never trusted my brain to work, but I *feel* that this is all so right. And truth is not nice, not nice or pleasant. In fact it's terrible and sad and grandly careless. But you must understand that I've got to do this my way even though I have no respect for my way which is sloppy and fumbling and indulgent. I have to look for myself in all the wrong places, crippled or not, and nobody else—and especially you—can do the looking and the not-finding for me. Please please please be patient with me and be strong enough to keep your strength away from me because that will surely rip the fabric of my trying. You can't know how hard I've had to work at being a good wife and a good mother—neither ever came naturally to me—and now before it's too late I must try to become a good *me*. That desperate woman in the mirror is what I made out of all the wants and needs that I have put down or thrown away and I have to unmake her or she will surely murder. You see, you *do* see, don't you David? If I can come through to the opposite side there'll be so much more of me to give—to give to you where I've never been able to, to give to the children and you know how I love them, to give and still have an abundance left over for myself. I don't know where or how I became so horribly malformed. I wonder whether everybody isn't really this way and I wonder why they lie and pretend to accept the total nothing of their lives. Or maybe they aren't pretending and it's just me that's crazy and unsatisfied. You remember I must have told you about the freak I saw once at the Stockbridge Fair who sewed buttons on his skin. Oh, people are so repulsive to me sometimes that I want to scream and stuff my mouth with my hands. But I have to try my own way. My friend (the cripple) also said that delight is a function of the digestion, but joy is angelic. I would like to find me in joy.

I think that I remember that I love you,

Letha

I read the letter three times, interspersing my readings with additional cups of coffee and cigarettes. I seized on all the phrases that attached me to Letha and I sickened over the last cool line, "I think that I remember that I love you." No hints, no clues, no mundane trivia about where she was, what she was doing, who she was seeing. All-night walks along the river and cripples and pigeons—the direct spiritual inventory of her soul, but not much news from the body. And a frantic directness, a kind of Euclidian psychic clarity that was frightening in its combination of bravery and fear. And how could I come to her and how could I keep myself away?

The day had settled into a hot August early afternoon, breezeless, humid, slow. The leaves on the few trees that I could see out the kitchen window hung parched and wrinkled like scorched laundry. The muted cacophony of the traffic on nearby Sixth Avenue beat out its tone and tempo with a defeated strangled weight as though the whole of Manhattan Island were stuck in the bottom of an almost empty jar of molasses. The thought of rain brooded like a delayed vengeance in the invisible globules of air that turned the whole atmosphere into a finely corded net. Between the screen and the upper-window sash a tired summer fly buzzed like a worn-out electric razor. I had no place to go now and nothing to do. Letha was pleading with me to leave her alone, the children were capably (albeit, erratically) taken care of, and I was without desire. I did not want to read, I did not want to think, I did not want to step again on the merry-go-round of eternal masquerades. I wanted to sleep with my eyes open. I wanted not to be hurt by anything from the outside. Je suis le roi de paysage qui pleut. My one line of Baudelaire. It rains across the country I remember. I groaned loudly in order to hear my own passive misery and I gazed with disgust at what was left of the cold synthetic coffee in my cup. Bravely I unfolded to a standing position and rinsed my face in cold water at the kitchen sink. And under the rush of the water from the tap I heard the insistent whirr of the doorbell. My instinct was to ignore it, to pretend it away. It was sheerly an accident that I was there anyway. But the bell did not believe in accidents and I finally opened the door to the visitor, who walked right by me with a deprecating nod and sat in the red-leather chair by the window.

"It took you a long time," he said. "Did I catch you in the bathroom?"

"No, you didn't."

"Then why is your face all wet?"

"Tears," I said. "Idle tears."

My visitor who was so comfortable among Ziggie's possessions was a burnt-almond-hued Negro, about my height and age, dressed in a natty grey-and-white-striped seersucker suit. He flaunted a neatly trimmed black goatee, and his face would have been unusually handsome except for a white scar that sickled across his left cheek. He was smoking a rakishly curved briar and when he crossed his legs to become more comfortable in the chair, I noticed that the grey-and-silver figures on his socks were a match to those on his tie. The smell of his tobacco was thickly sweet and he seemed to be regarding me with a good deal of private amusement.

"I don't think we know one another," he said grandly, welcoming me to his hospitality with a fine flourish of the pipe. "I'm Daniel Meleck. Perhaps you've heard Mr. Solchek mention me."

"Can't say that I have," I said. "I'm just using his apartment. My name is Riegel. David Riegel."

We shook hands, I having to lean awkwardly over the arm of his chair to clutch at his firm brown hand. This seemed to increase his amusement even more.

"Ziggie's not here right now," I said. "I know he's planning to be back around six, but I don't know where he is now."

"It makes no difference," he said. "I'm an unexpected guest anyway." He continued to look at me with that odd air of superiority and amusement and I could feel my bones becoming awkwardly jointed under his stare. "May I be rude?" he suddenly asked. "I'm a devoted student of human behavior and I'd like to ask you a rude question."

I sat down in the facing armchair acquiescently. "Be my guest, Mr. Meleck."

"Daniel, please," he said. "It's an old Biblical name."

"So's mine," I countered. "And that and ten cents will buy me a telephone call anywhere in New York. Ask away and we'll see what happens."

"Well—and truly *do* forgive my rudeness—why didn't you wipe your face before you answered the door? I really do find the behavior pattern quite fascinating."

I rubbed at my face with my hands but it was perfectly dry now. I didn't know why I hadn't. "I don't know," I said. "But you sure act as though you had some notions about it."

"No," he said. "Your action confuses me. If you had been expecting someone, you might have rushed to the door and paid no attention to your face. But you were a very long time in answering the door and you don't act as though you're waiting for anyone." He tapped at his pipe reflectively. "You might, of course, be that rare type of person who is completely oblivious to his creature appearance. But you've shaved this morning, your hair is relatively combed, and you're dressed neatly. Although, if I may say so, your style is distinctly passé."

"I'm sorry," I said. "I hate to be either passé or a source of confusion."

"No, come come come come. Don't waste your energies in meaningless aggressions. They're entirely natural, of course, but self-defeating. A small amount of paranoia never hurt anyone, but too much— One must be careful." He shook his pipe admonishingly.

"Excuse me, Mr. Meleck," I said. "I'm a little out of tune with the universe this afternoon, I'm sure, but why are you so all-fired eager to get into a polite fight with me? I ask because I too am a student of human behavior."

Meleck smiled broadly, exhibiting a double row of perfect teeth.

"Ah, Dav— if I may?—David. You have seen beneath my clumsy artifice. I am not only a student of human behavior, but I am a seeker after truth as well." He knocked the ashes of his pipe into a nearby ashtray and began methodically to ream the carbon crust with a small pearl-handled instrument. "Admit that you find me somewhat disconcerting," he said. "Just a trifle disconcerting."

"Okay, Daniel. We'll play it your way. You disconcert me just a trifle. So what?"

"And admit further that all Negroes make you uncomfortable. Especially what I might call 'Volkswagen Negroes' as distinguished from 'Used-Cadillac Negroes.' And most especially when they dress better than you. Admit that I am a distinct affront to your conscience and your ingrained sense of white superiority. And admit finally that in the battle between your conscience and your prejudice, your conscience wins only an overt victory, and that is why you are uncomfortable with me." And he sat back in his chair and laughed a deep easy laugh, having demonstrated something or other to his own eloquent satisfaction.

I was tired and I didn't want to argue with anybody. Maybe he was right. On top of all my other inestimable qualities, I was a secret racist, old Bayard Riegel, Grand Kleagle of Swampjuice County.

"Daniel, you've got me dead to rights," I said. "On the ol' rugged cross of the divine truth—hallelujah—I would have to confess that I would not, could not, ever ever consider marrying yo' sister. I might be able to talk my wife into it—she's not as reactionary as me—but it still wouldn't go. The children would demand their old pale Mommy no matter how many times I recited the Gettysburg Address."

Meleck laughed pleasantly from his chair. "Ah, you are a *humorist*, David." And then his voice fell into lecture rhythms. "It can be demonstrated, of course, that behavioristically the humorous attitude is the last desperate recourse before the disintegration of the ego. In the face of a stress situation there are only two possible *healthy* modes of response. One—" he held up a finger with a beautifully manicured pink nail—"one is to discharge one's energies in some active physical way. To run, to hit, to shout, to act. The action may be absurd, stupid, even self-injuring. But it does replenish the primary unity of the ego. You understand?"

I nodded wearily.

"Good. The second way—" two burnished fingers made an erect V in the air—"is to sublimate the energies directly into the passive action of ratiocination. To think, in other words. To observe and analyze the situation into its volatile components, weighing its variable pressures and measuring the probable directions of stress. Hence, to dissolve the stress situation into the absorption of the understanding, strengthening the ego in the process." Meleck tamped fresh tobacco into the pipe bowl. "You are still following me?"

I nodded again. "I follow. Lead on, Master."

"Now, as you can undoubtedly surmise from the emphases of my presentation, the second way—the way of thought—is the eminently superior alternative. But note that the first way at least functions to keep the ego intact. The humorous way, on the other hand, combines the weaknesses of both healthy responses without either of their strengths. It accepts the objective reality of the stress as does the first, or animal response, but it incorporates no active effort to alter it. It retains the passivity of the rational response, but it fails to shift the stimuli from objectivity to subjectivity—from reality to mind. In time the subject who habitually adopts the humorous strategy will die psychically of a starved ego." Meleck winced apologetically at his phrase. "I'm sorry to employ such imprecise terminology, but the technicalities of my system would be far beyond your comprehension."

"I'm sure they would be," I said, but Meleck seemed impervious to my sarcasm. "Anyway, I think I understand you so far. You mean that I should have hit you or spit or something—the animal response. Or I should have categorized you in terms of aggressive inferiorities—the deracinated Negro intellectual playing that popular parlor game called 'white-baiting' which is so much the liberal rage today. And if I'd done either of these things, I'd at least be feeding my poor hungry ego."

"Well, you seem to follow the main points in my theory," Meleck said grudgingly. "Although your illustrations are rather nastily chosen."

"Watch *your* aggressions," I said. "Sublimate, you know. But if I had done either of these two things, how would I or we be better off? I can't change you, you know. I can't change anything that *is.* And to turn my brain into a vacuum cleaner of understanding—Jesus, that seems stupid to me. All I want to do is—"

"What?" Meleck interrupted, leaning toward my chair. "What is all you want to do? I'm especially interested in motivational ideals anyway and it's just in the area of value systems that the sociological imagination can be most clarifying."

I ignored his professional eagerness and thought about the question carefully because I didn't want to say just words. It was true. I had found out over and over again that I couldn't change anything. Letha. My temperament. My good and bad luck. The deaths and dyings of those I loved. Myself. The projects I had started with explosive enthusiasm only to find them too difficult or dull or far out of reach of my peculiar energies. Pleasures that staled and pleasures that receded into pain the more closely they were approached. The porous slog of routine and time passing and busy extinction.

"All I want to do, I guess, is to get through each day without hurting anybody or anything too much, and not getting hurt too bad myself. That's all." It sounded like a pretty squashed-up ideal as I caught the playback in my ear.

"Is that really true?" Meleck asked. "Think it over a minute."

I thought it over. It *was* a damned ignoble raison d'être, but I didn't see how I could improve on it without turning it into some monstrous lie.

"Yes, I'm ashamed to say that it's really true," I said. "I'm not very proud of it, but it's the best I can do. Although you might just add this to keep the bets honest. Add 'and have a little fun along the way.' "

"A little fun?"

"Yes, a little bitty fun."

"That could be a very large addition, depending on how you define it, you know."

"I wouldn't be at all surprised," I said. "And I suspect, Daniel, that you're just the boy to define it."

"Maybe I am," he agreed. "But you humorous-response people don't like definitions." He laughed, and his scar caught the afternoon light like a golden scimitar. "David," he said, and then he listened to the sound of my name as though he were hearing it new and from a long distance away. "L'il David, go play on yo' harp."

He got out of the leather chair embarrassed, smoothing the wrinkles from the knees of his trousers. "Enough of this seminar in Interdynamic Group Exposure. My trained observational eye persuades me that you are without immediate plans. I should be honored if you would join me this afternoon in my cultural-educational pursuits. Naturally you would be my guest as far as monetary considerations were concerned."

"I can be seduced," I said. "What do you have in mind?"

"Well, my immediate intentions—" Daniel looked at his wristwatch and made silent calculations behind his smooth brow. "We might catch the two o'clock Bergini movie. He makes some very interesting visual correspondences between frustration and fantasy objects. And then I plan to attend Dr. Greene's lecture at four o'clock on Psychic Destiny Today. That's Cadmium Greene, you know, and it's really a closed lecture, but he doesn't mind auditors."

"Cadmium Greene," I said. "I've heard of him. I thought he was an art historian or something."

Daniel bridled. "Art historian! And I suppose Aristotle was a drama critic because he reviewed some plays." The scar glowed again, but this time with the sacred fire of the zealot-believer. "Dr. Greene is a Synopticon of World Knowledge. You must know his book, *The Mortuary of Love*?"

"I don't read contemporary fiction," I said. "Unless it's assigned."

"Fiction!" I had Daniel very close to an animal response. "Do I seem to be the kind of person who would read fiction?"

I had to admit that he was not.

"I have read some novels, of course," Daniel explained. "But I read them with specific things in mind. Like, for example, *Tom Sawyer*." He turned aggressively to me. "You've read *Tom Sawyer*, haven't you? What would you say was the most significant scene in that novel?"

"Jesus," I said. It had been years since I'd read the book and two different movie versions were all scrambled up in my memory. "I don't know," I said guardedly. "Maybe that famous whitewashing the fence bit. It's not one of my dearest novels."

"Of course," Daniel crowed triumphantly. "All you literary-type people remember the whitewashing scene. Which is just a piece of contrived theatricality. And right before that scene is one of the most remarkable pieces of psychological observation in nineteenth-century literature. I'll bet you don't even remember it."

"I most assuredly do not," I said.

"It's your training," said Daniel patronizingly. "I've been trained to observe. And that's the scene where this little boy—I can't remember his name, but it's not important—sails up the sidewalk toot-tooting away like a steamboat."

"Ah," I said. "A steamboat."

"That's right," Daniel said. "He toot-toots up the walk like a steamboat. He parks the steamboat and talks to the other boys and then he gets back into the steamboat and toot-toots away. Wonderful."

"Breath-taking," I said. "What's so damned wonderful about that?"

"Simply because it's pure documented observation," Daniel

said. "That boy isn't playing with an imaginary steamboat. He *is* a steamboat. And he stops being one for a minute to be a little boy and then he becomes a steamboat again. And we now know that in the middle of the nineteenth century in the Mississippi Valley, six- or seven-year-old boys were still capable of a complete identificational cathexis with objects of secondary sexual attraction. And most significant—" the pipe sliced the air— "they could destroy this cathexis at will and reestablish it without any traumatic dislocation."

"Hmm," I said. "I see."

Daniel polished the bowl of his pipe against the flanges of his nose until the smooth briar grain attained the same high gloss as his skin. We prepared to go out of the apartment.

"It's really a shame," he said. "The novelist could be enormously useful to us if he'd only take the trouble to observe accurately. Unfortunately it's the last thing he wants to do."

"Unfortunately," I said. "Sic transit gloria mundi."

I scrawled a black check on Ziggie's note, propped it back on the floor, and stuffed Letha's letter into my inside pocket; and Daniel and I took the air together, walking through Washington Square to the Eighth Street Playhouse. Why not, I thought. I had nothing to do and the theater would be afternoon-dark and air-conditioned. If I didn't like the movie, I just wouldn't read the subtitles. And for dessert—Cadmium Greene. Pistachio seagreen, Synopticon of World Knowledge, lecturing on 'Psychic Destiny Today.' O tempora o mores, Centurion Rigelus, there is after all a divinity which shapes our ends. And his messengers have a way of being dusky and dark. With tuberous noses. Or with eyes like grapes, I reminded myself. Of wrath and sepia desire. Cool in the warm places and warm in the cool. Wash me deep and winter thy hive. Riegel, Riegel, you wretched bastard. You are a crape grape with a drape shape.

The film was characteristic Bergini, and the box of popcorn

which Daniel and I shared in the dark was too greasy and sticky. He had paid for my ticket and I had nastily refused to argue the matter with him, aware that all I had to do was open my mouth to get a lecture on the anal fixation associated with money. The movie was depressing. Bergini's mastery of grotesque legerdemain was as deft as ever, but the incomparable craft seemed employed only in the services of an unmitigated phoniness. The scene where the bound priest is sexually manipulated by the dying tubercular ballet dancer and you have to interpret his thoughts from the way he clenches his hand on the rosary. Or the giant organ playing Buxtehude through the Kafkaesque sterile cells of the prison block, and when the tortured prisoners open their mouths to shriek they blend into a perfect Kyrie. So clever, such incredible talent—indeed, genius—and for what?

"Daniel," I said as we walked back toward Washington Square after the movie, "the trouble with you guys—you and Bergini and all the other clowns who are understanding and commenting on human behavior— The trouble is that you don't really believe in dreams."

"That's not at all true," he said. "I'm extremely interested in the total dream mechanism. It's fascinating observational material. And its connection with myth and folklore is no longer questioned by any serious student in the field. Why, I would be willing to say that—as an observer—I'm absolutely absorbed in dreams."

"That's what I mean," I said. "You observe them, but you don't *believe* them. You read them. Like a telephone book or a time table. You read them to get some information out of them. Something useful. Or like Bergini. He says, 'Look, here's a dream for you. I made it and you can watch it on my screen. And you better look damn carefully because I've hidden all kinds of meanings in it.' And sure, there are meanings in it. He put them there. And they're all fake because he doesn't believe in dreams and he hasn't the guts to put an honest genuine Bergini dream onto the screen."

I had made Daniel's face unhappy. "I don't think I understand you at all," he said. "Are you saying that you literally believe in dreams?"

"Sure," I said. "Every honest one, anyway. Every unexpurgated fairy tale or myth or tribal legend. Every day- or night dream that's caught me into a sick sweat or a lurch of excitement. Hell, I expect they're about the only things I truly do believe."

Daniel's unhappiness increased. We were walking through the Park, and he kicked morosely at a small wire fence. "This is extremely confusing," he said. "If you really mean what you seem to be saying, your position is completely untenable and irresponsible." He gave me an angry look. "Are you joking at me again?"

"Only a little bit," I said. "Us starved-ego people, we have to have a little nibble now and then too. But let me try to explain another way. You put your money on observation. I don't. You want to observe all the isolated events of Joe Cosmos at work, catalogue them, analyze them, and label them 'Classified and Known.' I don't deny that it's all very fashionable and industrious, but, as far as I can see, you end up just where you started. Lost and fragmented in a universe of lost and fragmented data. Me, I'm not buying it. The dream, on the other hand, that's something else. You don't have to look for it. You don't have to collect and arrange it. It just emerges. Jesus, it really collects us. It seeks us out, whether we like it or not. And it shapes us on its own design principles."

I wiped my forehead clean of sweat and noticed that my shirt was already sticky on my back in the short walk from Eighth Street. The mugginess of the day had intensified as though the whole atmosphere were being squeezed into a supersaturated sponge. The menace of a cathartic rain was poised with thunderbolts and dull flashes of heat lightning suspended like a glass bell over the city.

"Like, look," I continued. "We don't even know where the hell dreams come from. Maybe the glands, maybe the genes, maybe the collective experience of the race. Maybe God or his sister, the devil. But, you see, it doesn't matter from where. The important thing is that dreams have a design and an order in them that no man consciously made. They've got plots—beginnings, middles, and ends. The only goddamned thing in all nature with a naturally closed form. I'm serious, Daniel, I don't know anything else I'd even think of believing in. And the unpardonable sin is to falsify one of them."

We were passing the fountain near Garibaldi's statue. Its single waterspout jetted insistently to its zenith only to break and arc in a gentle defeated circular fall. Children in bathing suits or underwear shorts sported gratefully in the cool shallow water, chasing the silver spray as it undulated unpredictably in its fall. The concrete rim of the fountain was crowded with older people, some of them barefooted, all of them studded around the wheel of the fountain, drawn to the dramatic spurt and coruscating diffusion of the silvery dance.

"See, Daniel," I said, pointing to the fountain. "That's just a water dream. That's all and everything it is."

He shrugged me away. "Maybe you're not joking at me," he said. "But I don't know what you're talking about."

We crossed the street to a large, modern, unmistakably academic building with shuddering expanses of plate-glass window. Students of all descriptions were going in and out or standing in little circles on the sidewalks, some of them eating ice-cream cones.

"Some of what you said sounds like Cadmium Greene, though," Daniel continued. "Maybe you've got something in common with him."

"Alas, I probably do," I said. "I probably do, indeed."

The lecture hall on the second floor was very new, very modern, very ugly. I could almost smell a slight odor of disinfectant, some pedagogical formaldehyde to accompany the sterile green blackboards, the shiny uncarved-upon plastic-veneer seats with their foldable writing arms. The varnished floors were unscuffed and I had the feeling that the air was thoroughly filtered and renewed on an eight-minute cycle of constant revolution. What germ, I thought, what bacterium, what putrescent mold, what infectional grain of idea could possibly withstand such engineered antisepsis? The entire left side of the hall was windowed (the windows all sealed close in serene obedience to the hum of the air-conditioning units) and the bright open glass offered the seated students a stunningly clear view of a large grey warehouse across the street.

"Bartleby the Scrivener," I muttered to myself. "We're mass-producing a whole generation of Bartleby types. Like Barbie dolls."

"What's that?" Daniel asked. He slid into the seat next to mine.

"Nothing," I said, and I checked my watch. "Where's the old Cad? Maybe he's taking a holiday this afternoon."

"Dr. Greene's always a couple of minutes late," Daniel replied, chastising me for my levity with his tone of voice. "But he's never been known to miss a lecture."

The large room was almost full, the students ranging somewhat older than the normal-semester youth. The summer contingent, I thought. Like the mosquitoes and poison ivy and Douglas MacArthur. They always return. Librarians and schoolteachers earning a minuscule increment on their comically under-scaled paychecks. The graduate students—suave, eager, leisured, harried. The breathless accelerators. The perennial card carriers, No Credit, Audit, Withdrawal.

A trio of nuns in their cool white summer habits occupied

the front row seat, their pencils and sensitivities sharpened to small still points, alert to capture every syllable before it was sucked up into the acoustical tiles of the ceiling. Three large teen-age boys were reading comic books near the window. A petite girl, very stylish in a cotton frock with pink sheer stockings, was chewing daintily at a heavily mustarded meat sandwich. A boy in chinos and white shirt, slide rule clacking against his hip like a bayonet, charged up the aisle to take his seat, opening his loose-leaf notebook in studious anticipation. But don't knock it, Riegel, I warned. You and Admiral Rickover. It keeps you and them off the streets. It gets those good vitamins into your kids. And maybe it helps ultimately more than it hurts. We hope. Don't knock the dream that it is, Riegel. Thomas Jefferson and Horace Mann and only the census taker knows how many faceless faithful mothers and fathers who would have had their troubles spelling "education" much less explaining what it really *is*—how many had given up gratefully and cheerfully so that their overgrown louts of pigheaded sons and sex-ridden daughters could sit six hours a day in a heated schoolroom while they pushed their prematurely old joints into chilblains and arthritis and overdrove the complaining pumps of their hearts into a too-early death break. If it stinks it's not the dream that stinks. Don't knock it, big man. You especially don't have the right. So maybe the ladder doesn't really go anywhere and maybe the rungs are nothing but horizontal illusions, but it's a real honest dream that it is, and—as social dreams go—a goddamned good one.

The door at the front of the room banged open noisily and Cadmium Greene stomped to the raised platform where a small lectern rested on a table. He hauled a stuffed brown brief case in one hand and he lurched vigorously on a cane which was held in the other. I don't know what I had expected him to look like—the cripple had never entered my mind in his connection, and I was shocked to see him limp—but when I saw him I knew immediately that he looked like no one except himself. He looked to be in his late forties and he projected a strange fusion of intensity and composure, a grotesquely handsome power like that which you associate with some wildly uncontrolled Greek statuary in temporary arrest. His hair was thick, unkempt, curly—twisting in motion as though it were a physical extension of his muscles. His face was an even light pink with pale splotches on his cheeks and his mouth was over-mobile. The lips, very full and very red, tended to fall to one side when he stopped speaking and in that brief moment of facial repose, one caught his sensual—almost obscene—leering stance at the world. His shoulders were unusually broad, measured by the narrow width of the lectern, and his hands, which he used continually to orchestrate his speech, were wide and stubby—what we used to call "farmer's hands." In spite of the oppressive weather he wore a buff tweed sport jacket over his light-brown-gabardine slacks, and his left shoe was thicker by three or four inches than his normal right shoe. He shoveled his books on to the shelf under the lectern, strewed his notes along the top, hung the handle of his cane on the table edge, and, gripping the sides of the lectern with both hands, stared down at the class waiting for silence. His eyes were a fluid grey, deceptive, inhumanly concentrated, in constant movement. He looked directly at no one and yet he made everyone conscious of the uncanny contact of his eyes.

"Gentlemen, good afternoon," he began, ignoring the fact that more than half of his audience was female. The classroom became very quiet, the only sounds the riffling of note papers and some slight scuffling of feet toward the rear of the room. As he lectured, he paced continually, using the table as a brace while he gestured with his free hand. His voice was light and deep and violent, modulated under a virtuoso's control, and there was not a moment in his lecture when his presence and his speech did not fill the large room to amplitude. In fact, you could say that the large lecture hall was palpably cramped by Cadmium Greene.

"This afternoon's discussion topic bears the rather pretentious title 'Psychic Destiny Today.' I apologize for the pretentiousness, I do not apologize one whit for its calculated portentousness. For I am wholly convinced that there is no more important subject for us to confront than this very one. To confront with all the desperate artifices of our intelligences, our imaginations, and whatever primitive resources of brute courage and cunning are still left to us from the two-billion-year-old erosion of strengths that mankind has suffered under. For—as I see it—the question of our 'Psychic Destiny' subsumes within its radius of implication all the normally considered important questions of our time—the nagging problems of international social organizations, the bewildering fact of scientific indeterminacy which modern mathematics and physics have terrifyingly uncovered, the anarchic revolutions in form and theme that constitute our contemporary reports on the world. For this is the peculiar burden of our intellectual age, is it not? To be able to find no certainty anywhere. To look in vain in any of the established disciplines for the slightest resting point, for the smallest pinpoint of probability on which one can cast a pyramid of values. The peculiar burden of our time, to be crucified on a space-time axis while our bodies—our corpuscles and solar systems—are in violent erratic motion. To put it dramatically, we are in a position absolutely the reverse of Archimedes'. He yearned for a solid place on which he might set his feet *outside* the world so that he could move that solid unmovable sphere that imprisoned him. And we yearn for a solid place for our feet so that we can stop this insane acceleration, this wildfire burning into decay that marks our lives, our history, our metaphysical human destiny. The contour map of our century, is it not all too graphically found in Einstein's frightening predictions of the red shift in the hurtling heavens—that horrible and poetic astronomical sighting that parallels the great Shakespeare's earlier insight—'to be consumed with that which we are nourished by?' But while in prior ages this monstrous knowledge was confined to the possession of a few secluded geniuses—a dark hermetic Roger Bacon sealed away from the world in his brown cowl and saturnine humor, a Paracelsus, a mad Da Vinci pouring his vision into pigments which he knew would crumble and flake away, tortured spirits like the ice-cold Tycho Brahe, the perverse De Sade, that improper Victorian, E. B. Tylor—while in prior ages it was just the few, the elite, who were damned by their arcane wisdom, today we are all of us damned and doomed and the knowledge of our imminent fate presses at us with the latest headlines from Africa, with the latest messages to our cortexes from the dark and tropical continents of our own frustrate nervous systems."

His voice subsided in a long serpent's hiss and his lip fell to one side and he sneered at the class. I noticed that Daniel had leaned forward in his seat, his hands together on his lap as though he were praying, his whole demeanor intent on Cadmium Greene's words. He held a long silence as he studied the class and I could hear the squirreling scrape of ball-point pens and I noticed that the sun had disappeared and an ominous clutch of grey had squeezed the sky. Then Cadmium Greene straightened up from his menacing sneer and continued with an almost flippant buoyancy.

"Let us by way of example juxtapose some strange material. On the one hand, we have been examining in the past weeks that queer melange of a culture ideal which is crystallized in the image of The Explorer in modern western civilization. That figure of heroic daring and endeavor, relentlessly plunging into the unknown, conquering the unconquerable, crossing chartless seas, seducing impregnable women, subduing physical and then, later, psychological and spatial chaos to his human ordering hand. We have traced this image cluster from that caricature of rationality that we found in the late medieval devil figures of the morality plays and the popular lithography, threading through the mighty isolatoes of Christopher Marlowe, the mariners from Vespucci and Columbus to Magellan and the seventeenth-century buccaneers. We saw the image refracted of its physicality in the Latinate pederasty of Francis Bacon, in the Gallic cynicism of Montaigne, in the whimsical religiosity of Don Quixote. And we saw as the seventeenth century rolled into the eighteenth and the nineteenth that The Explorer retained his phallic thrust even as he abstained from his phallic duty. Focusing his massive energies to a point in which the male member is the true symbol of his purpose and movement, he performs the female function of settlement and colonization, of catalogue and constitutional program. The French philosophes, the early British empiricists, the Lavoisiers and Gay-Lussacs merge with the American Indian fighter, the frontiersman, the pioneer, to become hermaphroditic deities, great stucco Niobes weeping for the children that are always over the next mountain, beyond the next battle, behind the next concealing veil which hides truth from the sexless militant inquiring mind. We noticed that strange female despair that brings such dissimilar personalities as an Abraham Lincoln, a Byron, a Tsar Alexander the First, the weeping Mazzini, the incredibly martyred Freud into a choral mutuality of tears and lamentation. It is as though the male explorer hurtles valiantly through the first protecting membrane of discovery only to succumb to a triste ante coitum. There is a fatal broken circuit, a leakage of the vital energies, a guillotine swish of slice and cease! The thrust lurches, trembles, and balks, unable to continue its own desired momentum. The Explorer crumples into flabby lassitude, muttering Rilke's horrible self-condemning phrase, 'Jeder Engel ist schreklich!' And in female tears the stiff male rectitude is broken and mankind is left foundering in an agony of knotted frustration."

Cadmium Greene's face became a sudden mask of pain and he seized his cane and stamped it on the floor. "'Jeder Engel ist schreklich,'" he repeated. "Schreklich!" He lurched to the blackboard and drew a great stabbing arrow, using the side of the chalk and then he attacked the arrow with slashing canceling lines and he looked at his diagram with mocking satisfaction. Back at the podium he hung his cane again on the table edge and waited for a student to stop coughing. The sky had lowered outside even more and suddenly the banks of fluorescent tubes on the ceiling flowed into automatic light. Daniel blinked next to me at the sudden glare and Cadmium Greene bowed ironically and then continued.

"But remember also—remember that we have seen The Explorer figure not only as the abortive vehicle of man's ascending spirit—the human desire to know, to discover, to control—but also as a cowardly refugee who would escape from the blood bath. We have seen him as the pilgrim of shame who chooses a safer Amsterdam or Plymouth or Ellis Island for his precious religious bones—safer than the honest steel of an Archbishop Laud in his native green meadows. For here is that curious paradox, the forever unbalanceable equation in the metaphysics of courage. To explore the new frontier is to evade the older responsibilities of the native security. The great Napoleon—that sickly impotent half-man—" he spat these words from his mouth like writhing snakes— "he who is said to have weeped like an altar boy after his triumphal return from Elba. Might it not have been better for him to have wept when he first left Corsica? Might his later tears—his bitter tears at Waterloo, his bitter bitter tears at St. Helena—might these not have been the watery echoes of the Corsican tears that he lacked the courage to shed? The Corsican home that he lacked the manhood to live into? Ah, but look at Socrates, you may be saying—" Cadmium Greene shifted roles, becoming the voice of rational dissent in the classroom, acting out the parts in an insane vaudeville routine—"what about this primal exception, this Socrates? This full-grown Explorer refusing the treacherous Underground Railways of the craven spirit. Nay, he said. Though thou slay me, here will I stand. Do with me what my Athenian peers have provided. Nobility? Courage? Patriarchal wisdom? Perhaps. Perhaps. And perhaps not. Perhaps as Explorer he was already in permanent exile, a Cain of the intellect against whom every man's hand was rightly raised. The paradox, you see. It is neither an idle nor an academic one. It reflects that unfathomable split in the human soul which has bequeathed us the raging furies of dualism, dichotomy, double purpose everywhere. Matter-spirit, time-eternity, love-hate, good-evil, life-death. The human zodiac has only one meaningful emblem, and that is the enigmatic Gemini, the eternally joined and opposed twins who would move in different directions simultaneously, who would split us asunder in our moments of highest attempt."

Cadmium Greene stopped and contemplated the Gemini wistfully and I could almost see them hovering in the air, locked in an implacable opposition. He coughed slightly and cleared his throat and the class shifted haunches while he patted the notes on the lectern without looking at them. I bent toward Daniel to say something, but he waved me away, his attention wholly dedicated to the spellbinder on the podium. Suddenly a girl toward the front of the room whom I had vaguely noticed holding a handkerchief to her face seized this opportunity to get quietly to her feet and head for the back door. Cadmium Greene pointedly followed her progress up the aisle with a disgusted stare. The whole class turned to watch her exit and the massed attention of our glances broke against her like a sudden wave. She put her hand to her mouth and ran the last dozen steps to the door, letting it slam behind her. Cadmium Greene glared at the closed door, and his lips were tight and horizontal. Then the corner of his lip sagged down into the sneer, but when he spoke again, he snapped at his words like a dog trapped in its own ferocity.

"This point—this point that I have been trying to make in spite of these interruptions—is crucial to our understanding. We must—we must absorb its full intensity, because we cannot afford to gainsay its implications on our own terribly burdened destinies. Sir Isaac Newton took a great shuddering cosmic step forward in his daring construction of an absolutely eccentric, thoroughly irresponsible World Machine. The gentle Isaac is one of the great eighteenth-century Explorers, mighty pioneer, trail blazer into new mental worlds. And we are taught to revere him, to thank him, to place the laurel on his brow. But note well this gentle Isaac, this knight with the carmine hands. He fashions his intellectual machine and, as casual by-product or savage aim—who can tell?—he slaughters his father, Galileo, his father, Ptolemy. The new step taken can only follow the path of destruction, of violence, of murder. And if the past is necessarily the father of the future, the present can become future only by donning the horned hood of the son as hangman, the execrable parricide. Ah, perhaps now we understand—perhaps now we see why these phallic Explorers become blunted and impotent in their purpose. Perhaps that is why the rape is not consummated, the willing victim spread-eagled, tongue lolling with aroused lust, loins heaving with want, with need, with swallowing encompassing desire. The unappeased compliance to turn ashen, the surrender to become cold stony resistance. Just at the moment of true victory, the Napoleonic tears quell the raging fires and the forgotten guilt of parricide thwarts the act with an implacable jellied hand. 'The center cannot hold,' lamented the emasculated Yeats, but it was he and every other Explorer who had been unable to hold the center!"

He lurched again to the board and next to the splintered arrow drew a large chalk circle and then exploded it with stabbing thrusts of chalk. "Cannot hold," he shouted. "The center cannot hold!" And just as he lunged at the center of his decimated circle with one final sweeping stab of the chalk, the thunder which had been folded up in the sky cracked loose with a shattering rolling BOOM as though Cadmium Greene had pressed the desperate button and the echoes of its roar carved serried canyons of sound from the core of my fear. Within its vacuum it massed layers of frightening depth, gulches and gorges of unexplored being, and I felt ripped apart into many. I saw that Daniel's knuckles were ivory pink from the pressure of his clenched hands and I noticed that one of the nuns had instinctively felt for her cross when the thunder came. Cadmium Greene laughed wildly into the vacant place, and his cane fell to the floor when he tried to hang it back on the table edge. He left it there and he loomed over the lectern like a bleeding Greek hero flaunting the array of hostile armies drawn up to subdue him.

"Now," he shouted. "It's Now. Not past history which I am trying to make clear to you. It is the present moment. The Now. The Explorer has a new role, a new costume, a new argot. He wears a silver suit and he says not 'Cogito ergo sum,' but 'Roger, A-Okay.' Now he is an astronaut or a games theorist or an expert on nuclear fission or population explosion. The principle is unchanged. The slogan is the same tired overworked piece, 'You have nothing to lose but your chains.' Forgetting that one breaks something of one's own in order to break the tiniest link of one's chains. The newest exploration is of space. Our natural fecund world with its swamps and deserts, its rolling waters and continental land masses, this literal womb of mankind— What have we turned it into? A launching pad? A sterile Genoese harbor? A pencil-scrawled hypothesis, $E = mc^2$, from which we can extrapolate the extinction of human life? No, I'm not making value judgments. Blast off, I would say. Damn the torpedoes, full speed ahead. Gladly I would say this. I would give a papal blessing to the lethal tanks of the future. But our crippled astronauts, our wheeze-ridden Explorers, ride the pale horse of guilt in their lonely voyages, and they have always offered their heads to the glinting hooves before the final orgasmic breakthrough. Unless we can masculate them, masculate ourselves, insure the duration of the phallic drive, we are doomed to fail. Our 'Psychic Destinies'—they are fully comprised in the terrible female hieroglyphic of the Absolute Zero!"

He picked the cane off the floor and, without leaving the lecture table, traced an imaginary circle on the board over the scuffed fragments of powdered chalk. This time he rested the cane very carefully on the edge of the table, waiting for it to fall into balance before he addressed the class.

"But I said I wanted to juxtapose some strange and incongruous material." Cadmium Greene paused and smiled for the first time and his smile was an exposure of disease on his face. "On the one hand we have this very ambiguous, very pathetic, very comic culture image of The Explorer that we have been discussing today and for several weeks. And, on the other hand, the newspapers, especially the indelicate tabloids, have been regaling us with the details of two particularly horrifying crimes which occurred here in New York within the last week. The one, the case of the drunken obese mother who crushed and smothered her infant child under her own beery buttocks. The other, the four homosexual boys who used Coca-Cola bottles to cruelly violate and then bludgeon to death the virtuous maiden in Mosholu Park. I read these monstrous stories. You read them. We reconstructed the crimes on television and in the smudged photographs in the newspapers.

And we are socially shocked. Our social faces blanch and we murmur for troops of vigilantes, for guardian minute men of the night. But we keep a terrible secret from ourselves, don't we?" His voice became hushed and insinuating and his torso coiled into itself grotesquely. "We keep a very terrible secret from ourselves. Even as we murmur our outrage, we nurture a lovely delight in the suffocation of that puling infant child. We fondle our own imaginary Coca-Cola bottles. We hold within our own spotless bosoms a secret self that nuzzles its loathsome snout in blood. That is imbedded in the basic structures of our psyches like coral. And what is this secret self except the mongrel bastard offspring of the two diseased elements in modern man? The two running sores of our leprous state. Consciousness and Guilt." He pounded his two fists on the lectern, scattering his notes, which he hadn't looked at yet. "Yes, Consciousness and Guilt. The impotent fathering consciousness and guilt, the blood-bitten mother with the rending nails. For man was not always the crippled thing he is now. Once he knew a joy in his holy assault against life. The joy of the antelope in his rush against the wind. The joy of the jaguar as he ripped at the tough hide of his prey with gleaming savage teeth. The joy of the vicious catamount snarling into the western winter blizzard. Man knows no joy now. Squeezed between the calipers of his consciousness and his guilt, he prates of delight and contentment, reaching for his pipe and slippers while the feral wind whips at his television antenna. Nor, alas, can man know that joy again. The step once taken eradicates all paths of return and only in his forgotten dreams can he find the ancient visceral releases."

Cadmium Greene paused and rearranged his notes without looking at them. The shattering acreage of windows was awash with streaming rain and we might all have been in some hollow submarine chamber air-locked away from the menacing sea. Cadmium Greene had turned his profile toward the windows and the cold tubes of fluorescence cast a crown of briny light on his wild hair. His face when he turned back toward us was pressed beneath centuries of sad pain, and then in a volatile moment, the lip dropped and his teeth were sharp in his words.

"Nor can man discard his father Consciousness, gentlemen. Let him but try. Emergent, as we have noted, through eons of genetic and cultural adaptation, it is a salient part of his human definition and all attempts to destroy it end only in the paralysis of guilt. Lawrence, Miller, the pathetic yen for Zen—what are they but sickly suicides—the deceptively buoyant bubble of air in the veins? No, that is no true way out. But is it not strange that there has never been an eternal prohibition against matricide? Was it because none was needed? Is mother love so deeply ingrained in the animal nature as to make an injunction against mother slaughter unnecessary? The wisdom of the ages proscribes incest, although crippled humanity has always felt free to overstep this one forbidden boundary in order to bathe its putrid weaknesses in the Lethean baths of incestuous guilt. May it not be—may it just not be that the wisdom of the ages proscribed incest in order to encourage man to matricide? And is not matricide the only practical and possible response which phallic man can make to the hideous challenges of the present and future? Root out the impoverishing guilt within! Stamp it out! Destroy it! Kill the mother that saps our strength in order that we may at last take full possession of the willing mistress. Nature awaits the erect spirit—" Cadmium Greene stood as tall as he crippled could behind the lectern, trumpeting proudly to the far wall at the end of the room— "the truly manly man—waits trembling with desire for him. Nature, knowledge, space—they wait like virgin angels for the joy of the blood spilled sacredly. They await the new consciousness without guilt. And all things will be open to that new man. Interstellar distances will fold into centimeters before the thrust of his ardor. He will crush and he will create and his face will be blank of all expression save joy. The secret self within—the blood glutter, the deformed grotesque of our repressed desires will blend and fuse into perfect union with the entire psyche and mankind will walk his own universe for the first time since the mythical Fall from grace in full and proud possession of himself."

Cadmium Greene stopped with a stunned look on his face and then he read the time on his wristwatch as though it were a calendar and the mesmerized audience sighed back and rustled in their seats, beginning to shift books and notes. The rain had stopped as suddenly as it had begun, and one could feel the slow hiss of its invisible ascent beyond the sky. Daniel slowly brought his hands apart next to me and gripped his knees. Cadmium Greene stuffed his untouched notes and books back into his brief case, speaking in a more subdued pitch but with the same pressing violence.

"I see that we have come to the end of today's meeting. Next week I shall pick up from here to discuss the ancillary topic, 'The New Joy in Contemporary Art.' In the meantime I shall assume that you will have completed page twelve of your reading list by next week's meeting. Thank you, good afternoon."

And with a shuffle of movement and a last defiant glare at the class, he seized his brief case, retrieved his cane, took four long-striding, lurching steps to the door and disappeared.

My face was hot and I noticed without surprise that my pulse beat had quickened, there was a dried jelly of anticipation in my lower chest, and my parasympathetic nervous system had rallied to the ready. Physically I was waiting to hurtle violently through the hole which Cadmium Greene had punched into the serene afternoon. My muscles wanted to hit out, my teeth to tear, my blood to race and boil and spill.

A voice of intellectual protest from a student behind me dissipated some of the intense electricity. "Cheezis, page twelve on that goddamned reading list by next week. That's two whole books and eleven articles. Who the hell does he think *he* is anyway?"

The class was already dissolving to the exits, threading sluggishly along the irrigational canals of its own inertia, and Daniel was tamping tobacco into his pipe, the pale scar on his cheek glowing faintly. The sun was out again and the ceiling lights had drained off in silent obedience to some efficient mechanism of response. I got up from my chair carefully since my pants were slightly stuck to the shellac on the seat and I squeezed Daniel's arm in a friendly gesture.

"Wowie, he is a something," I said. "Is he always like this?"

"He is a great man," Daniel said. "A true teacher." He thought for some seconds, pursing his brow in fine brown wrinkles. "He was rather unusually agitated and perhaps overrhetorical this afternoon. As though he were disturbed about something." Daniel considered the enormity of the suggestion that his idol might be at the mercy of irresponsible human fate. The possibilities were simply too staggering to be entertained, so he stuffed his pipe more tightly with a poised thumb.

"You should have heard his lecture on the Medieval Squat," he said. "It was absolutely brilliant."

"It sounds it," I said. "What was it all about?"

"It's not easy to explain," Daniel answered. "A magnificent synthesis of the salient aspects of medieval culture in terms of the squatting image. You know, the system of fealty and vassalage, the psychology of the genuflection, Gothic architecture, the dominant modes of perverted sexual behavior, even the structure of the isorhythmic motet. All as manifestations of the physio-psychic attitude of the squat. And he demonstrated how this anal posture defined and determined the beginnings of usury, the Protestant reformation, and the ideological foundations of modern science. It was an incredible educational experience."

"I can well believe it," I said. "It doesn't do so bad even in summary. Do you know anything about Professor Greene—you know—personally? Like was he born with his foot like that or was it an accident? Is he married? Does he have kids? You know."

Daniel stiffened into a peculiar resentment. "He is a great teacher," he repeated. "There are always people who are unable to tolerate greatness because it accents their own paltry mediocrity. I refuse to listen to their dirty stories. I know Cadmium Greene from his lectures and from *The Mortuary of Love*. And that's more than enough to persuade me that he is a great man. I hear some of their filthy backbiting gossip and that just convinces me of their own poisonous envy." He stared defiantly at me. "You saw and heard the man. What do you have to ask me?"

"Mediocre curiosity," I said, soothing the distressed acolyte. "There's no question about it at all. He certainly is a something."

The classroom was almost emptied, the janitor waiting impatiently by the door to clean up and close up as we entered the corridor and headed for the stairs. On our left was a men's room, which I spotted with gratitude.

"Medieval Squat notwithstanding, friend," I said, "I've got to take a leak."

Daniel accompanied me into the tile-white bathroom, holy and dedicated with its serried banks of decorously curved urinals, its closed stalls and gleaming sinks. Cadmium Greene was indeed a something, I thought. A torrent, a jet, a twisted high-pressure hose of a flow, this aching release of a seagreen burst. He's mad, of course, I thought, the best and the worst kind of madness. The variety of madness that impales a white whale with the stake of his own self-hatred, or invents an alphabet in order to spell out his own self-curses, or digs at his heart with an ice axe when he's just a snowball-throw away from the misty summit of his achievement. His mother must be dead, sad beaten bitch. And now he can't kill her, the poor bastard, and of course he knows his doom. Oh, nosirree, Riegelo Rigoletto, I wouldn't be in his shoes—the thick or the thin of them—for nothing, no thank you. And I hope and pray that Letha is outside of the sweep of his murderous swing. Because when that awesome jet loses its pressure—and lose it it must if he's really human—and the walls of marble and porphyry are still uncracked and unstained, then where is he? What does he do then? Shake a last tear from his rod and smite the rock, but no Moses he. Better you than me, old Cad, old man. I elect ball bearings to roll to hell on. You can boil away on your own jet turbines.

I backed away from the urinal to zip up my pants but the zipper wouldn't budge. I tugged harder. It would move neither up nor down. I counted very slowly to ten, looking blankly at the frosted window, and then I tried it again. Nothing. The zipper was locked like a concentrated crab on the furled stuffed material of the fly and my pulling only served to secure its comic clutch. My Haspel jacket was too short to cover the gape in my world, and even had it been longer, it was nattily tailored to fall away toward the hips and flanks. Riegel, I thought, you have been had. You are a sitting queer duck and the birds will peck at you all the long way back to Christopher Street.

"What's the matter, David?" Daniel asked, drying his hands carefully on a roll towel.

"Nothing," I said. "Nothing, but my phallic thrust is blunted indeed. My goddamned fly is stuck is all. And Christ, I don't even have anything to hold in front of me. Like a brief case or something."

Daniel came over to help survey my clumsy humiliation. His face was concerned and studious, but his lips kept twitching at the corners.

"That's a terribly unfortunate thing, David. I know just how you feel," he said. "I always worry about things like that myself. As a matter of fact, I have special zippers—Claw Easy-Kwiks—sewn in all my trousers. You never know when something like that will happen."

I found that if I stood straight with my suit jacket buttoned and my pants belt tightened an extra notch, I was reasonably presentable until I took a step. Then the coat would flare and the material of my pants would follow the direction of immediate strain, the right-leg material parting to the right, the left-leg material riding to the left. From an absurd and wrinkled wound of synthetic textile I gaped.

" 'Tis not so deep as a well nor so wide as a church-door," I said. "But 'tis enough, 'twill serve."

I clutched the treacherous cloth in my fist and practiced a lurching loping bent-over walk in front of the large mirrors that lined the wall above the sinks.

"It's not so bad this way," I said. "Somebody stops me I can always explain that the cat's got my tongue. Or I lost my truss. Or I'm bleeding to death from internal wounds. People won't look at me anyway. They're embarrassed by suffering. I'll be the invisible man."

"Wait a minute," Daniel said. "I think I've got something."

He disappeared for two or three minutes, leaving me to assume various concealing postures in front of the mirrors. On his return he was quietly jubilant, bearing a magazine on his upturned palm. "I thought I remembered seeing something," he said. "There were two. The *Journal of Aesthetics and Art Criticism* and this."

"This" was a copy of *Ebony* magazine with a cover picture of a severely Anglican Negro churchman looking out of the page, with balefully suffering eyes, over a huge Biblical tome.

"I thought this would be less obtrusive and more suitable than the other," Daniel explained. "Also, it's somewhat larger."

So with *Ebony* awkwardly protecting my exposed crotch, we left the safety of the men's room, slowly navigating the stairs and emerging on the street. I found that I could hook my right thumb under my belt, holding the magazine in place with the four fingers of my right hand. This bestowed a kind of relaxed suavity to my appearance, I thought, the Man of Distinction on the point of delivering some succinct advice to sell short on soybeans in order to plow heavily in Industrials. Daniel was going east and I was going in the direction of the slowly sinking sun.

"I'm sorry to leave you in the lurch like this," Daniel said. "But I really must make this appointment."

"Think nothing of it," I said. "Man was destined to be alone in his highest and his lowest human moments. It's been a very pleasant afternoon—with it all—and I'm very grateful to you."

We made a ceremony of the hand-shaking, I switching my hands to effect the courtesy, the Anglican minister nodding his grief over our farewell. Daniel looked at him and then at me and he clucked deep in his throat and allowed a bare shadow of mirth on his dark face. "You're a walking picture of biracial amity, David," he said. "The NAACP would applaud you."

"Not to mention the B'nai Brith," I said.

We waved our good-bys and I walked slowly through the Park and across Sixth Avenue. I contrived an easy sauntering gait behind my *Ebony* shield which made me look as though I were in the last throes of severe constipation or badly chafed thighs, but no one except some incredulous children found me worthy of anything but a passing glance. Sure, I said to myself, you've got to be open, baby. I had recalled a small tailor shop at the corner of Ziggie's street and it was to this haven that I was heading for repairs. It's just a pit stop, I told myself, lurching ahead in second gear. Just a simple pit stop like all the speed kings take.

The shop was right where I had remembered it—Solomon's Sartorial Parlor—but the door was locked and the gooseneck lamp with its throat wrenched over the pressing machine was extinguished for the day. "Oi, Solomon, you can't do this to me," I breathed, pushing my face close to the glass and shading it with my hand to peer inside. The shop was quite clearly closed for the day, but I could hear the dulled syncopation of a radio playing in a back room and I pounded heavily on the glass until the radio stopped and someone finally lumbered to the door. Dressed in an undershirt and suspenders with heavy misshapen grey trousers, the sequestered inmate that I had summoned from his lair could only be Solomon himself, opening his door angrily just the length of the lock chain, eager to spit his disturbed imprecations at me, the alien intruder, the Nazi insult.

"Vat de ya crazy?" he thundered. "I'm closed! All shod up! Go vay before you smesh my gless!"

"I got a little trouble," I said, shouting through the door crack as plaintively as I could. "It'll just take a minute."

"*You* god a liddle trouble?" he said. "Who don't god trouble? De hull efternoon nobody should bodder to come to my bizness and you tink you god trouble. Go vay I'll call de police!"

"It's worse than trouble, Solomon," I said, seeing the door begin to close its three open inches. "It's tsoris I got. A little tsoris you can help me."

The three inches remained hesitantly open. "Vat kind tsoris?" he asked. "Chip or expansive?"

"For me it's expensive. For you it's cheap," I said. "I got the damned zipper on my fly stuck." And I backed away from the glass, lowering my buckler of *Ebony,* exposing my shame and discomfiture.

Solomon looked down at me through the glass, and his round thick face broke open into a wide crescent grin, displaying a row of gold inlays and nicotine-rotted gaps in his mouth. He laughed a kind of guttural snort and then unlocked the door, leading me into the shop.

"Trouble is trouble, but tsoris—dat's someding else," he said, and humming an unrecognizable tune under his breath, he had me slip out of my pants and stand shivering next to a full-length poster of a man in a dark-grey suit with umbrella and Homburg in a style that must have rocked the executive set circa 1936. He pulled my pants under the gooseneck lamp and made deft motions at them with a small pliers.

"I vorned dem," he said. "Ven dey foist come out mit de zipper, I vorned dem. I said den, 'Trouble. Dere's goin to be trouble from dis.' I said it den and I say so now. Me, I vouldn't have a zipper on a pair pents of mine, it should be made from gold. Now mit a buddon, you alvays know vat you got. A buddon, it's a piece honest moichandise. Mit a zipper, oi vay, you don't know from noddin."

He made a final adjustment with the pliers and pulled the zipper up and down its track, the silver teeth opening and closing in quick raspy breaths.

"So." He handed the pants back to me. "Now you can ged yourself into more trouble."

I accepted the pants gratefully and slipped them on. "Thanks, Solomon," I said. "Trouble but not tsoris."

He snorted his laugh at me again. "You tink you god a choice? Oi, hev you god a lot to loin."

With my armor repaired, my external wounds stitched and stanched, I returned to Ziggie's apartment to find my note untouched on the floor and that air of cumulative silence in the room which bespoke hours of undisturbed vacancy. It had been a long hot afternoon and it was too early to go to the Libido. I wanted not to think, and I wasn't hungry, so I took a long ice-cold shower, letting the spray bite into the back of my neck, purposely dulling the keen flashes of imagery my mind tossed up in front of me. I dried myself off, and, wrapping up in an immense towel, I lay on the bed to rest. I fell asleep almost instantly, between slow drips from the shower nozzle, inserting myself seductively within the intermittencies of splash and plop. And I dreamed.

I was walking on a high narrow wall no more than the width of my shoe and with her head over my right shoulder—the classic burping position—I was carrying Rosalie. But it was Rosalie as a baby of seven or eight months, her legs and arms thin enough to be encircled by my hand, her hair fine and meager, like a bird's. I could feel her heart beat against my chest and from time to time she would crane her head on her neck to look directly into my eyes with her knowing unbaby eyes—deep burnished brown and frightful. I was moving very slowly along the top of the wall, placing one foot in front of the other with fearful care, shifting my weight back and forth like an acrobat on the high wire, catching my balance tenuously, moving gropingly ahead. Something was behind me that I had to escape from and the wall was too high to jump off, especially while carrying the fragile tender burden of my daughter. It was dark—a twilight jungle dark—and the top of the wall was riven by slippery uneven vines or roots so that each footstep was a tortuous tentative foray into dangerous unknown territory. I was in a dank wet bath of perspiration and the threat behind me was coming closer and faster. Suddenly, below me, his head perhaps three feet beneath my feet, was a man—a German soldier in the frighteningly familiar jackboots, steel helmet, and SS green that all the ghastly newsreels of the thirties had imprinted on my mind. He was looking up at me, and his face was a clear etching in the gloom—a face that I did not know at all, but a face that was very near to mine. The high cheekbones, the clean-shaven fair-skinned chin and cheeks, the iron fold of straight flaxen hair cutting out at an angle from the heavy curved helmet, the eyes blue and straight and squinting into mine. His arms were reaching toward me, toward the top of the wall, and the movement behind me was scuttering nearer. I panicked at the sudden sight of him, my toe catching on a snaky tendril, and I lurched off balance, frantically clawing at the air to keep my footing, desperately pirouetting as I ponderously fell, holding Rosalie away from my body, my toe inextricably under the vine. And at the last moment in my fall, like a basketball player swooshing a foul shot, I dropped Rosalie directly into his green-clad reaching arms, the white burden floating down feather light, and he caught her with tenderness and his blue eyes locked on mine, and did his face change shape and the lip fall to one side and the eyes melt liquid and grey? Suddenly it was all gloom and then glowing horrid sepia and I quivered in cold fear and my head was in a net.

Ziggie had returned and dropped a wet washcloth on my face. He was snickering noisily at the foot of the bed.

"What ho!" he called. "What great hulk this? Sleeping Beauty, perchance? No, it's not built right. Moby Dick, perhaps? Shrouded in terry white, thrashing its murderous flukes. Sperm ahoy! The prize doubloon is mine!"

He danced a little jig around the room, his own loose version of a Nantucketer's hornpipe, and I caught him 'twixt horn and pipe with the still-damp cloth.

"Sit down, you horse's ass," I grunted. "For all you know, this is the first sleep I've had in twenty-four hours. Some people, they just got no respect for the dead."

"A thousand pardons, Herr Lazarus." Ziggie salaamed. "Gunga's humble joy at remarkable recovery make too strong medicine for native sense of unworthy inferiority. Gunga beg miserable forgiveness, Sahib, effendi. Bwana bwana bwana.

Baksheesh baksheesh baksheesh." He banged his forehead against the floor with an aching thump.

I straightened up on the pillow, feeling a little like a damp mummy as my dream receded into the tomb of dreams. "For Christ's sakes, give me a cigarette and tell me what you've found out. It just so happens that I have a little information myself."

Ziggie lit two cigarettes, gave me one, and quieted himself into a chair. He was now playing somebody from Homicide.

"9:02 A.M. Checked out of Christopher Street pad to stake out in East Sixties. No dice. Suspect cleared out last week, no forwarding address. Landlady unwilling to cooperate. Threw five fast slugs into lower left quadrant of chest cavity. She crumpled like Madame Ouspenskaya. Croaked out 'cara Italia' and hemorrhaged into a DOA. I carved a purple 'P' in her cheek to throw off the fuzz. Stupid bastards." Ziggie spit the cigarette smoke out of his mouth in disgust. "They'll go nuts trying to find somebody who pees purple."

Well, that figured. Letha must have moved out maybe five–six days ago. Probably went back from time to time to check on the mail. Or maybe she arranged with somebody to hold it for her. In the mountains, there you feel free.

"Good work, Knuckles," I said. "I may move you up to whorehouse collections. What did you find out about Greene?"

"Ah, C. Greene," Ziggie tasted the name in his mouth, savoring the drawn-out vowel sound as though it were a vaguely disreputable delicacy. He changed roles in his chair, become now the encyclopedic statistician, the brain truster with no trust. "C. Greene. Sehr geherte Herr Professor Doktor Cadmium Greene. A.B., Columbia; Wasserheim Fellowships to Heidelberg and the Sorbonne; Ph.D., Harvard. Member of the Medievalist Society, the International Orientalist Association, the American Philosophical Society, ex-Book Review Editor of the *Erannos Jahrbuch,* American representative in the UNESCO excavation teams at Lascaux and later in the Negev Desert. Presently associated with the Advanced School for Research. Author of numerous treatises in the specialized areas of archaeology, classical studies, medieval science, the Kabuki theater, and Sino-Russian trade relations. Also, and incidentally, author of the astonishingly popular Evergrave paperback, *The Mortuary of Love.*"

"Well done," I said. "Was he born with his gimp leg or did he earn it unnaturally?"

"Oho, David." Ziggie wiggled a finger at me. "You've not been relaxing."

"I've been mixing business with pleasure," I said. And I told him briefly about the visit of his friend Daniel Meleck and our attendance at the lecture. I mentioned the party of the night before without referring to Rennie. Ziggie assimilated my information without asking me any questions.

"This Cadmium Greene, David," he said. "He's no lightweight. I read a little piece of his once on the societal implications of the Achilles shield description and it's first-class work. And *The Mortuary of Love.* There's nothing flimsy about it, either."

"I don't dispute you," I said. "I did hear him lecture, you know. But it's not his *mind* that interests me right now. What kind of guy is he? I get the impression from Daniel that there are a lot of strange stories trailing around after him."

"Don't knock the mind, David." Ziggie's face was suddenly serious, and he studied the glowing tip of his cigarette. "You get somebody as intellectually vigorous as Cadmium Greene, his ideas can become vascular to him, you know. After a while he may not make any fine distinctions between his theories and his actions."

"Then God help his mother," I said. "Or, for that matter, any other woman who gets within knife distance of him."

Ziggie allowed himself a look of unusual respect in my direction. "I keep forgetting that you're not as dumb as you act, Dave," he said. "Well, here's the poop I've been able to pick up on the good Professor Greene. Only child, a small town in northern Connecticut, father a seemingly unsuccessful Congregationalist minister. His mother evidently took him over completely. Tutors, private schools, and all—both to avenge herself on poor old Daddy and to glory vicariously in the success that she got cheated out of."

"Archaeology and classical studies," I snorted. "Seems like a helluva success story for a frustrated woman. Even a vicarious one."

"That evidently was just the point," Ziggie said. "Mama Greene had a nice diplomatic political career all planned out. So when the young Cad gets out of Columbia, he joins the CP and spends a year with the Abraham Lincoln Brigade in Spain, effectively putting the squinch on Mother's rosy reveries."

"Ah," I said. "So that's where he got the bad foot?"

"No," Ziggie answered. "That he seems to have started with. And the CP wasn't as choosy as the Selective Service Boards. Anyway, the Spanish War business appears to have done Mama in. She wasn't buying any foreign Bolsheviks, she didn't give a genteel screw for the Asturian miners or the Spanish republic, and I expect that, in a pinch, she probably figured that Adolf had the right notions, even if his implementation was a wee bit crude."

"Well!" I blew out my surprise in a whoosh of cigarette smoke. "That adds a new wrinkle to Mr. Green, doesn't it? I'd never have figured him for a hot-eyed idealist of the thirties. Or any other time, either."

"Oh, he wasn't," Ziggie said. "Never underestimate the power of a woman, my boy. Chances are—if he thought about it all—the young Comrade's political ideas were about the same as his mother's. He wasn't fighting Fascists in Spain. He was fighting Elspeth Drury Greene."

"Maybe," I said. "Anyway, he won."

"He lost," Ziggie corrected me. "In the winter before the Brigade was moved out—on an early February morning, to be exact—the Reverend Doctor Doremus Nathaniel Greene was stuck on the ice in his Plymouth coupe between the garage and the sidewalk. And dainty Elspeth dutifully donned her weathered alpaca and overshoes to spray gravel under the spinning rear wheels. How it happened, nobody really knows—least of all the good Reverend himself. But the tires slipped and Elspeth slipped and the Plymouth slipped over her three times. Once was undoubtedly sufficient. The second two slips were probably for good luck."

"Aha, I see," I said, seeing nothing but looking into the murk for a light. "Guernica in Connecticut." I thought for a minute. "But that doesn't work out right," I said. "The returned ex-Comrade should classically have gone gunning for Papa. Mama's in the sepulcher by the sea, chaste and inviolate, safe now to be embraced with loving filial ardor. He should have taken off after the ravening wolf. I don't understand this reverse twist."

"Cadmium Greene is not a simple man," Ziggie said. "I suspect that he had effectively destroyed the good Reverend years before and he'd evidently learned in Spain that the sweet Elspeth was of a stock too tough and horny to be exploded by symbolic hand grenades. So when he got home with nothing to show for his European wanderjahre but a corridor of closed doors with neat signs saying 'Ex-Communists need not inquire,' and when he found that the impotent minister had stupidly skidded into his own rightful executioner's place—well, something very big must have closed in him then. Closed or dried up or fallen irretrievably out of place."

"Perhaps," I said. "He's not married, I suppose."

"Not now." Ziggie lit two more cigarettes and handed me one. "That's probably some of those stories that Daniel mentioned. He *was* married when he was at Harvard. A wench yclept Lola Spohr. I couldn't find out anything about her, but the newspaper reports called her dark-haired and beautiful. You can't tell too much from newspaper stories."

"What story? Why was she in the papers?"

"Oh, it was just a regular newspaper winter-accident story. It seems that the dark-haired beautiful Lola was helping her doctoral-candidate husband push their car up an icy incline when she was accidentally crushed under the rear wheels. New England ice is a very slippery variety."

"Indeed it is," I agreed. "And what has sweet Cadmium Greene been up to since?"

"His subsequent record," Ziggie said, "has been—if you'll forgive the pun—as pure as the undriven snow. No weddings, no hits, no burials. It is persistently rumored that he has a predilection for young men and that it kills him to give a good grade to a pretty female, but this is the kind of base canard that too often attaches itself to the bachelor American academic. He has been the recipient of multitudinous scholarly honors and he wears his plaudits with grace."

"With violent grace," I said, remembering. "Even the crazy painters swear by him. And you know what an illiterate horde they are."

"Yes, he has this knack," Ziggie said. "From what I could find out, he seems to be an intimate in almost every closed intellectual circle in the city. Not just artists, but editors and publishers, town planners, theater people—the whole quivering gamut of the marginal intelligentsia. In spite of, or because of, the dainty Elspeth, Cadmium Greene has contrived his own curious arrival."

"And an old bully for him," I said. "But what about me? Where in hell does this leave me?"

"At one further point which I have squirreled away for the end," Ziggie said puckishly. "He is no true story teller who would throw away his punch line while he's filling in the introductory material. Tomorrow night in his commodious mansion on the Island, Professor Greene is throwing a wing-ding of a masked ball. A costume party in celebration of his fiftieth birthday."

Ziggie coughed apologetically. "To be sure, this is not exactly his own idea, modest spirit that he is. But when he was pressed by a number of colleagues, friends, and associates who had formed a conspirational committee to effect this end, he quickly and almost graciously acquiesced. And you and I are just ripe for a costume ball, aren't we?"

I digested this new information wonderingly. "Ziggie," I said. "Did you— Is this party by any chance of what you might call a sudden determination? Has it been arranged for a long period of time or is it a kind of last-minute affair?"

"Strange that you should ask that, David." Ziggie smiled. "As a matter of fact, the Junta didn't really go into operation until very late this morning. But it worked very fast once it started. Very fast."

He scraped his cigarette into the ashtray. "One does a certain amount of reading in the library. One notes among other things inconsequentials like birthdates. One makes a phone call here, a phone call there. People love parties." He sighed loudly. "I do myself."

"Ziggie," I said. "You are a genius."

"It's true," he admitted. "But I'm damned if I can figure out what to wear. David, do you see me as more the Caliban or the Ariel type?"

"But what about invitations?" I asked. "You didn't work invitations for us too, did you?"

"Invitations, who needs them? This is a word-of-mouth deal. There'll be a small mob there, and in masks and costumes, who'll know the difference? Come one, come all. Bring your friends and neighbors if you like."

"I might just have to do that," I said. My watch showed a little after eight and I saw that it was time for me to re-enter the race. I dressed quickly, expertly hooking one of Ziggie's silk rep ties to renew my appearance.

"Aren't you the busy little bird," Ziggie said, watching me quizzically from his chair.

"Yeah, sure," I said, avoiding his steady eyes. "Look, I'll meet you here—say, eight thirty tomorrow night. All dressed and ready to go, okay?"

"Fine," he said. I could see a question rise to his lips and then fall back, a discarded ploy, the poisoned foil inert in the dust. "Tell me, David," he said. "How shall I recognize you in your festive guise?"

"There'll be no problem about that," I said. "Given the circumstances and in due deference to the nativity of Cadmium Greene, my costume is predetermined."

"Oh. What will you wear?"

I adjusted the knot on my new tie and started out the door. "Oh, come on, Ziggie. Get with it. I'll be wearing snow chains, of course."

And I walked toward the Libido admiring and rearranging the new kaleidoscopic pattern which Ziggie's information had introduced. Letha would have to be there. She was no more capable of by-passing a masquerade ball than Ziggie was. But in what capacity and to what end I couldn't know. At any rate, the costumes and the masks would make me legitimate. Be strong enough to keep your strength away from me, she'd written. But it wouldn't be *me* that would be there. I would be a bar of music, a dance step, a fragmented collage, hidden in crepe paper and yet completely unconcealed. We would meet without meeting, explore one another's undiscovered countries without the harsh sonorities of recognition, the weights and measures of balance and account book. It would be a trial in a fountain, a frittering frothy Maypole dance, and if the embroidered pole were insecurely set in a hastily dug trench, what was that to the dancers, what was that to the whirling pattern of the dance? Ah, Ziggie, I thought. You are truly a genius, a veritable genie in a bottle. And I broke into a most ungraceful undignified skip down Macdougal Street, eliciting sneers of adolescent scorn from the younger denizens of the Village, who were mortally affronted by any activity so patently frivolous, so spectacularly uncool.

Rennie was at Riley's table, her pink dress making an ice-cream clash of color next to Riley in his green raincoat. She noticed me as soon as I walked in the door, but she pretended not to, bending closer in conversation with Riley, looking up at me with a mock startle when I came over to the table. I shook Riley's hand and blew a kiss at Rennie (she wrinkled away from it) and I sat in the chair next to hers, gripping her left leg a little above the knee just for the pleasure and warmth of it.

"Mr. Riley," I said. "I don't want to be a tourist."

"That's the first step," he answered. "I suppose it's the biggest step."

"Look, I'm not kidding myself," I said. "I know I'm not there. I may never even get there, but I think I know the way. It's a matter of not caring, isn't it?"

He considered the question, holding me within the flashing radii of his round glasses. "It's a matter of not caring, *if you care,*" he said. "If you don't care to begin with, it's a matter of learning how to care. I'm not sure which is more difficult."

"Which war did you fight?" I asked. "The learning how to or the learning how not to?"

"Oh, I'm a special case," he said. "I've fought both wars.

Still fighting them." He made the mysterious movements beneath his raincoat to bring out a single cigarette and the bullet-shaped lighter. "You don't often run across the double-action tourist type like myself. I'm a very rare bird."

He lit the cigarette and the lighter disappeared beneath his coat. Rennie was listening to our elliptical conversation with a puzzled expression, but I kept her from interrupting by squeezing her leg in warning.

"Was once a wild Irish lad I knew," Riley said. "Wild as crab grass he was. Didn't give a flapdoodle for anything. Drank whisky and fought and whored around. A regular heller he was. Spit in his father's face. Left his mother keening on the yellow oilcloth like a banshee. Oh, he was a fine prince of a boy, he was. Used to smooch up with a little Protestant girl on the back porch while her boy friend played the piano in the front parlor. Oh, he was a very worthy fellow."

Riley didn't move while he talked, his shoulders turtled like huddled cliffs under the raincoat, the direction and expression of his eyes enigmatic in the twin whirlpools of light which his glasses made.

"Knew another young fellow too. Older I guess. He was a priest, a chaplain with the 184th Infantry. Wore the red and black hourglass patch on his left shoulder and the proud silver crosses on his lapels. A very military priest. A warrior-prince of the Church. And he was good at it too. Specialized in administering the sacraments under severe ground fire. And holding requiems for the dead. The 184th had a lot of dead. One day he shot up a whole case of communion wafers that the Quartermasters had flown in especially all the way from Guam. Just shot them up with a Browning automatic rifle. Hardly a very priestly thing to do."

Riley stumped out his cigarette and folded his arms across his chest. I shuffled uncertainly in my seat.

"What's Eliot's line?" I asked, trying to remember. " 'Teach us to care and not to care.' "

"It's a good line," Riley said. "But he never learned. Maybe that's why he could write it."

We seeped into the silence, the three of us, watching the smoke curling from our cigarettes, hearing the hollow caves of voices and clinked dishes all around us. Rennie's leg stiffened against my hand and she shifted forward in her seat.

"What in hell are you guys talking about anyway? I feel about as engagé in this conversation as the ashtray."

"Pardon us, little cabbage," I said. "Mr. Riley and I have been laying plans for the establishment of an Anti-Bureau de Tourisme. He's the President and I'm the controlling stockholder. We have declared total war against American Express, The Diners' Club, the Statler, the Hilton, Hertz, and every orange-domed Howard Johnson's that bleeds its dirty stream of curdled ketchup across the highways and byways of this our fair nation. Membership is absolutely free. All you have to do to join is rip up every charge card in your wallet. We will revolutionize the profile of the screaming eagle. He won't have a damned thing to scream at any more."

"Very funny," Rennie said. "You're both hilarious. This is what is called masculine humor."

"Women don't know anything about this," Riley said. He didn't smile. In fact, I realized that he rarely smiled. "Women never were tourists to begin with. They really don't have these problems, you see."

"Thank you, Riley," Rennie said. "Don't you men ever get bored living so close to our vegetable world?"

"No, really, Rennie," I interrupted. "We're not being pompous. At least, at the moment. Riley means this particular problem of tourism. It's a male problem, not a female one. That's all."

"Well, would somebody please explain it to me. I've had about as much male arrogance as I can take for a while." There was a shadow of hysteria in Rennie's tone that had nothing to do with the discussion.

Riley tapped on the table top with his knuckles, calling us to order. "In the beginning was the Word and the Word became flesh," he intoned. "And that's the literal beginning of the tourist problem. Adam is the created Word, the Logos, and the Word become flesh is Eve. And after the Fall, Adam is suspended between the two worlds of Word and Flesh. He's a tourist, a transient, a displaced person shuttling back and forth between two frontiers, neither of which will let him in. He's the imperfect spirit of Logos stewing and burning in his own damnable fleshpots."

"Well put," I said. "He's also the animal that laughs. Homo ludens."

"And Eve?" Rennie broke in. "She's what? A side of beef? A sheaf of wheat? A fertility symbol to be dragged out at the climax of the Mass? Christ, you men take a great self-satisfied pleasure in defining Woman so you can sit and pick apart your private body lice. And you always come up with the same definition. A mindless menstrual tide that's going to ebb and flow come hell or high water. And you take about as much responsibility for it as the kids who scale seashells on the beach. Oh, Jesus, you all make me sick!"

I tried to soothe her consternation but she wasn't having any of me. She just looked once at me and the sepia loathing was naked in her eyes. Riley, however, was unperturbed and firmly gentle.

"Hush now, mavourneen," he said, and there were traces of the brogue in his mouth. "The Woman has her problems, to be sure. But they're not the problems of the displaced tourist. They're more the problems of the unwanted orphan. The Woman needs to be loved from the outside so that she can love herself. The Man has to learn to love himself before he can love to the outside. It may seem like a thin hair of difference, but not when you weigh the soft tenderness of Our Blessed Lady against the hard justice of Her Son the Tiger."

He picked up his umbrella, the red-enameled ferrule glowing like a fire. "The good Lahd made a perfect Creation, but He didn't find it necessary or suitable to build comfort into it. He valued both joy and suffering as much higher virtues than the easy laziness of the sloth. And remember—" He tapped me on the shoulder with the tip of the umbrella. "He who pays the piper picks the tune." He nodded his head and tapped me again. "You can choose to sit it out if you want, but if you're going to dance, you dance to His tune and no other."

Riley tapped me once more on the shoulder and then leaned down and kissed Rennie softly on the forehead and began to move away from the table. I grabbed the ferrule of the umbrella to halt his exit.

"Thanks," I said. "Thank you, Michael."

His fine teeth gleamed in a broad smile and I looked directly into his blue eyes for the first time. They were as distant as the sky, as close to hand as the heavy depths of the sea. Our eyes held for a fraction of an eternal moment and he flourished his umbrella like a drum majorette before tucking it under his arm.

"You can call me Mike, David," he said and he smiled again. Then he marched out of the Libido like a green-armored parade and I had an uncanny sense for a second that my right hand was burned where I had held the umbrella.

"I still don't know what that was all about," Rennie said impatiently, unconsciously rubbing her forehead. "I never heard of Riley kissing anybody and I know he hasn't talked that articulately in years." She stopped rubbing her head and looked at me warily. "You have a nasty sneaking way with people, Riegel. You get into places you've got no business being. How did you know that his name was Mike, anyway? He's always been just plain Riley around here."

"A lucky guess, princess," I said. "What we used to call in pinochle a good speculation."

Rennie was strained and uneasy with me. She picked up her pocketbook and the gesture was self-protective and furious. "Don't play games with me, David," she spat. "I'm no doll or toy. I want some straight talk out of you."

"You call the shots, honey," I said. "You name it, I'll try to deliver."

"Oh, let's get the hell out of here. I'm sorry, David, I'm in a ragged way tonight." She put her hand in mine. "It's not your fault. You've been very sweet."

I paid the check and we left the coffee house, walking aimlessly from the lighted places to the dark, from the bright bubbles of activity where people laughed and jostled to the silent sleeping corridors of grey emptiness. We navigated the crooked old streets, the sudden recessed triangles of grass and trees, the shadowed corners where the faded neon blinked in methodical surprise. We walked on the broad avenues, the click-clack of our footsteps ringing the only sound in the canyons and gulches of stone, the traffic lights changing from red to green in oblivious obedience to the merciless clockwork within. The cross streets were ominous and imposing with their brooding ornate stoops, the warehouses and factories hanging high in the thin grey air, clean of human curve, bereft of human cry. A smell of moist ash was impregnated in the air, drawn from east and west on the savage currents of the foghorns, exploded into the streets through the iron gratings of the sudden subway roar, collected and dropped as from a giant scoop in the clatter-smash of a massive Diesel semi that cramped a sidestreet in a single gear-splitting rush. It was the time of night when the city returns to itself, secure in its stone-and-iron solitude. The trees and tidily begrudged patches of green were tightly chained within rusty iron fences, the see-saws in the playgrounds balanced and threatening in their horizontal agony. A swing swayed slowly back and forth, vacant, silent, amputated in the grey and black panes of darkness. The leaves under a glaring yellow street lamp were a thick vicious green, oily and palpable like a gouache. Squeezing the great rectangle of rock on either side, the two rivers chopped liquidly at their crests, biting patiently at the network of bridges which needled above them, at the wet cracked stone which held them to their channels. Far out in the harbor, cold in the warm night, the gleam from St. Ambrose lightship stabbed impotently in the ice-grey sea and two tiny red-and-green airplane flashers were lost in the roiling grey clouds. And we walked in silence, skirting from time to time the drunks and derelicts on the sidewalks and in the untended doorways—the fetid night plants in the city's stone.

We stopped finally at a bench by the river bank. Its green-painted wood was coated with the invisible sweat of the night, its silent wooden grief rocked by intermittent moans from passing scows, the jagged guttural rattle of the work-boats in the night. And we sat and huddled together for a warmth that might make a tiny heat in the city-cold night.

"Give me a cigarette, Riegel," Rennie said. And she lit it and blew the white smoke into the wisps of river fog which curled around us. "Okay," she said. "Now tell me about you. And tell me straight." She sat forward on the bench, looking at the river and I couldn't see her face.

"Whatever you want to know, baby," I said. "Barkis is willin'."

"Who are you? What are you doing? And what do you want from me?" She still wouldn't look at me. "And no bullshit, please."

"Okay," I said. "No bullshit. Well, I'm a schoolteacher from Boston. And I'm in New York at the moment trying to hunt down my errant wife. And managing to get kind of errant in the process myself. And I don't want anything from you except what you want to give. And that's about it, except I'm sorry."

I don't know what I was sorry about, but I *was* sorry. Whether for me or for Rennie or for just all of us, I don't know. Why do we have to say everything? Put things into words and fix them where they are unable to flow along the tender passages of the feelings? Why can't we merely hold ourselves in electric sentience and let life warm us like a river? I still couldn't see Rennie's face, the hot color of her eyes. She was taking long quick drags on the cigarette and then she snapped it disgustedly over the balustrade into the water. We watched the orange thread fall though the night and disappear.

"Crap," she said. "You're no different from anybody else, are you?" She was facing me now, but I was glad that her face was shaded by the dark. "You know, Riegel, you and your big intellectual problems about Man. You've got no variety at all, you men. You're all one big sloppy same thing. All your faces are the same when you get close enough. The same expression, the same weak brutality. You say the same goddamned things in almost exactly the same ways as though you invented them yourself. As though there were a training school to turn you out all the same. And you're so damned proud of your big potent virilities. As though anyone cared. As though anyone needs you for much."

"I'm sorry," I said.

"Oh, shut up! I even knew that that was coming too. That's all you're ever able to say. With all your words. I had the stupid idea that you might be a new kind of thing. That for just once I'd get a different technique, a different need. You didn't pant at me and tell me I was too good for you. And you didn't smirk around corners and tell me that you and me—we were the bad kind. You were kind of fun, you know. Kind of straight fun. But you turn out just the same as everybody else. Wifey is out rolling in the hay, so you want to bounce off the nearest knothole you can find to get yours back. Goddamn it—is that what being adults is? Dirty stupid adultery!"

"Whatever you say, Rennie," I said. "If you want to think that—"

"Oh, shut up, for Christ's sakes! Don't play humoring rational animal with me. I've been there already, you know." She took another cigarette from my side pocket and lit it herself, fumbling in her handbag with the matches. "You want to know about me? Shall I tell you about me?"

"I know about you," I said. "You don't have to tell me anything about you. You're one of the sweet ones of the earth." I didn't want to know about her. I had enough to know that I couldn't control and I didn't want any more. But she was talking elsewhere—to the sliding slosh of the river, to someone's ear that had never listened, that would never listen. That she would shout into with her last clay breath and it would never know.

"Don't kid yourself," she said. "I'll tell you about me. I'm a real doll, I am. A beauty, a doll. I'm married, you know. Does that surprise you?"

I thought about it. "No, I guess not. Lots of people do it. Anyway, I'm a little hard to surprise these days."

"Well, I am married. And he's sweet and kind and he has the patience and understanding of a saint. And he thinks I'm skating on the thin edge of a psychosis. When he talks to me his voice has that terrible therapeutic calm in it as though he's thinking if he hits the wrong pitch he'll shatter my brain like a wine glass."

"Is he wrong, Rennie? Are you that close to the edge?"

"Oh, who isn't, for Christ's sakes? Who isn't?" She turned nervously around on the bench, inspecting her face in her hand mirror by the muted light of a distant street lamp. "I *love* my husband, Riegel. He's the nicest man I've ever known. And I honestly and truly love my children. I'm telling you the God's honest truth."

"I believe you," I said, cupping her shoulder in my left palm.

"Then why can't I live with them and be happy? Or just be even neutral? Why, Riegel, *why?*"

"I don't know why, baby. I don't know anything," I said, searching desperately among all the words I had heard and read for something that would make sense and be honest, searching and discarding and finding nothing. We sat on the coarse painted wood, looking into the wispy dark, listening to the waters lap at the rock beneath our feet. The night was long, but a graded glow was beginning to rise in the eastern sky.

"You pick up your chips and you ante up for the next hand," I said.

"What does that mean, for God's sakes?"

"I'm not sure," I said. "It was something a friend once tried to teach me."

The glow on the horizon was spreading out in broad horizontal fans, imperceptibly glaring into false light.

"My mother," Rennie said. "She's one of those people with so much life that she throws two shadows."

"Oh," I said, trying to imagine Rennie with a mother.

"If she knew about me, she'd kill me. And while she was doing it, there wouldn't be the slightest expression of recognition on her face. She wouldn't even have to avoid looking at me while she did it." She turned her face toward me again, and her big eyes were wet. "Why, Riegel? Why can I stand that my husband knows about me? And even that some day the children will know? But I'd kill myself if my mother knew.

I'd kill myself rather than have her look at me and not see me."

"What about your father?" I said. "You don't mention him."

"Oh, him." She began to dab at her eyes with a handkerchief. "He died years before he died. He never counted at all."

The city noises, muted and indistinct in isolated sea wails and rumbles of traffic, were starting to quicken, to merge and blend into a still quiet but more definite blur of sound.

"Sex," I said. "It's not that all important really. Like Riley said. Lost tourists and unwanted orphans. And I can't love unless I'm whole inside and I can love myself. And you can't love yourself unless you're loved in the important undemandable ways. And we use one another just to keep above water. Coupled cripples pairing off a bad leg for a bad arm. A bad soul for a bad heart."

I helped Rennie off the bench and we smoothed the dampness from our clothes, turning to walk west in the streets of the false dawn.

"But you know," I said. "If a man could come to a woman whole in himself, he could really love. And if a woman had no need inside herself for his love—then—"

"Then what?"

"Then it wouldn't be sex or love at all. It would be way beyond that—a dream of joy. What the eye of love sees in itself. Why, baby, it would make us stop being children, that's what."

And we walked slowly back to Rennie's apartment, helping one another up and down the curbstones, crossing the streets with care for the early morning automobiles that sped heedless down the grey open thoroughfares.

# Interview

WRITERS AT WORK AND PLAY: XXXVI

*"Earl Rovit"*

*Our interview with Mr. Rovit took place in a hotel room in mid-Manhattan. When the interviewers arrived, Mr. Rovit was already present, hidden behind a large stand-up screen in one corner of the room. Judging by the smell of the room and the amount of cigar smoke that billowed over the screen during our conversation, Mr. Rovit is an inveterate devotee of the noxious weed. The windows were half open and the drum of city traffic, punctuated by the vagrant cries of pigeons, intro-*

*duced the only audial interruptions to our discussion. Mr. Rovit was exceptionally courteous in his answers, taking time to think before he spoke, speaking distinctly and emphatically, as though he were accustomed to using words. At times his volubility was lost to our tape recorders, but we have attempted to reconstruct the lacunae in the tapes as conscientiously as possible. The interviewers were unable to agree as to what kind of distinguishing regional accent flavored Mr. Rovit's speech, one holding it to be a variation of Rocky Mountain breeziness with a touch of Midwestern nasality, the other feeling certain that he had discerned an element of Upper Delta slovenliness. Impossible to represent on paper was the tone of joviality in Mr. Rovit's address. He chuckled and chortled constantly, and several times he giggled in a high-pitched nasal whinny. The interviewers are agreed, however, that the tone of his jocularity was geared to high-spiritedness rather than maliciousness.*

INTERVIEWER: Would you care to comment on your desire for anonymity, sir? You have gone to rather strenuous lengths to confuse your identity, not only in the context of your novel, but in the peculiar conditions under which this interview has been arranged.

ROVIT: Yes, I prefer to remain anonymous. I have what I consider to be ample reasons for doing so.

INTERVIEWER: There are pervasive rumors, I might say, that your desire for anonymity is based on the fact that you are a distinguished personage in your own right. It is said, for example, that you are actually a very respected theologian. Some say that you are engaged in a successful political career.

ROVIT: The two are not necessarily exclusive.

INTERVIEWER: No, of course not. Would you care to comment upon these rumors?

ROVIT: No, I'm sorry. I would prefer not to.

INTERVIEWER: We are rather interested in your choice of a nom de plume—that is, of your pseudonym, "Earl Rovit." Is there any particular significance or symbolism suggested in that name?

ROVIT: Oh, you mean as in Mark Twain or Lenin? No, I don't think so. At least not consciously. I chose a name that would be short enough to look attractive on a book jacket. I didn't want one that would be overcommon or too eccentric. So I just made it up. Earl Rovit. It may be that some industrious depth psychologist could find all kinds of things in it, but I, at any rate, am not aware of them. I just hope that there isn't anybody really named that. (Whinny) That's all I need, a *real* "Earl Rovit" nibbling at my royalties!

INTERVIEWER: Good, thank you. Now, Mr. Rovit, could you tell us something about your working operation. Do you use a typewriter? How many drafts do you make? Do you have regular working hours? You know, something about the sheer physicality of the creative experience?

ROVIT: Yes, I think I see what you want. Well, I always write on a typewriter. In fact, I write everything on a typewriter, including letters, notes to the milkman, etc. When I have to write anything by hand, my knuckles just clench up like a cholent. (Giggle) If you know what a cholent is. I like the solidity of a typewriter. When I'm working well—it's very rare—there's a physical rhythm between me and my typewriter. I'm kind of bouncing in my chair literally assaulting the keyboard. Most of the time, of course, it just sits there and I sit in front of it and we have nothing to say to one another. Like old married couples.

INTERVIEWER: Could you tell us how long the actual composition of *The Player King* took?

ROVIT: I can tell you almost exactly. It took a little over three months and ten years. It's my only novel, of course, but

I have a hunch that this would be my average gestation period for each novel.

INTERVIEWER: And did you work on the novel during this entire period of time?

ROVIT: Whenever I got the chance.

INTERVIEWER: And you lived in Paris most of the time while you were working?

ROVIT: Paris? I've hardly ever been in Paris in my life. And I dare say that I could find better things to do with myself than work on a novel if I were lucky enough to be in Paris. (Whinny) As a matter of fact, I did the largest bulk of the writing on a farm I own in Cornish, New Hampshire. I find, oddly enough, that I need an impoverished rural setting outside my window before I can visualize an urban landscape.

INTERVIEWER: Excuse me, Mr. Rovit, but I'm a little confused. In the Journal sections of your novel, you're quite explicit about being in Paris during the writing of the book.

ROVIT: No, no, no. That's not me. It's the writer of the journal that's supposed to be in Paris.

INTERVIEWER: Yes, of course, but doesn't he more or less represent you as the author of *The Player King*?

ROVIT: Represent me? How could he represent me? He's just a character in my novel. I'm not in my novel. I wrote it. It seems to me that a reader would have to be terribly unsophisticated to confuse the two of us. Daniel Defoe is not Moll Flanders, is he?

INTERVIEWER: I see. I'll have to think about this. Meanwhile, there has been a matter of some controversy in the critical reception of *The Player King*. You deliberately break into your narrative line, the David Riegel story, with various intruding devices—the journals and so on. Some readers feel a bit unhappy about this. Cheated, as it were, of the traditional illusion of reality which a novel ought to aim at. How do you justify this obviously purposive destruction of form?

ROVIT: Well, that's a very complicated subject and I doubt that I can offer a really satisfactory answer. If a reader feels that what you call my "devices" are intrusive, then I certainly can't justify them to him. But first I would suggest—just in passing—that nobody can destroy form anyway. If it's *there* at all, it's there because it has proved impervious to destruction. However, in terms of your question I would say this. It's my novel. I made it myself. And I had the notion that I ought to be able to do whatever I pleased in it. Like Fielding educating his readers on the fine points of the mock-heroic form. Or Thackeray addressing his readers directly. I like that. I like a writer to talk to me when I'm reading him. Maybe he has some interesting things to say that just won't fit into his particular story. So why shouldn't he just say them to his reader while he's got him quiet and undistracted?

That's only part of the answer, of course. Beyond this, it seems to me that I have been trying to learn the lessons that Lorca and Brecht have carved out in their revolutionary theater. Perhaps form is eternal—it's a nice notion, anyway—but the techniques of illusion have to be always changing according to the needs of the age. In their plays they deliberately open up their illusions to their audiences, inviting them to sit on their stages, help move scenery, and participate as players rather than bored spectators. And this strikes me as being awfully important. They showed us that it is possible to open the doors between the act of creation and what the esthetician calls the "sensitized perceiver" and still have a very healthy engagement. And my little devices may be attempts to achieve the same kind of effect.

INTERVIEWER: I think I understand what you're driving at, but I'd like a slight amplification on one point.

ROVIT: Ask and it shall be given.

INTERVIEWER: Well, as I understand your allusions to Lorca

and Brecht, you're talking about a different kind of "open door," so to speak. Many of your readers, at least, feel that your intrusions into the narrative line are closed rather than open doors. That they're too formidable. They don't invite the reader anywhere. They just close him out and confuse him. Do you see what I mean?

ROVIT: Yes, and of course again I can't defend myself against that kind of criticism. But let me try a different explanation. The most formidable doors in all architecture are the front doors of cathedrals and brothels. You know the famous doors of the Cathedral at Strasbourg, for instance. Incredibly massive and lacy. You'd never think of opening them. And I know a set of doors in a little bordello in Wilkes-Barre that would put the Brinks people to shame. But the point is, you can always get into a church or a brothel through a side door. Light or dark, feast day or work night. The front doors are come-ons, not come-throughs. They're to be admired and used as directional clues, not as entrances. I suppose, staying with the metaphor, that this is what a novel may have in common with churches and brothels. If you're going to observe them from the outside as esthetic objects or constructions of historical interest, then you find their doors forbidding. But if you have a need to get inside, then they're just a part of the total structure and you use them to discover the dingy way in. Without attempting to defend my own lack of craft, I should say that I had something of this sort in mind.

INTERVIEWER: Well, that's very interesting. You mentioned Lorca and Brecht. Are you especially concerned with the theater?

ROVIT: No, not any more. Having witnessed the supreme performance of a most magnificent Pocahontas in the days of my halcyon youth, I have found that the theater holds no joy for me any more.

INTERVIEWER: What about other writers? Do you feel particularly influenced by any? Who, for example, are your favorites?

ROVIT: I can humbly boast that I have been influenced by almost everything I have read. I love and envy all writers, but I do not conceive of writing as either a game of genealogical influences or a competitive barrage of typewriter clicking.

INTERVIEWER: You mentioned earlier that you own a farm in Cornish, New Hampshire. If my memory serves me right, there is a famous secluded writer who lives in Cornish—

ROVIT: Excuse me. I rent out my farm to lots of different writers. They like it up there because the living is cheap and you can get a direct dream to New York. I don't remember any of their names.

INTERVIEWER: This is perhaps an unfair question and you can choose to dodge it if you like. Since the question of identity seems to be central in your novel, could you tell us— Well, do you identify with any special character in *The Player King*?

ROVIT: Well, naturally, in some sense or other I have to identify with all of them. But if I understand the drift of your question correctly, I would say that I identify most completely with the woman in the white dress who weeps on the stairs somewhere toward the end of Chapter II. She represents for me an important resting place for myself in the novel.

INTERVIEWER: Thank you, that's very interesting. Would you be able to say—this is a dangerous question—could you tell us candidly what disappoints you most in the novel? What you would like to change or add if you could?

ROVIT: Now that's not really a question that I ought to answer. It would put you people out of business if we all did that. (Giggle) However, I would say two things. First, I didn't put any symbols into my novel. I had a whole bunch of them, you know—Freudian keys, Jungian roses, a little green wagon—things I'd been saving for a long time—and I got so involved in the writing that I just forgot to put them in. And, second, I desperately wanted to have a passage that would do the same thing in prose that Gluck's flute obbligato does in music. I don't know how many times I tried for it, but I always ended up with a bad imitation of Gilbert and Sullivan.

INTERVIEWER: Thank you, that's very candid of you. Are you presently engaged in a writing project that you'd like to talk about? A new novel? A play, perhaps?

ROVIT: Sorry, I don't care to discuss it.

INTERVIEWER: To go back to your comment about the author of the Journal sections being just another character in the novel. His name is Leo, isn't it?

ROVIT: Yes, I think so.

INTERVIEWER: Well, Leo is pretty certain that he is writing a novel, isn't he?

ROVIT: He hasn't the slightest doubt of it. At least, most of the time.

INTERVIEWER: And David Riegel is fairly certain that he is telling his own story?

ROVIT: Yes.

INTERVIEWER: Then—I wonder if you see what I'm driving at. If both Leo and David are so sure of their independent existences—and, after all, they're wrong, aren't they?—then—well, it's ridiculous, but—isn't it possible that you too—

ROVIT: That I'm also a character? Oh, yes, indeed, I'm quite a character. (Giggle) You can quite believe that.

INTERVIEWER: Hmm, I see. I think I see. Well, one final question which is not really as frivolous as it might appear. Do you by any chance happen to have a pimple on or near your nose?

ROVIT: (Giggle–Whinny)

*Rex Koenig*
*Roymi Kado*

# Journal

*27 May:* The day after my thirty-sixth birthday. Thirty-six. Swooping on the downslide of the Biblical roller-coaster offering. And how many men do you actually know who manage to collect the full ride, the three score and ten? Damn few, and those not among the nicest or the most humanly valuable. Not that it pays to brood over; quite the reverse, in fact. On principle I abhor and reject birthdays. Either every *now* is a new birthday or the term is a mere statistical convenience. Surely I am much newer today than I was ten years ago—much more open, much more exposed, much more possible now than then. (Although Eva would make me old to keep herself young.) And yet this truth is canceled by a grosser truth—the slow depreciation of the physical machine, sinews and ligatures stretched beyond easy resilience, gnarled knots of atrophy like log jams in the musculature, the steady drip of the life fluids exiting from the body's orifices like disappointed wedding guests. When the body is less and less a body of delight, what sordid stuffs must it find to nourish on? Almost every night before I fall asleep I am afraid that I will be dead in the morning. Every gruesome offal of hospital gossip that I have ever heard rehearses itself anew on my body's stage—the silent cancers, the quick arterial cramp, the valve, the membrane, the tissue that surrenders and betrays. The children gave me two Jacques Fath neckties to celebrate my age and Eva rejoiced in the adornment of the corpse. I know that she is in comic league with the undertaker, but the paralyzing thing is that she is unaware of her own murderous ferocity. Or do I create it out of my own fervor to live?

We struggle to think of birthdays as milestones, kilometer markers which measure how far we have traveled and how far yet we have to go. This is abominable, but the heavy inertia within us, the expendable cellular matter of our being insists on some false sureties of duration. "Unless soul clap its hands and sing," declaimed Yeats from the euphoric peaks of his new birth. But the physical death in his loins scooped the false mountain from beneath his illusory summits: "Nor is there singing-school, but studying monuments of its own magnificence." The orotund rhetoric saves it for poetry, but not for truth. When the body ages, it moves from activity to passivity. I do not welcome the music of hand-clapping in a graveyard.

Doren sent me a birthday present from Istanbul, a pair of Turkish touchstones—two round smooth stones to roll in one's fingers, to make a warmth in one's pocket. I didn't even know he knew my birthday and he is not the giving type. It's very strange. No note save the enigmatic "For Birth from Doren." Eva thinks it's meant to symbolize the Gemini of my zodiac, but Doren's mind is more devious than that. Gemini! That I, a natural Leo, should be born out of place in the astrology of character! The pathetic twin of the ravening lion is the lamb and if I do not slaughter him within me, he will swallow me in a bleat. Is Doren replacing with his gift something that he has stolen from me? Birthdays.

It's so easy to look backward, to connect the numbered dots of time into a vaguely meaningful curve of development, to measure the fatal pressures of this thrust and that condition. And is this not the paltry impotence of thought—to be always concerned with the past? To regard all action, human or otherwise, as a fait accompli, and to substitute fancied theorems for the heavy-footed fate of indeterminacy? Most of the pacifists I know keep large vicious dogs which they feed on wheat germ and whole milk. And the most eloquent advocates of the fluid life I find to be personally land-locked. Mann's Dr. Cornelius loved History because it was dead and I suspect that all life under the sterile glass of contemplation is not life at all, but a poor death mask which fools no one. Nor, Lord knows, is action a solution, either. The indeterminacy of the *now* is no romantic mistress to be seized and cajoled into compliance. Complete possibility makes action impossible. He who would ride the see-saw between action and thought merely substitutes the bondage of endless change for internment in an abstract contemplation camp. Fire or ice—we are free to will our deaths either way.

Or can we smash the vise of the either/or with the double engine of the both-and-neither? Words to soothe the death pangs of our birthdays?

Goddamn it, who would not be a shaman if the bellying

wings were to offer themselves and the icy distances to contract into a tiny heat?

Doren has been sending us a steady stream of color postcards to mark his wide crescent into the old lands. He travels eastward toward the dawn, toward the fecund beginnings, the photographs etching a more archaic, more depersonalized virility than any we now can know. My way is west, toward the backward beginnings, toward the harrowing personalization of consciousness, toward the modern weakness that we are rapidly losing the strength to bear. East and west, beginning and end—one elastic girdle of time without time, space within space. But we miss him—his acute intelligence, his uncanny perspicacity, his brutal energy. Partly because of his going, Paris has receded from us, leaving an island of familiarity and stale knowledges in its wake. That is, if he has really gone. I keep *almost* seeing him in unexpected places, his back turned in a brasserie, his silent loping walk at the end of an alley, his face averted through the rear window of a taxi. Twice I've come suddenly into a room where Eva has been alone and I would have sworn that he was there and I could almost see the shapes of his adder words diffusing in the air in front of the ornate Venetian mirror. I remember him once saying that the misery of civilization could be comprehended in the pathetic paradox that the Almighty (Blessed be He) labored powerfully to turn the Word into Flesh and mankind has since strained and twisted trying to force its poor flesh back into words. Eva maintains that she is glad that he is gone, but there are lines around her eyes which have never been there before, and I cannot read them.

And so we sink or rise into time—the manuscript pages becoming thicker and more oppressive, the weather finally warming into a very late spring. The glass enclosures on the sidewalk cafés have been taken down and stowed away for next winter, multicolored umbrellas sprouting up festively in their places. The gendarmerie have changed to their round white ridiculous summer caps, but they do not smile underneath them. Yesterday we took the children out to Versailles and we sat in the grand gardens while Mark and Lily dripped ice cream on the marble and trimmed grass. Mark wanted to know where the head of the bad king was kept and I told him I was wearing it on my shoulders. The children rode an ancient merry-go-round under the awesome stare of a very blank and white statue of Diana. Her helmet was weighted low over her forehead and I thought that now, as then, this is her kingdom and she rules without opposition here. And thus we must all strive to become citizens of some other country.

And whose voice speaks through me now? So many other voices, so many other rooms of transient possession. Is there one who possesses a lease hold or are we a collective union, a confederated babble of being—one after another elbowing his mean way for his moment with the microphone and spotlight. There is that in me, Whitman said, I know not what it is, but it is in me. Did he really know or did he make it up for play or salvation? Koestler calls it somewhere "the grammatical fiction," the socially constructed "I" that History and Psyche collaborate upon for their own convenience. Man needs a handy garbage pail to throw his kitchen experiences into, the dregs and peelings of our eatings and evacuations. Whose voice is mine? Is there an entity responsible for the saying and the said? And if there is none, no radical integer—single, simple, inviolate—then am I merely pushed across the page in a long, grotesque, mildly amusing prat fall? And to entertain whom? A reader who is also without?

# Four

Some nights, or so the old song goes, are made for love; but that one, or the remnant that was left of it, must have been especially tailored for fitful raggedness, for that gauzy glaucous state between sleep and wakefulness when dreams hover above the consciousness like visitors that are uncertain of their welcome and so they shift their weight from foot to foot beyond your reach, fearful to come in and too brazen or phlegmatic to wholly go away. At such a time the body becomes an entity entirely separate from the self; you can *feel* your liver, you can touch with unerring fingers the poised aneurism, the cellular decay in the brain tissue. You take a deep breath and you hold it tightly and you feel your body life beat in the pulses like a maddened prisoner in a box. The throat muscles stiffen, your temples riot in a cold throb, and the gulp of breath is forced back into the lungs and life has won or lost its match and the struggle begins anew. The awareness becomes more lucid, abstracted, as though you were bobbing in a crystal bubble above yourself. And the knowledge of the senses sinks into the dark, congeals into weight, into opacity. This, I take it, is what people mean when they say they tossed and turned all night. But my consciousness of the severe division in myself was too abrupt for such a description. My body tossed and turned but I was outside it. I could feel my hair growing silky and fine along the insides of my thighs, I could sense the dead flakes of my scalp, the churn and congestion of my blood in its channels. I was so conscious of my body that it and I were alien, were enemies, were connected only by that hostility that is the inevitable distance between that which knows and that which is known. I observed my flesh growing grey and I slept in submerged patches of time—eyeblinks between the black-and-white frames of a motion picture reel.

What in that lost fragment of time was dream and what was reality I could not hope or want to know. The visitation of demons, the bared teeth of a son, the lecherous curl of a lip in a daughter's leer. She seemed to be poised above me, her long conical breasts pendulous from their own weight, her face pallid in the lost light of the grey room, her eyes, her sepia wild eyes. It was a horror of bitter whispered curses, of obscenities turned loose from the clammy adhesion of tired flesh, of sweaty protestations of plunge and lurch, of entrance and stale broken-hearted release. The eyes, the terrible hurt eyes. The white outrage of the bicep side of the upper arm, the bluish hollows where the muscles had learned to sag, the lewd pressure of stomach and time-rippled straining thigh. Her thick breath seemed to be in my throat and I was strangling in hair, twisted and netted in hair, in mucous suck of lips, in sour skin. I burped for air in a closed bell jar and the eyes darkened and the side of my neck burned with pain. Mother death, daughter death, sister death desire. Evil wicked sister-soft. I reached up into consciousness and it dropped, silver grey, on my forehead. The side of my neck stung like a razor burn. My sheets were wadded into thin piles like dirty slush. I shivered in my wet and the room seemed to have changed its shape. I fondled the side of my throat as though I were nurturing a rare flower. My body, at any rate, seemed to have returned to me.

It was only when the window was squarely filled with the dull-yellow light of the unmistakable morning that I fell finally over the dark edge and found some three or four hours of clean blankness to disappear into. And even these were not completely vacant because voices and faces—or, better, echoes of voices and shadows of faces—pursued me on the margins of my dark awareness, talking, menacing, laughing with spite. I was reading a long book, reading swiftly and raptly, turning page after page because it was terribly important for me to find out what was going to happen. I could see the words lined out across the pages, but it was such a long book, so many more pages to read, and I feared that I would not be able to finish it in time. And I somehow knew even in my reading that it was a book that had never been written. That I was the author and the book was me. I tried to focus my attention in one great single concentrated squint to dissociate me from the reading, but it was impossible. I read with such languid engrossment that I was wholly a part of the process and there was no removed segment of consciousness to record and reflect upon. I was the reading and the writing and the words themselves and I had as little awareness of what the words meant as the words themselves did. And then, when I was suddenly at the very point of picking up my head to see a whole page in one revealing glance, I realized that I was dreaming and my sad revelation was just my waking up. And human voices wake us, and we drown, I groaned. Chambermaids *never* sing to me.

"ALLONS enfants de LA patrie—"

The voice from the next room was very high—preternaturally high, like a cat that has jumped up to a precarious branch and can't maneuver its way down again—as though it were stuck there, back arched and eyes defiantly glowing one notch below a screech out of everyone's—even its own—reach. But in spite of its height it, the voice, sustained a low piercing quality, like a kitchen knife between the clavicles. I lopped the pillow over my ears but the voice cut through the kapok, the pillow ticking, seeking armor plate to slice into pudding. I held my ears and my groin quivered and the foul shadow of the predawn madness passed over me leaving my spirit limp and clammy. Did I dream or was it—

"—de la PAtri-E—"

I shuddered and the shadow retreated. I threw back the sheets, feeling moistly like the Garde Républicaine, and I got out of bed. I let the window shade snap in a nerve-splitting crack and gingerly pulled on my pants as a first step toward piecing my morning soul together. The day had already advanced into heat. Like a mongrel bitch, I thought. Like a dry-tongued, ginger-colored bitch in full heat and the whole goddamned neighborhood is already one salivating yap in pursuit.

"—Le jour de GLWA-AH—"

I stumbled into the kitchen (mentally holding my ears) to find Rennie backed up against the icebox with her hands clasped behind her neck, her breasts and chest pushing violently against a too-small sweatshirt which advertised in faded lilac letters THE MONTROUGE BOYS CLUB, the rest of her squeezed into a once-white pair of sailor's dungarees. She was balanced on one bare foot and on the other she was rocking back and forth on a rolling pin. When she saw me, she made an instinctive covering motion, then seemingly thought better of it, reclasped her hands, and took up her broken song. She rolled back and forth some ten or twenty times and then alternated her feet, her face pomegranate red from the strain of her muscles and her singing.

"Good morning," I shouted over the screech. "Uh—bonjour, that is."

She maintained the rhythm of her feet, evidently considered the desirability of ignoring me, and without relaxing her posture, condescended to allow me entrance into the morning.

"Isometric exercises. Body tone. Latest thing."

"Oh," I said. "Fine." I backed off, clutching at my pants with one hand. "You stay right with it. I'd do it myself if you had another icebox." I kept backing off until I was out of the room. "I'll just grab a shower," I shouted. "Don't pay any attention to me."

Through the closed bathroom door I heard her launch into the "Internationale" and I ran both faucets hard in the sink to drown out the stridency of her revolutionary fervor. I rubbed the shaving soap into my face, making a thick frosty lather, and isometric exercises or no, I could see all too clearly that I wasn't young any more—not my skin or my bones or my chastened spirit. The red-rimmed eyes that glared dully at me while I shaved had delicate lavender blotches underneath them and the flesh of my face seemed old and thick to me. "Riegel, baby," I addressed myself. "I would not choose you if you were a chicken on the meat counter. No, I would not. You don't bounce so good any more. Elderly yet you ain't, but you are on the road. Oh yes, you most definitely are." The face in the mirror made no argument and we parted from one another with my cheeks scraped clean and red in mutual dislike. In the silent passage between sink and shower, Rennie's militant aubades sounded like castrated thunder, giving me a jagged series of high peaks against which I could measure my low morning mood.

"—The INter-nash-nul SO-O-O-VIET will SAVE the HU-man RACE—"

Showered and dressed I returned to a quiet kitchen to find the morning ritual concluded, coffee bubbling in the percolator, and two small places cleared on the cluttered kitchen table. Rennie was standing in front of the small narrow stove heating up some leftover pot roast in a large iron frying pan, carelessly burning the edges black while she concentrated on turning the bread on an old-fashioned stand-up toaster over a flame. The smell of burnt meat and carrots filled the kitchen with a greasy skein of smoke. I sucked at the clean taste of toothpaste on my back teeth and fastidiously scraped a piece of hardened egg yolk from my place at the table. Rennie glanced covertly at me and then studied her burning frying pan. I decorously transferred a drying brassière from the highest rung of my chair to the top of the icebox. I buttered a piece of toast and poured myself a cup of coffee, happy to refuse a serving of pot roast. Rennie set the frying pan down on the table, sat down opposite me, and began to pick at the charred ruins with a fork.

"Good morning, La Pasionaria," I said. "Sleep well?"

"I'm not complaining," she said. And then she looked straight at me for the first time that morning. She was facing the window and it may have been the morning light that added a golden tone to her brown eyes. "And you?"

"Fine. Fine," I said. Her question hung on the burnt smell in the air and then gently diffused. I hummed a few bars of the "Marseillaise." "This I take it is your regular dawn greeting?"

"Old Girl Scout songs," she said, putting a chewed piece of

fat back in the pan. "I revisit my innocent childhood in the morning."

"I guess that dates you," I said, wondering how old Rennie was. Her unlipsticked mouth was bracketed by an inverted V—two deep-scored lines that didn't completely disappear even when her face relaxed. The skin at her throat seemed to lie a little loose and there was a tautness at her temples and along the sharp ridge of her jaw. She must be about my age, I thought. A far more difficult thing for her than for me.

"Okay, let's get off this age bit." Rennie fluffed at the hair behind her ears. "You just walk softly and carry a big stick."

"Don't be stupid," I said. "You are eternal youth. You make me feel as though I were your big superannuated brother."

"Oh, drop dead."

Rennie poured herself some of the bitter overboiled coffee. The flick of hatred had gleamed again in her eyes and I felt a glowing glare of hostility in my own. We drank our coffee without talking, listening to the pigeons twittering outside the window and the morning clotheslines grating and whining on their reels. The coffee filled a vacant place in me and my irritation subsided. I enjoyed my first cigarette of the day, blowing the smoke nastily into the dusty leaves of an untended plant that stood on the window sill.

"Look," Rennie said. "I got an idea for today. Hot like it is. That is, if you want to."

"Whatever you say," I said. "I've kept my dance card open especially. I do have some plans for tonight—" I suddenly remembered them with a stomach-falling jolt. "But my day is clean and clear."

"Good. Then we'll go to the beach. I'm not working today and the trains run every half hour."

"Sure," I said. "It sounds dandy. In the ocean, there you feel free. Fact is, I'm a helluva swimmer."

"Then shut up and help me clean up this godawful mess,"

Rennie said, pushing her chair back and emptying the coffee grounds on her staunch but tired window plant.

I washed while she rearranged the clutter on the table and stacked the wet dishes in a sooty cupboard. The domestic routines of cleaning up and washing and our grotesque kitchen intimacy—the floor space was so constricted that we couldn't move without making soapy contact with one another—made me briefly sentimental. I remembered a morning breakfast with Letha when we had camped out on the banks of the Housatonic before we were married. It had been unseasonably cold and I couldn't get the damp kindling lit in the outdoor grate and she had brought a flaming brand from somebody else's fire and I had sulked all through breakfast. Or that terrible three-week period when Letha had got infected by a Wheat Germ and we had to eat trowel loads of "authentic" oatmeal every morning. And I remembered other breakfasts and kitchens. Man is at his best at breakfast, I thought. Or his worst, I corrected myself, recalling the grumphs and snarls of gallons of seized coffee and the metallic burn of frozen orange juice. Maybe it depends on the quality of the sleep that he rises from. Róheim says that sleep is the recurrent birth trauma, death's prior self that seals up all in rest. Sometimes it makes you new and sometimes it just shows you how terribly old and familiar you are. I dried my left hand on a damp dish cloth and pinched Rennie's behind.

"It's not bad," I said. "It's not bad to have a change every so often."

"Are you sure of that, Riegel?" Rennie paused over the wastepaper basket to watch my eyes for an answer.

"No. I don't know," I said. "Maybe it stinks. Maybe it's sloppy and it has no dignity. No human dignity. Which is all the dignity there is." I flourished the dish cloth like a banner and waved it over the sink. "Chameleons of the world, revolt! You have nothing to lose but your change!"

Our mood was scattered and we bumped around the tiny kitchen awkwardly.

"Well, what about you, Riegel?" Rennie asked. "Do you have any plans? What are you going to do?"

I told her briefly about Letha and Cadmium Greene, giving her a flippant outline of my grail quest in New York City and its possible denouement at the Grand Masked Ball that night. I was poking at the frying pan with a tortured ball of steel wool that kept shredding in my hand. "Anyway," I said, "I'm going back to Boston tomorrow. You do what you can, but there's no sense in beating a dead horse. Whether it wants to drink or not."

Rennie listened to me silently, a half smile hooking her lip from time to time. I had a moment of wondering whose side she would be on if it came to choosing up sides. Sisters of the Golden Circle. The Absolute Zero. How much man-hatred is the minimum requirement in the female recipe?

"So you're going to beard the fat old lion in his den tonight?" She lit a fresh cigarette and threw the match out the window. "Is that it? Do or die. High Noon. Custer's Last Stand?"

"I don't know," I said, ducking my head underneath her sarcasm. "I'll just have to see what happens." I held the pan up to the light. There were two or three small pocks of carbon which I couldn't scrape off. "People have a right to be, you know. To be whatever they are. It's maybe impossible to live up to, but you have to try. If you don't—hell, then everything's completely impossible."

Rennie released herself from her sarcasm and considered the burning end of her cigarette. "And you, Riegel? What are you trying to be?"

"Jesus, I don't know. Actually I think I'm basically a very simple person. But, you know what I'd like to be? I'd like to be a shaman, that's what I'd like to be."

"A shaman?" Rennie had begun dusting the pink wall telephone, pushing the cloth with her index finger into each of the dialing holes. The dial clicked off nine slow counts while she thought. "Shamans. Aren't they medicine men or something?"

"Something like," I said. "I don't know very much about them but I like what I hear. They mostly live around the Arctic Circle and each tribe has its own. The magic seems to be an inherited kind of deal—fathers to sons, you know. And sometimes the sons have to kill the fathers to get it. They have this double power of life and death. They can cure and they can kill. They go off into these flying trances—out of space and time—and they come down all loaded with potency. There was one I read about who made up his mind that he wanted this girl who lived with her husband and five brothers. So he ups and camps outside their cabin with a rifle for two weeks, picking them off one by one. And then he took the girl. There wasn't anybody who even tried to stop him."

Rennie was looking at me curiously and I smiled reassuringly.

"No, that's not why I'd like to be a shaman. It's that they become other people, other things, in these trances. They get a kind of knowledge and being while they're outside of themselves that seems to be absolutely unexplainable. They leave themselves, you see, and they're likely to become anything. Everything. Like maybe they work a connection to what we call the Unconsciousness in a particularly direct and immediate way. And the power they have is just the power that everybody has. Except they learn to use it."

Rennie threw her dust cloth onto the icebox and then she untangled it from the damp brassière. "Crazy," she said. "It sounds spooky to me. Astral bodies and ESP and all that jazz. I knew a Gurdjieff nut once who was all spiritual auras until he got his hands on you. It sounds like another racket to me."

"Maybe," I said. "I ain't never been there myself. And I

think women are disqualified anyway. Maybe the shaman has to go into his special trance just to experience what the woman has to begin with. Private identity can be murder for a man, you know. It's mostly something he has to break out of."

"Shit, Riegel! Are you back on women again? Don't they have identities either?"

"Not naturally," I said. "They have to work them up. And those women who make it—it's like a reward for damned hard labor. Like getting back into the Garden of Eden, I suppose. That's one of the reasons they love to be naked. With a man it's different. His body and his identity—well, you know—sometimes they're a prison for him."

"Jesus H. Christ, Riegel!" Rennie was authentically exasperated. "You got more goddamned categorical definitions for men and women than anybody I ever met. And the sad-sack thing is you don't know the first thing about women!"

"Oh, yes I do, glad baby," I said. "The first thing is the one thing I *do* know. And that's that they're different from men. And just you remember," I said, patting her lightly on the tight curve of her buttocks, "just you remember that a woman is physiologically open where a man is closed. That's of basic importance and don't you forget it."

"Thank you, Albert Einstein," Rennie said. "And if you think it's such a great pleasure to be open all the time, you got a hell of a lot to learn about women and shamans and everything else."

The kitchen was as neatened as it was possible to be without a team of dredgers to cart away the old brown paper bags which Rennie had stuffed between the icebox and the wall, and the cartons of carefully washed jars and bottles under the table. The telephone gleamed on the wall, beautifully dusted, and the icebox careened with a steady shake from its ancient motor. I switched on the radio in the other room in time to hear the last beautiful chords of the Gluck Flute Concerto. A sorghum voice lisped the enchantments of a new tranquilizer, and then static drowned out the overture to *The Mikado*. The apartment was small, unkempt, and overflowing with junk. Books, magazines, Mexican shawls, prints, ceramic bric-a-brac, a semidraped dressmaker's dummy behind the door, an empty birdcage over the radiator, some red-plastic toys strewn about on the floor. Out the one window you could see a small triangle of the Hudson through a frame of apartment houses and bridge girders. The river rode sluggishly this morning, squeezed low in its bed by the fetid pressure of the city heat. The sun was a nodule of flame in a vacant sky and I could feel the heat rising from the breezeless streets, slow, patient, and merciless like the fires of an atavistic Inca sacrifice and the bodies of the slain hung dry and limp in the ascending shimmering waves. Consumed with that which it was nourished by, I thought. Heat and air, fire and the scorched breath of life. To burn, to char, to sear. People walk slower on the concrete, their feet melting into stone, the noxious black smoke of the traffic exhaust coating their lungs, forming an impenetrable film behind their eyes, settling into the valves of the heart in thick viscous sludge. Cliff hangers, sodomites, crustaceans in concrete. I remembered the little pedagogical formula that I had used to differentiate between Dostoevsky and Tolstoy. Sodomy in the city; fornication in the country. And you had to be careful not to slur your voice on it. The city is a male structure, I thought. That's why women are terrified by it and love it so. Phallic, brutal, closed, impervious to rhythms and cycles of season and change. The city always dies from the center out. Never from the fringes in. Like a man. It organizes itself into a sluiced centrality and then it explodes. Slum clearance. Urban renewal. The metropolitan monkey glands. And it yearns for the meadow and the valley. The breasts of the mountain, the irrigational thighs of the cleft ravine.

Rennie broke in on my meandering from the open closet where she was surveying a rack of dresses. "What kind of costume are you going to wear tonight?" she asked.

"I hadn't thought about it," I said, thinking about it. "Maybe I'll just go as I am. Au naturel. That's masquerade enough."

She looked at me appraisingly. "I suppose we can fix you up." She measured my waist with the span of her hands. "I can borrow a pair of tights and an old ballet tunic that ought to fit. And we can put black spray in your hair." She squinted at me, imagining my appearance. "Sure, you'll be easy. A pair of sandals, and I have an old silver chain belt somewhere. That way, you'll be nothing in particular and you can be anything you want."

"The story of my life," I said. "I'll look like a spear-carrying extra who's lost his way to the opera house."

"Shit, you'll be fine," she said. "I just can't decide how I should go. You could have given me a little more warning on this thing. A woman takes a costume party very seriously."

"What in hell are you talking about? Nobody invited you, for Christ's sakes. I'm not going to this thing for *fun*, you know!"

"Well, I am," Rennie said deliberately. "So you better shut up about it and help me figure out a costume." She hid her hair with her hands and inspected herself in the mirror. "You son of a bitch! If you'd given me any time at all, I could have rented a wig. I've always wanted to wear a wig."

I explained eloquently that it was a man's job I had to perform at the ball. That it is a well-known fact that he travels fastest who travels alone. That where in good God's name did she think she was creeping on her crooked feet anyway. That the portcullis to Chapel Perilous opens only for the single rider. That Galahad could make the scene only because he didn't have a Guinevere on his back. My presentation was something less than persuasive. Rennie ignored my stammering protests with an expression of superior and amused disgust.

"Stay loose, Riegel," she said. "I won't cramp your style. Anyway, I think I have a right to see what your precious wife is like. I don't rent by the hour, you know." She bared her teeth at a small hand mirror, laying a piece of black felt above her lip for a mustache. Suddenly she looked very dangerous. The glint of her teeth, her lips drawn back and her chin sharp. Her eyes seemed thin—like dark tooled steel. Then she relaxed her face. "Even a cat can look at a queen, as the book says."

"From under a chair," I said, surrendering.

"From under what chair?"

"As I recall the story," I said, "the cat has to go under a chair to look at the queen."

"Queens shouldn't be screwing around under chairs," Rennie said and the wickedness leaped across her features for an instant. "Well, I won't guarantee any chairs, but this cat may just end up under the table."

"If you're so smart, why the hell aren't you rich?" I responded weakly.

But I guess I was glad after all that she had elected to come along. And not just because of the "et tu, Brute" angle, either. I was a David Riegel with her that Letha knew nothing about. Or if she'd once known, she'd long forgot. Rennie had her own saintly anchor of a husband tending the votive lights amidst the ruined choirs of their marriage. Where late the sweet birds no longer sang. And she didn't quite know me as pigeon. Not completely. Christ, the roles are too strictly drawn. One is to dance at the end of the chain, arms and feet flying in irresponsible helter-skelter, frenetically chasing the butterflies of the moment, the enticement in a calculated smile, the invitation in a voice tone, a gesture, a door slightly ajar. And the other is screwed to the fixed place, locked on the prudential rock, tugging at the chain with frozen hands, welded to the chain by a savage moral self-righteousness. And once the roles are cast, the drama moves on oiled wheels. The butterfly accelerates in a flutter of despair. The rock settles into bleak and ponderous tenacity. The glitter of the one snuffs out in a smoky puff of last flame. The other dissolves into cold grey petrifaction. The dark covers all and the chain rusts into the careless tide of repetition and time. And none of it matters at all. And none of it means anything except the anxious spasms of two human souls imprisoning themselves in their own revolting revolt. Fluidity is all, but how can you crack the rock to make it gush into fountain? Especially without a God to guide the Mosaic rod? Can fountains play—can they really play—under the illusory vaults of an astrophysical heaven? Has man the possibility of becoming truly human if divinity is truly dead? To flow or not to flow, that is sure enough the question, but is there a human answer any more?

I stopped and surveyed the dizzying ascent of my thought. Plato on a pismire, I brayed at myself. From a fart to the royal trump of doom in six easy steps. The fastest and smoothest ride in town. Step right up, ladies and gentlemen. No bumps. No rattles. Nonstop. You'll never even leave the ground. Goddamn it, you never even leave the ground.

"The hell with it, Rennie," I said. "We'll go it together. I'll be the pestle in your mortar, the shining Excalibur in your scabbard rock, the celery stalk impaled in your ice-cream scoop of potato salad. We'll go as 'Stuck Togetherness' until castration doth us part. And I will never never forsake you, you dim-witted Mrs. Macomber."

"Shut up," Rennie said. She had changed to a cotton shift dress for the street. "I'll just have to worry about my costume without any help from you. But we'd better get to the damn beach so I can tan out my bra straps for whatever I wear."

"Tan out everything," I said. "Just get a clamshell and you

can play Aphrodite rising from the waves. With all the rest of the clams. Hell, the only way you'll be able to tell one woman from the others at this goddamned barbecue will be by their pelvic distances."

And we locked up the apartment and headed for the beach, Huck Finn and Sister Jim chasing their tails out of a bigger Hannibal to a more tawdry Jackson's Island where the bathhouses were rentable by the quarter hour and the questionable pleasures of the Midway had been portaged to the very marges of the continental shelf. Beaches, I thought, as I winced my barefooted way on the hot sand, white and slightly paunchy if I let my stomach muscles go loose under my rented black-wool trunks. I bore a red-and-green-striped beach umbrella on my shoulder and I had an impulse to stop and lean against a nonexistent wall, to plead for water, to duck away from the insistent spears. The beach wasn't crowded except immediately in front of the whitewashed concession stands, and we walked beyond the lifeguards who were perched in their lookout towers like angular bronze birds in white-pith helmets. Beaches, I thought, staking my claim on an unruffled wimple of sand, quiet under the blazing sun, safe for a while from the riding breakers of waves which were low now as the tide changed from ebb to full. I twisted the thick wooden shaft of the umbrella into the soft sand and rolled out the rented blanket which smelled faintly of naphtha and citronella. I stretched out on my third of the blanket, white and suppliant beneath the overbearing sun. There was a dull red glow under my closed eyelids and the heavy sun pressed me to the hot blanket. I had forgotten how much I had missed the sun this dismal dissertational summer.

"Beaches," I drawled aloud toward Rennie, even my throat lazy in the bending warmth. "One of the last natural symbols left to modern civilization. The last physical frontier. Where land becomes sea, where sea becomes land. The mysterious passage from sameness to otherness. Beaches is wonderful."

"Shit," she said, not moving next to me. "And sand flies and broken glass and old tin. Very symbolic. My kid sister was raped on a beach. Mysterious passage, crap."

I raised myself on my elbows to look at her. "I'm sorry," I said.

"Why the hell should you be sorry, for Christ's sakes?" She rolled her bathing-suit straps down and lay on her stomach. "It happens sooner or later. With her it happened sooner. That's all."

I couldn't see her face which was turned to the other side. "Where were you when it happened?" I asked. "Were you with her?"

"Aren't you the old clairvoyant?" she said, her face still averted. "Yes, I was taking care of her. Real good care, huh?" She made a noise in her upper chest that was like a strangled giggle. "He wouldn't touch *me*. I wanted him to. But the sonofabitch, he had to have her."

"I'm sorry," I said again.

"Oh, can it," she said. "Sorry sorry sorry. He was sorry too. And me and my sister. And Daddy. Everybody was sorry. You're all alike. The only thing you know is rape. If you can't rape, you sulk and pout. And we're supposed to feel guilty about it. All that stupid crap about nothing but laying on top of a woman and forcing her to your dirt. And when you get past a certain age and the creeps with the sleazy shirts and the sideburns don't whistle at you, then you're all finished. Thrown away. Go get a knitting job with the Ladies Aid."

I couldn't see them but I knew her eyes would be sepia-wild again and her lips would have that half smile that would make her teeth show. I fixed my gaze at a knotted blue vein low on her ankle. "I have a daughter, you know," I said irrelevantly.

"So?"

"I'm scared. I'm scared for her."

Rennie rolled over to look at me. Her hair was loose and clotted with sand and sand had dried at the corners of her eyes. There was no pity in them. "Don't be scared for her. Be scared for *you.*"

I shook my head uncomprehendingly.

Rennie laughed at me. "You just don't understand, do you? It wasn't *that,* stupid. That was just a thing that happened then. I had learned to hate long before that. I was born hating you. All of you!"

"But what—"

"Oh, Christ, I don't want to talk about it. You wouldn't want to understand even if you could. Go on with your lecture about beaches. I don't know why I started with this anyway."

I lay back on the blanket and tried to put my head under the clean blaze of the sun as though to wash out the dirty things that had crawled into it. I let my hand touch Rennie's hip gently, but she wriggled away from it. "No, please. Talk about symbolic beaches. Please," she said.

"Oh, it seems stupid now," I said. "I was just thinking how many great beach scenes there are in modern literature, that's all. As though the modern writer is compelled to leave the city for the beach when he really wants to make an important statement. Whether he knows it or not. City scenes are fine for satire and psychology and all, but he runs like hell to the nearest beach when he wants a real confrontation of personality. That's all. It was just a kind of idea."

"I don't know," Rennie said. She seemed to be thinking it over and taunting me at the same time. "Matthew Arnold and Whitman . . . And the good J. Alfred, of course."

I hadn't remembered the Prufrock lines. My idle speculation was beginning to coagulate. "And Stephen Daedalus finding his vision of beauty on the banks of the Liffey. Or Proust with the girls at Balbec. Or that great scene where Aschenbach dies to death on the Lido. Or Meursault shooting the Arab. Why, Jesus, even what's-his-name, the banana-fish story. That's a hell of a beach scene."

"Coincidence," Rennie said. She was openly taunting me now, playing me like an eager fish that is so securely hooked that you can afford to give it slack. "Pure coincidence. If I bothered to remember as many books as you do, I could name you five mountaintop scenes or bathroom scenes or anything else. It doesn't mean anything."

"It has to mean something," I said. "There's no such thing as coincidence in literature. And these are all city writers. But they've got to get out to a beach at least once. They don't have any choice about it. Anyway, if I ever did write a novel, I'd have a beach scene in it."

Rennie scooped a little hole in the sand, sifting the sand from one hand to the other. "Is that what you're going to do? Are you going to write a novel?"

"Sure," I said. "Tomorrow. First thing after I brush my teeth."

"No, really, Riegel." Rennie had made a sieve of one hand and the flow of fine sand split into separate sprays as it cascaded through her fanned fingers. "You talk about novels all the time. Why don't you write one?"

I rolled over on my stomach to let the sun burn at my back. When I opened my eyes there were jumping black disks at the circumference of my vision. "There are many good reasons why I would not write a novel," I said.

"Among which are?"

"Among which are the following. First, I am too old and respectable for such nonsense. Second, I know too much about them. Third, I have nothing to say and I can't make anything up. And fourth, I don't even know well enough who I am to get a beginning point. Add to all this the fact that I'm not bright enough or brave enough and that I care too much and that's some of the reasons why I would not write a novel. And, anyway, there are far too many of them right now already."

The separate piles of sand under Rennie's hand were beginning to hump into one uneven pyramidal shape. We both watched it as though it were a serious construction. "That's something like the way I felt about having babies," Rennie said. "Before I had them, that is."

"That's a ridiculous analogy," I said. "Typical female logic. Babies are one thing and novels are another. It's impossible to get them confused."

Rennie swept her sand heap level and lay down under the shade from the umbrella. "Shit, you won't write a novel, Riegel, but not for the reasons you say. Because you're too scared and self-enclosed. And if you were a woman, you wouldn't be able to have a baby, either. All the doctors would tell you that you were perfectly healthy and you'd blame your husband, the poor bastard. When all the time it would be you, squeezing your knees together, terrified that you'd lose some precious part of yourself. Christ, you could write a novel, but you won't."

I sat up and glared at her. It was a stupid argument, but I was furious, both by her insistence that I would not write a novel (I certainly knew I wouldn't but I wanted it to be my choice) and her assurance that if I were female, I wouldn't be able to have babies. I felt at the moment that I could have billions of babies, a salmon spawn, the mackerel-crowded seas.

"Why don't *you* write a novel, then?" I sputtered. "Why don't you write a novel and leave me alone?"

"I already had my babies," she said smugly. "I've shown what I can do."

"Oh, Jesus Christ."

Rennie tilted the umbrella to rearrange the patch of shade,

broad red and green stripes serrating her upper body from the reflection of the sun through the coarse canvas material. She shook the sand from her thick hair.

"Look, Riegel," she said. "I'm not a very nice person. I probably never was. But when I was pregnant it was something else. I could forget my precious self and become really open. I mean *really* open, not just exposed. I kind of gave me up for a while so they could live in me. Isn't that what love is supposed to be, Riegel? You know all the words. Isn't that it? And don't think a woman is just a nest when she's pregnant, either." Her face was bright with her recollection. "I mean—well, we made one another, do you see? I mean, it was both of us making. Not just one way. I gave me up to them and I was more me than I have ever been. And if you can't understand that, you can't understand anything."

"I'm not talking about that," I said. "You change the subject so fast I don't know what I'm talking about. All I said was having babies and writing novels were different things, that's all."

Rennie closed her face to my argument. "You just go on and believe what you need to believe. But I should think that once a novel was started, you'd have to work the same way on it."

"But why the hell should anyone start one in the first place?"

"For love," Rennie said. "For love or for hate. They're the only things that people will give themselves up for."

"Jesus," I said, getting up and brushing the sand off me. "Anyway, if I ever write one, you damn well won't be in it. I can assure you of that."

"You won't have any choice," Rennie said. "You won't have any choice at all."

Rapes on the beach, novels and babies. A wild virago with eyes that could remind you of a tiger hiding behind a cocker spaniel. And me standing sandy like the Colossus of Rhodes with the beginnings of a moth hole in the crotch of a borrowed bathing suit. What was not possible in this new age of anxious complacency where each new moment was the new brightly packaged, market-researched product of a consumption economy dedicated to consume us all? The sun was savagely hot and the tide was beginning to slice more sharply into shore. Low chopping waves were cutting into the beach at a slight angle, breaking slightly before the shore to hiss into hungry foam. The horizon was long and low, and far out a freighter was steaming east, its smoke a blurry smudge on a clean blue sea and sky. My skin was tight and tingly in the sun.

"Come on, Rennie," I said, pulling her to her feet. "Pretend you're a little girl again."

She fixed her bathing cap, balding her head under the green rubber so that she looked for an instant like a lobotomy patient prepared for the table. She slapped my hand away from hers and ran for the sea. She ran with a stiff back, her legs skittering awkwardly on the loose sand, and I drew up beside her. We raced straight into the water as though we had made an unspoken pact that he who broke stride would lose everything. It was viciously cold in the first headlong plunge, the icy shock of the contact tearing at the blood and draining the skin away from the bone. I flailed at the water with my arms and legs, jackknifing like a porpoise, snorting and spitting the salt sea into light-refracting sprays until the unbearable shock receded into cold numbness and then, finally, a flowing bracing warmth, and I floated on my back easily and restfully, riding the swell of the water which had gentled itself to my body. Rennie was treading water near me, her face drained white under the bathing cap, and large colorless drops hung on her cheekbones like misplaced pendants. I splashed and ducked, diving deep to scoop at the spongy bottom, my skin as cold and wet as a fish, my body buoyant and wonderfully young in the illusion-making, ageless sea. I inhaled a deep breath and churned far out from shore in a fair Australian crawl (a little too much roll to the shoulders, mouth not quite correctly cupped into the hollow of the left collarbone for the quick snaps of air, but chest nicely arched and legs kicking beautifully from the thighs with just the right limber whip of ankle and instep). I returned more slowly in a clumsy mélange of backstroke, butterfly, and tired dog-paddle.

"Whoooosh!" I panted. "I can taste every goddamned cigarette I ever smoked!"

My arms and legs were heavy weighted from pulling and thrashing at the sea, and I breathed from a dry burning pocket in my lower chest, but as I bobbed my head to blow bubbles and salt spume, cupping my hands downward and funneling at the surface of the water to dredge small belching geysers, I felt spiritually pressed and dry-cleaned, the buttons of my soul securely sewed, the frayed places expertly treated with concealing vinegar and lemon juice. If I had had the breath I would have whooped like a triumphant loon. Rennie was squatting in about three feet of water, letting herself be rocked by the stronger current. Her face was thrown back to the sun, her breasts ridiculously pinched into the top of her bathing suit like a pair of inflatable water wings. She was making jellyfish motions with her hands and her lips had a bluish tinge.

The tide had crept farther into shore, the waves higher and more insistent, breaking with a white rolling crack between where we lolled on the cradle of waters and the yellow sand. The long curve of the beach sat on top of the water like a tenuous elongated golden crown, silent and assaulted by the majestic writhing of the ocean's coastline curls. Mighty Poseidon, I thought. Oh, you nasty seagreen Neptune, you are a very very big god and I would rather be on your side than against you.

"Come on," I said to Rennie. "Your lips are getting blue. We'd better dry off."

We kicked our way out of the tide, our legs churning the water white, and we ran easily back to the retreat of our red-and-green umbrella, scudding the water from our legs and arms, the fine sand coating our feet like a confectionery powder. My arms and back were already dry and hot from the sun when we reached the umbrella and I toweled my hair, feeling the sun burn on my back. My trunks were wet and cold and I dried my legs carefully where the black wool had dripped. Rennie was already on the blanket, her eyes abjectly closed to the sun's unabated glare. The sea had unstrung the tautness of her facial muscles and she seemed to be involved in some warm golden communion beyond my company and I felt fretful for something. I lit a cigarette, stowing a second behind my ear as a spare.

"I think I'll take a little stroll," I said. "I might just pick up one of these pretty little girls here."

"Don't strain yourself, Riegel," she drawled without opening her eyes. "Me and Letha, we wouldn't want you to come down with a hernia, you know. What the hell good would you be then?"

I didn't like Letha's name in her mouth, but I throttled my sarcastic response because I couldn't see where I had the right to protest. Instead, I squeezed some moisture from my trunks to trickle on her sun-dried legs. "Go to hell," she said indolently and threw a sandy clam shell in my direction. It missed and plopped flat at my feet. "Go to hell and don't bother to write!" She was almost asleep under the sun.

I surveyed the beach, preening a little like Balboa, and walked through the soft sand toward the water until I was standing on the hard cool margin flattened by relentless tides where the small stones were rounded and shells were embedded smooth on the surface. About two hundred yards away on my left was the crowded center of the beach, children splashing and playing with pails at the water's edge, sunglassed people squatting blanket to blanket, thermos to thermos, in the community pattern of a crazily knitted afghan. Behind them was the boardwalk with its whitewashed front of low buildings and concession stands. Civilization had moved to the sea. To dip its big toe into the water and chase back shivering to the humming warmth of its transistor radios. A child screamed with delight under the curling slap of a wave and the same transient wind brought me the coiled tail of a singing commercial. We hear human voices and we *do* drown, I thought. Oh, thou great sly wink of eternity, indeed. To my right the beach curved way out into the water ending about a half-mile distant in a thin spit of sand and rock where the high grasses came down to the sea. Except for a few brave scattered encampments, this part of the beach was clean of people, and the audacious sandspit with its waving grasses fingered into the sea as though it were a desolate archipelago in some savage communion with the ocean that it dared to split. I headed to the right, walking where the tide licked at the shore, pressing my feet into the just-damp clay where the earth asserted itself against my human pressure, rounding and smoothing my footprints with a careless inexorable ease. The sun was at my back and my bones were free and loose. I licked at the dried salt on my shoulder as I walked.

Horses, I thought. They train horses in the water's edge to strengthen their ankles. Black and shiny in the dawn, striking with a cantering spray the silver blanket of waters. Horses and water. No, horses and the silver-crested waves. Fluid synonyms in the mythic poem of Creation. Their manes and the way they toss their heads. And that they are in wild powerful motion and are not human. Not human, that's the important thing. Beauty and power are never human, even in people. A beautiful woman loses her humanness in her moments of true beauty, and there can only be moments of true beauty, like the single flashing fold of the wave fall. Beauty and power are symbolic definitions. Nonhuman ideals dreamed by human hearts. An igneous rock reshaped by a glacier. A musky-cupped flower. A torrent rising from the dank earth. Power must always corrupt and beauty dehumanize. Oh, what a gorgeous sea drift of weakness and ugliness—wens, warts, and slackened muscles, thou clobbered humanity, straining for a few flash moments of inhuman transcendence! God help us human clay, washed and abraded by the waves we seek to become. Christ was a great horse and his hooves outshone the sun and he ran well on water. But I'd still take Man o' War on a muddy track and give you three to five. Rennie has somewhat horse's eyes. Set right and lovely above her nose, but not in horses. Too large and glazed and dangerously blank of expression. Human expression, the only kind that is. What is it that horses see that makes their eyes so dead? And waves too. Eyes that large should make some human saying or be pinched from their sockets like grapes. That night driving the toll road in Maine near Scarborough Downs and out of the fog four horses abreast (they of the indubitable Apocalypse) galloping right up the middle of the white line toward me. Their heads and tails wild and high and their eyes caught in my long beams. And I was damned lucky to pull off the road before I thought, because even after they passed I didn't believe in them. Who believes in nightmares or night stallions on the ribboned turnpike where the toll booths are outlined in green light? But it was their eyes—their chalked lost eyes that unnerved me, long after the clack of their hooves on the asphalt had faded into my incredulous blood. What messengers of dread? What sweating harbingers of desire? White-combed horses and waves and waves of horses. And I will ride the tide, scattering the crest of the waters, my hair a river of sun, my body a terrible rolling breaker. Man can be a charging horse and a wave in his combing strength, oh my chevalier. And woman a horse. Letha a magnificent horse of supple undulation, warm-flanked and curved and flecked with moon-scented spray. The male horses of the sun and the pale white horse of the moon that you meet and ride once only. Dark stranger, fetlock and cannon bone, cleaving uncleft hoof. And the spavined swollen horses of the quotidian, rheumy and swatched with dung, belly bowed and beaten for a ration of mash, a rotted apple fall, windrift and salt.

I scuffed my feet through the tide, trying to walk where the water washed finger thick, but the currents were erratic and sometimes my feet were on dry hot land and sometimes the waves whipped over my shins. I was almost at my sand-spit, its shape elongated now from my new perspective, the grassed dunes ending in a small protective outcropping of rocky wall which formed a secluded inglenook against the sea. My cave of winds, I said. I hereby name and claim you as Riegel's Roofless Cave of Winds. The busy center of the beach was a tiny multicolored flag behind me and a seagull stood carelessly on the promontory of my cave, the sky bleak blue behind his dirty white ragged wings.

"Come on in, gull," I said. "I would carry you over my threshold, but you look like you smell from garbage. Come on, gull, old brother. We'll stake our claim together."

I clambered over a large piece of driftwood to enter my rock-enclosed sanctuary. In one corner were the burnt-out logs of an old fire, and three brown beer bottles filled with sand were propped upright on a low rocky ledge. They've jumped our claim, I said. The busybody bastards. Robinson Crusoe and the modern footprint. And when the new Christopher skids along the skin of the moon, whose dead fire and drained bottles will greet him? Echoes of what guitar and concupiscence wrested from the primeval wilderness, pounding their hammer of love to the pulse of the silent space and the steady drip of the liquid night? I picked up each bottle by its neck and deliberately threw them, one by one, over my wall and into the sea fringe. The Russians, I said. They beat us everywhere. And I sat on the driftwood and lit my spare cigarette from the stub of the smoked-out one, burning my fingers in a sharp commemorative pain. I sat back and smoked at the sky, lazy and yet tense in a sudden peculiar way. My friend, the seagull, gave a hoarse cry and sailed aloft and away, the ribbed vans of his wings unbelievably long and motionless in his soaring glide. I watched him disappear and watched the smoke of my cigarette wreathe the alien rock and sand.

The sun was hot and it sat on my head and barred my cave, making me prisoner of the vacant sky. The new De Sade of the beach, I thought. An ex-ninety-eight-pound weakling chained to the rock, moldering in the fat of his own unlived past, a wallowing off-white whale. My cave of winds was breezeless and eerily silent. The cramped telephone booth of the soul where some other John made long distance calls to nowhere. You're back, Riegel, I teased myself. You've wandered back to the primal synagogue of the sea, the legendary sunken synagogue where the prayers are chanted in sea syllables and the beaded mollusk studs the memorial wall. Yis-ga-dal v'yis-ka-dash sh'may ra-bo. Bow thy head and bend thy knee and render thanks to The Holy One, Blessed Be He. What is man, that thou art mindful of him? He is born in the morning and in the afternoon he withereth away. Let him rejoice in The Lord and sing praises to His Holy Name. Thanks. Gracias. Me and the graceless vertical rock and the requiem tide of the sea. A metaphysical missile launched for nowhere, orbiting beyond nowhere, transmitting poignantly garbled messages which ricochet off the icy barriers of nowhere into nothing.

*No, Riegel, Reb Nobody. That's too easy. Too fashionable. I would say rather too difficult.*

*So say it. But you must not believe it.*

*I'm not strong enough. It needs more strength than I was given.*

*Don't make yourself so small, you're not that big. Was given to you the same as was given to everybody.*

*Well that's not enough. For me or anybody. For me as everybody. I have just enough to see that there's nothing. That there's just nowhere and nothing. For this, strength? Who needs it?*

*Everybody. Everybody needs it and has it for their need. There's still a something else. And where there's a something else, there is also the possibility of a somewhere and a someplace.*

*Words. Words words words.*

*No, Riegel. Beneath words.*

*Beneath words is silence. Is nowhere.*

*Beneath words is the something else. Something that can't be said in words.*

*Say it near then. Say as close to it as you can.*

*A laugh. A pride. A true sob. A small dignity.*

*That's pretty skimpy. Or dangerous. And even if it were so, it's certainly not fair. Not just.*

*So read the small print already. On the back. Where the backbone is. Or isn't. And then you can wail into the wind.*

My cigarette had burned itself out and the wool of the bathing suit was beginning to chafe me badly around the crotch. I kneeled on the sand and dug a shallow burial pit for my cigarette, smoothing the sand and marking the place with my finger. Then, on a sudden impulse, I retrieved the beer bottles from the wash of the tide and I planted them carefully in an equilateral triangle around my cigarette-butt grave. What was it that Letha had once written me? "Memorial is constant for those who live alone because all *was* and *will be* is now." Maybe it doesn't quite apply, but is there anyone who lives un-alone? I looked down on my ceremony in the sand—mute, absurd, correct. Let him who is without sin throw the first beer bottle, I said. At his own glass house. I twisted my back and stretched my arms in the air, feeling the burned skin on my shoulders crinkle and tighten. You got a good burn, I said. You'll remember this day for a couple of weeks. With fire. Wispy freshets of cloud had formed on the low horizon and a short land breeze quickened, eddying into my recess, cooling the back of my neck. There was a sudden odor in my nostrils—pungent, familiar—a green smell from the deep roots of the earth. Basilica? It pressed together in a sudden blossom of scent and then it was gone and I pursued it unsuccessfully as the breeze shifted and the clean earth-free smell of the sea swept my cave. A new quiet settled on the rocks, allowing me to hear the far distant squeaking honks of the gulls in their riding. I climbed backward over the driftwood door, mesmerizing my three dead soldiers to keep perfect watch, to guard and to listen for me on the outflung bastions of my tentative bridge. Pray for me in the hour of my, I said to them. Of My. Which is to say, My Own.

I walked slowly back to our umbrella, squinting at the sun which was lower now in the sky, aware of the beginnings of a slow itching and grating rasp on my skin. Riegel, you stupid bastard, you have got yourself a beauty, you have. You will dance the lobster quadrille in the flesh tonight and the fish will suck at your claws. Something there is that's supposed to be good for a sunburn. Vinegar? Calamine? The sins of the flesh find their scarlet compensations, all right, all rightee. I ducked once in the water, flooding the long cracks in my back with cold brine, rubbing it into my eyes and ears and the crevices of my groin. You walk and you run, you dodge and circle in measured or frantic pace, and you never leave the hollow after all, the dull vacant place without sides.

Rennie had already folded up the umbrella and the blanket

by the time I reached her and we shuffled through the careless sand, leaving an unmarked emptiness behind us, an uncertain memory of where we had lain. We walked stiff with salt toward the bathhouse where our clothes waited in cold wire baskets marked by numbered metal tags. Once I turned to look back at the spit of sand within which was concealed my cave. It fingered steadily into the sea and the waving grasses above it were like hair.

The long ride back to Rennie's apartment was slow and tired and peculiarly separated. An important pipe had burst in the bathhouse and we had to sit in the train with the dried sand and salt, gritty and unflushed from pore and hair follicle, abrasive against the cracked-leather seats of the superannuated railroad coach. Rennie and I sat side by side, our flanks strenuously not touching, and I found that it was a major effort for me to respond to her with a bare minimum of civility. I wanted to leave the seat, go into another car, get off at the next rattling stop and rid myself of this bitter, scratchy life weed that the sea had draped around my neck. What had *she* to do with me, this dried-up agonizing left-over piece? This inaudible whine, this insatiable demand, this pretentious beggar, this Woman. Come on, entertain me, humor me, strawberries and rose blooms in January, give me what you promised, give me more. Come on, worm-man, give me what you promised never to give anyone. Give it now. Crawl into my heart, man, CRAWL. Crawl into the grave of my heart and I'll bury you up. All we want from you is your life—lick, spittle, and slop. And then we'll pay you good, you stupid humiliated bastard. Pay you good for your gentlemanly wince, your sag, your give.

I shuddered in fear at my own revulsion, hectoring myself like a collegiate debating team for my injustice, for my irrational disgust. And the magnanimous segment of my nature seconded the assault, joined in the judgment against me, elevating my companion to a high queendom of charitable elegance. To no avail. I pretended to doze in the hot varnish atmosphere of the old train, holding myself away from the body that was so close to mine as though it were an erect salted fish. Some nuns were nibbling at a cool conversation across the aisle and I tried to bathe my flushed mood in their white bird trough of harmless serenity. Our car lurched to a stop every five minutes, discharging the little fresh air that was left to us and taking on new reserves of soot and fetid heat. Rennie was leaning her cheek against the unopenable window pane, her chin propped on her elbow, her face resolutely away from mine. Her indifference to my mood, perhaps a hypersensitivity and not an indifference, softened me. Why not give, I thought. What are you saving it for? Precious little you have left if all that is left is you. Left, RIGHT, LEFT. I had a good wife and she LEFT. First they fire you, then they tire you, then, by golly, they LEFT. I moved my arm like a machine and gave Rennie's hand a squeeze—a friendly squeeze, a comrade's squeeze. She turned her face toward me and there was some mild affection in it underlying the mocking contempt. Her mouth framed the words "Screw you," but they seemed not unfriendly meant.

When we finally descended to the subway, the cramped subterranean air (spewed from how many grimy pouched mouths?) settled around us. It was newly noxious to my fresh sea lungs. I felt absurdly outraged, violated, I who was almost divinely elected, I who was Achilles and Patroclus to these grey people who had lived their day in the air-conditioned placidities of sidewalk and elevator shaft while I had struggled nakedly with the sea and sun. My fury at Rennie had sunk below my awareness and I pushed her through the turnstile as The Dependable Friend, the buddy with whom one had gone through the napalm and the torture tent. My face in the mirror of a chewing-gum machine was brick red and my hair was bleached and powerfully tangled. Against the red and under my eyebrows, which were now more silver than blond, my eyes were a shocking sky blue, cold and wonderfully remote from my glowing heat.

Our subway car swayed clumsily on its ashen route beneath the city and now we sat together, letting the curved weight of our bodies touch and meet in the erratic blinking of the lights. Two elderly men were conducting a fierce Yiddish argument in loud guttural voices, shouting to make themselves heard above the roar of the car. The smaller man clutched a worn padlocked brief case to his vest and his straggly mustache was wet from the spittle of his teeth. The other was completely bald—not just his head but his features as well—and he exuded a loathsome self-containment that was ice to the other's passion.

"Pinchik? Pinchik, that's also a cantor? Once I hoid from Pinchik a Kol Nidre and I foist understood why a pogrom!"

"Vaismir, and this is a man with ears in his head." The little man was on the verge of explosion. He beat at his brief case with his right fist. "To sit on, with ears. To wipe with toilet paper, those ears. From the divine Pinchik you hear like this, and from the frog Koussevitsky you pretend from music. By you a fart is a violin and when that godly Pinchik, may he rest in peace, sings like the angel of the Lord, you get diarrhea. May your piles bleed eternally."

"Tapeworm."

"Cancer smear."

"Dung beetle."

"Pork dropping."

They left the car at their stop, not missing a syllable in the debarkation, the short man lunging again and again into his antagonist, who moved with an angular glide, erect and unbrokenly brittle. Two small Puerto Rican boys chased up and down the aisle during the entire ride, stopping from time to time to seal their faces against the windows to watch the red lights in the careening darkness, shouting "rojo" when our car swept by a signal marker. The automatic doors swished open and swooshed shut to usher in and out the passengers with their folded copies of the *Mirror,* the *Vorwarts, La Presse,* the *Times,* the pressing underground news of the day in seditious Cyrillic script, stained with cheap printer's ink, oblivious to the cerulean pressures which gave subway surcease in their token ride. I tried to fix my mind's eye on the bright image of my sandspit but it had already become fuzzy in the murk of the tunneled world.

"Rojo!" one of the boys shouted, pointing at my face and giggling. The other boy caught the joke and was convulsed, trying with native gentility to hide his rudeness.

"Su madre," I said in my best Robert Jordan manner, and I winked at them, stunning them into embarrassed silence. "I *doan* provoke," I said to Rennie, giving it the Akim Tamiroff accent, but she had transferred to her own shuttle line, clicking off her private stops and starts of red and green.

"I could wear hoops," she said. "But they're an awful bother and they always bend in the worst places."

"Yes," I said, remembering the party. "In taxicabs, telephone booths, and especially in small latrines. They can get awful messy in small latrines."

"Oh, shut up," she said, not really listening to me. "You don't know how important the right costume is to a girl. I haven't been to a costume party since I was in high school and I had on so many petticoats that nobody could get near me. I love costume parties, but nobody has them any more."

"Don't kid yourself," I retorted pontifically. "We're always in a costume party. And the door prize is death. Everybody wins. Nobody ever loses."

Back at Rennie's I took a long shower, lathering my red flesh thick with soap, taking special care with the sore places—the tops of my feet, my scoured and puckered shoulders, the fronts of my shins and thighs. My genitals seemed shrunken from their contest with the sea, white and receding from the fiery forward thrust of the rest of my body. It must be a law, I thought. Riegel's Third Law of Thermodynamics. When man is cut off from nature, he concentrates all of his sensual life in the genitalia. The congested swell of his vitality, his knotted sea and sun tides—they contract into a long pocket of fury and nuzzle against the cotton double-weave of his Jockey shorts and the sturdy grip of the Talon fastener (sturdy now, I hope) and the rest of his unused flesh crawls into impeccable rigor mortis to stuff a shirt and crease a pants leg. But reverse the conditions, throw man back into nature, into the sea and sun swirl, and his kneecap throbs in ecstatic tremors, his very armpit breathes an Alexandrian musk. Ergo, Riegel's homely root remedy: Cast your seed no more in the subway, but into the seashore, and it will return a thousandfold. Hesitate not a moment longer! Now is already too late. Nature shrinks white and puny before the tropical growth of an aluminum civilization. We have too efficiently cultivated our pubic gardens in the dwarfed Japanese fashion and with each drainfall we lose another erg of stature. Buck Rogers of the twenty-fifth century, he of the anti-gravity belt, he will have but a pimple to point with. It could be worse, I thought. Better a pimple point than no point at all. Look on the sunny side, Mama always said.

All my sides were sunny sides, but except for a sandpaper rasp when my skin brushed against anything, I wasn't too uncomfortable. It will take about twenty-four hours, I thought, recalling previous sunburns. Then you'll really be crawling the walls for sure. Consider the next twenty-four hours a provisional postponement, not a reprieve. What's the difference, anyway, the graduate-school part of me said. The next twenty-four hours or minutes or seconds is always a provisional postponement. Never a reprieve. Sunburn or shadow burn, it comes out to the same thing. I turned on the cold water spray full force to shut me up, gasping in agony under the rinsing shock of the icy jet. And that will teach you, Riegel, I said to myself. As though you've ever learned anything anyway.

Rennie was very busy in party preparations, her sewing basket open and strewn on the long-suffering kitchen table, a great scurrying to and fro on collecting and rejecting visits to various neighbors in the apartment house. From an upstairs overweight ballet dancer (he had since plumped himself into interior decorating) she had secured for me a once-golden, now mustard-brown, set of tights and a mouse-grey tunic, sleeveless and inoffensively without shape. From across the hall had come a worn pair of sandals which she had inexpertly painted with silver nail polish. And the promised silver chain belt, each link a grotesquely carved Egyptian slave bowed under the weight of a pyramid of imitation silver, grasping at the buttocks of his bent-over brother. If I practiced a strict economy on my breathing, I would be perfectly fine. And my final touch, a bottle of jet-black hair spray ("nontoxic, safe for children and pets") with detailed instructions on the methods of application. Rennie herself was in a dressing gown, her hair captured in a hideous gauze drying bonnet, her face as greasy as Gertrude Ederle's with cleansing creams and skin revitalizers. She was alternately sewing and swearing at a swatch of black jersey which covered the table and drooped on the linoleum floor. She pushed the pieces of my costume at me distractedly.

"Go out and find us some masks, Riegel," she said. "Nothing fancy. Just the plain thin eye strips."

"Dominoes, they're called," I said. "It's important to know the names of things."

"Sure," she said. "Dominoes. And what do you think Letha will wear? What do you think her name will be?"

I glared at her and she bit nastily at the black thread in her hand. "Stay the hell out of my way for at least an hour," she said. "I got a million things to do and I hate to sew."

I gathered my dancing materials into a heap and left them in the other room. Sure, I said to myself. They all hate to sew, but Jesus God, they sure love to reap. And who pays the freight, picks up the pieces, takes all the blame? Jesus God. Not far around the corner from Rennie's building I found a small variety store which sold, among other things, party favors. The merchandise which was not party favors included a cornucopia of bewildering delights, hung, stacked and strewn in a musty smother of disarrangement like a Dickensian rag-and-bone shop. There were yellowed cardboard displays of presmoked calabash pipes, progressively longer and sharper jackknives, and gauntlets of keychains with every conceivable talisman and heraldic device known to the professional trade. There were shaving brushes made from genuine badger bristles, heavy-duty rubber flashlights, nipple shields for nursing mothers, reticules for silk stockings cut in the shape of outrageous lace panties, hard-boiled-egg slicers, dishtowels stenciled with scenes and homiletic phrases from the Old Testament ("An Apple a Day Keeps Eternity Away"), snake-skin belts, mousetraps and rat poison, sweatshirts stamped with the heads of famous composers, varieties of non-narcotic sleeping potions, medically approved "pep-up" pills, scattered back files of the *National Geographic,* the *Watchtower,* and *G-8 and His Battle Aces,* cracked dishes with the militant profile of General MacArthur embossed in imitation gilt, dusty cases of Moxie and Dr. Pepper, several hampers of "dry goods" (brassière inserts, pillow ticking, elastic hose, and discontinued models of ribbed corsetry), and an awesome higgledy-piggledy construction of canned soups topped with lethal-looking bottles of lye and disinfectant. I breathed the suffocated air in grateful wonderment, this fetid democratic emporium of American miracles so quickly dying to the time-study machinations of the modern business engineer, and I felt not that I had come home, but that there was a home for me somewhere on the shelves, in the counters, perhaps behind the nylon-Acrilan foul-weather suits that were squeezed cruelly on hangers in the back room. That if I sought sternly enough, I could someday find my place on the cardboard display, the shoe and boot boxes sized and stacked against the wall. But I shrugged my foolish metaphor away and bought the dominoes as ordered, discovering also a magnificent plastic Cyrano nose with a celluloid pimple on the end of it and a short black false beard. When I returned to the apartment Rennie was locked up in the bathroom, so I dyed my hair over the kitchen sink and dressed myself for the evening in the living room.

It could, I suppose, have been much worse. The tights had a treacherous tendency to stretch in places where I would rather they had held me in and they sagged where they might very well have not done so, but I reassured myself somewhat ruefully that this was not, after all, a competition of Apollo. Nor Dionysus either, I reminded myself. Not, at least, I hoped. My hair was as stiff as tarred hemp from the dye, but with the tunic close-belted around my waist and my silver sandals shining blotchily, I arched myself in front of the mirror and decided that I would do passably well as Hermes Trismegistus. If it were dark enough. When I affixed my nose and beard I gained both a more saturnine and bulbous cast—a clownish Iago, a brutally wicked Feste. The elastic bands of the beard and nose were uncomfortable on the back of my head, so I put them in an inside pocket of my tunic.

There's no rule, I thought. No rule that says you have to stay in the same costume all the time at a costume party. I pirouetted ungracefully in front of the mirror, foolishly well-pleased with myself and my garish ensemble. So must Cotton Mather have looked when he rode out to Salem for the famous witch-twitching. I took a professorial stance, arranging imaginary notes on a nonexistent podium, and I admired my absurd reflection like a dedicated moon calf. I should have been a pair of sagging jaws, I told myself, lecturing to floors of silent "C's." You'll have to do better than that, Riegel, old mouth, I warned myself. If you don't want to be flunked-sunk by C. Greene and black thy hair. Mistah Kurtz, he good. He lechers real good, he does. Like a French-horned horny goat. And to the best lecher belongs the spearls. Thank you, Andrew Jockstrap. I made an insinuating bow to the mirror and received a dark swooping curtsey in return. The dyed hair in the mirror was a shock which changed both the shape and the expression of my face to me. My inside self stayed blond, and outside I darkened like an agitated pool. The outside and the inside merged gently, then drew apart. Maybe I should drive a stake into my heart, I thought. A sharp green root biting at my red life. Maybe I already have, I said.

The water was running again in the bathroom and I knew that Rennie's one hour would doubtless stretch into two, but there was time, there was time. I wandered the room aimlessly, first trying the radio but finding no music except the dubious gland cries of teenagers, which I was pleased to squelch off. I picked idly through the scattered magazines and books but found nothing to hold my interest. The large drawer of the desk held a mare's nest of strewn papers—photographs, receipted bills, letters, match books. I riffled through the pictures, eager at first to investigate the yellowed images of Rennie's other lives, and then suddenly indifferent to them. Not curiosity, not guilt, not compliance—nothing connected me to the disordered contents of the drawer. I was as transient as the mailman; I was merely leaning against the doorjamb waiting for the registry slip to be signed. Way in the back of the drawer I noticed a bisque doll's head with movable eyes in the scooped-out sockets. The nose was badly chipped, and when I picked it up the weighted eyes swung back and forth and the cool porcelain lay suggestively in my palm. I put it back in its place carefully, feeling somehow tender to it, and I rammed the drawer shut.

I was possessed by a restless kind of energy, but I didn't want to read and I couldn't sit still. I played with some paper on the desk, drawing tight symmetrical arabesques, making lists of words and meaningless phrases, pushing nouns mercilessly into tortured adjectival positions. I wrote, "I have been spiced by the condiment sea," and then I crossed it out disgustedly. I can make a better poem than that, I said, and, effortlessly guiding the words into their own cramped patterns, I wrote:

> The basilisk of joy was gazeless not awry
> And the morning fell with heavy yellow eyes.
> Strike the fisher's bell to mark the hour.
> The hunter? Let him skin his raw delight
> For party trophy. 'Tis well to sacrament
> A wound so blind and water-sharp.

I scanned my lines unhappily, finding two dreadful metrical breaks and one that was just barely defensible. The imported Elizabethan cadences and the literary diction tromped into mangled silence whatever I might have wanted to say and I crumpled up the paper and threw it into the wastebasket. Riegel, old bard, I said. You have been heisted on the prongs of a belletristic education. You've sucked up so many words that they keep you away from yourself. You're a 175-pound lacuna in a plagiarized text. The sea girls, old brother—even if they *did* sing to you, how the hell would you hear them through your noise? Better had you been born ten years earlier so that you might have learned to believe in economics or psychology instead of literature. Marx might at least have saved you from this. Given you a smoother grip on the prophecies of Isaiah. Or the good Sigmund, that intrepid prince of the phallic profit. Nobody really gives a damn about saving the world. Not Karl or Sigmund or even the doughty Jonathan. All anybody wants to save is a relatively solid seat for his own precious ass. Which is precisely what the rules don't allow. Spiritual hemorrhoids, the one absolutely unpardonable sin—the incurable disease of man. And literature makes a precious poor stool for man to perch on in the anguish of his bowels. You believed in the aroma of rhythm and imagery and now you've learned to become an anal stench in your own nostrils. Write a novel? Not on your life. And who else's life do you have, hochim? Let's summon the devils to come up through the trap at the end of the fifth act, shouting with Faustus, "I'll burn my books," and still salvation will avert its frosty face, its best profile. Redemption, brittle Riegel, be so ashamed of thee. Suck on, old parasite. Leech to the arterial phrases of a schoolbook anthology, a Freshman Reader. Suck deep and swell up and dry. "A wound so blind and water-sharp." That's not too awfully bad. I wonder who I stole it from.

The old-fashioned bolt on the bathroom door ground roughly in the lock several times and Rennie made her entrance, posturing in front of me like a fashion model. You couldn't tell that her bra straps were tanned out, but it made no difference. She was dressed in tight black Danskins which hugged every swell and hollow of her body. Her head was encased in a black witches'-peak hood and she had drawn cat whiskers on her cheeks with an eyebrow pencil. From the base of her spine, whirling like the trailers on a Maypole when she turned, was a braid of green and black tails. She wore long black gloves, at the tips of which she had fixed pointed green fingernails. She was not just a cat. She was the Primordial Cat, somnolently dangerous and sinuously feline.

"How you like?" she asked, purring fiercely in front of me as she admired herself in the mirror.

"I like," I said. "You're the cat that wants to look at the king."

"The hell I am," she said, wheeling on one toe so that her tails whipped around and rested momentarily on her behind. "I am the Cat of Nine Tails."

"You'll have to wear a sign," I said. "There won't be no man with the concentration to count them all."

Rennie inspected my costume and grudgingly allowed that it would pass. "What the hell," she said. "It won't be too light there and people do a lot of drinking at costume parties."

"Thanks," I said. "That strong vote of confidence is just what I needed." I looked at Rennie again, trying to measure the purposeful expression in her eyes. "Cats, like women, are strange creatures," I said. "They almost always have reasons for what they do."

She spun around again for the mirror, her many tails provocatively whip lashing her rear end. "A cat can look at a king," she said. "Or a queen."

"All men are kings," I said. "Even me. And I suppose that all women are queens too. But what particular little regicides are you plotting in your furry little head?"

She made no immediate answer. She just purred in front of the mirror, arching her back and sharpening her claws. "Wouldn't it be funny," she said as though to herself, "wouldn't it be funny if Letha came as a mouse?"

"Oh, no!" I said. "You stay the hell out of my business. And you keep off Letha, you hear!" Rennie opened her lips, showing her teeth to the mirror. She let just the tip of her tongue protrude and she let it caress her teeth. "Look, you," I said. "Cats are very durable beasts, but they have two fatal weaknesses."

"Which are?"

"The first is curiosity," I said. "And it leads to the second. Which is that they drown easy. Do you understand me?"

"*Meeaoow,*" she said, unconvinced, scratching at my face with mock ferocity.

I folded my overworked Haspel into a shopping bag while Rennie checked the water and the gas, slipped into her raincoat, and locked up the apartment. We took a cab to Christopher Street, the driver eying my costume and Rennie's whiskers with a contemptuous sophistication that blanched me back into the kindergarten. He disdained even a crushing comment and he accepted my exorbitant tip with undisguised disgust at such a puny effort to gain his good grace. It was almost nine o'clock and the evening was darkening from violet to indigo, the electric bulbs and neons harder and more distinct as the sky lost its softness and became concentrated into night. I rang Ziggie's bell and the door was opened in a ceremonial flourish by a gorgeous apparition in linen.

The face was masked, but the obviously real goatee, the edge of a white scar crooking below the mask, and the odor of pipe tobacco in the room allowed no question as to what body there was beneath the swaddle of garishly chromatic robes and turban.

"Daniel," I said, seizing his hand. "You've gone and taken off your girdle. Jesus," I said, admiring him. "I'll bet you've ruined more sheets on this than the local Ku Klux Klan."

Daniel's voice was embarrassed as he led us into the room. "Ziggie persuaded me that it would be a good opportunity to make a closer contact with Professor Greene." He moved uncomfortably in his easy-flowing robes. "And we thought that within the rather noisy anonymity of this regalia, I would be free to observe behavior with virtual impunity."

"But what are you?" I asked. "I mean, are you supposed to represent something?"

"He is the famous Gaekwar of Baroda," Ziggie said, skipping into the room from the back of the apartment. He was dressed in jester's motley, complete with silver bells on the tips of his curved slippers and pointed hat, and in his hand he carried a belled scepter. He tapped Daniel on the point of his turban. "Rise, Gaekwar. Go and sin no more." He put the scepter between his legs and fixed a red-rubber flower to the front of his jacket, then straightened and preened in front of me. "What think'st thou, sire?" he said. "Am I not a most clownish clown, a pretty fool?"

"You are a veritable clod of a clown," I said. "An oafish, doltish fool of a fool. But it comes natural to you."

Ziggie made a graceful bow and squirted me with water from his toy flower. "For I will be the bells of the ball," he sang, tinkling all his bells and dancing around the room on the toes of his slippers. "Better that than the balls of the belle," he said, stopping in front of Rennie, who had been watching the scene with amusement. "Aha, my fair lady," he said. "There's been dirty work afoot." He turned to me accusingly. "So that's what you are, foul miscreant. You're what the cat dragged in. Introduce me to the cat, please."

I made the introductions and Rennie and Daniel sat down while Ziggie went into the kitchen to fix some drinks. I followed him there while he hummed over the ice cubes, shaking his bells from time to time with great appreciative glee. He examined my costume unenthusiastically.

"Well, I suppose it will be all right, David," he said. "Some people always look the same, even when they're sick. But with a mask on, you should be okay. And your friend the cat is quite a cat. Quite a cat."

He handed me a drink and went to bring the others into the front room. "By the way," he interrupted himself. "There's another letter for you. It's on the icebox."

It was a Special Delivery in Mama Sheva's handwriting. I had a flurried moment of panic because Mama Sheva used Special Delivery only for funerals, but if something were wrong with the children, she would have telephoned. Inside the bulky envelope was a note scribbled in pencil on a page torn from a philatelist journal and a second envelope, a Special Delivery letter to me in Letha's handwriting. Sure, I thought. We all suffer and the Post Office licks the bones. Mama Sheva's note was, like herself, bewildered and to the point.

I dont know what michigas you kids are doing but I dont like it. Rosalie has a rash on her back, I hope it isnt God forbid the measles, she says its the prickly heat, all her girlfriends have it. There a blessing, God bless them, but the Lord gave children to young people, they have the health to take care of them. Tell Letha I saw a stunning one shoulder white crepe in Filencs, it would look beautiful on her. Its only been marked down once, Ill wait. Why does she write you in Boston, at Special Delivery yet, I dont understand you kids? You leave the children they would think there orphans, God forbid, and you can tell me its none of my business—Im only a mother—but to me it smells from fish.

Mama

It wasn't hard to reconstruct her confusion, I supposedly vacationing from my dissertation with Letha in New York and Letha writing me Special Delivery letters to Boston. Mama

Sheva's suspicions were not easily aroused, as long as they didn't concern her directly. But once she did get an idea in her head, it assumed the monolithic permanence of an ancient ruin. It became ipso facto an object of historic and esthetic interest around and within which she conducted guided tours, and you could as little dispute the validity of her enshrined idea as you could deny the existence of Miami Beach. What could I tell her tomorrow when I got home, sunburned and spouseless? I fingered Letha's letter and drained the drink that Ziggie had left me. Tomorrow and tomorrow and tomorrow. For, as I had announced to Rennie, deciding it with an inexorable stamp at the moment of my saying, tomorrow I was going back to Boston, back to my splintered family, back to the unexcavatable Jonathan Edwards no matter what. Tonight I would dance once more on the Procrustean bed of fire, lithe and substanceless, a grinning coal in a madman's hearth. Tonight was fire and the blood that seeps outside of time, a moment snatched from the water, precious and somehow irrelevant. And tomorrow I would return to myself, quenched by the cold douche of the dawn, buttoned up and pinned down in the beige regimen of responsibilities and promises. So I would go back, but for what? To what? When a man takes off his belt, how long must he wait for his pants to fall? The milk sours and the cottage cheese turns rancid, and you vote no special accolade to the butter-and-egg man, the homogenized gonif! So I would pick up my mask, brush the dirt off my chest protector, squat once again behind home plate. For what? A welcome for the prodigal daughter, the fatted base runner, the adultress penitent and rampant with a shield of gules? A ninth-inning colloquy on the mound? A reconciliation? A divorce? What? I don't know, I screamed at myself. I don't make things happen. I just get happened to. And nobody can roll with the punches forever. Not even the sea.

I poured myself another large drink from Ziggie's bottle and

I opened Letha's letter, tearing the edge of the envelope carefully as though portentous things depended on my neatness. Mimetic magic, I thought. If you open the envelope without fraying the edges, everything will be all right. If you answer the telephone before the second ring, it will be good news. Hocus pocus, dominocus. It's what we've got instead of God, Brett said. Bullshit. Passivity tearfully regressing to a totemistic infancy to protect itself against its own excremental cowardice. Ah, Riegel, you know so many things to have a stupid ass's head. Letha's letter was short, unexpected, and characteristically ambiguous.

David—

I should arrive I think on Saturday about 4:00 P.M. South Station. I'm not sure about anything but I think it's right. Please meet me alone, sans kinder, because I have to talk to you. Kisses to the children.

Letha

Saturday. Tomorrow. Everybody's going home tomorrow. The cow and the cat and the fiddle. The Largo from Dvorak. This train's a goin'-home train, this train. I read the letter again, slowly like an exercise in explication de texte, testing the words for emotional resonances that would tell me what feeling was behind the words, concealed beneath the words, crying out of the silences. What does she think is *right?* The time, the place, the conversation? We shall sit on our graves and talk about the death of kings. Was her little fling all flung, the solid-fuel package burned out, the trajectory flattened into glide, an arrest, a need for emotional repose? Or would we, heart-to-heart, talk man-to-man? And this is the way it is, David—sensibly, rationally is. There's no sense in beating a dead seahorse, after all. And perhaps divorce is the kindest cut of all, the wise Solomon slash of outrageously twinned incompatibility. If thy right heart offend thee, cut it off. Until another death do us part apart. Call the marriage broker, the pustular one, and tell him we broke our bank. The bottom's dropped out of the market and the small businessmen are drowning in their red inkwells. Kisses for the children, but no smooch for thee, old wriggle-foot, old wrong adult, thy poor unkisséd virgin cheek.

I reread the letter once more, its studied vacuity of emotion sinking in my chest like a bathysphere. Then I tore it into shredded strips and let the pieces drip like parade paper into the wastebasket. Tonight was still a free ride on a maybe unmerry-go-round and Ziggie's bells were tinkling in the farther room. Not quite curfew yet, old flame coverer, I thought. The bells yet jingle afire and beyond time (the silver edges of their rings) is always now time. The flames consume in time (which we are nourished by), but out of time—in very now—they blaze hot and green. Moses and his burnished bush. Riegel and the fiery crucifixion tree. We hang pendulous from the cross-bitten height of our lowly earth to fall upward into selfhood. To plummet low and laden into a base and ridden self.

My friends were arguing loudly in the front room, so I carried Ziggie's bottle in to them for fuel and sacramental libation. Rennie had thrown her raincoat off and she sat coiled in her chair, a svelte shock of black jersey, haranguing the ludicrously painted sheets of Daniel Meleck, who puffed his pipe like a camouflaged pillbox under assault. Ziggie twisted on the rug between them, his jester's cap bobbing from one to the other like a swivel-necked spectator trapped in front of a ping-pong game. Their absurd costumes and their formal seriousness were grotesque elaborations on my mood. I swallowed them whole with voracious delight. They're mad, I decided. Magnificently, seriously, desperately insane and I (a skulking princeling in the dark of the hall-mirror)—I am the controlling madness, a canted megalomaniac planet fixing my satellites into their eccentric orbits. And who does not feel himself the same insane, I thought. In this mad century, secure from private haunt, who is not the off-center nucleus of a human world aswirl with the velocity of unappeasable desire? Whirl is king and Everyman a jocose gyration of askew and ascant. En garde, Father Cadmos. Let's set to for the perfumed spices which glitter their prizes on the continental shelf. Roar your sea-moan and I will make my human cry. I'll slice thy Gordian tide with snickersnee or fall asmile on the sui-seaside in my trying. Not farewell, but fare forward, voyageur.

Rennie was in the midst of launching a spirited female attack, emphasizing her words with scything slashes of green fingernail.

"It's that there isn't any space. No space between people. Everybody is so close to everybody else that they become everybody else. Nobody can be *anybody,* then. Don't you see what I mean?" She waved her hands exasperatedly. "If there's no space between people, then you haven't got any in-between room to *make* anything. Inside or outside."

Daniel sucked on his pipe deliberatively, gentling his goatee with the same hand that cupped the pipe bowl. When he spoke his voice was dry and formal, although I could tell that he was making a special effort to be kind.

"This outside-inside-in-between business doesn't make any sense to me," he said. "In fact, it all strikes me as rather hysterically subjective. People certainly do operate under controlling principles of group coagulation, of course. And I suppose that there does exist a subjective desire for an individual sphere of autonomous ego possession, or what you call 'space.' But I would suspect that whether one accepts or rejects this particular illusion, it's still completely irrelevant to the dynamics of human behavior." He rubbed the bowl of his pipe unconsciously, lovingly. "From a purely behavioristic point of view, I wouldn't want to go any further than that."

"*Irrelevant!*" Rennie was furious. "Then what in Jesus' name *is* relevant?" She stabbed at his sheets with her flying nails. "Tell me, then. When you're all alone, what are you, anyway? You know, when you're all just stuck in the dark of yourself? What are you then? A mirror? A nice shiny mirror that reflects nice shiny nothing?"

Daniel sighed deeply and worried at his teeth with his pipe stem. "Well, now you're shifting the abstractions to a different plane," he said. "But since you ask, I suppose what I try to be—whether I'm alone or not—would be more like a lens, I guess. As clean and clear a lens as I can manage." He pointed the pipe at Rennie in the traditional "stick-em-up" gesture. "Look, I just want to see what's there. What's really there in front of me. That's all."

Ziggie giggled happily on the floor between them, nodding his bells up and down in delight. "It's wonderful," he said. "They're wonderful. They both agree. Daniel just wants to be a naked eye, a—what was Emerson's phrase?—'a transparent eyeball.' And you, Rennie—" he shook his bells toward her—"you just want to be a naked 'I' with a capital 'I' with enough room around you so that people can admire how pretty you are. It's a true marriage of minds."

Daniel grunted disgustedly. "Our friend Ziggie has an unerring talent for destroying serious conversation."

"No," I said, seeing it all clear and complete in a single rhythmic flash. "No, Ziggie's right. They're really not so very different at all. Look—" I was hunting frantically for the words that might convey my monumental aperçu. "Look—a person needs to *be* and he needs to *know.* And he can't be while he's knowing, because you have to split yourself up in order to know. And you can't know while you're being, because in those moments you're too full of yourself to be conscious—or self-conscious, anyway. The ideal would be to fuse the positions."

"Oh, Christ, you're playing word games—intellectual Scrabble," Rennie said, lighting a cigarette with a vicious scratch of a match. "Daniel is as crazy as a loon, but at least he takes an honest position."

Daniel bowed ironically toward her. "Thank you," he said. "But it's not honest or dishonest. It's the only logical practical position. David has this literary notion of making the ego so acrobatic that the only effective option he has left is a sheer disintegration of personality. And your position—" the pipe pointed toward Rennie— "a typical female position, I might suggest—is absolute narcissism. Not that it isn't healthier than David's in the long run."

"All right," I said, taking a lecturing position in front of the fireplace, still full of my unspeakable revelation. "Let's change the metaphor. Suppose that it isn't a pool that Narcissus is looking into. Suppose it's a window. A real window that looks out into the world. And suppose this window is dark in some places and clear in others. That it distorts the view unevenly and sometimes even reflects your own face back to you. Then, you see—" I made fumbling explanatory gestures with my hands to demonstrate.

"Then you see—precisely nothing," Daniel said. "Nothing that has any objective validity."

"I don't know what you're talking about now," Rennie said, piqued. "You people can't even stay on the subject."

"But don't you see," I said. "That's a much better metaphor for what our problems really are. Sometimes we see clear and sometimes our vision gets all fouled up. Sometimes we think we're seeing the outside and we're just getting images of ourselves thrown back at us. And all I'm saying is that we have to learn to keep moving—always moving—behind the window. Sometimes close, sometimes way back, but always moving and juggling our faulty images into some maybe over-all view." I caught a glimpse of my unreal black hair in the mirror behind me, but I shrugged it away. "Jesus," I said. "You can't expect to look through a glass darkly unless you try to throw some damned dark looks yourself. It seems perfectly clear to me."

"Like mud," Rennie said, throwing a dark look at me.

Ziggie giggled again, happy in the argument. "Alice through the looking-glass darkly," he said. "You've got on the wrong costume tonight, David. You should have braids and a pinafore."

"Well, am I crazy?" I asked him. "I can't get through to them at all. Do *you* see what I mean?"

He corkscrewed to his feet and went around our little circle, filling our glasses from the bottle. "Yeees, I think I understand what you mean, David," he said. "And I might even agree with you, more or less. But it's not so simple as you seem to think it is. Or as easy. The worthy Gaekwar here quite correctly points out that the line between a flexible and a deranged personality is mighty slim." He shook his belled scepter like a conductor's baton. "Rennie is anxious because there isn't enough space when she's with people. And Daniel ought to worry a bit when he's all alone because there's too much space. But you—" the bells tinkled at me—"you have the worries both ways. Inside-outside. With and without. Maybe your position is possible, but even if it is, it would be pretty precarious."

"I accept the risks," I said grandiosely, although I wasn't sure that I understood what he meant.

"In a way," Ziggie continued, "you've got not only the launching problem—the getting out of self—but a major reentry problem too. The self that you leave isn't there when you come back, you know. You have to make it up all over again."

Dimly I began to perceive what he was teaching me. You

would have to be a God of constant creation but without a God's omnipotence or cold dispassion. "I see," I said slowly. "Yes, I see. But I don't think there's really a choice. And I can't understand how she and he can afford their positions. Especially him," I said, pointing at Daniel.

"Why?" Daniel said. "Why me especially? All I want to do is observe what's in front of me."

"But that's just the point," I said. "You're in front of you too. You're a very big part of what's there. And especially being a Negro."

Daniel stiffened. "From my professional point of view, my being Negro is a matter of pure happenstance. It has some personal interest to me, of course, but from an observational standpoint, it is without significance. I don't see with my skin, after all."

"Oh," I said, jumping to the attack. "You mean it's a kind of laboratory variable, like humidity or atmospheric pressure, which you have to make calculated allowances for."

"You might put it that way," Daniel said.

"Then you're crazy," I said. "The most pathetic kind of crazy." He tried to interrupt me but I wasn't giving an inch away. "Jesus, Daniel, of course you see with your skin. Everybody does. You don't have anything else to see with. Oh, goddamn it—" I could see that we were making no connection. He was inspecting his pipe as though trying to memorize its shape while some strange wind was howling far away. "Look," I said. "You want to observe human behavior? Fine. But from your position, you'll see all kinds of behavior, but nothing *human.* There's a damned big difference between human behavior and human *being.*"

I had got Daniel angry. Even his sheets seemed to have become more starched and cold-edged, but his voice was deeply controlled. "I dare say you can find some poetic difference between behavior and being," he said. "But I can't.

There's just what people do. That's behavior. Some of it's pretty good and a lot of it is disgusting, but I don't concern myself with that. *Being*—that's something else. That's a dirty word I used to hear preached at store-front revival meetings. Man's knowledge has progressed a little beyond that, you know."

Rennie had been following the argument disconnectedly, seemingly irritated at all of us for throwing her statement into academic orbit. "I don't follow most of this," she said. "But why should it make a difference whether Daniel is a Negro or anything else? I mean, if he's looking through a microscope, what he sees isn't going to be changed, is it? What do you want him to do? Wear a sign saying 'Negro'?"

"He's already wearing it," I said. "And it makes an existential difference. Just as your being a woman makes a difference. Or that I'm Jewish. Christ, Rennie—this is partly where that 'space' you were talking about comes from. If it comes at all. It makes somebodies out of everybody."

"Then you're just saying that people are determined by what they are physically and socially." Rennie groaned her distaste. "And that they damned well better accept their definitions and live inside them. You don't allow any freedom or growth."

"No," I said. "You got it backward. It's you and he who are denying man the right to be free. To change. You want everything to be still on the outside so you can move around on the inside. He wants to be quiet on the inside so he can watch the outside. And both of you commit yourselves to a sacred unbreakable fixity."

Daniel had retreated to his pipe and Rennie sniffed at me with contemptuous disdain. Again I sent a look of appeal to Ziggie. He grimaced puckishly and sliced with his belled scepter as though he were administering a fatal thrust with a fencing foil.

"Outside-inside. Take another stab at it, Dave," he said. "They have ears but they do not hear. Eyes but they will not see. Gracious, how often do you get a chance to deliver the Word to such resplendent flesh-worshippers of Baal?"

"All right," I said. "I'll give it another shot. One cannot choose to lay aside the burden of the Word." I reconsidered the line of the argument and I noticed again the shock of my new black hair reflected in the mirror. "Okay, let's try it this way," I said. "It's like these foolish costumes we're wearing, you see. We're in them, but they're not what we are. Like my being Jewish. Or Daniel's being Negro. Or somebody being tricked or betrayed by someone they trust and love. Or vice versa. None of these observable facts are intrinsically real, even though they do have a kind of reality."

I laughed and made a thespian's salute in my mouse-grey mustard-brown makeshift courtier's suit. "It's a costume," I said. "You wear it. And you wear it because you don't have any choice except to wear it. Somebody else put it on you and so you've got to wear it. But you wear it and you play behind it and you try to accommodate it to yourself, don't you see? You don't pretend that it's not there like the Emperor's underwear. You use it. Christ, it seems axiomatic to me."

Daniel tapped his pipe bowl clean into the ashtray, thinking into the grey ash which settled in light spilled heaps. "What about in the middle?" he asked suddenly. "At the nucleus of all this cloacal concealment? Is there something solid and unchanging there? Behind all the costumes?"

Ziggie laughed gleefully. "That Daniel," he said. "He do ask the nasty questions. How do you answer that one, David?"

"With fear and trembling," I said. "But I'll try."

I turned toward Daniel, realizing all at once how much more difficult it must be to have a dark skin in a white world than just a hooked nose and a three-thousand-year history of psychological circumcision. But the principle must be the same, I thought. It has to be. Even if my Hebraic costume is more devious and less physical than his darkness, and even if he can't or won't recognize the fact that I'm hidden behind what he thinks is myself—the principle has to be the same. And what's true for him as regards me—glorious Jesus—this must also be true as regards the good sanitary Anglo-Saxon world that I'm outside of. Hell, they must be inside their own costumes, too. Rennie. Cadmium Greene. The State Street bankers and the Beacon Hill dowagers, stiff and straight in their fur-topped overshoes, balancing their proper rectitude on the icy precipices of Joy Street. *We're all outside the world,* I thought with awe and unbelief. Since the expulsion from the Garden, the primal Diaspora. The insiders and the outsiders, the light-skinned and the dark-souled, all of us. A goddamned costume party and most of the players don't even know they're in a game. Don't even know that from their birthday suits in and out they're masked in crinolines of sham, in bedazzled definitions of disguise. Agonizing quest for identity, hell! Who, oh, who, oh, Lord? Who am I really and true? High-school metaphysics to impress the girl's locker room. The quest is agonizing only because the simple answer is so damned hard to accept. I'm not a single findable thing at all. I'm a Venetian Carnival, just like everybody else. A circus of improbable possibilities. And in the middle—in the center ring—inside the clown acts and under the trapeze passes, what? Remembered promises? A vacancy sign with a neatly printed warning that Strangers Need Not Apply? *What?*

"Well, Daniel," I said, speaking carefully and trying to keep in mind the sacred unfinished monstrosities that Jim Crow and Treblinka had been to us. "I don't know what's in the middle. Maybe it wouldn't be too good to know. Maybe you're not even supposed to know. Maybe it's death there—or a kind of life that would be fatal to the living. But I'm pretty sure that there's nothing solid and unchangeable there. That just doesn't make any sense to me. There's nothing else in the world that fixed and certain."

I paced around the room while I talked, stopping a moment by the window to wait for a group of drunken singers to swing around the corner, noisy and certain in their whisky happiness. I remembered suddenly one night years ago, right after I'd been discharged from the Army, walking around the Loop in Chicago at about three o'clock in the morning. And I had seen a middle-aged man dressed in a neat brown overcoat and grey-felt hat standing in the middle of a bridge over the Chicago River playing a bagpipe all by himself, wailing the weird notes into the middle of the city with as much military assurance as though he were standing review before Buckingham Palace.

"No," I continued. "So far as we know, there's nothing that's fixed and changeless anywhere in Nature. But that doesn't mean there's nothing in the middle. I like to think that there's something like a force field of steady potentiality. Not stability. Just free-floating possibility. Sometimes one direction becomes dominant and the others lie fallow. And maybe this force field is inherent in our temperaments when we're born. And maybe not. Maybe we create it as we go along, killing the lives within us that we don't want to live. Or the ones that we're afraid of. Or gambling on some that we conjure up out of thin air to back our bets. You know, like spraying a column of air and getting an illusion of substance."

I patted my black hair with a mustard-brown arm. The Egyptian slaves girdling my waist lurched upward with the gesture. I straightened my mouse-skin weskit and laughed at my mirror self. What was I trying to tell myself, the mock pedagogue?

"Actually, I don't think it makes much difference," I went on. "But the important thing—the human thing—it seems to me, is this. Somehow we have to learn and keep learning to let the life energies have maximum freedom to play with our potentialities and somehow we have to try to keep our self-awareness from being duped by any temporary domination of direction. I mean, we've got to be aware of our costumes even when we think we're down to the naked bone. And especially then."

Daniel had refilled his pipe and was looking toward the window, hidden in his mask and royal paraphernalia. Ziggie sat cross-legged, tailor-fashion, clinking the bells of his hat indolently from side to side. In her chair, coiled around a cigarette, Rennie hissed softly to herself. I felt stupid, conscious of having made a speech. And yet at the same time, I knew that I had said something to myself that I would have to live up to. Or down to. I started to apologize for my tirade, but I checked myself and took another drink.

Rennie ground her cigarette out thoughtfully and surrounded herself in the chair. "Maybe you're not completely crazy, Riegel," she said hesitantly. "Maybe just ninety per cent. But this fuzziness in the middle. That's hard to understand. I was taught to believe that every thought and action was important because it was final. Because you became whatever you did. You know, like laying bricks to make a wall. You remember the old story about the man who wore a mask for twenty years, and when he finally took it off, his face had the shape of the mask. I was taught that we make our own faces and we have a moral obligation to be consistent with them. And the worst sin is hypocrisy. I'm not that proud of the face that I've made for myself—" she blushed and lit another cigarette quickly while Daniel fumbled with his matches—"but I don't tell myself any lies about it. It just seems to me that what you're preaching is a kind of deliberate hypocrisy."

"Maybe I am," I said. "But hypocrisy—that's just another word, too. Or maybe it's a bigger sin to be a hypocrite to life than to just a face. Hell, look at the cosmetics industry. Faces are just masks anyway, aren't they? You know the question that the Zen Master asks? 'Show me the face that you had before you were born.' Maybe it's more important not to be hypocritical to that face. To that potentiality of face. Do you see?"

Rennie was reluctant in her cat costume. "Maybe women have a different surety, David. I just don't know."

I couldn't read Daniel's face behind his pipe, and whatever expression his eyes might have had was distorted by his papier-mâché mask. He waited for Rennie to return to her cigarette and he cleared his throat uncommittedly, but when he spoke his voice was filed to a sharp cutting edge. "Speaking strictly as an observer, David—and forgive my recourse to the ad hominem—I'd have to judge you as a pretty poor specimen of your own ideal. For one thing, you cover up an awful lot of self-pity and self-righteousness for the Masked Phantom program you've been propounding."

"Touché," I said, wincing. "A very palpable hit, indeed. But judge the message, not the messenger. I don't claim it's easy to live this way. It's impossibly hard, in fact. And I don't claim to be any model of performance. But, Jesus, I'm trying my best to learn how."

It was impossible to be certain because of his mask and the smoke and the way the shadows fell from the lamp, but I could have sworn that Daniel's eyes were slyly amused behind the oval slits in his cardboard domino.

"Maybe you can learn, David," he drawled. "Maybe you can. You might even be able to pick up some pointers from other people. Even from me."

I remembered his concealed delight with the *Ebony* magazine. "I don't doubt it," I said. "I don't doubt it at all."

The room was suddenly quiet and reflective and the Greenwich Village night noises drifted disconnectedly through the open window. Ziggie looked at each of us in turn with a sardonic smile on his face and then he rose to his feet like a gaudy campanile. "Perfesser," he said bowing to me, "I'm sure we've all appreciated your little sermon this evening and speaking for the collected brethren and cistern, I'd like to express our thanks."

I returned his bow silently, waiting for the poisoned arrows to strike.

"However, there are a couple of little points I'd like to explore somewhat further," he went on. "I'd hate to make a mistake on your road directions to Salvation City."

I nodded again without speaking, wondering how many pins he was going to stick into my lovely balloons.

"If I follow you correctly," Ziggie continued, "the Riegel Code bases itself on the principles of complete perverse self-consciousness and purposive deception. Right? Does it not follow then that the one absolutely verboten gesture in the Riegel system would be love or passion or whatever you want to call that anachronistic feeling that history makes so much of?"

"I don't know," I said. "I certainly didn't mean it to be."

"Well, let's examine it," Ziggie said, deft and casual as a surgeon. "You would require that every human or nonhuman contact be in some sense a *considered* one. In practice, a competition rather than an interaction. You have to be so busy fooling people that you could never feel them at all. Every man his own Houdini, insulated from the world by self-conceit and his little bag of tricks. Point one, then: a built-in factor of human isolation."

"Well, man is isolated anyway," I rejoined weakly. "That just makes my position the more realistic."

"Perhaps," Ziggie said. "Or maybe it's an elaborate rationalization for inherent cowardice. But let me move to point two. Passion or love—as differentiated from sheer animal lust—has traditionally been associated with a surrender of self and a direct confrontation with life. Now it's possible that this is all a romantic nostalgia that we can no longer afford, but love has been one of the few human values that people have been willing to subscribe to in some form or other. And the Riegel system, as I humbly read it, would make love impossible because your fluid self is by definition unsacrificeable, and the last damned thing you want to do is to interact with life directly and honestly."

He paused in his autopsy and jabbed at my chest with his scepter. "Ergo, no love, no self-sacrifice, no creative sharing. How does Shakespeare put it somewhere? 'The violence of either grief or joy/ Their own enactures with themselves destroy.' Except that you beat the bard to the punch by getting rid of the violence and the possibilities of grief and joy. Everything's possible in your world except anything human. That's a kind of heavy price to pay for a party costume methinks."

"Oh, Jesus suffering Christ," I said feebly, watching my sparkling creation settle into lumpish dust. "I must not have explained myself very well."

Ziggie smiled gently. "According to your principles, you're not supposed to, are you? That would be too honest."

"I mean," I said, forcing a false grin on my face. "I'm for love and all. I truly do believe in it. Whatever it is. I must have left something out. You know that's not what I mean."

Ziggie jiggled his bells again, receding into the jester's role with just a suspicion of a sharp scalpellike hook in the corners of his smile. "Yeess, I think you did leave something out," he drawled. "Small but slightly significant."

"Like what?" I asked. "What is it?"

"Call it humility," he said. "That last scrim of humility underneath all the veils. It used to be a pretty cardinal virtue once. I have a notion that it might still work pretty well."

I felt self-betrayed and disgusting. "I'll have to think about it," I said, putting a weak end to the conversation.

"You do that, David," Ziggie said. He collected the empty glasses and the bottle to bring them to the kitchen. "Or better, try feeling it instead of thinking. Sometimes the head can get in the way, you know."

Ziggie smiled at us all and straightened up the room while we checked our masquerade disguises in the mirrors without speaking. The black dye from my hair had streaked on to my cheeks and I looked sooty. Sooty and with a hollow shame pitting my stomach deep beneath my tawdry slave belt. Rennie was self-occupied, quiet in her own internal scrutiny, but Daniel clapped me on the shoulder with a friendly hand. He smelled of a warm trustworthy tobacco. He pushed his mask up on his forehead to wipe sweat from his eyebrows and his direct gaze at me was companionable and unaccusing.

"Let's go, man," he said. "You got to ride high between the notes."

"So they tell me." I smiled ruefully. "But friend, I am way down. I am as way down under the notes as you can go."

He chuckled and squeezed my shoulder. "When you get that far down," he said, "you don't even feel it any more. Man, you got rockets you ain't even used yet."

"Thanks," I said. "By the dawn's early light. And the star of Bethlehem. Not to mention the red white and blue."

"There are worse colors," Daniel said. "Like yellow. Take it from somebody who knows. Who's been there." He aimed a mock uppercut at my chin. "Who's been there, boy, and found that you can crawl out."

And Ziggie locked the ornate Victorian door to the apartment and we crowded through the dark hall and out into the street to flag down a taxi. A blinking red neon blotched our faces with a smoky glow and a dark breeze rode in from the sea, encircling us and pulling playfully at the folds of our costume cloth.

# Journal

*21 June:* The Day of the Summer Solstice. The sun-smudged marking of time in the engorged immensities of space. The longest day of the year, the blazing meridian point between the birth and the death, the annual dawn and the sad permanent dusk. The day in which we live longest in the light, fiery and consumed with that which we are nourished by. What a comical clown act to check human time against the sidereal clock. How silly and purposively ignorant we must be, if we are to be at all. Timeless seas, lap thy tides. Rain, resettle thy cruel shroud. Wash us clean to the mocking bone, since our desperation is beneath thy most generous contempt.

I speak directly to the elements these days (what *other* could understand me now?) and, once, last week I tried to hold a wall by its hand and my knuckles are still skinned and raw. I hold long unfinished conversations with Doren (imaginary ones, I think) and I make fine telling points to destroy him utterly. He listens and his obsidian eyes burn, but he doesn't move from the primitive rock of his hatred. He tells me (I put the words in his mouth) that I am soft and sentimental and I make a saint's parade to hide my fear and cowardice. I thunder back crushing refutations and he points to Eva reading a book among the corpses with flies crawling on her lips. Am I mad? Am I insanely cuckolded by some taint in my own blood flow? Some beast that dares to snarl inside me in spite of the heavy chains?

I push my novel more slowly now. Is it because I refuse to unkey the locks? I have no defenses inside me to still that terrible snarl. You cannot bribe teeth except with the heart's blood and I am afraid and empty. Eheu! So afraid and so cruel to my fear!

And we know now, in this our enlightened century, that the multiplication of vision is blindness. Each new scope and *ism* in the history of human understanding paints a thicker layer on our shadow-scape of sight. Man was given only two eyes in the chary economics of evolution—two to focus in one image by the golden rule of three. His temerity and sickness is to aspire to multiple sight, to become frenzied Argos of the hundred eyes (the tragic peacock's tale), to vie with Jehovah (The Great Eye That Eyes). The resplendent Joseph was buried in a pit and Oedipus knew the savage bite of his mother-wife's brooch against his eyeballs and sweet Gloucester, that stupid purblind father-man, he too. The sin of vision is punished by banishment from the sight of God's Eye, the sun, on the shortest or longest day in its golden coursing. ("And it was about the sixth hour, and there was a darkness over all the earth until the ninth hour. And the sun was darkened, and the veil of the temple was rent in the midst.") I had been working in the back room, which had darkened without my realizing it, and I came into the front room where Eva was sitting before the open French windows and the light hurt my eyes. She had a book on her lap that I had never seen and when I looked at the open page, it was blank. "What are you reading?" I asked her. And her eyes were sorrowful and I saw that she had grown more beautiful beyond my hands and she answered me. "You," she said. "I read you." And I closed the book hard on her fingers. "Make a drawing," I said. "Make a drawing in your empty book." And Mark ran to her and made an evil face at me (he looked like Doren all at once) and Lily laughed in the corner, kicking at the telephone bell.

I think something is in my eyes. I don't know what is in my eyes.

Last week I climbed to the high battlements of Notre Dame (I had to do something physical with my trapped corpse of a body) and I was caught at the top in a mighty afternoon thunderstorm—lightning, hail, and sulfurous torrents of rain. The gargoyles were spitting from the highest lonely places and the dark settled so close to my towers that I could barely see the rounded turrets of the Conciergerie across the square. Notre Dame and the Conciergerie, the cathedral and the dungeon, the axial basis of western civilization. The vertical pit with the slitted windows, claustrophobic, stone-smothered from the light, a sneering angel that looks like Eva skipping on the summit with a forked heel. Ad maiorem gloriam diaboli. God and the Devil (His Other Self) dividing the world between them as a woman splits herself to swallow up a man. Breastless angel and excremental gargoyle, Deus et Diabolus, protean shapes of the same awesome power, ordering, measuring, balancing the geometric designs of man's imprisonment and liberation (Doren's face, glutted with black rage when the warder pushed him out of the dungeon at Vincennes with a key as long as a rifle). Hollow architectural triumphs now, the pit and the tower, the reliquary gaol and the houses of worship which are now great stone coffins of prayer. There is no one to live in them any more; the dungeon become too small to house the criminality of man, the flying groined vaults too spacious for the little gods that we allow.

The penal pit is even more obsolete than the cathedral now (Eva mesmerized by the phallic bull carvings in the catacombs of Beauvais. Her uncanny look of tenderness before the Christ on the North Portal of Chartres, His face of agony desperate and uncomplaining like her father's). We now have the donjon en plein aire, the outdoor barbecue, the barbed-wire strung encampment where the bleak and the pinched huddle white and unstrung under the vacant sky. There is no need to banish the wicked from the sight of God's Eye. It has been plucked out of the heavens like a rotted grape and become a definable mass of flaming gases, so the bleak and the pinched can pierce their flesh on cold hooked steel under a wide unfettered sky and know a deprivation that man had never dared to imagine before. Open, vacant, colorless, arbitrarily undefined in straggling fenced perimeter, the inside merges with the outside. Space surrounds, insinuates, saturates. Man becomes catatonic animal, light becomes darkness, life flows into death and there is no passage, no transition, no change that is not unformed and changeless.

The dungeon created the cathedral, the gargoyle squatting on his loathesome hams gave slow birth to the angel. What can the sterile concentration camp engender? What could it possibly create, also in the open air? Perhaps to dream an impossible architectural vision, to cast an unetched engineering blueprint to balance the machined perfection of a Dachau, an Auschwitz—to imagine a modern antithesis, obverse and fully compensatory. The Un-Concentration Camp—a spielplatz of joyful disintegration, open to the sun and air, luxuriant in growth, as perverse in its full satiation of human desire as the concentration camp is efficient in its perverse oppression. A playground of opportunities and possibilities—polymorphous, sensual, expansive. A richly accessible body of delight to be swallowed and ingested where ripeness and readiness are always and all.

The gargoyles spat disconnected yellow streams of water and the other tourists crowded closer with me to the silent bells of Quasimodo's towers and the rolling dark came across the square until I couldn't see the Conciergerie at all and the last image to my eyes was the comic procession of steep green angels mounting the pitched roof toward what. I threw one of Doren's gift stones over the great balustrades into the square and now I only have one in my pocket, one half of a doublet to roll in my palm and press between my fingers.

The weather grows muggier and muggier every day and I don't even look at Doren's almost-daily postcards. I don't believe that he is truly away. I think I have him trapped inside me and I don't want him to get out. Eva says that he plans to return toward the end of next month, but he will be in a different country then. And us. The city changes with its tall windows pushed open. The living rooms and bedrooms move into the streets and the radios play for everyone on the block. And always at night, in every street, in every quartier, a single head silhouetted in front of a shadowed light, the body leaning against the iron guards high above the street, the city solitary waiting silently in his unhallowed concrete crèche. And each window, it sometimes seems, has a silent sash rope opening and closing it to me.

Eva goes to sleep early these nights as though she's storing up rest, her knees drawn up to her stomach out of her nightgown, her body coiled in an untouchable ball as she lies on her side on the far edge of the bed. She doesn't stir when I get into bed and her breath is long and even, but I am sure that she is awake. She let a greasy mountebank pierce her earlobes for earrings ("So that I won't lose any more in sewers," she said), but I do not take her hand in sleep.

Summer Solstice and the faint shimmer at the far end of the tunnel. Light, open air, the glow of fool's gold.

# Five

Cadmium Greene's house was about an hour's ride out on the Island. The cab-driver, somehow inveigled by Ziggie's casual mesmerism, threaded through the careening lines of expressway traffic like a sorcerer's needle, crosscutting the slow manicured roads where orange signals blinked at the crests of gentle grades and the large estates were set far back from the front gates under steady sheltering trees. We were never actually in sight of water, and yet the sea smell was sharp in my nostrils as though I had sewn a salt pouch of it under my tunic. Ziggie, the good husbandman, had thoughtfully packed another bottle in his jester's wallet and we sang as we drove, passing the bottle from hand to hand, the driver taking his regular turn with both bottle and choruses in a nasal rumble of oom-pah-pah and squealing tires. Ziggie sat half turned around in the front seat, directing the songs and the bouncing progress of the bottle, a crazed Laramie cowboy herding his loco cattle to Sedalia for grass and fresh water and the rattling boxcar ride across the great river. Rennie was between me and Daniel in the back seat, catching too much treble on the high harmony parts and scratching indiscriminately at both of us when the bottle lagged or the tempo straggled. We twanged and droned and whined through the Ole Chisolm Trail, lamenting the fortunes of the white-linened hero from Laredo and his myriad weather-and-fate-beaten brethren—ignorant, lonely, unaccomplished men whose smoked-out campfires and bitter whisky-drained lives had provided an opéra-bouffe setting for the ex-European children who clawed in factory grime at a despairing polyglot of tongues and uncivil city ordinances which they accepted eagerly without comprehension or love.

"Take my pony and face him to the West and we'll ride the prairie that we love the best." Can't you just hear America singing loud and clear? My grandfather, Reb Yankel, in what obliterated pigsty shtetl, spurring his silver-saddled pinto between mikvah and many-times-gutted study house, his sombrero tilted low to shade his eyes against the white Polish sun. Yankel the Pferd-Gonif, black-robed desperado of Lodz and Cracow, chanting the Shmena Esreh in the alkali dust churned by the Cossacks in their savage warpath charges. And Bubba Malyah, the one grandmother that I can barely remember, toothless in her black shawl—she knew that false teeth were a trick of the goyim to introduce trafe into clean Jewish mouths. A prematurely ancient woman with a young girl's blue eyes, unable all her adult life to speak more than a word of English, proud, tenacious, incapable of registering defeat or acquiescence or even simple joy. Sunday mornings (after the bagels, after the lox) my father would take me and my brother to visit her and she would feel our faces with her dried hands and she would pinch the flesh on our arms to see if we were healthy and firm. Pioneers, O Pioneers, sang Brooklyn Cowboy Walt, but if Lafayette really patted him on his head when he was a small boy at a Fourth of July parade, Bubba Malyah gave my brother and me an equally formidable desert blessing with a love pinch on the arm and a low-whispered "Fehgele." And we'll all ride the prairie that we love the best. Rennie's grandfather too, rounding up the dogies in his high round collar and carefully buttoned vest, peering at his account book through silver-framed spectacles while he measured out feed and salt and harness strappings in an Ohio general store, spitting hard-bitten Lutheran curses at the purple coyotes whose shadows loomed large and menacing on the gritty contours of the Black Hills. And Daniel's too, his grandparent too, another leathery-skinned, hunched-up sourdough, Indian fighter, frontier scout, doughty slaughterer of bison and passenger pigeon, holding the pass against flash flood, drought, and sidewinding rustler. Some old Mose or Amos or Hosea (dark prophetic names to blot the purple sage), riding his derelict mule, tall in the no-saddle, tending the scabrous cotton rows on meager-enough side meat and chitlings. Prophets, settlers, frontiersmen all—learning slowly (so terribly slowly) how to endure themselves and one another in the fierce grasp of their identities, which compelled a hatred for the goy, the furriner, the pale-hearted overweening white. And they and we and all our others sit enraptured before the thirty-foot-high movie mirror, ecstatically seeing ourselves, finding ourselves at last in the Virginian who pinches the ends of his hand-rolled Bull Durham and squints stoically at the color-splashed western sky beyond which laps the other sea, the impassable land's end.

Our taxi roved the gulches and arroyos of the sleeping land, following the lumpy bed of the Long Island Rail Road. The headlights swung and focused quickly, catching a tree, a dull-green mailbox, a bicycle tethered in front of a door, capturing the solid images of the day and releasing them casually into the darkness of our wake. Like the bird in the old Anglo-Saxon parable, I thought—my mind riding point on our spectral eastward westering. We ride a skittery lightning through the murky wastes of our lives, illuminating an image just long enough to see it falsely, to record it in our memory book of lies, to pretend a truth and a time lock of experience where there is none and no hope for any. That poor rider, man—just a false lock on the stage door of mock entrances and exits, an illusory system of sievelike barriers which channel remembrances and promises into jigsaw patterns of pseudo-meaning. Which some have died for, I reminded myself. And killed for, too. That last, a much more blazing emblem in an age of unbelief, an age of open locks, of bolts and hasps and rusted metal tumblers hanging idly and unclenched. Death is so much the easiest task today. Anybody can do it. Does it, in fact, as a regular part of the daily routine, an accustomed fatal station break between television shows, between the fall and rise of a voice tone, between the rinse and spin cycles of the automatic washer. Nor is there any lamb's blood in that antiseptic mechanism.

But to kill for. To initiate an action rather than to be acted upon. This is the rarity of murder in an age where we are all ripe to be slaughtered. Our modern birthright gives us a natural martyrdom from the sloughing off of the placenta. We chew Golgothan thorns with our teething rings and Zwieback. But to kill for a meaning. The murderer is blood high above the saint in our secret hierarchy of sanctification because he *does,* and we are done to. Great jokes from little ikons grow—the swastika, the cross, the rood, and the empty cup. Even murder in self-defense is beyond most of us—that Darwinian mist of a myth, diffusing like the ground fog which is our discoverable self. Self-defense? Which self to defend? Self-consciousness demands passivity, not passion, and death is the secret sharer whose huddled shape we cherish in the heart of our darkness. Six millions—six million me's—all my six million selves. They clambered into the sealed freight cars, they stacked their clothes in heaps like tombstones, they inhaled the patient gas numbly, docilely, willingly. And how many billions more, accepting their deaths passively on a thousand levels of disguised deprivation and destruction. If the red slayer think he slays, or if the slain think he is slain, they know not. They know not, indeed. Oh, Thanatos, Thanatos, wherefore art thou Thanatos? Thou most modern hero with a million faces, with a zillion guises, the slow seepage of your life vacuum adhering to the most trivial and sacred gestures and rhythms of our daily dyings. To arms, Rigoletto! Thou pimpled king in a nutshell, thou unlocked sluice, thou multiseried self! Definition is the putting of ends to, the establishment of limits and boundaries, the iron succession of the lock of death. Be juicy, Riegel. Burst! Be thou a compounded confusion, a welter and a seething boil. In a world of prepackaged, deep-frozen lumps, be thou a sauce, a goulash, a tzimmis, a gravy. Scatter the boundaries of your sad self-drippings and imitate the lapping-over slop of the sea. Seducer, pimp, cuckold, man—thy blood is thy kingdom and only you can be the party of usurpation. And if you're so goddamned spacious, Haroun-al-Raschid, why the hell aren't you even a little bit smart?

The taxi bounced into the gravel drive which led to Cadmium Greene's hybrid Italian Renaissance house and I grabbed the bottle from Daniel and drained the last scalding dregs. Mosquito flares had been set erratically around the front lawn and cars were parked crazily in the drive and on the well-tended greensward. Costumed figures milled in and out of the house and stringed music could be heard through the open lighted windows. From the outside the house looked like a beached pleasure ship, its white stuccoed walls rising like a sun-drained grounded keel. Near the hedge where we parked the car, a shaggy-maned lion was trying to cure an almost naked mannequin of the hiccoughs by holding her ears while she gulped at a bottle of beer. We squeezed out of the cab like clowns from a circus car, spilling over one another, adjusting our masks, our spangles, our sequins and papier-mâché. The cab-driver had turned his cap backward, the yellow brim protecting the nape of his neck like the scoop of a snow shovel, and Ziggie had given him a rubber monster's mask for his face. We were skipping, tripping, bobbling up the road, the echoes of our singing skittering like gravel under our feet.

"The play's the thing," shouted Ziggie, our cheerleader, waving his arms to the chant, "wherein we'll catch the conscience."

"King king king." We returned the line like a football chorus.

"King king king," screeched Rennie the cat, mincing at the words with her tongue. "Come on, you king."

The lion was beginning to creep down from the mannequin's ears in a lascivious descent and the green bushes were full of fireflies. The scent of the Sound was strong through the trees and the white façade of the house shone silver. Ziggie led us up the front steps to the door. Directly above the portal someone had Scotchtaped the book jacket of Cadmium Greene's astounding success, *The Mortuary of Love*, and the garish illustration, a pale nude reclining in a coffin, dangled over our heads as we trooped in to the party. Daniel saluted it with his pipe. "In hic signo vincemus," he said. The cabbie grunted and headed for the long buffet table in the entry hall, which was lined with brown-porcelain cups and bottles. We followed his lead, my pulses starting to trip-hammer as the adrenalin juiced through my system. Letha should be here and I would know her and then.

From the center hall we could see two large rooms which flanked it on either side, reluctantly fringed with colored streamers. The furniture was moved back to the walls and there were lit candles in the wall sconces and chandeliers. In the right-hand room, the smaller one that was normally I suppose the dining room, costumed figures danced or talked in groups, throwing wild candle shadows on the walls and ceilings. The left-hand room, much larger and more commodious, had the appearance of a medieval banquet hall. Blotches of moving shadow swam from the many candle flames against the raised beamed ceiling, reflecting off the leaded frames of the open French windows and settling in an uneasy murk on the square stones of the floor. In a large wall niche between two giant windows, a string ensemble in startling white dress suits impassively played Viennese waltz music into the smoky shadows. Their bodies were exaggeratedly stiff and only their bow-holding arms moved in the making of the music. The dancers, garishly painted and unreal in their disguises, swung through the 3/4 measures that had been irrevocably shattered with the fall of the Hapsburgs, and I imagined the laughing corpses of an Edgar Poe script executing the bleached steps of the dance of death over the timorous tomb of the world. At the very end of the room in front of a huge fireplace a throne had been erected on a raised dais. It was a Victorian hall ensemble—a single monstrous piece of mahogany comprising a hat and umbrella stand, a high bench for the removal of boots and overshoes, and a tall backing mirror. Heavy crape folds had been thrown over the varnished wood, and on the very top of the mirror a gilded branch was fixed like some pagan fetish. On the bench, sitting like Claudius chewing his lip in Olivier's *Hamlet*, was Cadmium Greene, our ungenial host, crowned with a tarnished golden crown, swaddled in a heavy velvet drape. He sat contemptuous on the pinnacle of the festive sepulcher, his mouth drooping to one side, and in the mirror behind his head the reflection of the candles and the fireflies outside the windows flickered like baleful moths of light. And on a stool at his feet, shimmering in white Egyptian cloth with broad gold borders along the hems, her jet-black hair knotted high in a cone, her face masked in a glittering golden mask, was a girl who might or might not have been Letha. I took a deep breath and backed out of the room to my friends, who were drinking at the buffet table.

"Well, Riegel?" Rennie called to me, giving me a brown cup of something which went down sweetly and then caught on fire in my limbs. "Is she or isn't she?"

I filled my cup again and drank quickly to see whether the fires would continue. "She is," I said. "Or she isn't. I can't tell from here. And it's crazy in there." I patted at my domino. "And this goddamn thing. I can't see very well through it."

Ziggie shook his bells and made a little dance skip. He had filched from a drunken somebody a child's ukulele and he had strung it across his back, like a medieval troubador. "When in doubt, attack!" he said, taking charge of the military strategy. He drew himself erect and issued the marching orders. "You and Rennie—" he pointed at us— "make a diversionary waltz around the floor. And see if you can gradually work yourself up close to The Enemy. Daniel—" The scepter leveled off at him and the Gaekwar sprang to attention. "You'll cover our flanks. If you stand next to the orchestra, you can dominate the whole room. Meanwhile our trusty charioteer will be out here under the whisky if we have to beat a hasty." Our trusty charioteer was squatting serenely next to the buffet eating big handfuls of olives and serrying his empty brown cups on the floor in the design of a parking lot. "And I," Ziggie continued,

"I'll maybe work a little infiltration into the upper echelons." We saluted him smartly and he bowed his head with embarrassed dignity. "Mes enfants," he said. "Remember St. Crispin's Day."

Rennie and I joined in a stiff waltz embrace and swung into the wheeling rhythm of the music. "*One* two three, *one* two three, *one* two three, *one* two three," I counted to myself, concentrating on the glide and turn of my left foot, remembering my wedding waltz and the years that had spun crazily away in between. The candlelight and the shadows whirled around and around and my unwilling body slowly inserted itself as a spoke in the giant wheel which made the stone floor into a rolling turntable, the beams of the ceiling and the leaded windows spinning, the other waltzing couples looming up in front of my eyes from nowhere to disappear into the blotched shadows and the dizzy turning perimeter of the dance. The musicians stroked their strings with a ludicrous white angularity, pulling us into the circular whirl of the chords, turning us into gaily colored double notes knotted to the golden strings which leashed us round and round in the waltz. I tried to focus my eyes on Rennie's nose, straining to hold on a single unmoving point around which I could turn without losing myself in the dizzy swirl of the room, but my eyes kept sliding down her cat's whiskers and off their axis, surrendering themselves to the revolution of the world, glossing over the images they caught like a gentle feather duster moving among the bric-a-brac. I saw Daniel standing straight and impossibly tall in his wildly painted sheets, a severe dark sentinel guarding the mummified orchestra. I saw Cadmium Greene's face, contemptuous and half averted as he sat his throne, his lip falling to the side, his eyes unmasked and thick with spite, the muscles under his cheek twisting like a corded serpent. I had a quick rolling glimpse of the Egyptian girl, her lissome back to the dancers, the subtle swell of her hips and buttocks turning my stomach into ooze as I sought to recognize her under herself. "Slimsome she was, fairy fa-grace and lightly," I quoted to myself, but then the image was gone and I had a brief sight of Ziggie's belled hat, and the fireflies darted around the room in a cycle of bright treachery.

"Well, is she or isn't she?" Rennie demanded, her question taking me momentarily out of the dance.

"I don't know," I said. "I think so, but I can't tell."

"Jesus Christ, Riegel," Rennie said. "You have to know your own wife. Dance us up there and ask her to waltz with you."

"I suppose so," I said. "But I'm scared."

"Poor baby," Rennie said. "And nobody but the old mangy cat to change your diapers for you."

We fell back into the dance and worked our way through the circling couples to the throne end of the room. It was like the game of Giant Steps as I tried to impose our rhythmic progress on the overweening rhythm of the dance—three steps forward and two steps backward, lurching into other couples, sucked backwards by the rise and fall of the beat which the musicians administered ruthlessly from their niche in the wall. A knight with a gleaming red cross on his breast jolted my elbow and we spun into his partner, a phosphorescent skeleton with enormous breasts and a cadaverous skull. I apologized to the vacant air as they swept away, and we fell out of the circuit of the dance into the emperor's foyer.

Ziggie was kneeling at the base of the dais, strumming the ukulele to the under rhythm of "Five Foot Two," and in a high nasal chant he was accompanying his strings, intoning the Easter trope, "Quem quaeritis in sepulchro, O Christicolae." Rennie picked up a bowl of flowers in her hands and, bearing it like a severed head, genuflected at Ziggie's side before the throne, her green tails fanning out behind her as from a great voluptuous fish. I got my breath back and willed the room to cease its dizzying spin, and I found myself face to face with Egypt.

She was Letha's height and Letha's shape, her full rounded bosom captured in the white cloth by a golden clasp of embracing serpents, her hips and stomach full and languorous beneath the easy give of the heavy linen. Her face was concealed, but I could see the rich plum of her lips and the almost indiscernible loosening of the skin of her throat. Her arms, bare to the shoulders, were round, and although there were clashing bracelets above her wrists, her fingers were without rings. I fell into an Elizabethan gesture of obeisance, certain without surety that I had found what I sought.

"Hail, Egypt," I said. "Hail, the topless towers of Ilium. All hail, musk and tamarisk, to the serpent queen far fairer than all."

"Far darker than all," she said imperiously. "Dark as the midnight's pit, the inside hollow of the grape, dark. Rise and proclaim yourself, nimble tongue."

I got to my feet, took a flower from Rennie's bowl—a yellow rose prematurely blossomed out in the close warmth of the room—and I laid it in her hand.

"I proclaim myself a naught to your all, fairest dark lady," I said, closing her fingers on the stem of the rose. "A love knot to your everything. I proclaim myself a weak back, a willing heart, a ripe rose to be crushed for the perfume. I am Antony of the wide continents, Antony the servile pawn of the Nile."

"The Nile needs no continence," she said. "And Antony is of weak heart except in war. Too easy to the scorpion sting of death." She looked at me measuringly. "Methinks his hair had more gold than thine. It is so long to remember. So long to remember clear."

"My hair has blackened through ages of grief, dark lady," I said, fixing the rose under the pin of her serpents, feeling the heat from her skin warming the white linen. "Through dark ages of loss and desire." I circled her back with my right arm. "Let us dance the ages more golden, oh sweetest fair, oh darkest light."

Her back crept away from my hand and she looked warningly up toward Cadmium Greene who was engaged with Rennie and Ziggie. "My master likes it not when I leave his hand," she said.

"The true mistress is masterless," I chided her, leading her out to the floor. "And you have already sailed away from me once without permission."

The orchestra had changed centuries to a fox trot and we danced close, her forehead under my chin, her white linen against my tights and tunic, and her hair smelled of herbs and spices and the salt sea. We danced without talking, circling the floor slowly and almost indolently. She certainly *felt* like Letha to my body's touch, but the candles threw a distorting light and the square flags of the stone floor were in strange disequilibrium under my sandaled feet. The music broke upon us like a freshet on a rock, eddying around our bodies and pushing us together into an island of motion.

"Yon Caesar," I said, nodding my chin in the direction of the throne. "He hath a lean and haunted look."

She craned her head back on her neck to look at me suspiciously, displaying at the very top of her throat a thin circlet of wrinkles that were whiter than the surrounding make-up. "It's the look of man," she said. "What would you have?"

"Something more of the child, perhaps." I shrugged. "I would not myself attend his ghost."

The suspicion grew on her face, tightening her lips like the mouth of a purse. "And who are you to keep my hours?" she said.

"Nothing, lady," I said. "Only a lover. Not more and not one whit less."

She inspected me with a long deliberate glance from beneath her concealing mask, and when she spoke, her voice was sharp and final under the music. "I will dance with you," she said. "But I shall know you not."

I bowed my acquiescence and we danced more slowly, cutting the beat in half, gliding our double steps together as though joined at the hips to dance on the glossed floors of our own creation. Others were dancing but I did not see them, felt them sometimes brushing by us like curtains in a breeze, the music and the motion and the unceasing fretful dance of the fireflies. And then the music stopped in a gradual sweep of strings and we faced each other on the margin of the floor. She dropped my hand and fondled the petals of the rose.

"It has no odor, my lady," I said. "The sweetest perfume would be pretentious to breathe where your breasts so softly sigh."

She regarded me again almost as though I were a puzzle. "My gratitude for the dance, Sir Knight," she said. "Good-by." And then, as if she were not aware of her action, she stretched slightly on her toes and touched my cheek with her fingers, reading my skin by Braille. I was standing alone on the floor, the abrasive tingle of her dress and her fingers cupped in the memory of my empty flesh. I looked around, but the white robe and the high-piled hair were out of sight. I saw Daniel by the orchestra niche making a congratulatory prizefighter's signal with his hands clasped together over his head. We joined at the buffet and toasted ourselves with two brown cups of liquor.

"Is she or isn't she, David?" he asked. "You danced as though you knew her."

"I don't know. I can't be sure," I said. "I think so, but—Jesus, I don't even know if I'm really me."

"Well, what about her voice, David? You can surely tell from her voice."

"I don't know," I repeated angrily. "She talks as though she were on the stage. And she keeps changing her inflections. I don't know anything."

"Okay," Daniel said smiling. "You're doing fine. Just stay in there." He helped me adjust my false nose and he gave an unnecessary pat to his perfect turban. "You need help, just holler," he said. "But frankly, boy. You're on your own, now."

I watched him wander into the other room, leaving me alone with my comic misery. Christ, I thought. How ridiculous can you be? But how can I tell if it *is* she when I'm just not sure? I danced my way back to the crape-clad throne, ignoring one proposition and a scattering of sneers and compliments on my solo performance. The Egyptian dress had vanished and Rennie was sitting to one side with the bowl of flowers in her lap, braiding a garland for an anemic pirate whose black patch kept slipping into his red false beard. Ziggie was singing at the foot of Cadmium Greene's bench, fingering the ukulele cursorily while the half-century-old birthday boy loomed down on him like a sea-beaten shoulder of rock. Ziggie was improvising verses, and although Cadmium Greene's face was disdainful, there was a hint of indulgence in his smile.

"For Orestes the sack of Troy
Was small solace
If Iphigenia really lost all
At Aulis."

Cadmium Greene snorted. "Your English metrics are an abomination," he said. "Do one in the Greek."

"Alas, my lord," Ziggie said. "My Greek has all congealed and I can't budge out of the middle mood. But my friend here —" He pointed at me. "He is a more foolish fool than I am. I am a mere professional fool, which means that I only profess foolishness. He, on the other hand—" He made a great flourish and handed me the ukulele. "He is an amateur fool. Which means that he is in love with foolishness."

I smiled an idiotic smile beneath my false nose and I waited with the ukulele in my hands.

"Well, play something," Cadmium Greene roared. He grabbed the hair on both sides of his head and squeezed at his skull, tilting the crown forward on to his forehead. "I have an absolute hell in my head!" he groaned. "Sing something that will soothe me."

"Only death has cool enough hands, sire," I said, and I improvised a limerick out of the dance and my mouse-grey courtier's rage.

"There once was a scholar serene
Whose growth was obsidianly obscene.
But a slip on the ice
Cut off a big slice
Of a footnote and heart-root of green."

Ziggie jumped high in the air, clapping his hands above his head and kicking his feet in exorbitant applause. "Is he not wondrous foolish, sire?" he shouted, slapping me on the face and pounding on the ukulele case.

Cadmium Greene's expression narrowed into puzzled malevolence, and like a girl awkwardly pitching a baseball, he threw his brown cup at me, the liquor staining my leg and the pieces smashing into slivers and shards of brittle china on the stone floor.

"You don't amuse me at all," he said. "What are you?"

"Just a lover," I answered. "A lover with a bursting nose and a soul of prose. I came to steal a single rose from your birthday. May I?"

Cadmium Greene studied me intently, methodically, and his grey eyes had frigid depths in them where nothing could live. He examined me slowly and acutely, but he seemed satisfied that there wasn't much to examine and he dismissed me from his attention as though I didn't exist at all. He dismissed the whole room in a disdainful shrug of his velvet drape—the dancing mummers, the music, the candle-flames, the dart of the fireflies which made a Byzantine aureole for his head in the dark mirror behind him.

"Lover," he spat disgustedly, spewing the word from his lips as though it were reptilian. "Roses. Dancing. Allurements of sex in a jade cemetery. There are no women to love. We have destroyed women. And women have destroyed sex. Sex. Eros. The one naked force of creation. The architect of the Eleusinian mysteries. The builder of the desert pyramids."

"I always thought that it was my ancestors who built the pyramids," I said. "Although nobody ever gave them credit for it."

He scowled briefly at me and then chose to ignore me, a massive flyswatter deigning to overlook the foolish impotent buzz, the busy unbusinesslike rasp through the uncaring air. Ziggie shot a quick look of warning at me, but I was sailing high above his look in my mustard-brown mouse-grey, and my cheek was warm where her hand had come to troth. Cadmium Greene continued his harangue, butting his head against the mirror behind him, his eyes ice in their sockets.

"Before the time of *things*—how long ago that was," he said, "when man lived before the time of things, Woman was sex and man suckled on her. Cleaved close. The pearl beyond price, because she was life to him." He snorted in revulsion. "Now Woman is another *thing* and she has exchanged her sex for vanity. Vanity," he emphasized. "It's a force that *things* respond to."

"So saith the preacher," I muttered under my breath.

"Vain *things*," he went on, his mouth twisting as though in pain. "Things. Tawdry items of self-possession for tentative sale. Junk on a bazaar counter. Pale sexless pearls that chill the skin to borrow human heat." He shook his fist and his voice was strangled. "A thing has no secret openings. No deep hidden places for a man to bruise, for a man to suck life out of. Just a thing. A closed-up bauble thing, stealing someone else's light, the cold lunar dark, Artemis cold naked under black cellophane."

"And Aphrodite taking a douche on a clamshell," I said. "So what? What do you want anyway, a hot bath? An electric massage? A geisha sugar-tit for your pyorrhea? Who promised you anything in the first place?"

Cadmium Greene rocked to a stop on his bench and glared down at me, again examining me with fierce detachment, his eyes fascinated by my spurious plastic nose. I snapped my finger at the pimple and beat a tattoo on the ukulele.

"Just a thing, sire," I said. "A fake pimpled thing, but it throbs red and hot and I live out of it."

He squeezed his head between his hands once more and groaned loudly. "Hell is where my ears pinch," he growled. "What are you, pimple?"

"I'm the carbuncular lover, my lord," I said. "The creditor who appears on birth-debt-days. Would you do penance in the snow like Henry before the turrets of Hildebrand? The snow is slippery and cold and my pimple is soothing warm. Do your sheets stay cold when you lay?"

He shook me away with his head, looking frantically around the room as though seeking someone who was not there. Finally his gaze rested on Rennie, who was trying to put her finished garland around the pirate's neck while he kept slapping at her buttocks with her green and black tails.

"You," Cadmium Greene roared. "You. Slut. Bring me a bowl of this drink. My throat burns."

Rennie repulsed the drunken pirate's boarding party and

ran off after the liquor. Ziggie took the ukulele back and tried to divert Cadmium Greene's attention from me, but he would have none of it.

"You," he shouted. "You, pimple. What do you think you know that makes your mouth so loud? What do you know that I haven't thrown away as trash years ago?"

"Maybe one thing, sire," I said. "Something that you never even found to throw away. Maybe to laugh at yourself because you're so funny." I broke into an uncontrollable giggle, pointing up at him as though I were sighting the North Star. "You're so funny. Like my pimple."

Ziggie took my arm in the restraining grip of the lock-ward. "He's moon and moth mad, my lord," he apologized. "His wife ran off with a merman barnacles ago and his brain has become salt-flecked. We carry him to revels and birthday feasts to stop his weeping."

"She was light and fair, my love," I said. "A feather in the bed, a new straw broom in the closet. A hound saw her running some days ago in this forest and I seek her way."

Ziggie gave me a soft wailing background of a Welsh ballad of unrequited love and early death and Cadmium Greene took great slurping gulps like a horse from the bowl Rennie had brought, eying us both with spite and befuddlement.

"My wattled house is small, sire," I continued. "Just three tweeters, one woofer, and a portable chemical toilet. But I am lonely without her and I cannot reach the high cobwebs on the ceiling and my instalment payments are in default. I loved her before her breasts were budded and I thought that her plump grown breasts were a present to me for my love. She sleeps badly at night and I bring her warm milk in the morning." A real unsought tear welled in my eye and slipped below my mask and my voice was almost a sob. I could have collapsed on a tearful bed of weeping and drowned forever, but I leaned on the sea and remembered myself. "So much milk to stand sour beside her fresh-made bed," I continued. "Oh, help me to find her, my lord. She has hair between her legs and she looks like black silk stockings thrown across the counterpane when she sleeps."

Cadmium Greene finished the bowl and tossed it down to me. I held it awkwardly against my chest. His eyes had changed expression again, but I could not read them. I thought that there was a tinge of wonder in his face, but the mad fireflies were dancing more wildly in the dark mirror and they drained his light away from him. He laughed, however, when he spoke—the too-loud, uncertain laugh of a man who has no belief in laughter.

"You commence to amuse me, pimple," he said. "You play a harmless game, whatever game it is you play." He pointed at the room, at the accelerated pitch of the merry-making. "This is a birthday party, not a wake. Take any wench you like and slop her with your sour milk."

I fell to my knees, crowning myself with the inverted bowl. "Your munificence knows no bounds, sire," I said. "I shall start on the kitchen help."

And she was suddenly there, standing next to Rennie, observing our tableau as though it were a movie, but I couldn't tell what reel she had walked in on. She had changed costume to French Empire, her breasts almost squeezed out of her bodice by the high gathered waist, her hair hidden in a high blond Pompadour wig, her face powdered white to match the white lace of her heavy draped skirts. There were two black beauty marks pasted to her cheeks and she stood small and stiff on her high heels, a narrow silver domino hiding her eyes. In her hand she carried the yellow rose, its blossomed head drooping on the short stem. She *was* Letha. She had to be. Or was she? My visceral responses to her identity were sharp and sure, but I couldn't be certain. There was the rage of the liquor, the grotesque pitch of the costume party, my own undiminished shock at being black-haired and disguised, improvising surreal verses on a shifting revolving stage. Rennie was conducting a careful female appraisal of this Antoinette, this slight, almost diminutive Maintenon, and her black cat's back arched as she threw a questioning glance at me. I shrugged my confusion back to her and remembered my immediate role.

"Your bowl returned, sire," I said, tossing the bowl up to Cadmium Greene, who caught it clumsily in his lap. "Lest your concupiscence run over," I said. I turned raucously to the Empire gown. "But here's a likely scullion for my potato peeler. Come on, Kate, let's keel the goddamn pot."

I took her hand, the one that held the rose, and led her firmly to the floor, adapting the oversmooth banalities of the dance orchestra to the tinkling suggestions of a minuet, an infrangible Dresden clockwork in the dust of the antiquary's shelf. She followed me with a small resistance, turning her head to look back at the throne, but either Cadmium Greene nodded his assent or she herself decided that it wasn't worth the trouble to protest. We danced a careful dance, giving our concentration to the patterns that we shared rather than to one another. I had made her uneasy and I gloried in the fear that I had raised in her, whether she was Letha or not. I kissed the hand that held the yellow rose, the hand that I held as we danced.

"Madame," I said. "You carry my flower in your hand as you carry my heart in your heart. Our love has a long stem and its roots run deep."

"You are forward," she said, and did her voice have a slight lisping accent, a tiny vestige of a sea change in a journey from a long way away? "Your head," she said, "can fall as easily as the flower's. I pay my gardeners very well. I like my verdure to be pruned and cropped."

"Our national disease, I'm told," I said. "But with you, it is le droit de la reine. Myself, I would choose to eat your cake and have it too. You inspire me with hunger, Sans Souci."

She backed off away from me as though she were trying to put me into a sharper focus. "There is that in you," she said, "that I do not know. That I do not think I like."

"Oh, you'll find it likable when you get to know it," I said. "It's what gave Mimi such cold cold hands. It rattles a little like the tumbrils, but it's been very rusty. Don't, Madame," I said. "Don't spurn our little treasure. It's ours, after all, to enjoy."

"I don't like you to talk to me like that," she said. "You use words too well. You could play the coward in danger and write a brave letter afterward. I know too awfully well the hollow lies that words can't cover up."

I was stroking her back, keeping time to the music, smoothing a mole that grew low between the shoulder blades. Letha had such a mole on her back, but I couldn't remember whether it was in the same place. "You must have had a good teacher," I said. "To have learned so much about the sham of words."

"I've earned my degrees," she said. "All men are good teachers of that."

I unfastened my false nose and returned it to my inside pocket. "Let me at least defend myself," I said. "Or, at least, let me defend words, the precious word. Word sham is word sham, yes. But not necessarily deception. Words can also be promissory notes. A man can try to redeem his promises, his honeyed words. To hold himself to himself."

"What would make him do that?" she asked. "Why should he try to do such a rare thing?"

"Maybe for a woman," I said. "Or a rose. Or even for himself. A man too can have his strangenesses."

She settled back into the dance, looking at me thoughtfully, holding her head away from my shoulder. "What do you do?"

she asked. "What do you do when you're not making speeches out of a costume?"

"Ah." I made a mock moan. "The pretty lady will not play with me. Was it not ever thus? I'm a simple man, Madame," I said. "I try to cultivate my own small garden, which, alas, has lately gone to seed. And I rehearse the speeches that I would not dare to utter save with a concealing mask at a costume ball."

"No," she said. "I'll not play. Who are you? How do I know you? I won't play your game."

I could not then—nor can I even now—weigh all the ambiguities. If she was, indeed, Letha, how could she not know me, costume and hair dye or any other device or disguise notwithstanding? To live and sleep by my side for almost ten years, to learn my walk, my stance, the flab below my chin, my every cramp and nuance as she knew her own memorized face. Impossible! But then, I too should not have been uncertain about her. And I had even come looking for her, seeking her out of the mummers, and I was not sure. Or did she know, and like Daniel with his masks and masks, was she merely playing a game on a higher dimension? And yet it wasn't important at the time—she or me—masks within masks, truth beneath words and words beyond truth. And if she were not, after all, Letha, then who could she have been? What frantic eidolon of my buried passional life had I projected into flesh and black shadow?

"Madame," I said. "You ask more questions than man can answer. I come as an imposter to cherish the bright kernel which is denied. I'm a misunderstood musician. You know me. You've heard my famous Concerto for Electrocardiograph and Corpse. It's sheer murder, that piece."

"Stop it, stop it, stop it," she said. "Leave me alone."

"Come on, you'll recognize me in a minute," I said, holding her tightly in the dance. "I'm really a simple millionaire, the sole owner and stockholder in a giant truss-rental corporation. We're nation-wide, Madame," I said, gearing my voice to a carnie's pitch. "You can pick one up in any corner of these United States and drop it off anywhere. No charge, no grief, no questions asked. I give succor to the weak-loined. I am king of the ruptured. Hernia victims all over the country bless me for my staunch support. I throw my holdings at your feet."

I tried to prostrate myself on the floor before her, but she struggled with me and wouldn't let me go down. "Stop it, you're making a scene," she said. "You're a fool."

"Of course," I said. "And that's how you know me."

The set was coming to an end and I danced toward a darkened corner. Some of the candles were beginning to gutter out, low and splattering in the hot wax. Her elaborate gown held her body away from mine and her face was removed under the wig and unyielding in its white-powder mask. I was incited by her remoteness and I felt pushed by a tide, powerful with a borrowed power.

"You are cold and difficult, Madame," I said. "But I can burn you. And in your next costume you will be naked to me."

She tried to struggle free from my arms as the music stopped, but I had locked her hands behind her back and I pressed a long kiss to her lips. She fought briefly and then tolerated the kiss like ice until I let her go. When we broke apart she was furious and beautiful in her gown. There was a high red in her cheeks even through the powder and the rose was partially crushed in her hand.

"You're nothing to me," she said, revulsion twisting her face under the mask. "Do you understand? You're everybody. You're nothing. But—" and she waved in the direction of Cadmium Greene's mock throne—"you stay away from *him*. You hear me. You leave him alone."

"He's a big boy, my lady," I said. "He's a big fifty-year-old boy. He can take very good care of himself, I hear."

Exasperated, she discovered herself shaking the flower violently at me, and when she saw what she was doing she threw it on the floor in disgust. While I picked it up to fasten on my tunic, she wheeled her skirts around and marched angrily to the far end of the room. A dignified little royal march, a tumbril march, I thought. Even though her pompadour had fallen slightly askew and the black roots of her hair displayed themselves beneath the blond.

I walked outside to the lawn through a tall terrace door. A large garden in the informal style, bordered by a thick hedge, flanked the house on this side. A small dark building—a toolhouse or a potting shed—was set at the far end, and some of the costumed guests danced or sat on the grass in the green shadows. Although it must have been already very late, the party had not yet reached its apex. The drive and the front lawn were still jammed with parked silent cars and whatever it was that Cadmium Greene had distilled into the little brown cups seemed sufficient fuel to sustain the night. Our amorous lion had passed out on the grass and his mannequin was sitting quietly on a stone bench. She rested one of her feet on his severed lion's head and the plastic teeth gleamed against her patent-leather shoe. I took a slow walk around the house, smoking a cigarette, taking care to avoid the bushes and the dark recesses where the sounds of giggles and sighs suggested that nocturnal unmaskings were taking place. There was no moon tonight, but fuzzy clusters of cloud were scudding low in the sky, damping the night with a moist silver sheen. As I passed the windows of the large room, the stringed music washed at me like spray, the inside shapes and dancing shadows floating like an aquarium dream, and I laughed drunkenly inside my head. Riegel! Riegel, you bastard! You who were with me at Mylae. Hey, come on, you Gefilte-Fisher-King, you dry fly, you limber casting rod. Shan't he, shan't he, oh, shan't he ever? You're damned right he shall.

You've hooked the sea, oh King, and you shall have rain for tea.

I was just going to move away from the window when my attention was suddenly focused at a tall mirror on the opposite wall. It cast back to me at a slight angle a recessed corner of the room that seemed to be behind Cadmium Greene's throne. The black curved shape, the tails, the outrageously feline gesticulations—there was no doubt as to Rennie's identity. Nor the other's also—the flounced Empire skirts and the haughty stance of one who is accused or unexpectedly confronted. That damned treacherous Rennie! I couldn't move from my ridiculously indirect post of observation for fear that they would have disappeared by the time I got back into the hall. And dancers blocked my view from time to time while the flickering candle flames distorted and concealed even as they falsely illuminated. Were they chatting, gossiping, arguing, exchanging recipes, confidences, diseases? Rennie emphasized some point, stabbing with her finger at the lacy bodice of the other's gown. And she, in turn, leaned closer, her blond pompadour contrasting with the black jersey of the cat costume. Their faces were very near together for talk. They could have been nibbling at the opposite halves of the same apple, and all at once, terrified, I felt my skin go stiff and red, felt my flesh take on a grainy white texture, felt myself scream from some interior mouth as the teeth bit deep and my substance dissolved in the juices of my terrible fear. And then some interior ear—some deep-lying receptor floating in the very pit of me—caught the scream, caught it and translated its pitch, its inhuman unvaried cadence, its sacred agony: "*Me. The self. The middle of the self. That which is afraid of its death. Which weeps eternally for its own death.*" I stumbled away from the window. I held on to my stomach with both hands as though I had been disemboweled and I was trying to stuff myself back into myself. There was a film of clammy sweat over all my skin. I sat down on the grass and breathed with panting avidity at the damp summer air. I trembled all over and the soughing branches of the unseen trees shook with me. And after a moment, convinced that this was the bravest thing I had ever done, I stood up on my feet and marched around in a small circle, sending orders to my limbs, running a check on the casualties, the damage, the debris of myself. My face was cold in the distant sea breezes and there was a quivering spasm in my breast, but the assault was over —if assault it had truly been. When I returned to the window the mirror was empty. I leaned against a column and collected the scattered segments of my being. A near miss, that, I said to myself, half convinced that I had gone mad, and about equally half convinced that I had made it all up. As I started to return to the house I remembered my still unused false beard. I might as well ring all the changes, I thought. A pimpled nose, a cheap braid of ersatz face hair, rumpled clothes from an attic trunk. Bravado, lies, rhetoric squatting on the throne of courage, drunken fire masquerading as passion. Oh, what a compendium of talents is man, indeed, that thou art mindful of him. And when the heat is on, he surely do squeal, don't he? God help us, manunkind.

With my beard fixed in an arrogant thrust, my head thrown back in caricatured profile of the princely Freud, I went back into the royal hall. Cadmium Greene had descended from his throne. He sat on the raised dais, his crown at his feet, his hair wild. There were red stains on his cheeks and his purple cloak had slipped back from his shoulders. Daniel and Ziggie both sat attendance on him and Rennie walked up with another bowl of liquor as I approached. His voice had become thicker, almost slurred, and there was a look of cunning on his face that suited the sinister droop of his lips too well. He took a long draught from the bowl and welcomed me with a roar.

"Oh ho! Pimple is back. Make a place for the pimple!" He narrowed his eyes drunkenly at me and I could see fine pale veins beneath the grey. "No, he's not a pimple any more. He's reformed. Now he's a beard. Pimple has grown up into a beard. And, pray, what will you be tomorrow, pimple?"

"An ash, sire," I said. "Even as will you."

"You'll always be a pimple," he said, drinking again from the bowl. "Pimples don't change. They just come to a head and leak pus."

"Sure, an it please you, my lord," I said.

"Nothing pleases me," Cadmium Greene said. "Nothing at all." He lumbered to his feet using Ziggie as a brace and he stood wild and unsteady searching the room with haunted eyes. "Where is she?" he grunted almost inaudibly. "Where is she now?"

"Where is who, my lord?" I said. "I have become expert in finding what is lost."

"You have had experience," he said. "But fire does not burn in ashes. Could you kill if the want were enough?"

"Only myself," I said. "I could not want another's life that much. I sometimes think I have a surfeit of my own."

"And if you had a loss rather than a surfeit? What then, pimple? Could you kill then?"

"I doubt that there are any losses in nature that are remediable," I said. "Life leaks away and all our fury cannot suck it back. But the surfeit remains and this is trouble enough for us to swim in."

Cadmium Greene tinkled the bells on Ziggie's cap in sarcastic applause, addressing himself to Ziggie and Daniel as though I were not present. "Did you hear?" he said. "He's a case of mistaken identity. We thought the pimple was a poet, but he's grown a beard and become a philosopher. Epictetus in a nutshell. The pimple was more attractive."

"I always aim to please," I said, taking off the beard and putting it back in my tunic. I struck an attitude for Cadmium Greene.

"What are you now?" he asked. "What disguise is this?"

"Man," I said. "The last impenetrable disguise. The barefaced lie." I rubbed at my face with my open palms and made the conjuror's demonstration that there was nothing up my sleeves. "See," I said. "Now I'm like you."

He looked at me, measuring his face in my face, threatening me with a dreadful contempt. I smiled into his furious scowl. "No," he said. "Your mirror doesn't fit me at all. I am like no one." He turned away, lurching around Ziggie, scanning the room but not finding what he sought. "Where is she?" he said. "I want to dance."

Rennie circled in front of him, pivoting slowly, provocatively, on one toe, arching her arms above her head. "I am a very good dancer," she said. "Once I won a cup for the Charleston. And my Black Bottom is considered spectacular."

Cadmium Greene searched the room one more time and then inspected the new offer. "Sluts are always in long supply," he said. "In famine, war, and time of plenty. The one certain economic factor in the progressive pustule of history."

"Oh, Mr. Greene," Rennie warbled. "You're so romantic."

Cadmium Greene snorted and transferred his weight to Rennie's shoulder. They moved out on the dance floor, he leaning on her, a heavy purple column, powerfully dependent. I picked up his crown and settled it on my head. The orchestra was playing a fandango and I was surprised to see that Cadmium Greene danced well, even with his crippled foot. He swung and reversed and stamped his feet with a brutal grace, using Rennie as both dancing partner and mobile support. He moved like a stallion, his shoulders wide-boned and his eyes flashing white. As the Latin tempo of the music increased, the other dancers on the floor fell out of the pattern, ringing the twirling figures of Rennie and Cadmium Greene, clapping their hands in a wide circle to the accelerating beat. Most of the candles had sputtered out and the large room was in semidarkness, the glooming shadows trapped in the tropical rhythms of the dance, in the half-sweet rapid motion of the after time when the dulled sun races with the night to bridge the ascending horizon. I found myself clapping my hands along with the others, whether in response to the pervasive rhythm or in begrudging approbation for this brutal display of violence and grace. I saw that both Ziggie and Daniel were also applauding in rhythm, Daniel particularly tall and rapt.

And then I knew that she was present also, sensing her from the chill along the nape of my neck before I turned around to see her. She had mounted the vacant throne seat while we were all watching the floor and she was sitting casually, one leg tucked up under her on the high bench, her eyes watching the festivities as though the performance and the rhythmic applause were for her amusement, for her own negligent delectation. She was almost naked on the throne, sparsely costumed in a bikini with green leaves fixed to the scant cloth, her hair loose and falling almost to the small of her back. Around her face, Moslem fashion, she had wrapped a light-green gauze scarf, and while she sat, she drummed impatiently against the wood with her free foot. She looked down into my gaze and we were alone outside the maelstrom of the dance.

"You planning any more costume changes?" I asked. "If so, you might be able to use this." I threw the yellow rose up to her lap. "It won't cover much, but every little bit helps."

She tucked the rose under the top band of her bikini bottom. The blossom nodded against her navel. "You don't like my costume," she said mincingly. "I think it's very becoming."

"You know I don't like it," I said. "I expect that's why you wore it. I suppose I should find that flattering."

"Find what you will," she said. "You may have stolen a crown, but it doesn't change you. A crown doesn't make you a king."

"And a throne doesn't make you profound," I said. "It's you who'll make me a king."

The music ceased in a clashing crescendo of "olé's" and hand clapping and Rennie and Cadmium Greene were escorted back to the dais by the applauding crowd. The exertions of the dance had colored his face to match his purple robes, and he was panting heavily, leaning his weight cruelly upon Rennie's shoulder. Some of the mummers made an abortive beginning to the choruses of "Happy Birthday to You," but their voices withered and fell silent under Cadmium Green's glare. "Speech," someone called, and others took up the chant, huddling around the front of the dais. Cadmium Greene stretched out his arm for silence, waiting until the crowd was quiet before he spoke.

"You expect me to thank you for coming to my birthday," he said. "I did not ask you and I prefer to celebrate myself alone, so I have no thanks to offer you."

"Good old Cadmium," cried a drunken voice. "A real sweet guy."

"But if I don't give you my thanks, I can give you my heartfelt curses," Cadmium Greene continued, eying the crowd with unembarrassed hatred. They rustled uncertainly before him, determined to believe that he was making an elaborate joke and soon they would be able to laugh at themselves with him. "Yes, curses," he repeated, savoring the expulsive rancor in the word. "In a remote province of Manchukuo, it is the custom on birthdays for the celebrant to spit on all those who have befriended him during the year. No one has ever befriended me, but I would adapt the custom to spit on all of you. I am like none of you and you all disgust me."

He picked up the bowl and toasted himself long and heartily while the crowd dispersed with nervous laughter and hesitant applause. As he put the bowl aside, he saw that she had returned, that she was sitting on his throne, her foot swinging indolently like a pendulum.

"Slut," he roared at her. "Where were you when I wanted you?"

She didn't move in the chair, heedless of his words. I felt myself brace to jump between them, to stuff his mouth with his cloak, but she sat on the high bench, unmoved.

"You hear me!" he shouted. "You hear me when I speak!"

He looked around furiously, his face gone from purple to black, and he caught up the bowl like a shot put, bringing it behind his head in position to hurl. She turned her head like a cat, looked curiously at him, and then she turned away. His whole body tightened in a writhing spasm. An animal howl of rage erupted from his throat and I saw his shoulders clench as though he were going to send the bowl crashing through the air and I plucked it out of his hand from behind his back. He stood frozen in space, one hand still on Rennie's shoulder, the other poised empty behind his head, his face contorted with some kind of frustration and misery that no human should behold, much less display. In the moment of almost darkness, his hair seemed to be twisting in pain and we might all have been chiseled out of some sea-ferned scaly rock.

"Your crown, sire," I said, removing the crown from my head and presenting it to him with an awkward pageboy flourish. "And now the restoration of my kingdom. *My* crown, which you were going to throw away." I put the bowl back on my head. Some few drops of the liquor left in the bowl dripped down over my ears and were cool on my cheeks.

Cadmium Greene looked at me as though I were an insect. Then he looked up at her and then he looked long at me. He laughed raspily. "A lunatic hero," he said, directing his voice up to the throne. "You've found yourself a valiant knight, doltish and daft." He turned back to me. "And what do you think you've won, pimple? What do you think this door prize is worth?" He looked back at her appraisingly. "She doesn't hide much. You should be able to tell what she is."

She sat above us both, her foot tapping, her eyes scarfed and smoldering. The fireflies filled the mirror behind her head.

"I think she is fire and love," I said, looking up at her. "Growth and green change like the rainbow. She is beautiful and her face can be hard, but I think it can be soft also."

Cadmium Greene laughed spitefully, laughed long without mirth, his laughter becoming a strangled drunken cough and his breath erupting in slow and violent heaves. He sat heavily on the edge of the dais, tearing the black jersey of Rennie's arm as he clawed his way down. He sat ponderously, a leaden giant, squeezing at his temples with both hands, his tongue loose in his mouth. I had not realized how titanically spent he was, burnt out, not so much with the liquor as with some inward fire that you could almost see licking at the backs of his eyes. I would not have been incredulous at that point to have seen flames jet from his nostrils and mouth, searing the air in front of him with a dry stale heat.

He caught me with his eyes and the corner of his lip sneered at me contemptuously and yet for a second there was something that was almost like affection in his glance. "Scrape away everything, hero," he muttered, his words almost inaudible. "Scrape away the dross and the fat and the gaseous vapors. The lies. The illusions. The myths small men pack their frustrations in." His words were almost drooled out and his mouth had gone slack, but his voice was still resonant, even in husky whispers. "Scrape it all away, hero. And you're still left with *that.*" He made a spastic shrug with his head toward the throne above him, and his eyes burned with grey glacial flames. "Oh—" his voice was a groan in his throat—"there's still *that* left beneath everything."

"And what is that?" Ziggie asked, bending down beside him to catch his words.

"The horror of *that,*" Cadmium Greene gurgled, laughing or sobbing with his mouth all loose, repeating his shrug toward the seated figure on the throne. "That's what's always left to man."

"What was it he said?" Ziggie asked. "I couldn't make out the word."

"He said *honor,*" Daniel said. "He said that honor was always left to man."

Cadmium Greene snorted in the beginning of his drunken sleep, cradling his head in his arms against the rough wood of the dais, his tarnished crown teetering on the wild hair at the back of his skull. His body was stiff and braced, even in sleep, and he seemed to be straining against the dais, bent to push the wooden framework of the world off its precarious axis. Rennie helped me arrange the velvet robe around him and we shifted his weight so that he would be more comfortable. The room was almost completely dark now and the fireflies were coming through the windows—the outside coming into the inside—dancing to the white surreal music, which I realized with a shock had never ceased. And then I saw that she had descended from the throne and she was stroking the velvet on his shoulder with a tender abstracted hand. She sighed and very deliberately lifted the crown from his head and placed it beside him on the dais. It gleamed there like burnished copper in the night.

The music and the dancing continued, flowing over and around the huddled purple sleeper like slow easy water breaking over and around an unmovable rock. The music and the dancing were more gentle, more quiet, more accommodated to the dark inexorable pitch of the night, the cantilevered panoply of late stars that fell slowly down the indigo steeps of the heavens toward the caverns of dawn. Daniel had sat down next to Cadmium Greene, lighting his pipe for the first time since we had arrived at the party, a vigilant guard wreathing himself and his royal keep in pungent tobacco smoke. Rennie had moved away with Ziggie and I was alone with her, outside the tobacco smoke and the music, outside the darting fireflied world. I took her wrist and we danced slowly into the music, weaving a dark circuit among the other shadows in their slow unfathomable orbits. Beneath her scarf she seemed to be biting at her underlip as we danced.

"Why?" she said, and there was a note of resigned despair in her question. "Why did you have to come? Why did you have to do this?"

I couldn't tell if she knew me, and I knew also with a flash of demonic absurdity that unless she knew me, I could not tell if I knew her. We moved around the floor like painted pieces in a game and I thought that the most pathetic arrogance was to believe that one knew the game, that one was actually manipulating the moves and arranging the humorous confrontations and dolorous denouements. There was, to be sure, a game. How could one gainsay that? But who was the player and who was the played? And what slow hands would meet with shattering response to applaud the play, to witness the stumbling beginnings and pathetic ends?

"I'm sorry, lady," I said. "The choice was not mine. I was moved to come for love. And whatever hateful thing I have done, this also out of love."

"Love," she said as though she were tracing the word out on her fingers, following half-obliterated chalk marks on a rain-stained wall. "Love. It used to be a lovely word. What can you know about love? What can you really know about me?"

"I shan't apologize for the love," I said. "I have loved you deeply, truly, knowingly, since He took you from my side. I have been willed to you since His Will smashed your form into being. Since He made you Other. Since He made us into broken twain."

"Who took? Who made? Who? What are you talking about?" She pulled at her scarf, loosening it a little at her throat. "*Who* took me from your side? What desperate nonsense are you casting me in?"

"He. The only He That Is," I said. "He made me to fall asleep and He took a rib from my side and He fashioned you therefrom. Can you have forgotten already that we were once one?"

She laughed nervously as though she had been given a release, as though she had been offered a new part, not the one that she had been lusting after, but a good one, a playable role. We danced through the open French doors out on the terrace, circling the columns and the stone benches, dancing past the windows which no longer gave forth light. We danced easily, matching our steps, leaving the terrace for the garden, the grass cool and moist and soft to our dance.

"Oh," she laughed. "Adam. I didn't know you in your dark. You've put on weight and you've grown much older."

"Life is more exacting outside the garden," I said. "Although it has its compensations. But I'd know you anywhere, Eve. You've never changed."

"You think I'm—" she giggled and put her hand over her mouth. "Poor Adam," she said. "You never *could* tell your own true wife. I'm not Eve, silly. I'm Lilith, your oldest dearest friend. Don't you see how long my hair is? And wild?"

"Lilith," I said. "My first and truest own. You've been a long time away. Welcome home, my heart."

"This is not home," she said. "I have no home. Except the night and the shadow pools. And it's time for me to go now."

She tried to pull herself out of my embrace, tried to move her feet out of the rhythms of the dance, but I held her to me.

"No, not yet," I said. "I've searched too long to find you and the dawn is not yet. We both have time."

"Well, yes. The dawn is still away," she said, nodding at the eastern sky. "But you shouldn't be out here. You should be home with your Eve."

"Ah, I can't," I said. "She's got this date with a serpent and it wouldn't do for me to come barging in on them. History would never forgive me. Come, dance with me, Lilith, and let's fade like the fireflies while the night drains grey."

We danced on the grass, warmly and sinuously entwined, our smooth skin become bark and our limbs encircling like woody vines. She laid her head on my shoulder, where it grew and rooted, and we moved through the grass all one piece, riding the rise and fall of the earth swell on delicate porous feet, and the night damp ascended to our nostrils, sweet and heavy and aching with want. I tucked my fingers beneath the elastic of her bikini, following the rippled glide of her flanks with my palm as her hips and thighs moved to my slow dancing lead. She tightened her arm around my neck and we were an ancient tree, growing centuries with every step in slow rhythmic circles, adding sweet age and latent power with every sure steady ring. A light wash of smeary silver fog stained the eastern horizon, drowning the distant stars on the hem of the night, and as we danced and grew together, the fog began to rise, pulling the false banners of the dawn beneath it, invisible now, but heavy and cold with foreboding presence. The lap of the sea air had a more acrid bite in the sour mouth of the fog. I pressed closer to hold back the sky, pushing my lips at the green gauze of her face, breathing needfully, desirously into the green. She made a tiny movement of retreat, a slight flicker of reluctance to leave the pattern of the dance, and I could feel the conflict of her muscles with my hand, and then she pressed back at me and we were warm and rhythmed in a motionless dance.

"No, not here," she said. "Come with me."

She took my hand and led me across the grass and through the bark shadows of the trees to the potting shed, which smelled of old wood and deep primordial earth. There were no windows and the old door swung open easily to the touch and I had to stoop down low to keep my head free of the twisted nails and splintered beams which roofed the top. With the door closed behind us we were in the absolute blind dark and I fumbled for her, seeking her in our darkness, teaching myself her ways with the touch of my new fingers and her reaching arms. And we found one another in the unmasked dark as the unknowing earth revolved in ever-dizzying cycles and the whole false-lit universe pitched at an infinite velocity away from its boundaries, beyond its measured sureties and wry beginnings.

The cold yellow light woke me harshly, slatting through the long cracks in the crumbling walls of the shed, striping me with sun and morning shadow and hurting my eyes even while I slept. My head ached like misery and the skin on my back was tight and painful from my sunburn. My left cheek was pressed flat against the crumpled earth and I opened my eyes to find the yellow rose curled around my right ear in a pale Dionysian joke. I was alone in the shed between rakes and pitchforks, my feet pushing at a huge burlap bag of warm seed, and above my head, hanging from a single rusty spike, was a menacing pair of garden shears. THE GREAT AWAKENING, I thought, reading my mind's words in capital letters, half the lurid caption on a Temperance poster, the other half fiery with the crabbed spirit of Edwards' burning homiletic on "Sinners in the Hands of an Angry God." Get up, Riegel, you sot. Rise and shine and seize the day. I counted my feet and my arms and I crawled backwards out of the shed—stiffly, protestingly, aghast at the monstrosity of the full resplendent dawn, the sun already completely rounded and glaring ugly above the low trees. I brushed myself as clean as I could, scraping at some humus that had stained my tights and become crusted under the collar of my tunic. I peered back once more into the shed, wondering if I had truly left anything there, wondering what was dream and what was reality, and what parts of reality were not, after all, dream. The grass was wet with dew and my sandals were saturated within four or five steps. Oh, you're a pretty picture, you are, I said to me. A sodden sotted morning song, an aubade in dirty water colors. A shame the children can't see you in your full moral glory. You're an animated catechism, a soapstone Tablet of broken Law. Regard your father, children. Observe him well if you would lead the good life. Ugghh. An acid belch of revulsion soured my stomach and rose to my throat. Observe him very well. Paradise through parricide. Morality is what you feel good after. The living embodiment of Thou Shalt Not, you vertiginous bulwark, you paltry wriggle-heart.

Our cab was still parked in front of the house with three or four other stalwart vehicles, and our cab driver, stiff and insensible, lay prone on the gravel near the left rear wheel of the cab, asleep like the Cornish Giant. The true Arabian horseman, I thought. With his brown alcoholic life streaming out of him, doubled—nay, trebled—up in pain, he must have held his breast together with his hands and crawled back to his faithful steed for the one last white gallop across the desert sands. And now he lies noble and transmogrified at the tomb of his abandoned mount. A lazy early morning bee sniffed at his upright nose, but the nostrils deigned not even to twitch under the investigating buzz. In the back seat of the cab Rennie was curled asleep under her raincoat, and Daniel snored erect in the front, sitting tall, his costume barely wrinkled, his mask still firmly in place. And where is our lost leader, I wondered, circling the cab and looking about on the front drive. Could he have succumbed to the ragings of the night, he of the undeviating blood? And then I heard the unmelodic tune of a kazatzky whistled off beat, and Ziggie, hatless and with his hair neatly combed, skipped up the walk, a pot of coffee in one hand and a stack of cups balanced neatly in the other.

"Buon giorno, Lothario," he chirped. "The morn in russet mantle clad, walks o'er the dew of yon high eastern hill."

"Good morning, friend," I said. "I was afraid we'd lost you."

"Not the old Zig-Zag," he said. "He don't lose easy. I would have worried about *you,* but I figured you didn't have enough sense to get into real trouble. Join me in a good-morning quaff?"

He offered me a cup, taking another himself, and he propped the pot steady in the cabbie's yellow cap.

"It smells wonderful," I said. "Where'd you get it?"

"All modern houses without exception possess kitchens," Ziggie said. "And where there are kitchens, there is a distinct possiblity of coffee. Cheers."

We drank the steaming coffee slowly, testing it gingerly with our lips, sipping at it with pleasure. Ziggie watched me curiously, his attitude inviting me to talk, but I diverted his attention to the sleeping cab driver.

"Why, man," I said. "He doth bestride the narrow world like a Colossus, a Stonehenge, a granite outcropping from the dark side of the moon."

"He is humble," Ziggie agreed, admiring the stoic composure of our prostrate friend. "Humble and beautiful as a corpse. But he is ours and we love him."

We fell silent and concentrated on our coffee. "It was quite a night," I hazarded, uncertain of what or how much I wanted to say.

"Quite," he echoed. And seeing that I was not going to offer anything more, he picked up the conversation by himself. "Yes, indeedy. Quite. And your friend the cat was the cynosure of multitudinous attentions. Which is to say that she had a scratching good time."

"Fine," I said. "She had it coming to her."

"I'll say," he said. "From all directions, as a matter of fact." He laughed and poured some more coffee. "Her cup of milk flowed over and over and over. And even the imperturbable Daniel. I could have sworn I saw him dancing with a live woman." Ziggie giggled irrepressibly. "But I'm sure I was drunk."

I laughed too, abstractedly. "It sounds like a wonderful party. The kind I've always wanted to go to."

"Well, maybe it was," he said. And then he looked directly at me. "And was it successful by your reckoning?"

"I don't know," I said, trying to think my way clear to myself. "I'm not sure what I really wanted to happen and I don't know exactly what did happen. But I do feel somewhat resolved. In some way, anyway."

"A rare thing," Ziggie said, and we drank our coffee and listened to the raucous staccato of the birds and the distant sound of a bus shifting gears on a steep grade. The early morning sounds were dissonant and vaguely accusing to me.

"I mean," I continued, groping for some verbal entrance to the labyrinth of my feelings. "How can you know anything important? You know, successful or failure, right or wrong? There's just what is."

Ziggie stretched his legs and walked around the cab to inspect the sleepers. Then he sat down again on the concrete shelf that bordered the gravel drive. "Okay, David," he said. "What do you need? Old Doctor Solchek at your service."

"Thanks," I said smiling. "But I don't need that kind of help. I can make it on my own, I think. It's just that there's nothing to measure anything by."

"A very real problem," Ziggie said. We were both silent for a time and the birds sounded strident and startling in their empty amphitheatre of air. "I do have an offering, though," Ziggie continued. "My appropriated motto for hot August mornings. 'I am good; God is not good.' Do you know the idea?"

"It sounds vaguely familiar," I said. "I'm not much interested in God."

"But you are interested in 'I,' " Ziggie rejoined. "It comes down to the same thing."

"Have it your way," I said. "Theology doesn't make any sense to me except at night. Some nights."

"So stop pretending it isn't night," Ziggie said. "There's a hell of a lot in that little sentence."

" 'I am good; God is not good,' " I repeated. "It has a kind of nice balance to it, but I get no bells. I'm afraid it doesn't do anything for me."

Ziggie ignored my flippancy and his face gathered into the same kind of intensity I had seen when he was talking about silences. "It's a damned interesting notion," he said. "Notice it doesn't say that God is bad. It merely says that neither good nor evil can be attributed to God. And it doesn't really say that I am good. It just suggests that the attributes of good and evil are potentially adherent to me."

"Okay. If you want to read it that way," I said. "But I can't see where I'm much better off. According to this, all a man has to do is say that he's good. And he's got it made. Isn't that right?"

"Maybe," Ziggie said. His eyes were strangely stern and I had the feeling that I was being interviewed for a job I didn't want very much.

"But what if a man lies?" I said. "Suppose, for example, I go around coveting my neighbor's wife and ass and all that, and then I wash my hands good and announce to all and sundry that I've been a very good boy? What the hell kind of measuring is involved in that?"

"I can think of worse kinds," Ziggie said. "In the first place, you'd have to be a pretty rare bird—pathological or saintlike —to be able to say it. To be able to have the kind of self-serenity that could come out with approbation for yourself in such a situation. And second, even if you could, you'd at least be accepting the notion of the good. You'd be placing yourself within a moral referent—which is itself a value. Do you see?"

"No, I don't think I see that," I said. "At least I can't understand how it could apply to anything I know."

We sat quiet for some time, I examining the dark brown streaks of coffee at the bottom of my cup and trying vainly to connect this book talk of morality with the things that I had known and felt in these past frenzied days. Ziggie had scooped up a handful of gravel from the drive and was scattering it in lazy arcs across the wet grass. We were both startled to hear the front door of Cadmium Greene's house slam shut and the hollow clack of heels against stone. Down the steps and toward us on the gravel drive approached a figure in a clown's suit, the banal blotches of yellow and red contrasting violently with the white stucco and green grass, the figure moving swiftly but mechanically forward, erect, stiff, and vaguely formal as though driven by some ruthless clockwork of gears and wheels. As it came nearer we saw that it was a girl—perhaps not quite twenty, perhaps not quite as balefully pathetic as the sick fall of my stomach told me she was. The baggy pants and the scalp-tight canvas wig with the double strands of straggly red hair degendered her in some outrageous act of defloration. Her face was deeply streaked through her thick pancake make-up and I was unutterably shocked to see not only that she was young, but that her eyes, tearless and staring straight ahead, expressed the proud pain of some willing flagellant who has been whipped beyond even the extremities of desire. She may or may not have seen us, although she passed close enough so that I could have caught her wrist, impeded her measured advance by merely stretching out my arm. She passed us by without even deigning to heed us as spectators, inserted herself behind the wheel of an open sports car, made one swooping backward burst, and then roared out of the driveway. We listened to the receding motor for several minutes, its high-compression whine stilling the birds and the early morning crickets into an awed surcease of their graceless noisy litany.

"Look," Ziggie said, facing me again as the sound drained away. "This is important. The big problem in morality is getting people to believe that their actions are at all susceptible to a moral judgment. Once you manage that, you've done everything. Regardless of how wrong you or I may think any particular judgment is. Just let a man say 'I am good,' and you've already demonstrated the existence of morality to him. Ipso facto. Where he goes from there is strictly between him and God."

"But now you're sneaking God back in," I said. "That's not fair argument. It gives you private channels of information that I don't have."

Ziggie leaned back on his haunches, hugging himself under the knees. "You do an awful lot of protesting about God," he said. "That's usually a tell-tale sign. But if it makes you happier, just substitute another word. Life or love or sex or any other undefinable quality of experience. Maybe death is the biggest word." He rocked back and forth on the curvature of his spine. "After all, whatever we mean by God is just the sum indefinable total of all these."

"Jesus Christ, I don't want to argue with you," I said. "Go get yourself a plump young Jesuit and sharpen your fangs on him." I thought over his notions on morality, wondering and testing myself for signs of goodness. "Goddamn it, what a time to have to live in," I said. "Good old Jonathan Edwards. He didn't have it so bad with his Original Sin. Things were at least clear cut. Good and evil, milchik and fleischik, and when you put butter on a meat dish you knew you had sinned and you had to get the rabbi to come and repurify everything. For a fee. At least a man knew where he stood."

"Don't kid yourself," Ziggie said, releasing his knees from his two-handed grip. "A man only knew where he would be buried. In fact, I suspect that Original Sin was probably a metaphor for someone like Edwards. For any man who wanted to stand up in life. A way of talking beyond the ethical dualisms that most people use as moral strait jackets. I wouldn't be at all surprised if maybe Edwards was playing the same game of metaphysical charades that you and Daniel were talking about last night. The same game that so many others have played without always admitting it."

I got to my feet and stretched my cramped muscles, surprised at Ziggie's connection, feeling the burn on my skin and remembering through the associations of my body the windless shrine of my beer-bottle-guarded grave. "This game, Ziggie," I said. "Who do you play it against? God?"

Ziggie laughed and rose to his feet also. "Good Lord, no," he said. "You play it against yourself. You play *with* God against yourself. That's how God is created."

His words skipped into my head, hovered portentously beyond my neural traces, and then slid meaninglessly away. What has all this to do with me, I thought. Words and casuistries and Yeshiva-student theories, the ping-pong game of concepts and cunning syllogisms which anyone with a fair memory and an irresponsible attitude toward life and logic can play. I'm no mystic, no Rambam, no matador of metaphysical chess. As soon say, "God is evil; I am not evil." It explains a helluva lot more. And with greater justice, too. But there had been a surge of my blood, a willingness in some inchoate area of my unknown vitals to accept the groove, to become settled in a truth that one could lean on. Hell, the question is not a matter of knowledge anyway, but simply "who cares." My inner dialectic was broken by a gruff bear's voice from the cab.

"I smell coffee." It was Daniel sniffing out the open window, and Rennie stirred at his voice and poked her face out of the raincoat, her skin white and puffy beneath her eyes.

I joined Daniel and Rennie for a second cup. We all sat on the grass without much talk, engaged in our own thoughts or nonthoughts while the cab driver slept unmoving on the gravel beside us. His face with its morning beard heavy and greasy in stubble was turned directly to the sun like a heliotrope, but except for the slow heave and fall of his leather jacket, he might have been a leftover corpse on a battlefield, a hulk, a mass, a ponderous negation of the morning dawn and the night before. Ziggie gathered up the cups and the pot when we were through and arranged them on the front steps in a diagonal slash of metal and china. The nude on the book jacket had been ravished with lipstick, but she still dangled bravely in her sepulcher above the portal. Cadmium Greene's house was as silent as a derelict hull, as remote and austere as some gaudy coral reef glistening salt white in a never-tasted sea. I glanced quickly in a window, but the pane of glass had caught the low-rising sun and all I could see was reflected fire or blood or the delicate flush of a rose blossom.

Under Ziggie's direction, Daniel and I carried the cab driver clumsily into the back seat, pillowing his head against the arm rest and twisting his feet in pretzel turns so that they would rest on the jump seat. Rennie sat beside him, reaching across his hulked body from time to time to flick ashes into the ashtray, and when she missed, the grey tubes of ash lay on his leather coat like moulted age. Ziggie drove and Daniel and I sat with him in the front seat. The sound of the motor churning into a start was like a healthy heartbeat near the strangely cadaverous house, and the rear wheels spun gravel into the grass as we shot through the gate. I suddenly realized that I could no longer smell the sea, that I hadn't smelled it since I woke up. The wind must have shifted. Ziggie drove slowly, wearing the cabbie's hat with the brim peaked low to shade his eyes on sudden hairpin turns when the sun would glide through the branches of a tree or over a billboard to glare viciously red into the windshield. We didn't talk very much on the ride. We watched the ribbon of road wind into expressway, watched the oncoming traffic escape from the city on this hot August Saturday morning as we approached the impossible skyscape that hung in the morning haze.

"You may as well drop me off first," Rennie said, leaning over the seat to give Ziggie directions. I tried to catch her eye, but it was self-absorbed.

Free of bridges and the main circular arteries, the avenues and cross streets were unimpeded and quiet, the hum of the summer heat heavy and subduing on the asphalt and concrete. Puerto Rican children were already sucking at ice-cream cones and Cokes bought from God knows what desolate variety stores, and there was an air of calm and inaction as though the city had decided to consecrate Saturday morning in a heavy sweaty sleep. Ziggie parked in front of Rennie's apartment house and I walked with her to the elevator in the lobby.

"So, how did you do, Riegel?" she asked, facing me in front of the brass doors of the elevator. "Did you find what you were looking for?"

I shrugged my shoulders. "Does anybody?" I said. "And would it be such a good thing if you did?"

"Ooohh," she breathed sarcastically, and she was suddenly back in her feline costume—a cat with claws and glowing sepia eyes. "A very high tone this morning," she said. "I guess that answers my question. Tough titty, buster."

"Maybe. Maybe not," I said. "Or maybe that's all there really is." And through the cat I saw or felt again the dark levels of poised sinuous assault, the purr deep in the throat which could turn to electric hiss and spit, the loving grip of the even white teeth against the top of the lower lip. And then I remembered the weird mirrored colloquy I had witnessed, the shining pompadour and the black cat's hood sharing a secret entente on the destiny of man. And then I realized that not I but my fear had remembered. "Look, Rennie," I said. "I saw you speaking to her last night. Did you— What did you—" I didn't know how to frame the question.

Rennie pressed the call button for the elevator. "Girl talk, Riegel. Just girl talk. You wouldn't be interested." She examined the sharp green points of her fingernails as though she were making a weapons inspection, and the smile she threw me was an unlovely thing. The steel door of the elevator slid open and she started inside.

"Wait a minute," I said. "Uh—look, Ziggie will return these things of yours." I indicated my badly rumpled, stained costume. "And Jesus, Rennie—"

"Yeees, David?" Her voice went up on the syllables, whether in an ascending rise of contempt or a note of strange plaintiveness I could not tell.

I realized that there was nothing that I could say, that there was nothing I wanted to give her, that we had gone too far or come too close for pretense or friendliness. That my gratitude to her was highly ambiguous and that she knew it and was waiting defensively for me to say or do precisely the wrong, the unacceptable thing. Whatever thing I said or did. So I kissed her good-by, the weasel role which is man's, I trying to put in the kiss that quality of fear and desire I felt for her, she turning her cheek to my mouth, making the kiss an awkward brotherly peck, a Judas garden kiss. She entered the elevator and faced me, her raincoat draped like a cape over her shoulders.

"Like we say here in New York. Ring me up when you're in town."

I nodded eagerly, seizing on the straw of social amenity, knowing that I would drown like a plummet if this were my sole stay. The steel door was sliding shut when I remembered and I held it from closing. "Look," I said. "If you run into Michael Riley, give him my best. Tell him—"

"Tell him what?"

"Tell him— Oh, I don't know. Just give him my best."

The door slid shut and the old cable mechanism grated and creaked and the red In Use light went on and I watched it, listening to the whine and metallic complaint of the greased steel, and then the sound ceased and the light went out. I returned to the cab, dissatisfied and yet somehow glad at the parting. The street was full of the sun and children were playing stickball between the traffic.

When we dropped Daniel off at the Square, he shook hands very formally with me, his eyes reserved and unreadable in their descending layers of brown. "Good luck to you, David," he said. And then he smiled suddenly, warmly. "May I say that you have been a distinct educational experience?"

"You can say it," I said. "Just don't put any money on it."

We gripped hands again and I touched his shoulder in a gesture of farewell. Ziggie and I watched him skirt a row of ashcans, stately and impervious in his royal masquerade robes. A small boy chased a ball in front of his path, stopped and stared incredulously at him, and then ran back into an alley leaving the red ball spinning in the gutter. Daniel never broke his stride and I imagined the chuckle that he muted within his throat, the totally amused guffaw that buried itself behind the stiffness of his laryngeal dignity.

Ziggie out-feinted a large delivery van with a flourish of horns and hand waving, and we slid into a legal parking place on Sixth Avenue around the corner from Christopher Street. He reluctantly hung the yellow cap on the rear-view mirror and I twisted my false nose and beard around the spokes of the steering wheel. Ziggie stuffed the cab keys into the pocket of the leather jacket along with several neatly folded bills, and we shut the doors carefully. The cabbie shifted slightly in his sleep, gurgled low in his throat once, and slept on. I wondered what he would make of the night when he awoke, what wild stories he would tell his unbelieving wife, his friends. What wilder stories he would tell himself, fearful to believe or disbelieve. Who drives the horses of the sun shall lord it but a day, I quoted to myself. But, oh Lord, what a day!

Ziggie's apartment was cool and dark, with the shades drawn against the sun, and I searched in vain for some sign or hint that would testify to my previous occupancy, to some familiar past, to a vestige of myself left over, revealed, and waiting for me to pick it up and put it back where it belonged. There was nothing. Several ashtrays brimming over with dry butts, a whisky glass on the mantel, the old-fashioned green shades pulled taut to the window sills, the sun filtered on the rugs and along the spines of the books in the bookcases. There was really nothing of me here, any more than there would have been on the platform of a subway station that I could stand on five days a week, and every time it would receive and reject me with complete anonymous impersonality, and I could stick to the tiled roof like a wad of chewing gum and I would still be impermanent, transient, merely passing through. I took a shave and showered thoroughly, scrubbing the black hair dye out of my scalp with painstaking care. My shirt grated against my tender back and I had a new awareness of my shoulder blades and the raw fury of my shins. Arrayed once more in my redoubtable beige suit, my regimental tie loosely knotted and mounting firmly to my chin, I surveyed myself in the mirror. My cheeks and forehead were burned coppery pink and my hair wouldn't sit down properly under the brush, but I was familiar to myself again. I made a grotesque clown's face in the mirror, exposing my nicotine-yellowed teeth and corrugating my brow into a half-dozen parallel furrows, but the face that grimaced back at me was without surprises and was indubitably my own.

When I joined Ziggie in the kitchen, the coffee was already perked and poured out. He sat in front of his cup reading the newspaper.

"Nu, David?" he said, pushing a cup toward me. "So what are your plans?"

I looked at my watch. "There's an eleven o'clock for Boston which gets in a little after three. In her letter Letha said she'd be at South Station at four. I guess I'd damn well better make that eleven o'clock train."

"And then?" Ziggie said. "And then what?"

"Then will be then," I said. I swallowed half the coffee in one gulp. "You got to be open, baby."

Ziggie folded his newspaper and tucked it neatly on top of the refrigerator. "It *was* Letha last night," he said. "It was, wasn't it? It had to be."

I shrugged. "I just don't know for sure," I said. "Maybe yes, maybe no. I guess I don't know what has to be any more."

"Well, are you sure she'll be on that train?" Ziggie persisted. "You're kind of betting heavily into a blind deck, you know."

"Honest to God, Ziggie—" I smiled— "*your* God. I'm just not sure of anything. Except that I'll be at South Station at four o'clock, flowers and summer greetings in hand."

He looked at his watch and ran some water into his empty coffee cup. "Is there anything you'd like me to do, Dave? You know I'd be glad to."

"Sweetheart," I said. "You've already done everything." I recalled the old tune and crooned it at him with exaggerated schmaltz. "Just stay as sweet as you are, as sweet as you are, don't let a thing ever change you." I was embarrassed to say good-by and blunderingly uncertain how to tell him what I felt and thought. "Look," I said. "We'll keep in touch, huh?"

"Sure, Dave. Of course."

"And you give 'em hell at that Yeshiva, you hear? You give 'em bloody rabbinical hell!"

We shook hands awkwardly and I bulldozed a beige exit out the door, plowing a path to the corner of Sixth Avenue without seeing before I discovered that my cheeks were wet and there was a fuzzy glaze in my eyes that made it hard for me to focus. I wiped my face with my palm and I licked salt from my fingers, savoring the taste with awe and thanksgiving.

The eleven o'clock left the Manhattan tunnels of the New York, New Haven & Hartford right on schedule (Hamilton watch time) and I was aboard—wrinkled, casual, grooved in my slot that was racing east and north at better than sixty miles an hour like some automated coin or slug or gyrating pinball. I hadn't even time to buy my ticket, running down to the lower level of Grand Central, elbowing past the bored guard at the track entrance, entering the train while the great iron wheels were spitting steam and the locomotive was already beginning to chug asthmatically from its sooty berth. There weren't many people in my car (who would be going to Boston on a Saturday morning?) and I went to the end reserved for smoking, where I half reclined on the leatherette cocktail-lounge seats that the railroads had admiringly copied from the airlines. I kept sneaking glances at the mirror on the end wall of the car to see if my hair was black or blond or what. I tried to make a pattern out of the past few days, but my mind resisted the probe of memory like skin crawling away from a clammy touch, and I found that I could remember much more clearly things from my far-away past than the happenings of the past hours and days. Hey, involuntary memory, I cried, where is thy sting? Hey, Proust, where is thy victory? I turned to the future, then, trying to project an order upon it, but my mind ground to a stop at the far end of the track some two hundred miles ahead of me, following the ribboned steel along the coastline until it would buckle to a grimy bumper end in Boston. In South Station at four o'clock.

"Then will be then" was fine stuff for an audience—resonant, mouthy, a deliberate open stance, but it gave a hollow substance for me to chew upon all alone. Was she or wasn't she Letha? If she was, did she or didn't she know me, her demon lover, her full-married dissertational stalemate? And would she or wouldn't she be arriving at South Station later this afternoon, bright and summery on the four o'clock train with her suitcase stuffed with presents for the children, a covered basket of goodies under her arm for old brainsick Papa of the shorn teeth, old Man of Sorrows with a crown of horns. Sweet Jesus, I should have been a ragged Talmudist, scuttling across the floors of Holy Sees, to be able to work out the infinite variable number of alternatives, each with its own particular urgency and crying need, each insoluble conundrum weeping and laughing from the same sourceless mouth. If she wasn't Letha, then Letha didn't know that I knew. Or didn't know *what* I didn't know, I corrected myself despairingly. And we were right back at the beginning, except what new prison did that encase me in? My mind recoiled from the impossible corridor of closed rooms, each door firmly locked and bolted and the keys in nobody's possession because the doors hadn't been locked on purpose. They had just swung shut the way a good door is built to do. And they locked because when honestly built doors shut, swinging free and noiseless on their hinges, they lock. These lived-through doors anyway, and there's no going back through them.

But say she was Letha, say anyway she was. Then she had either recognized or not recognized me in my fool's masquerade. And if she had or hadn't, what then? A different corridor of equally locked rooms, a floor above or a floor below, the plumbing and the wiring running vertically, toilet to toilet, fuse box to hidden fuse box. If she hadn't known me in the rushing green turmoil of her dream, then it would be the same for me as though she hadn't been Letha at all. Almost. That I had dreamed a journey and a dance and a desperate dialogue from a park bench in Boston Common while the fountain sprayed on heedless children, and this landscape slipping south behind me now was the scorched backwash of my sleep and soon I would yawn and wake to the unseized day. But if it were she, she would have had to know me. You can't deny that, can you? My mind simulated the closed corridors, denials gliding nebulously away on the worn piling of the carpets. Would you swear to know her, Riegel? Could you sit in the witness box and swear to her face in the obdurate face of her denial, her face looking curiously, fearfully, unknowingly at yours? It takes two to know one, fool or wise man, harlot or princess. And if she didn't know you, then you have not known her, and you are still unattached and floating, unself-knowing, a disengaged mote in the cold eyebeam of unilluminating light. No, you have no keys to unlock those doors, no keys for thy kingdom, miter and triple crown, none.

I went to the men's room and washed my face hard and slow, rubbing cold water into my eyes, trying to knead some sense, some order, into my skull from the outside since the inside offered no hope in its opaque ramifications of possibility on possibility. My face looking back at me from the mirror was essentially friendly, but removed and unrevealing. It smiled at my smile and it frowned at my frown, but it had no message of its own to deliver and it mocked at my research with an implacable flexibility of response. There's not a damn thing in nature that's unknown, but thinking will make it so, I thought. Unknown and forever unknowable. And so tangled in its indeterminate valences as to elude for always the swinging net, the four-square jiffy-quick trap of the mind's best endeavors. Think about unimportant things, unliving things, abstract corpses of ideas. That's what thought is for. The inchworm of the brain which we look at with great rose-tinted magnifying glasses. Put the worm to work at its own lousy anthill, Riegel. That's what thought is for, you inteffectual. I stuck my tongue out at my mirror image, closing my eyes in order to refute the reciprocal insult from the glass and I returned to my seat ridiculously proud in my small victory.

We were leaving Connecticut, beginning to knife through the marsh coast of Rhode Island to Roger Williams' illusory Providence, and I marveled anew at Edwards' savage fury against those latitudinarians of the spirit who had assaulted his rock-ribbed soul, who had offered the palliatives of an easy digestion and a liberal toothlessness as substitutes for the athletic adventures of the stripped human consciousness in struggle with an inhuman God. And suddenly I began to see where Jonathan Edwards might be hit, the Puritan pugilist dropping his guard. Where he might yield an opening, the structure of his thought so logical and well-ordered as to be logically insane. To be a poetic metaphor of possibility, human possibility, erected on the comical keystone of an outrageous ambiguity. Complete, thorough, absolute determinism—a willed and willing surrender of the human footstep to the parade of divine events, a vital compliance to the life force that brooked no collusion with automatism or mechanism. Psychological or otherwise, I reminded myself. No pre-Freudian he, except in history. I found an envelope in my pocket (the envelope that Letha's long letter had come in—what better heart to inscribe upon?) and I scribbled diagrammatical notes to myself on the back and along the edges. Intransigent thought structures that I had bounced off for over a year—a psychology of the affections that was puerile and antique except where it was ultramodern, a metaphysics which had never come close enough to the earth to receive a name—suddenly everything began to block itself out into patterns like recondite images in a poem come all at once to life. I saw that it was ultimately as a poet that Edwards saved himself, forcing a magnificent conceptual shield between his lean pliant self and the terrifying immensities of space that were bounded by a Glory beyond Glory, an Almighty Father who knew not Love.

"*Active* passivity," I wrote, underlining the first word with such force that the nib of my pen tore through the paper and dripped ink on my pants leg. The great unlocking key was in the adjective, in the modifying effect on the determinism by the moral *action,* that small word (denied by many to exist) which transformed passivity into passion, which glorified the determined sacrifice beyond all determination, which cut a tiny slice of space in the tight-hewn structures of logic through which moral universes could multiply into infinitude. For the first time, and that all at once, I saw the beginning and end of my dissertation, saw it workable and demanding to be worked, releasing it from the soul-deadening boxes of the card catalogue, the heavy-footed trudge of bibliography and source and influence hunt. Jonathan baby, I thought. I've busted your Calvinistic back, you bastard, you secret Jew. I'm on the inside now and I will turn you inside out from where you have been hiding in the neat blue volumes of the Yale edition. Because you really weren't a philosopher at all, were you? And what you made was not the logical thing you pretended. It was just a mere magnificent human thing, that's all. Call it by its right name, I thought. They tossed you out of your pulpit and they ignored you in England (where there were some who should have understood—impious Age of Pope, laggard Age of Swift) and you cultivated your little Indian garden without rancor or protest (oh, you sly Protestant) and you saved it all for the great trapeze act, the moral reverberation of your soul. Oh, Jonathan baby, I will do you good. I will walk the tightrope with you and spell out the spaces that you cunning made. Even though they'll probably reject it. Even though they'll find it "Ingeniously argued but based on unscholarly assumptions." This is not what we meant at all. This (fingering the neat bundle of manuscript pages with the footnotes marching in battalions of black at the bottom of each page), this (sliding it back across the desk with a disdainful white academic hand), this is not it at all. But there is an interesting note in the current *Corpus Scholasticae* on some Edwardian sources in Duns Scotus. You might just take a look at it. But it doesn't matter, Sir Professor. It doesn't matter at all. I will do it for Jonathan and for the sake of my own immortal soul and when it is done, I shall have committed my own small moral act.

I shook my head and observed myself wonderingly. There was a tight chain of bubbles surging in my chest and I was eager all over to begin what I had been eluding for so long. I looked at the back of my envelope, the writing barely decipherable with its charging arrows and cryptic ideographs, and I smiled at it and at myself and put it back in my pocket. The train was entering the long series of trainyards, passing Back Bay, and the city that I knew so well was unfamiliar to me in its convulsive urban renewal and my alien worm's-eye view from the railroad bed. So be it, I said, feeling an emphasis of finality in some deep-lying synapse that was now unutterably thankfully closed. So be it. Whatever else I may or may not have accomplished on this journey or dream of a journey, this I now have. I departed from the green of the Common barren and I am returning pregnant, heavy with child. I am the willing victim of an Immaculate Conception and, Jonathan baby, I will carry you under my heart for two full semesters and I will push you screaming into a world that couldn't, but couldn't, care less. I counted the months on my fingers. It will be May, blessed infant mine. Gather ye rosebuds then in May. We'll celebrate our birthing days together. I will deliver you, wisest philosopher, as the great American poet manqué, and I in turn (who am essentially a poet at my doggeregal heart) will become a Doctor of Philosophy. A fair exchange is a royal bargain. It's Unser Amerika, Jonathan. You can't fight it, so we might as well join it.

The train lurched to a halt in a pig's squeal of air brakes and neck jolting as the sudden stop of the locomotive transferred itself backward through the coupled cars. It's all right, I thought. The engineer just didn't realize that we'd come to the end of the line. He only had two hundred and fifteen miles to prepare for this. He was merely playing it safe, poor sod. I patted the envelope in my pocket and went out into the station. According to the notice on the Arrivals Board, the train that Letha would or would not be on was scheduled in "On Time," in fifty minutes. Track Sixteen. Track Sixteen and never been missed, I sang to myself, my inner voice a little hysterical in its intensities, and I perched on a stool at the lunch counter for a sandwich and a milkshake. I ate slowly, chewing everything very carefully, even the froth from the milkshake, swallowing the tasteless food deliberately, as though it might weigh down the lightness in my chest and stomach. At the far end of the station was a flower shop and I walked toward it with great empty leisure, forcing myself to browse over the souvenirs and magazines and paperback displays which gave the huge waiting room the appearance of a tawdry bazaar. *The Mortuary of Love* leaped to my attention, its jacket nude familiar like an old locker-room companion. You'll have to read that book, Riegel, I said. Or maybe the old Cad will rewrite it. I started to buy a copy and then I stopped myself. There'll be time, Riegel, I said. Time for a hundred more revisions. We'll see.

The florist specialized in roses, the fragile flower of rivals and debauches. Behind the green glass chilled to protect the blossoms from the warm fetid air of the station were vases of roses, tight-budded young yellow and red roses with long stems. I thought between the two colors and then, as though I were making an absolutely irretrievable move, I bought a half-dozen of the red ones. Wrapped in thin green tissue with ferns, the deep red of the blossoms flamed like buried life. I held them by the stems, heads down, as I had been taught years ago, and I strolled toward Track Sixteen. How should I be, I wondered. Intense? Ardent? Casual? Casual will be best, the moderate weather of all seasons. I shall hold my roses gracefully across my chest and lean against a girder, long and half collapsed, like Jimmy Stewart. She shall come flushed and distracted off the train and she shall see me on my girder and she shall say, "David!" And I shall smile slowly, my grin of welcoming delight breaking across my Midwestern American face in slow motion, and I shall untangle myself and move toward her and I shall hold her in my arms and say, "*Dar*ling! It's *so* good to have you back!" I moved toward the track entrance, savoring my welcoming scene with an idiotic simper on my face. There was an unusually large crowd clustered around Tracks 14–16 as I came closer, and I checked my watch against the huge station clock. Ten minutes to go. No, I can work a better greeting than that. Somehow I'll get out on the platform and I'll spot her first coming down the train steps with her suitcase. And she'll see me as I'm coming toward her and she'll call, "David!" And I'll surround her like light and I'll clutch her to me and say, "Here am I, Letha! Here am I!" And we'll kiss so tight that we'll squeeze the roses flat between our bodies.

It *was* an enormous amount of people huddling around in front of my track entrance, mostly women, and far too many just to meet an ordinary summer afternoon train from New York. As I oriented myself on the fringes of the crowd I realized that it was not Track Sixteen that drew them, but Track Fourteen, where the trains come in from Cape Cod. And then I noticed a large white-cardboard sign, hand-lettered in blue, fixed with wire above the track entrance. "CAMP SEAGULL." On either side of the name were two blue Stars of David with what was probably meant to be the curved blue wings of a gull soaring around in the middle of each. And in smaller letters in the lower right-hand corner, the name "MAX SEGAL, DIRECTOR." I groaned and reinspected the crowd with miserable foreknowledge. The summer-camp season was coming to an August end and I would have to fight for Letha through a mob of returned delinquent children and ungrateful graceless mothers. Maybe they'll come *after* Letha's train, I prayed. Please, God. Let it be after Letha's train. My prayers were answered in what amounted to celestial curb service. A whistle blew and the high-pitched treble of children's voices announced the sun-browned returnees from Camp Seagull, marching in a column of hand-holding two's. They marched out of the track entrance and into the crowd, their voices splitting the arched vault of the waiting-room like a barrage of Lilliputian needles against a great palpitating eardrum:

"Hail, sweet Seagull, champion bird,
Hail, bright Seagull, sweetest word,
We, thy sons with hearts so true,
Pledge ourselves fore'er to you."

Max—he must have been Max—in a screaming white T shirt embossed with the same eccentric gull imprisoned in a Star of David, a lanyard with a whistle on it hanging around his neck, his arms and head baked obscenely brown by the sun, led the chorus in a whisky baritone as he funneled the children into the waiting crowd like bunched raisins into a whirling cake batter.

> "Hail to thee, oh, dear Camp Seagull
> With thy colors blue and white,
> We will keep thy standards regal
> In the day and darkest night."

So must the Jewish section of Hiroshima have looked, I thought. When The Bomb hit. It was stupendous. Children and mothers flying in all directions, fishing poles, tennis rackets, boxes and suitcases loosely knotted with yellow cord, stacks of thumbed, dog-eared comic books, odd shapes of bleached driftwood with lampshades teetering on them, a wild wonderful melange of multi-madonnas with children and Max's white teeth gleaming in a rich broad smile within and above everything.

"My Arthur! Where's my Arthur?"

"Roger Rosenthal! Has anybody seen Roger Rosenthal?"

"But, darling, it's a lovely ashtray!" (A large splintered clamshell with the paint still sticky.) "Daddy will be so happy with it."

A small dark boy in a far-too-large T shirt (his unhappy seagull was soaring somewhere above the general vicinity of his groin) was weeping on the margins of the crowd, wiping at his eyes manfully with a first-baseman's mitt. Someone's precious shell weeping on the sand, unpicked-up, unmet, unfound. A knot of older boys were exchanging thunderous punches on the arm and breath-stifling whacks on the back, tendering their own boyish farewells to the glories of the summer. Max's voice boomed above the turmoil as he shouted like a circus vendor, "Get 'em fast! Get 'em hot! Get 'em while they're red hot! Going! Going! Gone!"

I was beginning to struggle against a wave of hysterical laughter that was coming to crest at the base of my throat when I felt my arm grabbed in a longshoreman's grip and I turned to see a short round woman, fearfully powdered and trussed as though she were ready for the spit, her tiny pig's eyes squinting up at me. In her wake she held a tearful eight- or nine-year-old, who I would have judged outweighed me by about ten pounds.

"You Milton's counsellor, ain't you?" she said, not relaxing her grip on my arm by one foot-pound.

I smiled patronizingly at her mistake. She probably wanted to give Milton's counsellor an extra tip for feeding her round brown salami so well. "No, I'm sorry. I'm not," I said. "He's probably around there somewhere." I gestured in the direction of the thickest crowd.

She kept her gaze fixed on my eyes and she had my arm like a lobster trap. "Well, it don't make no difference," she said. "You're one of those mishugginah counsellors anyway."

Before I could protest my innocence, she had thrust an evil-looking turtle about the size of a baseball into my empty hand. "This," she said, "I can live in my house without, thank you."

The turtle slid his head around and looked at both of us and then hooded his eyes and retracted his head into his shell. A particularly incompetently sketched gull and star was streaked on his green horned back. The woman released my arm and anchored Milton in one motion, gave me a final porcine glare, and waddled away.

I started to protest, but she was already out of hearing distance (never having been in listening distance) and from the corner of my eye I could see a fresh trickle of people coming out of the entrance to Track Sixteen. I tucked the turtle under my arm like a football, and, with my roses held lowered like a lance in the other hand, I ran toward the stream of bright afternoon light that was seeping through the open gate.

# Journal

*23 July:* Finished. I am done. The Novel is complete and I have committed a moral action. I have projected a flexible promise into the future and I have redeemed my promise with the blood currency of my naked being. Aha, Leo, see. You have inscribed a moral codex into the Book of Acts and it is done no matter what else. Not just a novel, but a strategic confrontation of life. Sing, Leo. Clap your hands and sing. You make a paunchy, pedantic El Cid, Leo, but you too are racing eternally along the beach and your blood has crusted beneath the white leaves of your book. The print. The fine print, Leo.

God slays himself with every leaf that flies, and Hell is more than half of Paradise. You are master of a large Hades, Leo. What Persephone thine? A novel. A Chickamauga of the spirit. A moral action.

But have *I* been touched by the fire, the bad cess and murrain of the ghostly skirmishers? Sometimes I think that I am not touched at all, crouched in the slit trench of my bubbled concealment like a helmeted fetus, absorbing the shrapnel and the burnt cordite, transforming the outside howl of violence into private nourishment and illusory strength. I wear torn flesh on my lapel like a boutonniere and I whistle George M. Cohan melodies into the dying cries. Over there. And sometimes I think that I have been pillaged by a careless mighty life that has picked me up and used me as one squeezes a fruit for its juice. That I am empty, blasted, stunned, my blank forehead smashed against a cathedral dome, my weary viscera invaded by a shadowed corner of a café where an elderly couple sip Perrier and hold hands against the fall of night.

I feather the manuscript with the tips of my fingers (my Maginot Line, my foxhole, my pit of snakes) and it all seems like a dream. And when I look away from the leaves I seem the dream.

Ah, but it is all behind now, thank God. Far far behind now. (So strange to think that a moment ago, an hour ago, yesterday—any cadaverous tick of the past is absolutely equal in death with millenniums and eons ago. That I have met with death and wrestled him to a draw and carved my quivering moment into eternal form.) And now I am undone. Now I can stuff Doren's laughter with paper pulp and lined words and he will not tender me thanks for them. The gifts that one offers gladly are the quickest spurned because people would rather steal than be given. What more pungent insult than the unsolicited gift, eh, Leo? The world, it will be a little uncomfortable with my gift, eh? That one can smile and smile and— Be done. As I am indeed done. Oh, you will receive rare thanks, Leo. The sound of one hand clapping while the other protects its privates. And he will no longer burn into me.

And it makes no difference whether it is a good or a bad novel, this gift—this gifted curse. Who would have the effrontery to weigh a moral action on a butcher's scale? In its dead inarticulate shape it is just an incitement for potential responses. (I have no responses to it. How could I?) A moral action is its own good if it has held to the fatal harmony which it creates sui generis in the dark processive tides of its secret being. And I alone know the measure of those dread proportions. I, Paracelsus. I, the wan God, inscrutable at the center of my light. Like the Lord I have labored and I survey my handiwork and find it good. And if I have laid waste to vast territories of myself in the making, now I can send my legions back into the Sudetenlands that I have temporarily sacrificed. Ah, Leo, thou art truly exalted and hallowed hast thou named thy name! I welcome the holy future with salivation—the new order with yearning desire. I found a scrap of paper which had fallen from Eva's pocketbook. She had written three times, each line larger and blacker than the first, "Je suiverai mon coeur." Perhaps I have neglected her these past months (how much more have I neglected myself!). But what marching armies can afford to assign special convoys for their camp followers! Such a paltry neglect to leave a woman to her own resources in a Paris where the Seine curls its sinuous necklace of flowing light around the throat of the most desirable city in the world. Oh, I am full—full of me. I want to eat figs and dates in a silken tent and be serenaded with soft scarves and the jangle of brass against the flesh. Eva should be home soon and the children will be late from the special Guignol. I shall buy flowers—some red roses—and that fine dusty bottle of Armagnac that I pass in the vintner's window every day and Eva and I shall celebrate my soul.

But I shall have stark canyons of space in my life—great screaming hollows of nothingness—without my novel. Have I left anything to explore in myself? What corners to turn, what veins of adamant to trace to their sources? Oh, Leo Leo Leo, can you not rest easy on the hiatus rock of your achievement? Your blood will weep soon enough; you have not left the dried earth yet—not all of you. Relax. Rest easy. Gorge and glut and wallow. For now you can fill the empty spaces with laughter and demonic holiday. The bleating lion will lie down with the roaring sheep and you will be a blessed menagerie of peaceful madness. And Eva will bring chunks of bleeding meat to feed you and Mark will have a measure to hold himself to. Ah, it is good to nuzzle the fringes of well-earned sleep and savor the dreams that will come. Lily will be melon-breasted in my sleep and her eyes will know me—not Doren—deeply. To be completed and made whole, I and my novel, and to know the direct joy of the last fallen curtain. Hubris, Leo. That last is named shroud and you have larger amphitheaters than the grave to fill before you shall be wrapped therein. Rapt, Leo. Oh, I am rapt indeed. And stamped for spatial delivery to the Pleiades and beyond.

No. NO! No, it's not right at all. I'll kill her. Or him. Him especially. My friend, my dark twinning brother. She is nothing. Dough, clouds, a mindless response. Him. Him I will kill. Oh, stupid stupid Leo. To forget that the world doth move. It's so clear when you bother to look at it. To reconstruct the moves—one after another—foredoomed and foresworn—a steep stupid promenade of cliché and banality like the great steps at Odessa. Of course, he *must* be back in Paris. Maybe he never went away at all and what I thought was my madness was mere comical lucidity. She has never been like this—never. Planned, purposive, deliberate. Cold. Cold in her speech and face. Not hysterical or passionate. Cold as the blue paint on her eyelids. As though she had seen all the hands and knew that her trump was good. Cold and cruel, my Eva. Pull yourself together, Leo (which one?). First you must see clear, that when you strike, the aim will be as true as your hatred.

I bought the brandy and the roses. I shaved and put on one of my new ties (she has *never* asked me why I hadn't worn them!) and she came home but she didn't notice my difference. I followed her from room to room like a chafed eunuch. (I didn't want to have to say out of nowhere that I had finished the novel. She could have said a million things. "How's the work going, Leo?" "Did you write well today?" Anything. But the impetus had to come from her and I would have told her that I was finished and we would celebrate my soul. My soul? She murdered it years ago.) And then I saw that she was dressing to go out again. The blue lace that she saves for special attractions. I asked her where she was going, my celebration already gurgling down the drain of my throat. "Out," she said. "I can't stay inside here with you." And she didn't look at me while she fixed her make-up and drew her comb through her hair. And I got sarcastic and as though I had poked a seemingly dead fire with a stick, suddenly we were in flames, terrible words striking like snakes between us (could she have meant her words?). And from somewhere I dragged Doren and I confronted her directly with him (I don't remember exactly what brutal way I said it) and she was standing at the door like ice and there was blue on her eyelids and when I said Doren's name I was immediately sorry because her face got hard (and there must have been something else I should have said that would have made it soft). And she turned to me all bitter and untouchable and said, "Oh, Leo, you've made yourself something hateful. You're just a mask of hate." And she was gone. I wanted to scream after her down the stairs—me, the delicate juggler of words. To shout, "You, Eva! You, *you're* the pimple on the ass of our marriage! You, not me! You're the cause, the disease, the silent infection!" But she was gone and I was left with the Armagnac and the roses that she never even saw.

I don't know. I just don't know at all. Is she on a rendezvous, a tryst? Is it my friend Doren? Somebody else? When the girl brought the children home, they asked for Mummy and I said that she was out. Mark looked strangely at me and wouldn't kiss me good night. Lily saw the half-empty brandy bottle and demanded to have some, and when I wouldn't let her she went to bed crying. Both my children do my weeping for me, even though they think it's their own. Is it Doren or somebody else? She could even be having a Lesbian affair, my Eva, my cross. That little Angélique, shorter even than Eva but with enormous breasts and she looks like a mouse, soft and small and crawly. I said she looked like someone with an obscene soul, so of course Eva made it her business to meet her for a coffee whenever she could manage. Or Félice, the charwoman, corroded from a hundred years of hot water and lye and a million stairs to wash. Oh, she'd make a fine Baudelairian companion, filth for filth to wallow in. But she could do it. She could do these dirty things. Float in sewers of scum and slime with blue paint on her eyelids and her hair neatly combed.

Hate, indeed. I am good. *I once was.*

Or Doren. I don't want to think of Doren. A novel is a moral action. A strategic confrontation of life. I will not think of Doren. My touchstone is on the table, white and inert near the roses (I should put them in water so that they can die slowly). But what have I done to myself (which one?)? What has happened inside me in my madnesses? Unconnected parts of me fly around like sticky paper adhering to all the corrupt surfaces that my imagination can dredge up from the slime. I am Doren. Félice. Angélique. The dirty Eva that I never married. Eva has just gone out for the evening. To the theater I think she said. A concert. A walk along the quais. To window shop along the Faubourg St. Honore. She is my Eva. To love, honor, and obey me. I've pushed myself too far and I've splintered my brain like old coffin wood. Silly pandemonic Leo. Eva will be back soon. In a few minutes. It's getting late and she worries about the children in the night. About Mark's nightmares. I have worked too hard, too long, and I have drunk too much celebrated Armagnac. She will be home by the next time the bells ring the hour. The Métro has closed down for the night, but I will hear her cab door slam in the street and when she opens the downstairs door, the air pressure will make our front door shake on its old lock. She will be home soon and I have just dreamed another dream. A novel is a moral action and my spirit needs a rest from this sprint which has prolonged itself into a losing marathon.

Or Doren. Félice, Angélique. Ménage à trois. À quatre. Dirty dirty writhings in a foreign alien language. Filthy intrigues and betrayals and you, Leo, are the hateful novelist. You compose the script and cast the characters and write them into their roles. Secretly. By silences and insinuating provocations. You are outside and inside, Leo, pusher and pushed, you immoral actor, you player with lives and deaths. You take all the parts yourself and you react each to each—player and played, the king, the king maker, the regicide, and the hideous crowned beast. Your kingdom is split into a million pieces, shining broken shards of revolt and revulsion, and I don't know where you are hiding, Leo. I don't want to know *what* you are. I think I would have to hate what you are. The next chiming of the bells, the next bell will ring her home—stepping softly so as not to disturb, surprised and glad to find me up (company for tea or hot cocoa to sleep on), happy to disavow the argument at the door, consumed with that which we are nourished by. Hamlet and Lear were gay. The next bell, you'll see, Leo (which one?).

Oh, Leo, Leo, Leo! Good Lord, Leo, why have you forsaken me? Why, Leo?

# Outscape

So, macher, you're a big deal. A big man. You wrote a novel.

*We* wrote a novel. Don't try to weasel out on me now. You're in this just as much as I am and don't you forget it.

You, me, what difference does it make? Two times nothing is the same nothing as one times nothing. You want we should hire a bookkeeper? So look at him. One novel and already he's a corporation.

All right, all right. But just don't you forget that you were there too. You got as much blame for this as me. I'm not playing fall guy for anybody. And especially not for you.

Blame, shmame. Who remembers anything?

Somebody could remember.

Oi, are you a shlemiel! Did anybody remember that skinny guy?

What skinny guy?

See, you don't even remember. That skinny guy who thought he was God or something. He was a real tough piece of meat too.

Which one? The guy in the sand with all the bugs? I think I remember him. And then there was the one who sat in front of that tree. Just sat and sat and sat. But he wasn't skinny. He had this big roll on his belly, remember? There's been an awful lot of them.

You see, that's what I mean. Nobody remembers past the next day. Even us. The wound closes into a brown mouth and nobody knows from nothing. Hero today, gonif tomorrow.

You're punning in two languages again. Damn it, I warned you about that. It's a dead giveaway.

You can't give the dead away. We almost went broke in that business before we started doing this.

Sure, be the big comedian. I have to do all the worrying for us. You won't be so smart if they find out.

Look, golem, relax. Nobody's going to find out. Who's to know?

Somebody could know. We have to protect ourselves, for Christ's sakes. They could close us up like a tomb. Like a book.

Jesus, I picked myself a real live one. Somebody could remember, somebody could know. Somebody could this and somebody could that. Believe me, they don't know us from Adam.

Sure, you talk. They'd never find *you*. But they could put their hands on me quick enough if they wanted to.

Look, you're making a big mishmash but out of nothing. I'm

telling you, they don't know nothing, they don't remember nothing, they don't even know what we done.

You keep saying that. But somebody must know.

Somebody again. Please to believe me from the bottom of my heart. They don't even know that anything happened. For them there isn't a shade, a particle of difference.

You really believe that?

I know that.

Then why did we go to all this trouble for? What good is it?

Vaizmir, do you have a goyishe kop! With you I have to explain like with a baby. You *do* know where babies come from, don't you?

Sure. From God.

So you know something. You have at least a small capacity of understanding. Now strain it a little and think.

I can't think. I'm upset. I heard about a man he had a perforated bowel. Can you imagine? So just tell me. What's the sense of all this if nobody knows what we done?

All right, so listen.

I'm listening.

When across the throat of the chicken the shochet goes PHUUUT with his knife, does the chicken know what happened?

Go ask him. I'm not a chicken.

Don't be so sure. But it's the *principle* anyway I'm talking. You stuff it in a basket and it's flip-flopping around, it thinks it's a king. So you say, How do you do, Your Majesty, and the shochet wipes his knife on his yarmalka, and one two three, the head is on one side the basket and the feet on the other. You understand?

A little bit. A little bit I understand. It's a cheap dirty trick.

Nu, so write a complaint. But it works. It always works. What do you think happens when you laugh?

I don't laugh any more. This job has ruined my sense of humor.

So weep then. You got that many tears to spare, I can keep you busy a long time, believe me.

*Ugghh,* I'm beginning to see it now. Like that skinny guy. Now I remember that skinny guy. Flip-flopping in a basket. He put up a pretty good fight.

Him? Oh, sure. He wasn't so easy. But when he got it—

It thundered. I remember. It got dark and there was a big loud crack in the sky. So that's why we have to go through all this?

That's why.

You should pardon me, it's a lousy job.

So who's arguing? But it's steady. And you got no choice.

Me neither? Don't I have a choice if I want to?

Try it and see. But don't hang by your thumbs.

There are worse positions—I suppose you're right.

Believe me, I sometimes wish I wasn't.

Yeah? That I won't buy. You love this dirty business. You'd kill yourself before you got out of it.

So, believe what you want to believe. It makes you happy, it makes you a bigger man to wish all the blood on my hands, so wish! Suit yourself, partner.

Suit myself? I wish I could. Oi, do I wish I could! So, the hell with it. Please to deal me another hand and this time keep your dirty fingers off the bottom of the deck—